"Take me to your room again, Adam. Let me be your woman."

Heartbeats. Coiling, throbbing need. And Adam heard himself saying softly, "Is that what you want, Angel? To be my woman, like your mother was Camp Meredith's woman?"

Everything froze within her, and he saw it in her eyes.

Adam knew what he had said, but he couldn't stop. The time for coyness and games had passed; it had gone too far.

"I can teach you to love, Angel," he said hoarsely. "I can show you the best of what it's like between a man and a woman, the best it can ever be. I can make you my woman, and you won't be sorry. But is that what you want?"

ALSO BY LEIGH BRISTOL

Amber Skies
Hearts of Fire
Scarlet Sunrise
Silver Twilight
Sunswept
Twice Blessed

Leigh Bristol

Angel

WARNER BOOKS

A Time Warner Company

WARNER BOOKS EDITION

Cover design by Diane Luger
Cover illustration by Jean Targete

Warner Books, Inc.
1271 Avenue of the Americas
New York, N.Y. 10020

 A Time Warner Company

Printed in the United States of America

First Printing: April, 1992

10 9 8 7 6 5 4 3 2 1

CHAPTER

One

1886

HE might never have found her if he hadn't used the last of his coffee that morning and run out of tobacco late that afternoon. There were a lot of things a man could do without on the trail: good food, fresh water, clean clothes, a bed to rest on at night, and a friendly sun over his head when he woke up in the morning. It was even conceivable that for a short while a man could do without coffee or cigarettes—but not both.

It was a little before sundown when Adam Wood rode into Little Horse, Colorado. It had been raining for three days straight and the streets of the little town were a mess; mud sucked at his horse's hooves and splashed up over his pants legs, which were so filthy that their original color wasn't discernible anymore. He was soaked clear through, cold, and miserable. Although the rain had lightened to a drizzle, water still dripped off the brim of his hat and ran down the back of his neck and everything he owned smelled of mildew. Nothing had ever looked as inviting to him as the yellow glow from the windows of the general store—unless it was the sign across the street that advertised ROOMS AND MEALS.

He hitched his horse outside the store and stepped ankle deep in mud when he swung down. He was too tired even to swear. He made a cursory effort to scrape his boots on the boardwalk before he went inside, and took off his hat. Tonight he'd have a hot meal, a bath, and a roof over his head for the first time in over a week. But first he'd do what he had come here to do.

It was almost closing time, and the proprietor looked at him in dismay as he tracked mud across the freshly swept floor. "Something I can do for you?"

"Yeah. A pound of coffee and a tin of tobacco."

It was warm inside the store and smelled of dusty bolts of cloth and sharp cheese. Adam suddenly realized how hungry he was. "Cut me off a nickel's worth of that cheese, too, will you?"

A little happier now that the sale was mounting up, the storekeeper put the tobacco and coffee on the counter and removed the glass dome from the cheese wheel. "You been on the road a long time?"

"Yeah," Adam responded absently. "A long time."

He was examining a shelf of knickknacks near the window: ladies' fans, brass candlesticks, painted bowls. A porcelain music box caught his eye and he picked it up, smiling at the tinny little waltz it played when he opened the lid. Consuelo would have liked that. She liked all things pretty and delicate, and whenever Adam held something beautiful in his hands he thought of her. For a moment he actually considered buying the music box, just for the sake of the smile in her eyes when he presented it to her.

Then he closed the lid abruptly and returned the box to the shelf. What use would she have for a trinket when he couldn't bring her the one thing she really wanted?

"Got a girl back home?" The man at the counter inquired. "We got some mighty pretty things, make a nice present for a little lady."

Adam grunted noncommittally and picked up a wooden letter box. He had no real interest in the box and his stomach was beginning to remind him of the hot meal that awaited him across the street. But it had been a long time since he had been in a store, and he liked touching nice things and thinking about better times.

He started to return the box to the shelf when the craftsman's mark on the underside caught his eye. That was another habit he had picked up, looking for the mark, never really expecting to find it. This time he couldn't believe what he saw.

He looked at it for a long time, then brought the box over to the counter. "You know the fellow that made this?"

The proprietor adjusted his wire glasses and squinted at the small mark Adam pointed out. "Why, yeah. Yeah, as a matter of fact I do. Name of Haber, Jeremiah Haber. Comes through here about twice a year, selling his goods. Does nice work, too, ain't too many like him around these parts. Now, you take this piece here..."

Adam tried to keep the impatience out of his voice. "Does he have a girl with him?"

The man looked at first surprised, then a little suspicious.

"Yeah, his daughter. Pretty little thing, been traveling with him as long as I remember."

"I don't reckon you'd know where they are now, would you?"

The suspicion in the other man's eyes was definite now. "You a friend of theirs?"

Adam replied simply, "Yes."

The man behind the counter seemed to debate for a moment, but something about Adam's face apparently convinced him that he was harmless. Few people ever lied to Adam; that was something he had learned to count on.

"This time of year, they're usually down on the Platte. Heard 'em say something about Green River last time they was in."

"Green River," Adam repeated. "Where is that?"

"About forty miles east. Course, like I say, they move around a lot."

Adam looked out the window at the gray, dying day. It had started to rain again, fat drops splashing in two-foot puddles, streaking down the flanks of his mud-spattered horse. He'd have to get a fresh mount and ride all night. Even then, the chances of finding them there were not very promising. The yellow lamps from the hotel across the way beckoned. Forty miles . . .

His shoulders were set in resignation as he turned away from the window and back to the proprietor. "I reckon you'd better wrap up some soda crackers with that cheese," he said.

He bought the letter box, too. It cost him two dollars, but with any luck at all, it would be worth it.

* * *

Angel Haber watched the man across the table from her with mounting disdain. He was sweating bullets, and the eyes that studied the cards in his hand had the look of a trapped rabbit. She might have been moved to pity, but she was too overcome with disgust. Any man who couldn't take care of himself better than that ought not to get in the game.

"All right, poker face," she said impatiently. "What's it going to be? You in or out?"

The man's eyes kept darting toward the door, as though he expected God to come walking in with a handful of cash to bail him out. His Adam's apple bobbed nervously as he fingered the cards, then fumbled with the remaining two coins at his elbow. "Look," he said, "I'm about busted. If somebody could spot me a five . . ."

Red Cragor, on his left, snorted out a laugh. "Now, why in Sam Hill should we want to do that, stranger?"

"Because most of the money in that there pot is mine!"

Jimbo Katz, who was next to Angel, joined Red's laughter. "Mister, you ain't got nothing in your hand that's worth five dollars for me to see. How about you, Angel?"

Angel replied with a shrug, "Not one of you fellas have got anything in your hands or anywhere else I'd pay money to see."

That produced another outburst of laughter and a few of the expected bawdy jokes, but the interchange stopped just short of becoming rank. Nobody went too far with Angel. For one thing, they liked her and wanted her money in the next game. For another, it was common knowledge that nobody in three counties could match her with a knife. For another . . . she was Angel.

Green River wasn't much of a town, and the Lone Bull

wasn't much of a saloon. But they had something nobody else had: Angel. She had been coming to the Lone Bull for three months now, and that was long enough for the customers to claim a proprietary interest. They admired her, they watched out for her, they talked about her the way a proud rancher would about a sweet piece of grazing land. There wasn't a man in town who wasn't just a little bit in love with her. She was theirs.

She came every night and sat at the center table, thumbing out her cards, waiting for a game. She wasn't averse to letting a man buy her a drink or two, but that was all. She came to play. The men came to watch the way her breasts curved and thrust against the soft material of her dress, or, when she was in a sassy mood and wore a low-cut number, like tonight, to admire the curve of her white shoulders and the play of shadows across her collarbone until their mouths went dry and their vision blurred. They sat and watched the gleam of smoky lamplight on her black curls and memorized the delicate curve of her jawline and waited all night, sometimes, for the spark of a smile from those big navy blue eyes or the upward turn of her lips. They played, too, and most of the time they lost. Angel let them win once in a while, just to keep them coming back, but she didn't have to. They would have come back anyway.

Nobody minded if she seemed more interested in the cards than in them, nobody cared if her tone was short and her language sometimes coarser than a cowpoke's after six months on the trail; it didn't bother them if the light in her eyes was more often green than flirtatious laughter. She was Angel, and the air of disdain she projected made her more desirable, the rough edges made her more intriguing.

She said now, "Are we going to play this game or sit here and talk about it all night? It's late, I gotta get home."

Red said, "Looks like you're out, stranger. I got—" He started to lay down his cards, but the stranger caught his arm.

"Wait!" The look in his eyes was desperate as he quickly released Red's arm and fumbled in his pocket. "Look. I got something here that's worth a lot more than five dollars." He drew out a piece of jewelry and dropped it on the table with a clunk. His eyes were fever bright and anxious as he looked from each of the two men to Angel. "Well?"

Red and Jimbo shrugged and left it up to Angel. Neither one of them had more than two dollars in the pot and weren't sitting at the table for the sake of the game. The stranger had lost a lot of money, true, but Angel had covered most of it. It really came down to the two of them.

Angel looked at the gaudy piece of metal the stranger had thrown in the pot and tightened her lips against exasperation. It was some kind of cross, she could tell, too big to be pretty, pasted with pieces of colored glass and suspended on a dull black chain that looked big enough to hold a cowbell. She frowned in annoyance and shook her head. "Now what am I going to do with a beat-up old piece of tin and glass? Don't you have anything else?"

"Glass?" The man almost choked over the word, and once again he threw a quick look over his shoulder, toward the door. "I'm telling you, lady, this is worth—"

"Oh, hell, put it in the pot." Angel thumbed her cards impatiently. "I'll cover you for it. What've you got?"

There was a visible sag to his shoulders as he lay down his hand. "Three aces."

"Hell, no wonder you wanted to stay in," Red muttered, and tossed down his cards. "Beats me."

"Me too," Jimbo said. "Pair of jacks."

The stranger was already reaching for the pot, the sweat rolling down his face like rain.

Angel said quietly, "Guess it beats me, too." She deliberately fanned her hand on the table. "All I've got is a pair ... of aces."

Lightning quick, Red's hand slammed down on the stranger's arm with enough force to break it as he raked in the pot. In the same instant Jimbo's gun was in his hand.

"You son of a bitch," Jimbo said. "I don't know where you come from, but around here the deck we play with only has four aces."

Panic flamed in the man's eyes and his face lost its color. "Hey, wait a minute! You ain't accusing me? There's gotta be some kind of mistake." All the while his eyes were darting desperately back and forth from the pot to Jimbo's gun, and then he made his real mistake. He looked straight at Angel and demanded, "What about her? She was the one with the extra ace, wasn't she?"

Doubtless Jimbo would have shot him if Red hadn't lost his temper and backsided the stranger across the face. In the moment his arm was released, the stranger had a chance to grab for the pot again but all he caught was the cross before he was slammed backward out of his chair, and then both Jimbo and Red were on him. Not half a minute passed before the cheering at the other tables turned into active participation, and the stranger never had a chance.

Angel quickly gathered up the money before it was spilled, counting it with a practiced eye. Twenty-five dollars and some change. Not bad. *Not bad?* a silently jubilant voice practically shouted inside her. This was the biggest haul she had made all month. The stranger was not only a bad poker player and a worse cheater, but he carried far too much money on him for his own good. A few more nights like this one and she'd have a good start on getting out of this little dirtwater town.

She carefully tucked the money inside her bodice and stood up. By that time Will, the bartender, was breaking up the fight and there wasn't much left of the stranger except a huddled lump of battered flesh. Angel picked up her skirts to step around him. She was wearing her only clean petti-coat and she didn't want to get blood on the hem.

Will shouted, "Will somebody get this pile of pig piss out of my saloon before Miss Angel has to step on him?"

Two men came forward reluctantly and lifted the uncon-scious man by the arms and legs, edging him toward the door.

"Miss Angel."

Angel turned, and Red Cragor stood behind her, his knuckles bloodied and his face flushed with victory, looking shy and excited and more than a little pleased with himself as he held out the tin cross to her. "I reckon this is yours."

Angel took it from him, her lips turning down dryly as she glanced at the man who was just now being tossed out the door. "I should let the poor son of a coyote keep it," she muttered. But she couldn't do that, of course. There was a principle involved, and besides, the piece of jewelry felt heavy in her hand, as though it might be lined with nickel. It could be worth something after all.

She shrugged. "Stupid people don't deserve to be rich." She stuffed the bulky ornament into her reticule and pulled the drawstring. "Thanks, Red. Good night, boys," she called to the room at large. "Pleasure doing business with you."

Her exit was followed with a chorus of "Good night, Miss Angel." and "Me and you tomorrow, Miss Angel."

She had to step over the stranger when she got outside, and she swore softly as her petticoat brushed across his face. It looked as if she was going to have to rinse out her whites tonight after all.

She walked half a block east, until the crowd from the saloon thinned out and the piano music faded into the background, then she slipped into the alley between the Feed and Seed and Watkins Livery & Tack. She opened her reticule, fumbled past the bulky piece of jewelry, and drew out a small bottle of toilet water. Quickly she took a draw on the bottle, rinsed her mouth, and spat, erasing the faint scent of the whiskey she had had earlier. Then she gathered up her hair, which had been arranged in a provocative mass of curls over one shoulder for the evening, wound it into a knot at the back of her neck, and stabbed it into place with two hairpins. She tugged up the bodice of her dress, pulled up the sleeves so that they covered her shoulders, and lowered the hem of her dress two inches by tugging out the tucks in her waistband. She shook out the folds of her big, faded cotton shawl and draped it over her hair, fastening it at the shoulder with a hat pin so that she was covered modestly from head to knee. Then she stepped back onto the street.

Moments later she ran up the three steps of the little shack at the edge of town and opened the door. "Papa!" she called breathlessly. "I'm home!"

The lamp was burning low to conserve fuel, and Jeremiah Haber was silhouetted before it, leaning low over the table with a book in his hands. He put the book down immediately when she called and turned, a smile lighting his face.

"You're going to ruin your eyes," she scolded, and hurried over to turn up the lamp. Almost immediately she wished she hadn't done so.

He wasn't an old man, but in the harsh light of the lamp he looked like one. His skin was too tight for his face, stretched over bones and cartilage like tissue paper that highlighted the tiny veins in his nose and the deep sockets under his eyes. His hair was thin, too, limp grayish strands that strained to cover the top of his head, and his hands and arms were like the skeletal branches of a tree poking through the sleeves of his jacket. He was far, far too thin.

But the grip of his hand was strong as it squeezed hers and the light in his eyes vanquished the shadows for a moment as he said, "I was getting worried."

She kissed his cheek. "I'm sorry I'm so late, Papa. The Widow Sims wanted me to stay and polish the dining-room floor. She's having out-of-town company tomorrow."

She stepped behind the curtain that separated the portion of the one-room shack that was her bedroom from the rest of the house, removing her shawl.

"I don't like you working so hard," he fretted. "And staying out after dark with all kinds of riffraff wandering the streets . . ."

Angel checked the small spotted mirror to make sure her hair was in place, then removed the knife from her garter and slipped it quickly beneath her pillow. She took the roll of money from her bodice. "And look, Papa." She hurried back to the outer room, her face flushed with excitement as she knelt beside him. "I got paid today—and she gave me extra for doing the floors! With what we've got saved, this will make almost fifty dollars!''

Surprise and respect replaced the concern on his face. ''That much?''

Angel nodded, sitting back on her heels as she pried up the loose floorboard by the stove. ''I'm going out to Mason's farm tomorrow and buy us a leg of lamb for dinner. And maybe some of those sweet green peas you like so much. Won't it be a treat to eat something besides stew for a change? I'll bet that will pick up your appetite!''

She retrieved the mason jar from underneath the floorboard, unscrewed the top, and placed the roll of bills and coins inside with the others. It was almost full. Soon . . .

She replaced the jar in its dark hiding place. ''It won't be much longer now, Papa,'' she said. ''We're going to get out of here. We'll go west, to California like you said. We might even see the ocean before snow flies!''

His eyes sparkled. ''The snow never flies in California, Angel, not where we're going. But Lord have mercy on me, it would be good to see the ocean before another winter passes.''

His eyes took on that soft, faraway look as they always did when he spoke of California, and Angel laid her hand upon his knee. She was not sure she believed in California, with its endless summers and golden beaches, but she loved it when that look came into his eyes. When he looked like that, she *almost* believed it, and that was good enough.

He patted her hand briefly and winked at her. ''You're not the only one with a surprise tonight.'' He reached for his canes and slowly, painfully hoisted himself to his feet. ''I've been busy today, too.''

Angel watched him cross the room, leaning heavily on

the canes, and it was all she could do to keep herself from getting up to help. His legs were paining him more these days; it was the dampness. But the cough seemed to be getting better, and as soon as they got to a warmer climate it would be gone altogether. She was sure of it.

He made his way over to the larder and bent down to reach inside. Balancing on his canes, he turned around, holding a cloth-covered object about six inches high.

"Papa, what is it?"

Angel replaced the floorboard and went to him, taking the object from him. He watched expectantly as she removed the cloth.

Angel looked at the work of art in her hands with a mixture of tenderness and despair. It was a sea gull, perfectly carved from fragrant cedar, its wings spread, its neck arched, its feet balanced on a piece of driftwood. It was exquisitely worked, complete in every detail, breathtakingly lovely . . . and perfectly worthless.

He was constantly turning out little things like this. Sea gulls, egrets, sandpipers, pelicans—birds no one had heard of and nobody in these parts would pay good money for even if they had. They took him hours to do, sometimes days. He would comb the lumberyard for scraps of only the most flawless wood, would sand it and shape it and bring life to the dead wood with his knife, then he would polish it with the oils of his own hands until it glowed, and give it to Angel to sell in town. Angel filled a basket with the little wooden pieces and sometimes she managed to sell one for a few pennies to someone just passing through, but most of the time she ended up giving them away to children or, though it broke her heart to do so, burning them behind the blacksmith's shop.

Once Jeremiah Haber had made tables and chairs, even china cabinets and chests, and they had been able actually to sell those to mercantiles and farmers. They hadn't made enough to live on, but it had made him feel as though he were contributing. But then his shoulders and back had started to weaken, and he couldn't stand as long as he once could, and he'd had to content himself with smaller items. Letter boxes, fruit bowls, pen and ink stands ... now little birds.

Angel looked up at him, a smile trembling on her lips. "It's beautiful, Papa," she said softly.

"Do you think you'll be able to sell it? It's bigger than the others, I know—"

"Oh yes," she assured him quickly. "It'll bring ten dollars at least!"

"Ten dollars?" He looked astonished. "That much? Why, a man could buy a good saddle for that!"

Angel laughed, and carefully set the figurine on the mantelpiece. "Not anymore, Papa. Nobody gets anything for nothing these days. And you've got to charge a lot; that way people will think they're getting something important."

"Still, I don't want you overcharging folks. It's not right, and I won't have you getting greedy."

She smiled and slipped her arm through his, guiding him back to his chair. "Well, all right. I'll take seven dollars if I have to. But it's worth a lot more. Now sit down for a while, talk to me. Do you want something to eat? I think there's some coffee left from supper, and a little bit of pie."

Jeremiah smiled at her fondly as he lowered himself into the chair. "No, nothing. Come sit beside me. You've been scurrying around all day; I've hardly got to look at you."

She sat near him, leaning her arms on the table. "Tell me a story."

He chuckled. "Lord, child, haven't you heard all the stories I've got to tell by now?"

"Tell me about the ocean," she insisted. "I love to hear about how it was when you grew up."

That wonderful, faraway look came into his eyes as he said, "Well now, you know the ocean where I come from is a sight different from the one on this side of the country. My folks were fishermen. . . ."

Angel listened with only part of her mind, for he was right: she had heard the story many, many times. She asked for it these days not so much for her pleasure in hearing but for his pleasure in telling. And because she liked the sound of his voice when it was like this, low and peaceful and filled with good memories. And she liked the way all the lines smoothed out of his face when he looked back at his childhood.

Angel didn't have much of a childhood to look back on. She remembered the mission where she grew up and the nuns gliding and swooping around like big scarecrows. She hadn't liked it much, because the nuns had sharp voices and made her kneel for hours on stone floors saying prayers she didn't understand.

Then there was the fire, and a lot of children died; the rest were farmed out to state homes across the country. Angel hadn't spent long in the orphanage, but it had been a harsh, dark place. After a month or so, a man and a woman came to take her and a boy named Robbie to live with them. The man who ran the orphanage made it sound like they were very lucky, but as soon as they got into the wagon, their new parents made it clear that they didn't much care for children. They didn't have any of their own, and the man needed a farm hand. The woman needed help around the house. For almost a year Angel fetched water and scrubbed walls and weeded the garden and washed clothes and made biscuits and, in the hot summer, walked behind the plow with Robbie. She was only eight, but she wasn't a child then.

Then one day Robbie fell out of the hay loft and broke his neck. The woman cried a little when they buried him, but the man just said he would go into town the next day and see about getting another boy. That night, Angel struck out on her own.

She was small, and she was quick. She could steal apples off a cart without ever being caught, and lift a watch out of a man's pocket without his even feeling it. She could hide in the hay on railroad cars and no one would even know she was there. Sometimes she remembered things the sisters used to say about God frowning on sinners and reaching out to smite them, but after a while she stopped worrying about God. She figured He had stopped worrying about her a long time ago.

Eventually she found semi-honest employment sweeping up around a saloon, and that was where she learned to play poker. She learned other things, too, like the fact that drunken men rarely paid as much attention to their cards as to their whiskey, and how easy it was to help herself to the contents of a man's pocket when his trousers were hanging on the bedpost of some whore's room.

She was twelve when she joined up with a group of traveling whores whose specialty was entertaining the gentleman at the mining camps. She was still small and nobody paid her much mind; it was a simple thing to relieve a miner of his excess cash or dust while he was otherwise occupied with one of the girls, dividing the proceeds later between herself and the other girls. She never took it all, and had an uncanny skill for discerning just how much would be readily missed, and in this way she avoided detection all across the Dakotas and into Colorado.

Until one night her luck ran out and she was saved from the hands of half-a-dozen angry miners by the intervention of a tall, bony man named Jeremiah Haber. He was a cabinetmaker from Maine who had it in his head to make a fortune in the silver mines, and he held the men off with a shotgun while he packed Angel, bruised and battered and too scared to fight back, into his wagon.

It took Angel weeks to get her strength back, and all the while she kept expecting worse from Jeremiah than she had received at the hands of the miners. He was never anything but kind to her, but she refused to be taken off guard by that kindness. She accepted every mouthful of food grudgingly, she watched his every movement warily; she stole a knife and started carrying it in her boot. As soon as she was able, she ran away.

She was lost for four days and nights in the mountains, and she almost died. When Jeremiah found her she was on the verge of collapse from dehydration and exposure, and once again he nursed her back to health. But he did not try to force her to go back with him. He left her food and water and directions to the nearest settlement and started to ride away. Angel knew it was probably a trick, but anything was better than being alone in the mountains. She went with him.

He took her to Denver, and left her with a preacher's wife who wore fresh-smelling calico and crisp white aprons.

Angel overheard him promising to send the woman money for her board and education, and that was when she began to suspect that Jeremiah Haber was nothing more than he appeared to be—a good man with no more sense than to take up a half-wild orphan and give her a chance to grow to adulthood. When he left town, she followed him.

She had already observed from her travels with Jeremiah that he was not a very trail-wise man. He would invite strangers into their camp and then pretend not to notice the next morning when a side of bacon—and the stranger—were gone. His cooking was so bad that even the coyotes avoided the scraps around the fire, and he couldn't find water in a stump after a hard rain. He never remembered to load his rifle until after the deer was gone, and it was an amazing thing to Angel that he had made it this far west. If he was to continue to survive, it was obvious that he needed someone like her along.

They made a hand-to-mouth living working silver for several years, but it was clear that they would never get rich. Jeremiah didn't have the gumption to fight for the biggest claims, and when he did strike a vein what did he do but spread the good word to every passerby, feeling it was his duty to let others share the bonanza. Many was the time that Angel had to sharpen up her poker skills for the sake of a new wagon wheel, or promise some greedy-eyed snake favors she had no intention of delivering for a grubstake to the next town. Jeremiah frequently questioned these unexpected turns of fortune, but Angel always had a convincing answer, one that he had no option but to believe. At some point, without her knowing exactly how it happened, his peace of mind had become very important to her, and she didn't want him to be disappointed in her.

She didn't remember when she had started calling him Papa; after a time it seemed as though he had never been anything else to her. He taught her to read and filled her head with stories of heroes and heroines in faraway places. He showed her how to dress and act and talk as a young lady should, and in the camps where there were families she went to school with the other children. When they were near a town he made her go to church and infuriated her by putting their last dollar in the collection plate. When they were doing well and a neighbor wasn't, he would quietly give away half their provisions and refuse supper the next day by claiming he wasn't hungry. He was perhaps the biggest fool Angel had ever met, and it was a well-known fact that fools were the favored children of God. But Angel didn't trust God to look after her papa; that was her job.

When Jeremiah's legs were crushed by an ore cart, times became tougher and money shorter. For a while Angel actually tried to make an honest living by scrubbing floors and serving meals, but impatience got the better of her. It was stupid to spend ten hours on her hands and knees when she could make twice as much in half the time at a poker table. The world belonged to those smart enough to take advantage of it, and Angel was one of the smart ones.

Even after Jeremiah started selling furniture from town to town out of the back of a cart, the money situation hadn't improved. Jeremiah simply was not a businessman, and Angel had to fight and scrounge for every penny saved lest it find its way into some wastrel's pocket. He had never really recovered from the accident, and every winter he seemed to get older, frailer. Two years ago Angel had decided that California was no longer just a dream; it was a necessity.

She smiled as she kissed her papa on the cheek and left him to prepare for bed. She was thinking about the money in the jar under the floorboard. It wasn't enough yet for two train tickets to California, but it was closer than they had ever been. And she still had that chunky piece of jewelry the stranger had pawned off on her; maybe by tomorrow he would have come up with the five dollars to redeem it. If not, she'd polish it up a little and sell it to the Episcopal minister as a present for his wife. She chuckled a little at the thought of the fat-chested minister's wife sporting that ugly mass of metal and glass, but anything was possible. She'd ask ten dollars for it. No, twelve. Preachers always had more money than they had any use for.

She was feeling very pleased with herself as she blew out the lamp and got into bed. She'd promised Papa she would take him to the lumberyard first thing in the morning. He could spend hours there happily roaming around by himself, and that would give her a chance to do some shopping and see if she could get her money's worth out of that cross. She might even stop by the train depot and pick up a timetable, just to give them something to look at at night while they were daydreaming.

For the first time in a long, long while, things were looking up.

It was almost dawn by the time Casey and Jenks found Reedy Sims sleeping off his night's misfortune in the livery. Finding him wasn't hard, he'd left a trail as clear as mud tracks through the snow from here to Pueblo; stopping themselves from shooting him on sight was the hard part.

Casey grabbed Reedy by the collar and hauled him to his feet, slamming him against the back wall with a force that made the horse in the next stall rear and squeal. His face was covered with blood, his right jaw swollen to twice its normal size, and one eye was puffed shut. The other eye showed nothing but wild terror.

"Looks like somebody got to him before we did," commented Jenks, and there was cold disappointment in his tone. He stood a little to one side, his gun drawn and his trigger finger itching.

Casey pushed the back of his hand into Reedy's throat until the other man's good eye bulged. "All right, you thieving son of a bitch. Where is it?"

"I don't know what you're—"

Casey drew back and kicked him in the stomach. He heard a couple of ribs crack and Reedy collapsed in a writhing mass on the floor.

"Shoot him," Casey demanded, and Jenks pulled back the hammer on his gun.

"No, wait!" Reedy screamed. He flung up his hands as though to ward off the bullet. "I don't have it, God is my witness, don't shoot!"

Casey said, "You know what happens to a man that steals from his own partners, don't you?" He punctuated his words with another kick, and Reedy screamed. *"Don't you?"*

"I didn't steal it! I was just taking it to Denver, like we planned, to sell it, and then I was going to bring you boys your share—"

"Shoot him," Casey repeated.

"No!" Reedy pressed himself against the wall, hands upraised, sobbing.

"Where is it?" Jenks demanded emotionlessly.

"I—I don't have it—"

Casey drew back his foot again and Reedy screamed, "But I know where it is! I can't get it—we can get it— and then everything will be like we planned!"

Casey said, "Where is it?"

Reedy took a shuddering, hitching breath, and blotted his forehead with his sleeve. "The saloon—the Lone Bull...There was a woman by the name of Angel. I was playing poker...and I lost it."

"You lost it," Casey repeated.

There was only the slightest inflection of disgust to Jenks's voice as he added, "To a *woman*?"

Reedy nodded urgently. "But I was going to get it back. I know where to find her. We can—"

"Shoot him," Casey said and turned away.

This time, Jenks did.

CHAPTER

Two

A DAM was hitching his horse to the rail outside the Green River Hotel when he saw her. He hadn't closed his eyes in twenty-four hours; the last good night's sleep he'd had was more than a week ago. He was bleary-eyed with exhaustion, aching in every bone, and too tired to think straight. At first he didn't believe what his eyes told him.

She was climbing down from a plank wagon, switching up her faded calico skirts to clear the wheel, and for a moment she was directly facing him. Her dark hair was pulled back at the nape with a ribbon and fanned her shoulders with a knot of curls. Her eyes were deep, deep blue, her skin was faintly golden. And her face . . . He could have been looking at Consuelo Gomez as she was twenty-five years ago and for a moment

23

the resemblance was so strong that Adam's breath caught.

He had been searching for three years. Sometimes the trail was so cold, and the cause seemed so hopeless, that he'd returned to Consuelo in defeat, hoping to persuade her to abandon the quest. Invariably her quiet smile and the distant sadness in her eyes would send him searching again. He had never really expected to see journey's end. Sometimes he envisioned himself as one of those knights from the old country in the stories that Tori told her children: searching and searching all his life for something that didn't exist until finally he grew old and died without having found it.

He had tracked down the mission where the baby had been brought; he had even found one of the nuns who'd been reassigned to San Antonio after the fire. There had only been ten children under her care and she remembered them all. The baby brought who had been born on Passover eve they had named Angel and she had grown to be a vision of her name. She had survived the fire and been sent to an orphanage in Wichita. The nun did not know what had become of her after that.

Adam went to Wichita. The records of ten years ago were still in evidence, which was a miracle in itself, and he talked to the couple who had adopted her. It didn't take him long to understand why she had run away. That was the first time he had gone back in defeat. The child had lived to be eight years old; that much he knew. There was no way of guessing what had become of her after that, if she had even survived. She could be anywhere in the country.

But the look in Consuelo's eyes wouldn't let him give up.

Ten months ago he had stumbled across the name of Jeremiah Haber, a woodworker, and the girl he called his daughter whose name was Angel. It was an unusual name. Could there be two women with dark hair and blue eyes of approximately the same age who were named Angel? It was a long shot, but he couldn't go back to Consuelo again empty-handed.

And now she was standing not twenty feet from him, and it wasn't a long shot at all. It was Consuelo's daughter. After all these years, against odds too great to name, he had found her.

Without moving—without, in fact, being able to move— he watched her secure the reins and walk into the saloon. Even after the door had swung closed behind her, he stood staring at the place she had been.

And then, as abruptly as if he had been doused with a pail of ice water, the stupor left him. He wasn't tired anymore, he wasn't hungry, and he wasn't cold. He was within a few steps of the end of a three-year journey, and he quickly crossed the street after her.

Will was mopping up the bar when Angel came in, and he was the only one in the place. He looked startled to see her, and before she could even say hello he demanded, "What are you doing in here, Miss Angel?"

The saloon was a spooky place in the daytime, scarred with shadows and smelling of sour whiskey and stale smoke. The silence echoed, and the slats on the windows cast bars across the sawdust floor. Angel wished she had saved her errand for the night, but as usual impatience had gotten the best of her. Papa was safely tucked away at the lumberyard, and when she went to pick him up she wanted to have an extra five or ten dollars to show him. She wanted to celebrate with a big dinner tonight, and she wanted him to feel as though they could afford it without digging into the savings.

She said, "I was wondering if you might have any idea where I could find that stranger—the one I was playing with last night. Did he leave town already?"

Will came quickly around the bar, looking nervously over her shoulder at the door. "You ought not to be here, Miss Angel. A couple of men've been around already this morning, looking for you and asking lots of questions about that game last night. They was bad-looking men, Miss Angel."

Angel frowned and tried to ignore the shiver of uneasiness that went up her spine. "Looking for me? What did they want?"

Will shook his head. "I don't know, but they was up to no good, you can bet that. They seemed mighty interested in that do-dad you won off that stranger."

"This—" She started to lift up her reticule, where the cross was still stored, but caught herself just in time. Two men were looking for her and asking about it? Maybe they'd be interested in buying it. Maybe they'd just want to take it. She would have to think about this.

She said absently, "Thanks, Will."

He touched her arm. "I don't think you'd better come back here tonight, Miss Angel." He glanced again toward the door. "That stranger—he was found dead this morning. Shot through the head."

The first thing that crossed her mind was a dispassionate regret that one source for getting her money back was eliminated. The second thing was to wonder what, if anything, the murder of a stranger had to do with her.

She shrugged and said, "Well, he wasn't a real likable fellow. I reckon he must've cheated the wrong man after he got done here."

"Maybe," Will agreed reluctantly. "But I still don't like it, him being dead and them bad men turning up like that, asking about you. You be careful."

"I will," she answered, for by now it had occurred to her that the two men looking for her might be the law. And the last thing she needed now, when things were going so well here, was a run-in with the law.

She left the saloon just as a man was coming in. She didn't pay any attention to him until that split second when he stopped and said, "Excuse me—" And then she knew all about him she needed to know. She kept walking.

He said, "Miss, could you wait a minute?"

She walked faster.

He followed.

She ducked into the side alley but he was faster than she expected. She had barely gotten the knife out of her boot before he was upon her. His hand fell on her shoulder and she whirled, rounding on him with a swift kick to the inside of his calf. His balance and recovery speed were remarkable, and he barely stumbled backward before lashing out at her with his right hand, snatching for the knife. She brought the blade up in a swift killing motion that was meant to slice his palm to the bone but once again she miscalculated; either he had anticipated her movement or he was the luckiest man alive, for in the split instant before blade met flesh his swipe changed direction and the knife sliced only air.

She backed a step away from him, the knife held close to her body and ready to lunge. She was breathing hard, and so was he. His hat was hanging by its cord on his neck, the hair on his forehead was wet with perspiration, and he remained in a semicrouch before her with his palms held upward.

He said, "Hold on a minute. I'm not going to hurt you. Just . . . put that knife away. I just want to talk to you."

He watched her eyes, not the knife, which generated a small measure of respect in Angel even though it put her at a disadvantage. She circled slowly to the left, and he turned with her, maintaining his position. She said softly, "Talk."

"My name is Adam Wood. I've come a long way to find you. I just want to ask you some questions. Believe me, you don't need the knife."

He had a low, soothing voice, the kind that would be good with cattle and spooked horses. Angel was neither.

She made an abrupt upward motion with the knife and in the split second when his eyes followed the movement she had her chance. She thrust her foot between his ankles, forcing him to stumble back against the wall, and in an instant her knife was at his throat.

"All right, Adam Wood," she whispered. "Ask your questions."

His hands were upraised and his eyes reflected the normal startlement of a man who suddenly finds himself in such a position. She could see the rise and fall of his chest with his breath but otherwise he was very still. And far too calm for her liking.

He said quietly, "If you're going to cut my throat, the quickest way to do it is to slice from left to right. Poking me with the point isn't doing anything but making me mad."

Angel's hand tightened in reflex temper and she pricked

the soft flesh at the hollow of his throat with the blade, drawing blood. He didn't even flinch.

She eased the pressure a little. "What do you want from me?" she demanded.

His eyes moved deliberately to the knife, and he didn't answer.

"Where's your partner? Why are you following me?"

Still nothing.

Angel was beginning to have her doubts about Will's assessment of her situation. This man did not look dangerous; certainly there was nothing about him to strike fear into the heart of a man who had seen as many bad men as Will had in his lifetime. He was trail-worn and muddy, that was true; a stubble of light-colored beard roughened his cheeks, and his eyes were bloodshot with fatigue. He had hair the color of summer wheat, longish in back and flattened on top where his hat had pressed it down, and his eyes were blue—not hard blue, like gunmetal, but mild blue, like dawn. His face had a hint of boyishness to it, with the shadow of something like innocence that would bring out the mothering instinct in women; but that meant nothing. Angel had heard that Billy the Kid had had a face that could melt hearts on sight but he had killed fifty men in cold blood before he finally met his match. As for this one . . . he was no kid. There was a leanness to his face that tempered the prettiness, and behind those soft eyes was a man who thought quick and stayed cool, and who had known his share of hard times. He might be peaceful, and he might even be honest. But he was not harmless.

On the other hand, the gunbelt on his hip looked as though it was worn for more than decoration. He could have come around the alley with his gun drawn, or he could have whipped it out before she got a hold on her knife, or at any time since. Wondering why he had not done so made her curious enough to take the knife away from his throat—just an inch or two—and take half a step backward.

"What do you want from me?" she repeated harshly.

He relaxed his shoulders and let his hands drop midway, but still kept them well away from his belt. "Is your name Angel Haber?"

She didn't answer.

"Were you raised in the Mission de Jesus outside of Santa Fe?"

That caught her off guard. The knife wavered, and he saw it.

"After the mission burned down, were you sent to an orphanage in Wichita, where a couple named Gregor adopted you and—"

"Who told you that?" she interrupted hoarsely. The knife sagged in her hand. "Who the hell are you?"

He dropped his hands to his sides. "My name is Adam Wood," he replied simply. "Your mother sent me to find you."

For a moment Angel's head reeled. Her mother. She had been six years old before she even knew children had mothers. After that, whenever she heard the word *mother* she got a jumbled-up impression of the Virgin Mary and the mother superior in her head. *Mother.* The word was meaningless to her.

Of course she knew that some woman had birthed her, some woman had abandoned her. She thought about that woman about as often as a tom thought about the alleycat that had weaned him; it had nothing to do with her. Now this man strolled up to her and expected her to believe her *mother* . . .

Abruptly, the knife was a solid weight in her hand again and she jerked it upright into a defensive position. "You cactus-sucking liar," she said, her voice low. "What do you really want with me? Where is your partner?"

He looked weary and impatient and . . . something else. Disappointed. He looked at her, and he looked disappointed. He said, "I don't know what you're talking about. I don't have a partner, and I just told you what I want with you. I've spent three years looking for you. Your mother wants to see you. She sent me to bring you back."

It was all Angel could do to keep from bursting into laughter. The story was almost absurd enough to be true. He expected her to believe that after all these years some woman had sent him to track her down and bring her back . . . back to where? And for what purpose? He really expected her to just go along with him because he said so?

She said, "Listen to me, you louse-eaten spawn of a wild dog. I'm not interested in whatever you're selling, so stop going around town asking questions about me and stop following me. I'll let you off easy this time, but if I see your face again I'm calling the sheriff—if I don't carve a hole in your hide first. Now get out of here."

He looked at her steadily for a moment. Then he said, "I'm tired. I need a bath and something to eat and about forty winks in a good bed. I know where you are, and I'll be back. Though right now I'm not sure why I should."

He reached into his pocket and Angel jerked the knife toward him. But all he did was withdraw something small and flat, and toss it on the ground. He said, "I'll be at the hotel, if you want to talk."

And he turned and walked away.

When he was gone, Angel did not resheathe the knife. Still keeping a careful eye out for an ambush, she reached down and picked up the object on the ground. It was a daguerrotype of a woman...no, not just a woman. A woman with rich dark hair and compelling eyes and a certain lift to her chin, a familiar shape to her mouth and nose...

It wasn't just a woman. It was she.

Angel was thoughtful and subdued as she picked up Jeremiah at the lumberyard. She pretended an interest in the small blocks of wood he had selected and asked the expected questions about each one, but she could not concentrate on his replies. Adam Wood. Was it possible he was telling the truth? Was there really a woman out there claiming to be Angel's mother, and had she really sent this man to find her? It made no sense to Angel. What kind of crazy bitch would do something like that? And what for?

To add to the confusion, Angel had returned to the saloon as soon as she was sure Adam was gone and asked Will if he was one of the men who had been asking about her earlier. Will looked surprised, and described a couple of characters as different from Adam Wood as a jackrabbit from a field mouse. Will had never seen Adam Wood before he had followed Angel out the saloon door, and as far as Will knew he hadn't been asking anybody questions about her.

So either Will was crazy, or now there were three men she didn't know who were after her. Angel was no stranger to trouble; she could recognize it by its smell, and sliding out of its sight was second nature to her. But this was different. Trouble, yes, but slippery and strange. She couldn't quite figure it out.

A prickle of uneasiness touched the back of her neck as she climbed onto the wagon and took up the reins. Maybe it was time to move on, after all. The money she had saved would get them as far as Denver, and Denver was a wide-open town. There would be plenty of chances for money to fall into her pocket there, and it would be easy to get lost in the crowd. She had hoped to wait until Papa was a little stronger, but...

Jeremiah said, "What's troubling your mind, little girl? What happened while you were in town today?"

A glib lie was on her lips, but his quiet hazel eyes were patient and too knowing. She didn't want to lie about this, and there was no reason to. If they had to move fast, it might be easier if he was prepared.

She shifted the reins to one hand and reached into her reticule. She drew out, not the cross, but the daguerrotype. She said, "I met a man who said he had been sent to find me. He gave me this."

Jeremiah took the picture in his long craftsman's fingers and she saw his eyes widen as he looked at it. It had not been her imagination. The resemblance was clear.

"Why..." He looked from the picture to her in pleased astonishment. "When did you get this made? How did this stranger get a hold of it?"

Angel replied, "He said it was my mother. He said she was looking for me and wants to see me."

Angel wasn't sure what reaction she had expected, but she was certain that it was not the slow light of wonder and joy that spread over his face as he returned his eyes to the picture. "Good Lord have mercy," he said softly. "It is. After all these years . . . it's a miracle."

Angel said sharply, "He could be lying."

"With this picture as proof?" He shook his head. "Not likely." He looked at her, a smile glowing across his too-thin, too-frail face, excitement sparkling in his eyes. "Angel, honey, do you know what this means? You've got a family, a real family, and they want you back!"

"You're my family," she returned shortly, and picked up the reins with a snap. There was an anger inside her, and a hurting, that she could not quite understand.

Jeremiah grasped the side of the wagon as the team lurched into motion. "What else did he say?" he asked eagerly. "Did he tell you anything about this woman? When are you going to meet her?"

"Never." Angel kept her eyes fixed on the road. "I've got no use for her, any more than she had for me eighteen years ago."

"Angel, you can't mean that." The shock and hurt in his voice was the strongest weapon he had. He was disappointed in her. "It's your mother. . . ."

"Maybe." She had to tighten her hands on the reins to keep the harshness out of her voice, and the horses bucked their heads in protest. Forcefully, she relaxed her shoulders and reached across the seat to pat Jeremiah's hand. "Anyway," she said, "it doesn't matter. We're doing just fine the way we are, aren't we? Who needs some drifter coming into town and stirring up trouble?"

He did not respond; no doubt he had learned by now that when Angel took that tone—firm but sweet—there was no point in arguing with her. But a troubled frown played around his brow, and the disappointment didn't leave his eyes.

The house they rented had been in Green River before there was a Green River, and the only reason it was still standing was because it had been built by one of the founders, and their descendants still owned most of the town. It was made of mud and logs, with oilpaper for windows and a dirt-and-stick chimney that caught on fire once a month; Angel figured nobody had lived in it for years except mice before she came along and offered three dollars a month for it. She had cleaned out the weeds that blocked the light from the windows, patched the oilpaper, and rechinked the logs against the draft. It wasn't much, but it was home, and when Angel pulled up in the yard and saw the front door hanging crookedly on its hinges, the oilpaper torn from the front window and flapping in the breeze, an outrage went through her that left her momentarily weak.

She jerked on the brake and leaped out of the wagon, her knife ready in her hand. "Stay here!" she commanded Jeremiah hoarsely.

"Angel, don't—"

She was already at the door.

They were gone, she could tell that even before she stepped inside. The small room had been torn apart. The curtain of her sleeping area was flung against the stove, and her mattress and Jeremiah's were shredded and tossed across the room. Bedsteads were overturned, cooking pots swept from the shelves, the contents of the larder poured over the floor—flour, cornmeal, and sugar trailed from one end of the small room to the other. The small box that contained Jeremiah's woodworking tools had been crushed and emptied on the floor, and the table and chairs lay brokenly on their sides. Pillow feathers stirred under her feet as she moved inside, broken glass crunched.

Angel looked at the devastation and felt a sickness go through her, followed quickly by a fury so great that she almost choked on it. *Damn them! Damn their black stinking souls to hell for all eternity . . .* And it wasn't so much anger over what they had done that surged and clawed through her, but the fact that they had gotten away before she had a chance at them.

And then panic slammed through her chest, and she scrambled over the table and chairs to the floor beside the stove. She dropped to her knees and began to sweep away the pillow feathers and the flour with her hands, but it was no use. The loose floorboard had been pried up, the mason jar was gone.

She sat there staring at the empty hole for a long time. She couldn't breathe, couldn't even think, the black well of shock and loss inside her was so deep. Rage, pain, horror . . . desperation.

And then she heard a clatter and a scuffle of movement behind her. "Angel, what . . . Oh, my dear God."

Jeremiah stood at the door, leaning on his canes, and as his eyes went over the room he seemed to grow smaller, to dwindle into shock like dry paper curling in a fire. His veined hands tightened on the canes in impotence and despair, and the hurt and confusion in his eyes stabbed at Angel's stomach.

"Why?" he whispered. "We have nothing . . . we've done nothing. . . ."

A stranger, shot dead. Two men looking for her. Adam Wood.

Angel got up quickly and crossed the room, taking

Jeremiah by the arm. "Come on," she said. "Get in the wagon, and hurry. We're going back to town."

Adam was shaving when the knock came on the door. The bath hadn't restored him much, and the steak and eggs had tasted like dust. He kept thinking about that girl, Consuelo's daughter.

He tried to tell himself he'd made a mistake, that he had the wrong girl. He'd made a mistake all right, and that had been three years ago when he first agreed to undertake this quest. But there was no doubt in his mind that the dark-haired little hellcat who'd tried to carve him up in the alley was the child Consuelo had given birth to. The one he was supposed to take back to Casa Verde and present to Consuelo as the daughter she had mourned and loved and dreamed about all these years.

He should have been prepared, he knew. A girl raised in an orphanage, on her own since she was nine . . . What had he expected? A socialite with satin ribbons in her hair and finishing-school manners? It was a wonder she had even lived to see eighteen, and as for what she had become in the meantime—well, he should have been prepared.

But he hadn't been. He had agreed to find the girl for Consuelo for no more compelling reason than that she had asked him, and he had never once considered the consequences. The only question remaining was what he was to do now. It was clear that the girl didn't want to come with him and had no interest in her mother or anything else other than herself. He couldn't force her. He didn't *want* to force her. He could not have come all this way, searched all this time, only to drag back a wildcat kicking and screaming who would, as likely as not, spit in her mother's face the minute he got her home.

Perhaps it would be kinder, all things considered, to simply tell Consuelo that the girl was dead.

When the knock came on his door he knew it had to be her; no one else knew he was here. He wiped the shaving lather off his face, tossed the towel aside, and took his time pulling on a shirt. She had knocked three times before he opened the door.

Looking at her now, close up and without a knife at his throat, the resemblance to Consuelo was so strong that it was, for a moment, disorienting. She was so beautiful that his chest ached. The proud lines of her gentle, aristocratic face, the startling depths of her eyes, the rich sweep of raven-black hair, so lustrous and alive that it seemed to gleam with an inner light of its own. The curve of her lips, the tilt of her chin, the flow of her shoulders and the way she held herself, with a grace and ease of movement that caused the eyes of men to follow her helplessly when she crossed a room. It was Consuelo ... and it was only an illusion.

Angel pushed past him without waiting for an invitation and took two striding steps across the room, then turned and faced him. "So where is this bitch that claims to be my mother?" she demanded.

He felt a sharp jolt of disappointment. The woman with hard blue eyes and carelessly arranged dark hair who stood across from him now was not beautiful. Consuelo was beautiful. This girl was not elegant or graceful or compelling. She was not Consuelo; she was barely even a poor shadow of her. Dressed in rags and begging on a street corner, the mother would have outshone the whelp like a gas globe against a matchstick. There was no comparison; Adam could not imagine why he had ever thought there was one.

He buttoned his sleeves and pushed the door closed with his foot. "Didn't anybody ever teach you better than to come barging into strange men's hotel rooms?"

Angel ignored him. At first she had thought he might be responsible for what had been done to her house, but the notion had left her before she reached his room. Any man who could afford to check into a hotel just to have a bath didn't need her fifty dollars; besides, he hadn't had time to get to the house, do the damage, find the money, and get back here again looking fine enough for a Saturday-night social. Besides, now that he was all spruced up, with his hair brushed out and his whiskers scraped off and dressed in a checked shirt and clean cotton pants . . . he just didn't look like the kind that would get pleasure out of ripping the stuffing out of an old man's mattress. Angel didn't make snap judgments and she still didn't trust him much beyond what she could see, but she knew about men. And this one wasn't a thief.

She repeated, "Where is she?"

He went over to the basin and rinsed out his razor, drying it carefully on a towel before putting it away. "At a place called Casa Verde. New Mexico."

New Mexico. Her eyes narrowed a little. It wasn't exactly the direction in which she wanted to go, but it was better than nothing. And to get to New Mexico, they would have to go through Denver. To get to anywhere from here, they'd have to go to Denver.

She said, "What does she want with me after all these years?"

His blue eyes were mildly assessing, his expression obscure. "I think," he replied, "she misses you."

With an effort, Angel forced back the retort that boiled up in her throat like bile. "And all I have to do is go and see her, right?"

"That's right."

"And you're paying for it?"

There was almost a flicker of surprise, or amusement, in his eyes. "That's right."

Jeremiah was waiting in the wagon downstairs, and she did not like to leave him unattended for so long. She said, "I'm not going anywhere without my papa."

That did surprise Adam, but he couldn't exactly say why, and he tried not to show it. He merely nodded.

She turned for the door. "There's a train leaving for Denver in an hour. We'll meet you at the station."

And then she was gone.

Adam stood there frowning at the door. The matter, it appeared, was out of his hands. She was coming with him of her own free will, the endless search was over, Consuelo would have her daughter back. He should have been relieved, but he wasn't. He felt as though he was about to make the biggest mistake of his life.

CHAPTER

Three

CASEY and Jenks stood in the shadows of the depot, watching the girl.

"You think she's got it on her?"

"Got to," Casey replied briefly. Casey lit a cigarette and tossed the match over the side of the platform, into the dust. "Why else would she be leaving town in such a hurry?"

There were two men with her now, and that made Jenks uneasy. The cripple wouldn't be any problem, but the young one...he could be a hired gun. They hadn't counted on that.

"I say we take her now."

Casey looked at him in disgust. "In front of all these people? You ain't got the brains God give a gopher. Biggest

41

mistake I ever made in my life was teaming up with you."

Jenks's jaw muscle tensed and his fingers flexed on his gunbelt. "That can be fixed."

Casey gave the smaller man one last impatient glance and tossed the cigarette away. Jenks was half-crazy and not good for much besides drawing and aiming, but Casey still needed him. He said, "Keep it in your holster, hoss. There'll be plenty of time on the train."

He waited until the girl and the young man turned to help the cripple into the car, then he sauntered toward the ticket window.

Just before the train pulled out of the station, Jeremiah complained of thirst and sent Angel in search of a cup of water. He eased himself onto the bench seat, stretching out his legs as comfortably as possible, and motioned Adam to sit beside him.

He said without preamble, "Nobody who's ever known Angel took her for a fool, and I've known her longer than any man alive. If she's willing to go halfway across the country with you, I reckon she's got reason to trust you and I'd be the last one to doubt her thinking on the matter. Still, I want you to look me in the eye and tell me you're who you say you are and that you're taking my girl to meet her mother."

Adam's respect for the older man eased up a notch. He had been puzzled by the relationship between Angel and Jeremiah Haber from the start, and he hadn't seen anything in the past half-hour to help him put the pieces together. It didn't make sense that a girl like Angel would stay with a crippled man twice her age, and he couldn't figure out what kind of hold Haber had on her. Nor did he understand why

Angel had insisted on bringing him along, or why he had agreed to it. Jeremiah's question now reflected nothing more than a father's concern for his daughter's safety, and that eased Adam's mind a little. It still didn't make a lot of sense, but it made matters less complicated.

He met Jeremiah's gaze and answered, "Three years ago her mother came to me and told me a secret she'd kept for fifteen years. She asked me to find the daughter she'd left to be raised by the sisters at the Mission de Jesus, and bring her back to her. The mission burned down in seventy-one, and she lost track of the child. I've been hunting for three years."

Jeremiah closed his eyes slowly, smiling. The hand of God had once again intervened in his darkest hour, bringing a miracle in the form of this Adam Wood. No matter what happened to him now, Angel would be safe. She had a family who loved her, missed her, wanted to take care of her. He could breathe his last, secure in the knowledge that Angel would never be alone.

His eyes stung with a mist of tears when he opened them again, but he was too old and too tired to worry about things like that. He said, "And is she a good woman? Will Angel be happy with her?"

"She's the finest woman I've ever known," Adam replied sincerely and hoped that answer would suffice. As for Angel's happiness, that was of far less importance to him than Consuelo's disappointment. But he was touched by Jeremiah's concern. Apparently Angel had gotten a great deal more than she deserved when this man had taken her under his protection.

Jeremiah asked, "Why did she wait so long?"

That was a question that had occurred to Adam more than

once, and he was not entirely sure he knew the answer. He said, "A lot of things changed for Consuelo in those last few years. Angel's father . . ." He looked at Jeremiah quickly, not wanting to hurt his feelings by referring to the man who had a genuine right to call Angel his daughter. But Jeremiah merely smiled and nodded, and Adam went on, "He died. Angel has a half-sister, and she got married. Maybe it would have been hard for Consuelo to bring Angel home before then. Maybe . . . missing Angel's father made her think how short life is. I don't know."

This new information seemed to hearten Jeremiah even further. "A sister," he repeated, his eyes filled with wonder and contentment. "An entire ready-made family. This is good. So good."

He leaned back against the seat, his hands folded around his cane, and contemplated the vision he had of Angel's future for a long time, smiling. Then he looked back at Adam, his expression slowly sobering.

"I'm an old man," he said, "and my health isn't very good. I might not even make it to California, I know that. But now that you're here, my girl will see the ocean, just like I promised. Whether I'm there or not, you'll see to it."

The reference to California confused Adam and he started to question, but then Angel was there. It seemed to Adam she interrupted a little too quickly with, "I had to go all the way to the back of the train to find the water barrel. Here, Papa. I tried not to spill too much."

The gentleness with which she treated the old man surprised Adam, even though he had seen her transform from a spitting wildcat to a dutiful daughter at the station.

How deep did this act of hers go? And which one was the act?

Jeremiah drank from the dipper and returned it to her, patting her hand affectionately. The engine released a blast of steam and started to pull away from the station. Angel said, "I'll take the dipper back."

"I'll walk with you," Adam volunteered casually, and got out of his seat.

"Good idea." Jeremiah smiled at his daughter. "A young one as pretty as you ought not go wandering around the train by yourself."

Adam followed her all the way to the back of the train, where she returned the dipper to the water barrel, without saying a word. Then he opened the door that led to the platform outside the caboose, took a firm grip on her arm, and guided her through.

She jerked her arm away as soon as she had her footing. "Keep your goddamn hands to yourself. Just because you think you managed to worm your way onto Papa's good side doesn't give you the right to go pushing me around. What do you want with me anyway?"

Adam reached into his pocket for papers and tobacco. "I don't think your 'papa' would be too happy to hear you using that kind of language," he drawled. "Didn't he ever wash your mouth out with soap?"

She scowled at him and turned to look out over the rail, watching the ragtag jumble of boxes and buildings that was Green River disappear slowly behind.

"Of course," Adam went on, guarding the paper against the wind with one hand as he carefully sprinkled tobacco onto it with the other, "I wouldn't be surprised but there was a lot of things he wouldn't approve of if he knew. Like you sitting in a saloon every night when you're supposed to be out— What is it you're supposed to be doing, anyway? I didn't have time to find out that much.''

She shot him a sharp look. "You leave my papa out of this. And don't you go carrying your filthy tales back to him either."

Adam drew the paper across his tongue and rolled it into a tube. "You seem mighty fond of him."

Even the mention of her papa's name caused a change in Angel; Adam could see it in the way her shoulders relaxed, and the tight line of her profile eased. "He's the only good man I ever knew," she replied simply. And then she looked at Adam, her eyes hard once again. "And I'll see the man in hell who ever tries to hurt him."

Adam struck a match, shielding it with his cupped hand, and brought it to the cigarette. He never took his eyes off her; he was beginning to suspect that he couldn't afford to.

He shook out the match and let it drop, then said quietly, "What the hell is your story, Angel Haber? Why were you so all-fired anxious to get out of town? Why are you dragging that old man along? What kind of scheme are you trying to pull?"

Her indignation was so well feigned that even he was almost taken in. "You're the one that thought I'd kiss your feet for bringing me word about a mama I didn't even know I had. Seems to me if anybody's got a right to be asking questions, it's me!"

"But you haven't," he pointed out, drawing on the smoke, still watching her. "You haven't asked her name or what happened to your real father or why she's sent for you after all these years or even why she gave you up. I think that's because you don't have any intention of going back to New Mexico with me.''

She started to brush past him, but he caught her arm, jerking her back. She fought, and he let her, holding his grip until she either decided she was wasting her energy or that a bruised arm wasn't worth the effort. When she settled down, glaring fire at him, he said, his voice very low, ''Now listen here, little girl. I've had a hell of a week and a worse night. I'm in no mood to put up with tantrums, and if you think just because I've come this far to get you I won't set you off in the middle of the desert if you push me too far, think again. You used me to get you out of town, and that's just fine. It'll stay fine as long as you remember I'm in charge now. I'll put up with a lot, but I've got a lot more important things to worry about than what happens to you. So just mind your manners from now on.''

He released her arm, and she slowly rubbed away the imprint of his fingers. There might have been a glimmer of respect in her eyes, but it was hard to tell behind the hatred.

He leaned back against the rail. ''Why did you tell the old man we were going to California?''

She lifted her chin and informed him, ''Because that's where we're going.''

Adam tried to prevent it, but the shadow of a smile curved his lips. He had to admire her gall, if nothing else. ''Your mother is in New Mexico.''

''I don't have a mother!'' She practically spat the words at him. ''That old man in there is the only family I've ever had and he comes first, do you understand that? We're going to California!''

She whirled to go back inside, but he inquired mildly, "Why California?"

She stopped but did not turn around. Her shoulders sagged a little, then straightened. "He's got some crazy idea about seeing the ocean." Her voice was gruff. "He's been talking about it ever since I've known him. And it's warm out there. He needs a warm place."

Adam said nothing for a moment. "How do you expect to get there?"

Her neck stiffened again. "Don't you worry about that." She pulled open the heavy door of the caboose. "Once we get to Denver . . . just don't you worry about it."

With a flounce of her skirts, she stepped inside and slammed the door closed behind her.

Angel moved through the adjoining car and on to the platform of the next before she paused to take a deep breath. She flexed her fingers, which had been curled so tightly into fists that the nails bit her palms, and relaxed her shoulders. That had been close. She hadn't expected Adam Wood to see through her plans so quickly, and she must be careful not to underestimate him in the future.

He had asked *how* she intended to get to California, but he hadn't made any threats to stop her. He probably figured he didn't have to. If he was so all-fired smart he already knew that she didn't have the first idea what she was going to do once she reached Denver.

Absently she brought her hand to her neck, where the chain of the cross dug into her flesh as though an anvil were suspended from it. She had buttoned the neck of her gown up high so that the chain wouldn't show and wore the cross against her skin, fastening her shawl around her shoulders so its bulky outline wouldn't show through her clothes. The arms of the pendant were digging into her breasts and she was sure it had already stained her underwear black, but it was all she had left of any value at all. Maybe, once in Denver, she could bargain it for a room and a meal until she had time to form a plan.

She heard the door from the car behind her open, and she quickly moved across the platform toward the forward car. She had had enough of Adam Wood for one day, and if she didn't hurry he would take the seat next to Papa and she'd have to spend the rest of the trip worrying about what he would say to the older man.

Rough hands grabbed her just as she reached the door. Instinctively she jabbed backward with her elbow and her foot, and heard a yelp as her elbow met its target. She swung around, grabbing for the knife in her boot, but before she could reach it her arms were grabbed again and jerked back painfully. There were two men, not one. And neither of them was Adam Wood.

She twisted, she kicked out, desperately she tried to free her hand long enough to grab her knife. She had only fleeting glimpses of the two men. The one who held her arms pinned behind her back was short, wiry, and rat-faced, with yellow teeth and glittering eyes; the other one was tall and stocky, and it was he who jerked her reticule off her arm, tearing the strings, and ripped it open.

"All right, little lady." He was breathing hard. "Just settle yourself down. We're going to get what we come for and then you can be on your way."

He snatched out the meager contents of her reticule and let them scatter on the platform—a tattered hankie with violets painted on it that her papa had given her one Christmas, three pennies, her ticket receipt to Denver . . . and the daguerrotype of the woman who was supposed to be her mother. Angel gave a muted, involuntary cry of rage as he tossed the daguerrotype onto the platform along with the rest of her belongings, and kicked out hard enough to strike him in the shins.

He lunged at her, rage darkening his face. "Where is it, bitch? Where'd you hide it?"

"I don't know what you're talking about!"

"The cross, goddammit!"

"Strip her," the man who was holding her arms suggested. His breath was hot and foul on her neck. "She's got to have it on her."

"Let go of me, you filthy dog!"

Suddenly the big man was pulled away from her. She never saw Adam coming, but when the grip on her arms loosened a fraction in that startled moment she kicked backward and heard a scream as her heel dug into soft flesh. She jerked free and snatched her knife from her boot, slicing upward. The blade met its target and the small man stumbled backward against the rail just as Adam swung the bigger one forward. Under the impact the rail snapped, and both men fell. There was no scream, no crash; just the splintering of the rail, the rush of the wind, and silence.

Adam turned to her, breathing hard. There was a small trickle of blood on his lip, but otherwise he appeared unharmed. His shoulders were tight, his fists still clenched, and he appeared to be waiting for her to say something.

What Angel said was, harshly, "I didn't need your help."

He dabbed at the blood on his lip with the back of his hand. "So I noticed."

She resheathed her knife and bent to pick up the scattered contents of her reticule. Her hands were shaking, and she didn't want him to see. Her heart was pounding so hard that it hurt her chest.

He bent to help her, and their hands reached for the daguerrotype at the same time. She jerked her hand back, stuffing the handkerchief and the pennies back into the torn cloth of her reticule. He held out the daguerrotype, and she hesitated for a long time. Then she snatched it from him and placed it carelessly inside her reticule.

He stood up. "I'll walk you back to your seat." His voice was stiff. "I think you'd better stay there for the rest of the trip."

She straightened and met him stare for stare. "You keep your mouth shut about this to my papa. I'm not having him upset."

Adam opened the door to the forward car and waited for her to precede him. She did, and they did not say another word to each other.

Late in the afternoon, when Jeremiah was sleeping and Adam was pretending to, Angel left her seat on the pretense of using the chamber pot. In the tiny closet where the facility was stored, with only a sliver of sunlight through a high window to light her way, Angel knelt on the floor and removed the cross from around her neck. She spat on the hem of her petticoat and used it to scrub at a corner of the cross. The black coating wiped away easily, revealing a smooth gleaming surface underneath.

It wasn't tin. It wasn't lead. It was silver. Solid silver.

Angel's mouth was dry as she held the artifact in her hands. Silver. Nobody would glue glass beads to silver.

Rubies, half the size of pigeon's eggs, one on each arm of the cross, and a center starburst of pearls, real pearls, filigreed in what could only be gold.

She pressed it to her chest, closing her eyes, trying to steady her breathing. She stayed like that for a long, long time.

It was real. It was hers. And it was worth a bloody fortune.

CHAPTER

Four

D ENVER was a reckless, sprawling town with streets big enough to drive a herd through, lights in every window, and music coming from every doorway. It was the biggest town Angel had ever been in and seemed crowded with opportunities and danger. Anyone could hide here. Anyone could stalk here. Anyone could step out of an alleyway with a gun or a knife and be gone before the victim's body fell.

And when Angel stepped off the train as the last gray shades of dusk were giving over to night, she was thinking about the alleyways, and not the lights. She was wearing a fortune around her neck and it lay so heavily between her breasts that she could hardly breathe. She had no idea of its monetary value, but she knew it was worth killing for. She knew that in five years of working the mines, she and

Jeremiah had not pulled out enough silver to make even one arm of the cross. She knew rubies did not grow on trees and pearls weren't sold in the kind of stores she usually frequented. She knew that she was very likely wearing around her neck more money than she had ever seen in her life, or possibly even dreamed of.

But there was a dead man back in Green River. And two men, whether dead or alive, who would have done their best to dispose of her in the same way if they had had the chance. All she wanted to do was get rid of the cross and fill her hands with the cool weight of minted gold, and she wanted it so badly that her fingers ached. But she had to be very, very careful.

Her mind was racing and her eyes were busy moving back and forth, taking in every detail of everything within her range of vision, and she almost didn't notice when Jeremiah stumbled on the steps behind her as they descended to the platform. Adam caught his arm and Angel quickly moved to take his place, angry with herself for not paying attention.

Jeremiah chuckled and tried to wave her away. "Stop your fussing child; can't an old man miss a step in the dark?"

"You're tired, Papa." Angel's voice was calm, but a prickle of alarm and guilt touched her as she looked at him. His face was gray and haggard and his breathing seemed labored. She had been so preoccupied that she hadn't noticed before . . . which was another reason to get rid of the cross as soon as possible, and exchange it for money—lots of money, money that would enable them to travel to California in style and maybe even buy a house. A house on the ocean. Her papa would like that.

Adam said, "You'll feel better after a hot meal and a good night's sleep, sir. The conductor said the next train won't be leaving till morning, so we'll have to put up here overnight."

Angel shot a quick glance at him, and the weight on her chest felt heavier than ever. Adam Wood. With everything else that had happened, she had almost forgotten about him and his stupid plans to take her to New Mexico. He was a nuisance hardly worth bothering over in light of everything else, but she had already learned that underestimating him could be a mistake. Somehow she had to get rid of him. Somehow, between now and tomorrow morning, she had to sell the cross and get herself and her papa on the train to California without Adam Wood's ever knowing about it.

And that, she was sure, would test her wits to their fullest capacity.

The Haygood Hotel was not the fanciest place in town— not the one where the rich cattle barons and railroad men stayed—but it was a far cry from the Green River Hotel with its five cubbyhole rooms and iron cots. To Angel's dismay, Adam booked a room for Jeremiah and himself, and a separate one for her, which would make it harder for her and her papa to slip out of town without Adam's noticing.

She spoke up quickly. "Papa's not well and needs to rest. He'll need a room of his own."

"Nonsense!" Jeremiah protested. "I'll not have this man out of pocket—"

"Three rooms," Angel informed the clerk firmly.

Angel could feel Adam's eyes on her and she had a strong suspicion that he knew exactly what she was up to, and why. Her heart beat a little faster, but she met his gaze without wavering.

Jeremiah insisted, "Angel, don't be foolish. There's no reason to pay for a third room. It's far too extravagant."

Angel said coolly, not moving her eyes from Adam's, "He can afford it."

After a moment, Adam turned back to the clerk and counted out more bills to pay for the third room. Jeremiah was still apologizing as the clerk handed over the keys—three rooms on the second floor, one right next to another.

They ate supper in the hotel dining room, but Angel barely tasted what was on her plate. She was busy formulating and rejecting plans, and it seemed as though every time she looked up, Adam's cool blue eyes were on her, distant and observing, almost as though he were reading her mind. It was unnerving.

When she couldn't stand it anymore she put down her fork with a snap and demanded, "What are you staring at? Do I have food on my face or something?"

Adam murmured, "Sorry." But he didn't look sorry. And he didn't stop staring.

Jeremiah made an embarrassed little sound in his throat. "You'll have to forgive Angel, Mr. Wood. We're not used to being around folks much, and I guess maybe I didn't pay as much attention to her manners as I should've."

Angel said shortly, "Don't you apologize for me, Papa, not to this cowboy or anybody else. My manners are just fine. It's *his* that could use some fixing."

Before Jeremiah could answer Adam replied, "You're right. It's rude to stare, but I couldn't help it. You look so much like your mother."

That wasn't strictly true. The resemblance to Consuelo

was still there, but it seemed to grow shallower by the minute. But that was not why Adam had been staring. He was remembering those two men on the train, and how Angel had whipped the knife out of her boot and watched them both go over the rail without even breathing hard. She had escaped rape by a hair's breadth and barely seemed to notice. She had watched two men go over the rail of a moving train without wincing. This country bred some tough women; Adam knew that. But Angel Haber was something else.

All through supper she had been staring at her plate as though trying to figure out a way to turn steak and potatoes into gold. He had seen that same look in the eyes of gamblers, thieves, and ice-blooded killers, and it didn't look right on the face of a young girl. But then nothing about Angel was exactly right.

Angel surprised him again by saying abruptly, "We have a long trip ahead of us tomorrow and Papa needs his rest. We should go to bed now."

Jeremiah hesitated, but as Angel got to her feet he agreed. "I am tired. But there's no reason you two young people have to go up. Angel..." There was an oddly purposeful urging in his eyes as he turned to her. "Why don't you stay and have some pie? Keep Mr. Wood company while he finishes his coffee?"

Angel said ungraciously, "I'm not hungry."

Jeremiah once again looked embarrassed, which irritated Angel. He turned to Adam rather awkwardly, "Good night, Mr. Wood. And—thank you."

It infuriated Angel that her papa should have to thank Adam Wood for anything. But more annoying was the smile that played with the corners of Adam's lips as he stood up.

"Good night, sir." He inclined his head slightly to Angel. "Miss Angel. I'll see you both for breakfast."

It was possible that Angel could have imagined the slight mocking spark in Adam's eyes with those words, but she didn't think so. She took Jeremiah's arm firmly. "Come on, Papa. Let's go."

"I wish you wouldn't be so short with Mr. Wood," Jeremiah reprimanded gently as they went up the stairs. "He's never been anything but polite to you."

"Too polite," Angel returned. She caught the dusty skirts of her traveling dress in one hand while guiding Jeremiah's arm with the other. "It's the slippery ones you have to watch out for."

"He's been very generous with you—with us. He didn't have to bring me along, you know—"

"Oh yes he did." They had reached Jeremiah's door, and Angel inserted the key. "I told him I wouldn't come without you."

Jeremiah was silent as she stepped inside, lit the lamp, and swept the room with a critical eye. The bed was covered with a green counterpane and the mattress didn't sag too badly; the water pitcher was filled and the narrow chest of drawers appeared to have been dusted recently. It didn't seem like much to Angel for two dollars a night, but she knew that any criticism would only open the way for Jeremiah to start protesting the extravagance of the third room again. Besides, it wasn't any of her concern, how Adam Wood chose to waste his money.

She gave a curt nod of her head. "I guess it will do for one night." She crossed the room and tugged the window open a few inches, admitting a stream of fresh night air and the sounds of piano playing and voices from the saloon across the street. "Will the noise bother you?"

"Angel," Jeremiah said quietly, and with a sigh. "I never could control you, and I reckon it's too late in life for me to try now."

She looked at him, surprised by the sad, weary look on his face. He lowered himself carefully to the edge of the bed, balancing himself with his canes, and Angel went over to him. His eyes were clear and strong as he looked at her, but something about them made her swallow back the platitude she had been about to utter. She hesitated a few feet before him, uncertain.

He said, "I didn't ask you what happened back in Green River. Our house is torn apart and the next thing I know we're on a train to Denver with a stranger who says he was sent by your mother...and maybe I don't want to know why. Maybe there's been a lot of things, over the years, I didn't want to know."

Angel felt her chest tighten and she wanted to say something, but he didn't give her a chance. There was a strength in his voice that she had heard all too rarely over the years as he said, "But things are different now, Angel. This Adam Wood—he's a good man. You've got a real family waiting for you. Maybe I haven't always done the best for you, maybe I haven't been much of a pa—"

Then she couldn't stay silent. "No, Papa—"

She took a step toward him, but he held up a hand. His expression was determined. "But you've got a chance now. A chance for all the things I couldn't give you. I'm not going to let you throw that chance away, Angel. It would break my heart to see you throw it away."

Angel knelt beside him, placing her hand lightly on his

knee. "Don't worry, Papa," she said. "The bad times are over, and nothing is going to hurt us now. I promise you that."

He looked into her eyes, and he saw the truth behind the promise. What he didn't know was that the truth had nothing to do with Adam Wood or the mother he was supposedly taking her to meet, but that didn't matter. The bad times *were* over, and Angel could take care of them both now.

He smiled and touched her cheek. "Adam Wood is a decent man," he said. "A girl your age can't be too quick about turning her back on a decent man. They don't come along all that often."

Angel felt a bubble of startled laughter burst through her throat. "Papa, don't be crazy! You—"

But suddenly Jeremiah started to cough, and her amusement turned to swift, sharp alarm. It was a terrible paroxysm, worse than he had had in a long time. He doubled over with it and his face turned dark red; he gasped for breath and each breath set off new rattling in his chest. The hoarse, choking sounds he made seemed as though they would tear him apart.

Angel poured a glass of water with shaking hands and hurried back to him, holding his shoulders, offering him the drink. He waved it away.

"I'll get a doctor," she said quickly.

He caught her hand. "No." He was breathing shallowly, but the worst of the spasm seemed to have passed. "No. Just—tired, that's all."

Angel watched him anxiously, her heart jumping and fluttering in her throat, but after a while he seemed stronger.

He reached for the water glass, but his hands were shaking too badly to hold it. Angel helped him take a drink.

His breath still came hesitantly, but not as painfully as before. He managed a weak smile, and Angel helped him to lie back against the pillows. She brushed her hand across his cool, damp forehead. "It's just too much excitement for one day," she soothed him. "You'll feel better after a good night's sleep. And when we get to California . . ."

A shadow passed over his eyes and she thought he was about to say something. She thought she knew what he was about to say and she didn't want to hear it; she *couldn't* hear it. So she turned away quickly and began tugging off his boots. "When we get to California," she continued brightly, and perhaps a little too loudly, "all that sunshine is going to suck the sickness right out of you. You'll feel twenty years younger, you'll see. Everything's going to be just fine."

She shook out a blanket and spread it over his legs and then looked at him, almost afraid of what she would see on his face. But he was smiling, and he extended his hand to her. She came quickly, closing her fingers around his, trying not to notice how tired he looked, how odd his color was.

He said raspily, "Even twenty years younger I'd still— be an old man." He closed his eyes, and Angel had to bend close to hear the next words. "It'd sure make me happy . . . to see you settled with somebody. A good man, to take care of you."

"I can take care of myself, Papa," she said softly. But his breathing was even, his eyelids did not flutter. He was asleep.

She leaned forward and kissed his cheek. "I can take care of us both," she said.

Angel went to her room, more shaken than she liked to admit. He *wasn't* old. And he wasn't that sick. He was just tired, that was all. The winter had been hard and that drafty old cabin hadn't done his lungs any good. As soon as they got to California...

California. If ever there had been a doubt about what she had to do, there was no longer. Tomorrow they were getting on the train that was headed west, not south, and not Adam Wood or anybody else was going to stop them.

Angel rechecked the lock on the door, drew the window curtains tightly, then dragged a chair in front of the door and propped it underneath the doorknob. Then she sat in the center of the bed and, with hands that were only a little unsteady, pulled the heavy chain over her head.

She held the cross in both hands, staring at it for a moment. Just feeling its weight in her hands, just looking at it, gave her a thrill of power that was almost dizzying. It was still dirty, black, and ugly, and even the small corner that she had cleaned was dull with tarnish, but when she turned it just right the lamplight caught the fire in the depths of one of the rubies, and her heart beat faster.

Jeremiah was all the time talking about the ways of God and the hand of destiny; she had never paid much attention to that before. But now she was holding destiny in her hands, and whether or not God had had anything to do with it, a miracle had fallen into her lap. She had promised her papa she wouldn't turn her back on this chance. And she wouldn't.

Over supper she had decided that the only thing she could do was to take it to a jeweler. Denver was a big town, and she was sure there were shops that dealt in the buying and selling of fine merchandise such as this. Of course they were all closed now, and it was not going to be easy to sneak past Adam Wood in the morning to go in search of one.

The prospect of flashing the cross all over town, trying to get a good price, made her uneasy, and after what had happened on the train it was probably the stupidest thing she could do. Of course, with Adam Wood on her trail it was not very likely that she would have time to shop for the best price, but how could she settle for less? A chance like this wouldn't come again. This was her miracle, and she had to make the most of it.

She had only one alternative. She might not be able to find anyone tonight who could buy the cross, but in a town this size it shouldn't be impossible to find somebody who'd be willing to give her a good price for one ruby. She'd claim she was selling the setting of her grandmother's engagement ring or something. No one would be able to trace the cross or her; she would have enough money for the fare to California and still have the majority of it left to sell. And, most important, she could be out of Adam's sight before he even knew she was gone.

Diligently she set to work with her knife, prying at the setting of the left-sided ruby.

An hour and a half later she gave up. Her hands were blistered, the point of her knife was dull, and her voice was hoarse from muttering frustrated oaths. The rubies wouldn't budge. The pearls wouldn't budge. Even the gold filigree, which looked as delicate as lace, was solid enough to be molded from iron.

"God *damn* Adam Wood anyway," she muttered, and tossed the cross angrily on the bed. Without him dogging her every step she would have time . . . time to shop around, time to make discreet inquiries, time to be careful. Time to think.

She got up and began to pace the room. Tomorrow morning he would expect her to meekly board the train with him . . . a train that was not going to California but to New Mexico. If she refused, her papa would want to know why. If she refused, she'd never get Adam Wood off her trail. For all she knew, he could be after the cross just like those two men on the train had been. . . .

The thought occurred to her with a suddenness that made her heart slam against her chest in a surge of panic and anger that she hadn't considered the possibility before. The way he had just happened to show up, asking questions about her and telling wild tales about a long-lost mother, persuading her to come with him, cozying up to Jeremiah . . .

But after a moment her heartbeat slowed and the prickle of gooseflesh along the back of her neck smoothed down. No, if he wanted the cross, if he even knew she had it, he would have taken it by now. There was no reason for him to get her out of town if the cross was all he wanted, and he had helped her with the two men on the train. No, she was pretty sure Adam Wood was just what he appeared to be . . . but that didn't mean he was any less of a problem. And there was no point in taking chances.

After a moment she picked up the cross, balancing it in her hand thoughtfully. Then she slipped it over her head again, tucked it inside her bodice, and refastened her shawl so that the outline wouldn't show. She sat down to formulate her plan.

She had to get rid of Adam Wood. And she had to do it tonight.

There were some tricks one never forgot, and how to open a locked door without a key was one of them. A twist of wire pulled from her bed springs inserted into the keyhole, a muffled snap, and the door to Adam Wood's door swung open. Smothering the creak of hinges with her hand, Angel stepped soundlessly inside.

It was three o'clock in the morning, and the hotel was as quiet as death. Even a city the size of Denver eventually slept, and the last tinkle of the piano, the last clip-clop of horses' hooves, had long since died away. Angel's bare feet made no sound on the wood floor, and she had removed her cotton petticoat and stockings so that they wouldn't rustle when she walked. Her breathing was as soft as the night. She stood against the door for a long time, picking shapes out of shadows.

She could see his long form beneath the blankets on the bed, sleeping silently. His gunbelt and his hat were on the bedpost, his trousers flung across a chair. The saddlebags that he carried instead of a valise were on the floor near the bed. Her feet made no sound as she moved across the room.

She did not look at the bed. Men, like animals, had instincts that seemed to operate even when they were sleeping, and she concentrated on completing her task swiftly and silently, directing no attention to him and hoping to draw none to herself. Her sensitive fingers felt the weight of folded bills in the pocket of his trousers, and, satisfied, she draped them over her arm. But she could afford to take no chances; he might have something of value in his saddlebags. Carefully she inched closer to the bed and bent to pick them up. They were heavy, and she held her breath as she slowly, so very slowly, lifted them off the floor.

Suddenly she wished she had brought some kind of weapon. Her plan would only work if he awoke in the morning to find himself without money or clothes, and by the time he was able to summon help she and her papa would be long gone. That was putting entirely too much faith in chance, and if she could knock him out and tie him up while he slept, that chance would be eliminated. She cursed herself for not thinking of that before. If he awoke as soon as she left the room . . . If he awoke now . . .

If he awoke now it was very possible that he would shoot her where she stood. And although every moment she lingered in his room tightened a new knot of urgency in her chest, being shot for a thief was not a chance she was willing to take. She had to get his gun.

Still deliberately avoiding looking at his sleeping figure, looking at nothing except the gunbelt on the bedpost, she crept around the bed. The saddlebags dragged over her shoulder and with every step she held her breath, afraid some unexpected rattle or clatter of their contents would wake him. The gunbelt was on the right side, on the head post, where a single move could put his pistol in his hand. Angel counted off the steps. Seven . . . eight . . . nine . . .

She reached to slide the revolver from its holster, and her hand closed around air. The gunbelt was empty.

A cold sickness sank to the pit of her stomach even before she heard the sharp click of a hammer behind her. "Well, Miss Angel," drawled Adam Wood. "What a surprise."

Angel's shoulders stiffened; slowly she turned around. He was sitting deep in the shadows of a heavy stuffed chair in the corner behind the door. Even now she had to strain to distinguish his form from that of the chair. She moved her eyes to the bed. Pillows. There were nothing but pillows beneath the blankets, arranged in the shape of a man.

She said flatly, "I knew I should have brought a club."

The flare of a match made her squint and turn away, but by the time the lamplight dispersed its quiet glow around the room she was able to look him in the face again.

He was leaning back in the chair with one ankle resting on his opposite knee, wearing nothing but a faded red union suit and boots. She cursed herself for not noticing the missing boots before. They should have been right beside his bed, and the fact that they weren't should have alerted her immediately. There was no question about it: she just wasn't as sharp as she used to be, and the realization made her angry.

She demanded, "Are you going to shoot me?"

The gun was propped casually against his upraised knee, hammer back, aimed directly at her. Without blinking an eye, Adam shifted the barrel a fraction of an inch and pulled the trigger. It clicked harmlessly.

"I was afraid the temptation would be too much," he said, "so I took out the bullets." He put the gun on the table beside the lamp and stood up. "What do you want with my pants, anyway?"

Angel did not answer. He was standing between her and the door; there was no way she could get past him—even if she *did* have a club. Fury churned low and hot in her chest. She wasn't used to being outsmarted. She wasn't used to losing. And she didn't know how to give up.

So she slid into her best poker face and replied in a tone that was just as easy and casual as his, "You're so smart. You figure it out."

He shrugged one shoulder. "Seems to me it might have something to do with taking my money and leaving me stranded. The only thing that surprises me is why you didn't try to cut my throat and have it done with."

"Maybe I should have," she admitted. "How did you know?"

"I was a Texas Ranger for five years, sheriff of a town that needed some hard cleaning up for three. After a while, it just comes naturally."

She nodded. "That explains a lot. I reckon you want your things back."

She slid her hand under the strap of his saddlebags, as though to drop them to the floor, and when she had a good grip on them she lunged forward and swung the saddlebags at him in a movement so fierce and unexpected that he couldn't possibly have predicted it . . . but he did.

He stepped into her move and ducked, taking the full blow of the weighted bags on his hip, which stopped her forward momentum. In the same moment he swept his foot around her ankle and pushed on her shoulders. She hit the floor hard enough to knock her breath away and the next thing she knew she was flat on her back, crushed beneath his weight, wheezing for air and staring into his angry blue eyes.

For a moment her struggle for breath was so painful that spots danced before her eyes and she didn't know anything except the desperate, futile gasps that dragged through her throat. Then air trickled into her lungs, her chest expanded with a gulp, her head cleared. And she felt the pressure of his thighs against hers, the weight of his abdomen across her middle, hard fingers gripping her wrists and his chest crushing her breasts, making them ache. Fleetingly she was aware of the shape of his body, long and lean and protected only by the thin flannel underwear, and of the heat of his breath on her cheek, and of his scent—shaving soap and tobacco. And she thought about how fine his eyes looked, charged with the spark of anger, and how strong his hands were, but those were barely whispers in the back of her consciousness, and it wasn't the thrill of danger that made her heart suddenly lurch and pound. It was fear, genuine and pure, because if he shifted even a fraction he would be sure to feel the shape of the cross between her breasts; even now he might already have spotted the chain.

She hissed, "Get off me, you animal, or I swear to God I'll scream the house down."

He replied in a low voice, "No jury in the state would convict me."

But in a swift and economical movement he rolled away and jerked her to her feet. Still holding her wrists, he swung her around and pushed her into the chair, so hard that she bounced as her buttocks hit the cushion. But she did not give him the satisfaction of trying to escape again. She sat there rubbing her bruised wrists and glaring at him as he stepped away.

He thrust his fingers through his hair, pushing back the section that had fallen over his forehead. He said, "I'm getting mighty tired of this, lady. I've done more fighting in the past two days than I've done in the past three years and I'll tell you the truth, it's starting to wear on my nerves. So let's just get it over with right now. What the hell is your problem?"

Angel said spitefully, "You're a fool. I've spent half my life running from men like you and none of them's ever caught me yet. You can't make me go where I don't want to go."

Very much to Angel's surprise, he agreed with her. "No, I reckon I can't. You'd rather I'd just leave you stranded in Denver."

It was on the tip of her tongue to exclaim "Yes!" but she caught herself in time. She didn't trust this man; he was entirely too quick with the traps. And the way his mood changed from one minute to the other—first shooting fire, then quiet and agreeable, then studying her like a bug on a leaf, then narrowing his eyes like he could read her mind . . . she knew what to expect from him next, and that was dangerous.

She lifted her chin coolly and said nothing.

He walked over to the chair where he'd left his shirt and vest hung neatly by the shoulders over the back of the chair. She had never before known a man who was so careful with his clothes. There was something unnatural about that, and only another cause for suspicion. Even her papa, who was the only civilized man she'd ever met, didn't go to the trouble to hang up his shirt by the shoulders at night.

Adam took the makings from his vest pocket and began to roll a cigarette. The door was unguarded, and she could have left. But there was no point now. Her plan was spoiled, and for perhaps the first time in her life, she didn't have another one.

But then, she had never before had to plan for the disposition of a fortune. She had never had so much to be so careful about. And she had never met a man who came as close to being her match as Adam Wood did.

He took his time about lighting the cigarette. Finally he struck a match and a thin trail of smoke and sulfur scented the room. He turned and said, "What if I took you to California?"

Immediately she sensed another trap. Her eyes narrowed. "Why should you do that?"

"You said that's where you wanted to go."

Much against her will, her mind began to race. California. San Francisco. There were big stores and banks in San Francisco, lots of rich people. Next to the big cities back east, she couldn't ask for a better place to try to sell the cross. And California wouldn't just be an overnight stay; she could take her time shopping for a good deal. Once she got to California, she wouldn't have to worry about Adam Wood anymore. He could go or stay or threaten her at gunpoint but he couldn't make her leave; no one could. She'd be a rich woman, and she could hire men to take care of him if she had to.

Those last few moments with Jeremiah came back to her with a sickening chill. He needed sunshine and dry air, and he needed it now. What if she couldn't sell the cross in

Denver at all? What if those men came back, or more just like them? How much time—Jeremiah's time—did she have to waste?

California, on Adam Wood's money, with his tickets. She could have her cake and eat it too. It was almost too good to be true.

And that was precisely why she did not answer him and kept her face carefully blank. Nobody gave away something for nothing.

He sat on the edge of the bed, one ankle propped across the opposite knee, smoking, watching her. A lot of men would have looked silly, walking around in their underwear with the baggy crotch and sagging bottom; most men would have been embarrassed. Adam Wood hardly seemed to notice, and he didn't look silly at all. His self-confidence was unnerving.

He said at last, "Look. I learned how to track and trail from one of the best men in the country. I found you once, and I'll find you again, you can count on that. But the fact of the matter is, it's a lot of trouble and I don't want to. So let's just make it easy on ourselves and strike a deal."

A deal. Now they were getting down to it. "What kind of deal?"

He drew on the cigarette and exhaled. He didn't seem to be watching her quite as carefully as before. "I take you and the old man to California, show you the sights, drive out to the ocean. Then you come on back to New Mexico with me and meet your mother. From there you're on your own, you don't even have to stay if you don't want to. You just have to meet her."

It was too easy. Far too easy. Her eyes narrowed again. "What's in it for you?"

He didn't respond right away, and she thought he was thinking up a lie. But when he looked at her she saw nothing but plain truth in his eyes, and that irritated her beyond all reason.

"I can't take you home like this," he said frankly. "You're in bad need of some taming, Angel Haber, and maybe a little detour to California will give you time to calm down. Leastwise, maybe you won't be so likely to pull a knife on your own ma the first time you set eyes on her." He shrugged. "A lot of people figure the best way to break a horse is to ride him till he drops. Me, I figure a little sugar and a low voice does the job quicker—and it's a lot easier on the saddle muscles. So if taking you to California is what it takes to get the poison out of your bite, that's what's in it for me."

"You're the biggest goddammed fool I ever met," Angel said, and if she had been closer she would have spat on him.

Then he added, "Besides, it'll give you a chance to fix yourself up a little. Buy some dresses, maybe learn some manners."

He was goading her, and she knew it. Her fingernails dug into her palm and her jaw hurt from gritting her teeth, but she kept her temper. He had outwitted her once today; he wasn't going to do so again.

She said in an even tone, "She must be paying you a lot, this woman that misses her precious baby so much she'd send you halfway around the country looking for me." She couldn't keep the venom out of her tone. "Is she rich?"

He glanced at the tip of his cigarette and knocked the ashes to the floor. "No," he answered. "She's got enough, I guess, but she's not rich. And she's not paying me anything. Just expenses."

Again, she half-suspected he was telling the truth, and curiosity got the better of her. "Then why are you doing this? If you had any brains at all you'd just find a girl and pay her to pretend to be me. Why go to all this trouble?"

He looked at her and answered simply, "Because I made a promise."

Then she *knew* he was telling the truth, and that unsettled her. What kind of man would spend three years chasing down a girl he didn't even know for the sake of nothing more than a promise? Now he was offering to take her and her papa to California free of charge and all he asked in return was that she help him keep his promise. What kind of world did this man live in, anyway? She didn't know quite how to deal with him, and she didn't like getting into a game when she didn't know the rules.

She stood up and walked a few steps toward the window, her hands clasped lightly before her. There was a trick in this; there had to be. Or maybe there wasn't, and that possibility disturbed her more than the first.

She said, "So she's not rich. But she's just hoity-toity enough for you to be ashamed for her to see me like I am."

"I didn't say that."

"You said I needed fixing up."

"I said you needed manners."

She turned on him. "Well, let me tell you something, mister. I've got along just fine for eighteen years the way I am and I'm not about to change now—not for her or anybody else. You can take me the way I am because that's all you're going to get."

He flipped the butt of the cigarette into the washbasin and stood up. "Does that mean we have a deal?"

Angel's heart was beating hard. She had known from the beginning that she didn't have a choice. Whatever he was up to, she would take her chances. And if he wasn't up to anything at all . . . well, then he deserved what he got.

She said, "San Francisco. It has to be San Francisco. There's an ocean there."

He nodded. "And then to New Mexico."

She hesitated only a moment. "Yes."

"I have your word?"

She lifted her chin, and her eyes were hard. "Yes."

He smiled. "Your word's not worth spit, is it?"

She looked at him for another moment, then said, "No."

She turned and left the room.

CHAPTER

Five

BEFORE leaving Green River, Adam had reluctantly telegraphed Consuelo, saying only that the girl had been located and they were departing for Denver to make connections home. Now that the plans had changed, he knew he had to send another message, and he wished he had not sent the first one at all.

There was a telegram waiting for him at the office, as he had been almost certain there would be. It said: AM OVERJOYED STOP VICTORIA SAYS GO IN STYLE STOP DRAFT AWAITING AT DENVER BANK STOP CONSUELO.

Adam stood frowning at the yellow slip of paper for a time, both amused and disturbed. Victoria, or Tori as she was called by everyone except Consuelo, was Angel's half-sister. She was the heiress of Casa Verde, one of the richest spreads in New Mexico, and married to Adam's best

76

friend and ex-partner, Ethan Cantrell. For a long time, Adam knew, Tori had resented Consuelo, her father's publicly acknowledged mistress, and it was only after Tori's marriage that an uneasy peace began to grow between the two women. After the death of Camp Meredith, Tori's—and Angel's— father, Consuelo had accepted Tori's invitation to live at Casa Verde, and with the birth of Tori's and Ethan's three children, Consuelo had become more and more a part of the family.

But Tori was a headstrong, fiery-spirited woman, fiercely protective of her family and unyielding about the way things ought to be done. Adam had never expected her to welcome a sister she had never even heard of before, especially since that sister was the issue of her father's illegitimate liaison with a woman Tori had once disliked intensely. Telling Tori about the child must have been difficult for Consuelo, and Adam knew she never would have done it without the encouragement of the telegram he had sent from Green River, which all but promised that her long-lost daughter would be arriving on her doorstep within days.

Now it was no longer Consuelo's secret, but a hoped-for possibility that might never come to pass. Now the entire family was involved, painful wounds from the past were being opened, questions that had been too long unanswered were being asked . . . and all for the sake of Angel Haber.

Apparently, Tori was taking the news well, far better than Adam had expected, and the bank draft was her way of sending out a welcome to the sister she had never met. How would she feel when she met that sister? Tori Cantrell was a good-hearted woman, but her generosity had strict limits. She had little tolerance for deception or fools, and her benevolence ended where the peace of her family was threatened.

Bringing Angel Haber into Tori's home would be like putting two rattlesnakes in a burlap bag.

Adam owed a lot to Tori and Ethan. Although there wasn't that much difference in their ages, Ethan had practically raised Adam from a wild young boy hell-bent on self-destruction to a thoughtful man with eyes clear to see the future. It was Ethan who had persuaded Adam to stay in Dry Wells as sheriff, and it was from Ethan's breeding stock that Adam had built himself a nice little herd of cutting horses that became the basis of one of the finest ranches in the Hatchet Mountains . . . or at least it had been, until he had left on this mindless quest to find a girl he wished to God had stayed lost the rest of her life.

Still, the horses kept breeding and he had good hands to break them; Ethan kept selling them and the money kept piling up in the bank at Dry Wells. Adam could well have afforded the expenses of this journey himself, but Consuelo kept insisting upon contributing, and now there was Tori. She would be hurt and insulted if he didn't cash her draft, but it grated on him to do so. He didn't think Tori would thank him much when—and if—he brought home her wayward sister.

After a moment he crumpled the telegram and sent a return message: SOME DELAY STOP GOING BY WAY OF FRISCO STOP LETTER FOLLOWS STOP ADAM.

He hated to write letters almost as much as he hated riding in the rain, but he didn't have much choice. There was no way he could explain the events of the past two days in the amount of space on a telegram form. He wasn't sure he'd be able to explain it even with a whole ream of paper.

Angel was waiting for him in the lobby when Adam

returned to the hotel, and he was ashamed of the disappointment he felt. But he had discovered that it was easier to chase her than to try to hold on to her, and, unfair as it was, he would rather tell Consuelo he had lost her again than that he was bringing her home.

She was wearing the same dark blue traveling dress she had worn yesterday, although the dust had been sponged off and most of the wrinkles pressed out. Her hair was coiled away from her face and held neatly in place by a net, the paisley shawl fastened high at her neck, and the strings of her tattered, freshly mended reticule were wound tightly around her fingers. As far as Adam knew, she did not own a hat or gloves. But even dressed as plainly—even severely—as she was she made a striking picture, pacing back and forth from the door to the window. That dark, shiny hair, those startling blue eyes, the high cheekbones and creamy peach-colored skin . . . Not one man passed whose eyes weren't diverted, who didn't tip his hat or nod to her, and even on the street Adam saw men slow their steps and linger by the window.

She was beautiful, Adam had always known that. Her mother was beautiful. Consuelo could snare a man in her eyes and bring him to his knees; she could turn her head and make the world spin. Angel had that . . . and something more. Her beauty was wild and fresh, as darkly dangerous as a thorny rose and just as entrancing. He wondered if she had any idea of the command over men she carried in that slim, compact figure, of the power she could wield with a lift of her eyebrow or a twist of her hand; certainly she had never tried to use any of her wiles on him. For the first time he found himself wondering what he would do if she did, and it was an unsettling speculation.

Jeremiah was with her, sitting on the edge of a chair with his hands propped on his canes, watching her indulgently. Every once in a while Angel would stop and speak to him, or pat his hand, then resume her impatient pacing. As always, Adam was puzzled by their odd companionship, for it was clear who was taking care of whom, and he had little doubt that it had always been that way. Surely a girl who could find compassion in her heart for a crippled old man couldn't be all bad. There must be something of her mother in her.

He crossed the lobby and Angel whirled on him. "Where have you been?" she demanded. "The man at the desk said the train leaves at ten! We're going to miss it!"

Adam was surprised, then confused, to see a spark of fear behind the anger in her eyes. After what she had tried to do last night, she was actually afraid that he had gone off and left her. He had never come close to understanding women, but this one was beyond even trying to figure out.

He said, "I had some business. Have you had breakfast?"

"Yes." She picked up her valise and Jeremiah's. "I put it on your bill. Now let's go."

Adam smiled as he took the two cases from her. "Don't worry. I've taken a lot of trains in my day and not one of them's ever left on time."

"That's what I tried to tell her," Jeremiah put in. "But you know females—born impatient."

"Good morning, sir." Adam shifted the valises to one hand and reached out to help him up, but Jeremiah managed on his own. "I've got a buggy waiting outside to take us to the station. It's a pretty far walk."

"Well at least you thought of *that*," Angel declared scornfully and marched toward the door.

Adam met Jeremiah's helpless, apologetic look and chuck-led softly. The two of them followed at a slower pace.

Until Angel actually boarded the train she wasn't sure she had done the right thing. Maybe that schoolboy, good-as-gold act Adam Wood put on was just that—an act. Maybe he was baiting the trap with this promise of California and she was a fool for believing him. When she got on board he might have thugs waiting to tie her up, or the train that was supposed to be going to California would be going to New Mexico instead. She knew she was taking a chance; the only question was whether it would be worth it. And when she saw the train she knew the answer was yes.

It was the grandest thing she had ever seen. Unlike the spur line they had traveled to Denver, the Denver–Frisco Bay was a big, prosperous railroad that dressed up its trains like a big-city woman in high-button shoes. The Pullman cars were painted a rich, sleek brown, and the interiors were more luxurious than Angel had ever imagined possible in a conveyance. Yesterday they had sat on hard slatted benches; today they settled into the parlor car in roomy armchairs, with forest-green upholstery and a deep green and ruby tapestry carpet underfoot. There were green velvet curtains on the windows and green velvet draperies swagged back at either end of the car, tied with gold tasseled cords. The ceiling and walls were inlaid with rich, polished wood, and there were gas lamps with fluted shades on the walls.

Angel tried her best to hide her awe, but it wasn't easy.

So this, she thought, *is how the rich folks travel*. No broken wagon wheels, no sludging through knee-deep mud to coax a stubborn mule, no aching back and bruised bottom and blistered fingers from driving a team across rutted roads. Suddenly the weight of the cross between her breasts did not feel like an anvil; it glowed against her skin with a warmth that almost burned. *This* was her ticket out. In only a matter of days she would be one of the rich. Never again would she wrap Jeremiah's legs in blankets against the chill of dawn as she harnessed up the team. Never again would they huddle beneath a leaky wagon to wait out a storm. This was the life she was born for, the world of the privileged, about which she had barely known enough to dream. Now that that world was within her reach, her head swam with anticipation.

When Jeremiah was settled in a chair next to the window, Adam asked her politely if she would like to look around the train.

Angel didn't want to say yes, and she didn't like it when he got that mannerly look on his face, like a father indulging an excited child. But she knew he wouldn't let her go off by herself, not after what had happened on the last train. And she did want to look around. So she inclined her head coolly and stepped beside him into the aisle.

He offered his arm to her, and, observing the way the other ladies in their feathered bonnets and bustles held on to their male escorts' arms, Angel placed her hand on his elbow. She felt like a dog on a lead but after a while was too excited to care.

He took her through the sleeping cars, where beds were arranged like double rows of shelves on either side of the aisle. Each bed was fully curtained, so that one could even change clothes in privacy, and there was one car for women and another for men. Angel had never imagined that there would be beds on the train, and she thought the arrangement was ingenious. There was a lavatory with a sink, mirror, commode, and running water; Angel had heard about fancy hotels that offered such amenities but she had never stayed in one. Adam, however, appeared not to find any of it unusual, so she refrained from comment.

There was a smoking car, decorated with red velvet lounges and brass spittoons, where men had already gathered, talking loudly and filling the air with the pungent blue fog of big cigars. They stopped talking as she went by, and their eyes followed her. That didn't bother Angel; she was accustomed to men looking at her. What she wasn't used to was having another man holding her arm while they did so, and she could feel the tightening of Adam's muscles beneath her fingers. He seemed almost to grow taller, and his stride became more deliberate and slower, so that she was forced to walk more closely to him. She was annoyed until she glanced at him, and then she was confused. His eyes were cool and capable, the set of his jaw strong, his stance . . . possessive. There was no other word for it. The other men deferred to him, averting their eyes or nodding politely, sweeping off their hats or stubbing out their cigars as she passed by. That made her feel powerful. Almost queenly. On Adam Wood's arm the men looked at her not as though she was something good to look at, but as if she were a lady. She had never known that feeling before, and she liked it.

Other passengers were strolling about, and she found herself imitating the way the fancily dressed ladies held their heads and minced their steps. She wanted to run from car to car, pressing her hands against the windows and exclaiming out loud, tilting her head back to view the dazzling array of lights from the glass chandeliers, tracing the textured patterns on the wall . . . but only once was she unable to suppress a muffled cry of delight, and that was when they came to the buffet car.

It was as grand as the inside of a church, with patterned fabric on the walls and a ceiling formed of different shades of wood put together in an intricate design that peaked at the top. The carpet was thicker and lusher even than that in the parlor car and reflected the colors of the burnished gold, cut-velvet draperies that marked the entrance and exit of the car. There was a big, curving bar at one end, adorned with a silver tea set. Tables and low, upholstered chairs were drawn up in groups. It smelled like furniture polish and candle wax.

"What do they do here?" she inquired, running her fingers lightly along the highly polished bar.

Adam shrugged. "Play cards, drink, talk, I guess. In the afternoon they serve tea."

She glanced at him sharply. "You guess? I thought you'd been on trains before."

"None as fancy as this," he admitted. "I can't even say I've been in too many hotels that were as well turned out as this."

Angel smiled smugly and felt a little better. After that, she wasn't quite so careful to restrain her enthusiasm, and she asked a great many more questions.

He wasn't sure how long the trip would take, but he thought it would be less than a week. Yes, there would be stops on the way, but none overnight. No, it didn't cost extra to eat in the dining car with its rows of white-covered tables decorated with little vases of flowers and candles; but when he told her there were over twenty things to choose from on the menu, she didn't believe him.

At the end of the train was an observation car, framed in plate-glass windows and set up with chairs and sofas and little tables for the passengers' comfort, and that was where they found themselves when the train pulled away from the station. It was also where a great many of the other passengers had gathered, waving to friends and relatives and straining for their last glimpse of the town they were leaving behind.

Outside the car was an observation platform, also set up with chairs and tables. Not many passengers wanted to risk their fancy traveling clothes to the soot and dust flung up in the train's wake, so it was almost empty. Oblivious, Angel pushed through the crush of the observation car and opened the door to the platform.

As the train picked up speed and the rocking motion settled into a steady sway, the mud and clutter of Denver was left behind. Rocky, open countryside swept by on either side, the sun sprayed on her face, and the wind streamed through her hair. Exhilaration that was almost unbearable gripped her, and freedom tasted like sunshine and wind and coal oil. Had life ever been so good? A thousand miles from here to California, open land, unimpeded escape. And at the end of the journey, Paradise. Riches. A house with hundreds of windows, and so much sunshine that Jeremiah would never be cold again. Silk dresses, soft leather boots, real feather mattresses. A table that was never empty. All her life Jeremiah had told her, "Ask and you shall receive." She had waited a long time and she had done a lot of asking, but now it was her turn. She was receiving.

The train rounded a bend and her vision was filled with the soaring panorama of the Rocky Mountains. Huge and rugged, blue in the distance and capped with snow, the vista was so magnificent that it took her breath away.

"It's something, isn't it?" Adam commented quietly behind her, and she looked at him, startled. She had almost forgotten about him.

She turned back to the rail. "Do you think we'll see any buffalo?" she asked, trying not to sound too eager.

"I doubt it. Most of the buffalo have been killed off around these parts. You might see some antelope, though, and coyotes and wildcats if the train noise doesn't scare them off. You ever been across the Rockies?"

She shook her head. "I've never traveled much. What about you?"

"Made it as far as Wyoming, once. Cheyenne. But I never hit California." He smiled. "This'll be a first for both of us."

She turned, leaning against the rail with her hands braced behind her, and observed him thoughtfully. "You're a peculiar man, Adam Wood. Anybody ever tell you that?"

He clamped his hat down on his head against the wind and squinted into the sun. "Can't say that they have."

"Well, you are." She looked at him a moment longer, his long tight arms braced forward against the rail, his back straight and his shoulders broad, his face set in relaxed, contemplative lines as he took in the mountain view. No sidearms were allowed on the train, and some men would have looked vulnerable, even naked, without their pistols strapped to their hips. Adam did not. He looked confident and in control, and the absence of the bulky gunbelt only drew her attention to the lean planes of his pelvis, and pants that fit him better than any man's ought to.

She demanded abruptly, "You got a girl back home?"

He hesitated only a moment. "No."

"How come?"

He still didn't take his eyes off the mountains. "I got better things to do with my time than chase women."

"You chased me far enough."

He looked at her then, and the slow, sparkling grin that spread across his face brought an unexpected tingle to her cheeks. "Yeah," he agreed. "I reckon I did."

Angel jerked her eyes away, annoyed and at the same time unaccountably pleased. Men didn't tease her. Men didn't flirt with her. In all her life, she wasn't sure she had ever known a man who was capable of either. But she should have known that Adam Wood couldn't be counted on to do the expected.

"You haven't caught me yet," she reminded him.

"Can't say as how I'd ever want to. I reckon any man who ever caught you'd have his hands full."

She could still feel his eyes on her, laughing, she thought. That was a new experience, too—being laughed at. She wasn't sure she liked it.

She said, with all possible dignity, "Papa will be missing me. I'm going back."

Adam let his eyes linger for perhaps a moment too long on the graceful line of her retreating back and the sway of her hips, and then he followed.

Adam spent most of the afternoon watching Angel from his seat across the aisle, sometimes openly, sometimes covertly. She had insisted that Jeremiah take the window seat, although she spent most of her time leaning over him, exclaiming softly as she pointed out some new passing wonder in the scenery beyond. Adam could almost see Jeremiah growing stronger and more vital, drawing life from Angel's enthusiasm, and the process amazed him. They laughed softly together and exchanged low, animated conversations that Adam could not hear; the two of them, wrapped in a world of their own, were a sight to behold. Angel's eyes sparkled, her cheeks glowed, she was a young girl the way young girls were supposed to be, alive with hope and vibrancy and utterly enchanting to the casual onlooker. Strangers smiled indulgently when they passed her, and Adam, as he watched her, felt a mixture of amazement and protectiveness and—yes, even jealousy— that he could not quite define.

Adam was accustomed to women reacting to him in a certain, predictable way. He was not quite sure why, and was certain it was nothing he did on purpose, but females usually took to him right off. They liked him, trusted him, and most times they gave their hearts far too easily. That he had nothing to give in return was not his fault, and if sometimes he took advantage of whatever it was about him that women liked . . . well, that was not his fault either. He had learned that when all was sorted out in the end, life was an even swap, and nobody gave something for nothing.

Angel Haber was the first woman he hadn't been able to bend around to his way of thinking with a few gentle words, the first woman who hadn't gone soft when he smiled at her, the first woman who had ever fought him so long and so hard over anything . . . the first, that was, since her mother. But Consuelo was different, and always had been. Angel was just a girl, bad-tempered, foul-mouthed, and more than a little dangerous. Yet, he found himself wondering what he would have to do to get her eyes to sparkle that way for him, and to make her laugh the way she did with Jeremiah. He wondered too why it was suddenly so important that she stop lying to him.

Perhaps it was because Angel reminded him of what Consuelo must once have been like, before Camp Meredith and the passage of years had taken their toll. Perhaps it was something else. But the journey that had begun as an odious duty with little hope of a satisfactory conclusion now took on more of a challenge for him. Just because he liked to see Angel smile.

When they went to the dining car that evening good spirits prevailed, and it was a vastly different meal from the one they had shared the night before in the hotel. Jeremiah talked about the changes in rail transportation that had taken place over the past twenty years, and Adam found the old man's stories fascinating. Angel's eyes went wide when she looked at the menu, and she ordered seven courses, beginning with mock turtle soup and ending with two desserts—a cream custard with brandied peaches and a slice of chocolate cake that almost overran the cut-glass plate on which it was served. Jeremiah admonished her when she ordered a second glass of wine and she demured modestly, but her maidenly act didn't fool Adam. He had a feeling that she could hold her liquor with the best of men, and the knowledge amused him.

Angel was not unaware of the way Adam had been watching her all day, but she didn't care. The feast and festivity all around her had sharpened her senses; she wanted to try it all, taste it all, hold it all against her breast with a greedy delight, and no one—not even Adam Wood—could diminish her pleasure in the world that was opening up before her. Jeremiah was happy; he hadn't coughed all day. Adam, despite his apparent inability to take his eyes off her, seemed to have relaxed his guard by dinnertime. When he left to go to the smoking car it was almost as though he had made a public declaration of her freedom, and Angel's spirits soared.

She sat sipping coffee across the table from her papa, but her eyes kept returning to the folded bills Adam had left on the table for the steward. When Jeremiah announced his intentions to retire for the night, Angel stood up to walk him to the sleeping car. But before she left the table she surreptitiously swept up the folded bills and tucked them away in her reticule.

When Angel had first learned to gamble she had done it for the money. Even now, her first and foremost reason for sitting down at a poker table was to put bread and meat on the dinner table . . . but over the years a new element had been added, so gradually that she was almost unaware of it. When she took up a deck of cards and met the eyes of three or four men across the table, she was a soldier in a war she knew how to win. She met the enemy on her own battlefield and she always had the edge. There was power in that. She liked to watch that speculative, man-woman gleam in her opponents' eyes turn to respect. She liked to see them struggle to keep their attention on their cards when she shifted her shoulders or tossed her head. And she liked the sound the money made when she raked it across the table, and the way it felt between her fingers. But mostly she liked the power, the excitement, the certainty of knowing that this was one game she could always win.

She did not need the money tonight. If all went well in San Francisco, she would never need to turn a hand of cards again. But like a starving child who stuffs his pocket with pastries at a banquet, she could take no chances. Tonight she needed to win . . . and more.

For when she walked into the elegant buffet car with its carved ceiling and glittering chandeliers and black stewards in white coats scurrying back and forth to serve the whims of the rich, she *belonged*. The blue traveling dress and modest hair net disappeared, and in her mind she was wearing a bright red satin dress with a bustle and train, its cleavage cut into a heart shape over her breasts, and a diamond choker at her throat. Her hair was swept up and adorned with pearls and feathers, her hands encased in long white gloves. When she walked into the room, conversation stopped, and the eyes of every man there turned to follow her. They saw beauty, they saw wealth, they saw *power*.

In her dark blue traveling dress Angel walked into the buffet car, her head held high, her eyes sweeping the crowd with a cool elegance with just a hint of a smile. Conversations did not stop, but some of them faltered. The stewards looked at one another in confusion. The eyes of men followed her, yes, some in admiration, some in annoyance. There were no other women present.

Angel's eyes moved from group to group. Some of the men were old, some young. Some of them were dressed in dark coats or city suits, some were as casually attired as Adam. But all of them had money, and were ready to lose it. Out of the corner of her eye she saw a steward approaching her hesitantly, but a man at the table to the right gave a slight lift of his hand and stopped him. The man smiled at her, and she approached the table.

Three men rose to their feet as she stopped before them.

"Gentlemen," she said. "Good evening. I wonder if any of you would be interested in a game of poker?"

Someone pulled out a chair for her.

Adam didn't know why it took him so long to figure out where she was. At least he didn't waste any time making inquiries of the sleeping-car steward; even on short acquaintance he knew her too well to imagine that she would do anything so sensible as to retire early. He looked through the dining car, the parlor car, and the observation car and its outside platform. With each failure he grew more irritated with himself. It was not his job to be her keeper, and she could hardly have escaped the train. But he kept remembering how childlike she had looked this afternoon, her cheeks flushed by the sun and her eyes bright with excitement. He remembered two ruffians and a fight between cars, and how she could draw attention to herself just by walking through a room. He thought about how little sense she had when it came to her safety, and he thought about the kinds of characters who occupied the cheap seats near the back of the train.

By the time he reached the buffet car, Adam's nerves were as tight as a drum skin and he was boiling mad. When he saw her sitting at a table with three sharp-looking men and a hand of cards fanned between her fingers, he had to wait, and make himself stand still, until the urge to leap across the floor and snatch her up by the hair had passed.

He walked casually to the table, staying out of Angel's range of vision until he had read the faces of every man there. He nodded acknowledgment to each one in turn, and they watched him warily. When the man on Angel's left raised the bet, Adam stepped forward smoothly, took the cards from Angel's hand, and laid them face down on the table.

"Sorry, gents," he said. "The lady folds."

He gripped her arm, pulled her up, and led her away before anyone at the table had time to raise an objection, before Angel could utter so much as a syllable.

In the safety of the corridor behind the velvet curtains she jerked her arm free. Her eyes were blazing. "How dare you! You have no right—"

"That's right," he shot back. Adam lost his temper rarely, but once done it was best to let it go. And his temper had been straining to burst since the moment he had met Angel Haber. "I don't have any right to tell you how to live your life, and it's not my job to keep you out of trouble; but I'm doing it anyway."

She gave him a look filled with scorn and turned to go back into the car. He caught her arm and whirled her around with a force that made her petticoat flare.

"You go back in there," he told her, his voice low, "tonight or any other night, and I swear I'll turn you over my knee and tan your hide."

She wrenched her arm away furiously, but behind the outrage in her eyes was a flicker of caution. "I don't need you watching over me and I don't need you telling me what to do! If there's one place I can take care of myself it's in a game of cards and—''

He interrupted her with a short bark of laughter, but his eyes did not smile. ''Lady, you were so far over your head in there you would've drowned in another minute and you're too stupid to even know it! Maybe you can handle yourself with half-drunk cowboys and miners who never learned to count past five, but those men were professionals. They ride the rails like they used to ride the riverboats, just looking for a mark like you.''

''I was winning!''

''They would've taken you for everything you had, and when they found out you didn't have anything . . .'' His eyes narrowed, sweeping over her body, and he didn't finish.

Angel clenched her jaw and met his gaze without flinching. ''I always win.''

He examined her speculatively. ''Do you cheat?''

She lifted her chin. ''Sometimes.''

One corner of Adam's lips curved upward, and the anger faded from his eyes. ''Then maybe I should've left you to them. If there's one thing this world doesn't need, it's another card cheater.'' He cocked his head and looked at her sardonically. ''I wonder what Papa would think of his little girl if he could see you now.''

Angel's nostrils flared. His anger she could stand, even his amusement, but his mockery—particularly when associated with her papa—bit into her bones. She had already taken too much from him, for the sake of promises and appearances; she didn't have to stand there and listen to his carefully veiled threats as well. She didn't *have* to.

''Oh, it's so easy for you, isn't it?'' She clenched her

fists to keep her voice from shaking. "Mr. Holier-than-God Texas Ranger up on your high horse looking down at poor sinners like me! What do you know about me *or* my papa—you in your ten-dollar suits and your fancy dining cars with two forks at every plate! Did *you* ever scrape rocks out of the ground until your fingers bled and then go to bed hungry because somebody better off than you had gotten to the good ore first? Did you ever pick the mold off the last piece of bread and then have to fight somebody off with a knife for the privilege of eating it? Don't tell me how to act or what to do or how to think because you don't *know* what it's like in my life!"

As he listened his eyes lost their amusement and he grew very quiet, but Angel felt no satisfaction from that. She scarcely noticed.

He said, "Are you so sure?"

"Yes!" she spat at him. "Yes, I'm sure because I know you, I know your kind. You make things easy for yourself by saying this is right and this is wrong and this is the way things should be and you don't even notice it when they're not. You're weak, Adam Wood. You think things are going to be fine as long as you mind the law and do what you're told and keep your promises and tip your hat to ladies and do what's *right*. But let me tell you something—people like you wouldn't last long in this world without people like me to take care of them. I know how to fight, and I know how to cheat, and I know how to do what it takes to get by. And I'm not ashamed of it. So you can just stop looking down your nose at me, you hear?"

Angel stopped, her chest heaving and her eyes glittering, and Adam looked at her for a long solemn moment. She didn't like it when he looked at her like that, as though he were seeing inside her. She wished she hadn't said so much; she wished she hadn't said anything at all. She wished the corridor were not so narrow and that he was not standing so close. His legs were brushing her skirts and she had no place to go without backing up. She would not do that.

A slow, sad smile came into his eyes and he said, "Let me tell you something. I came from a dirt-poor family where a piece of bread—moldy or not—would have been a treat for supper. There were eight boys and one pair of shoes between us. Not one of us knew how to read or write. I learned how to fight with a knife between my teeth and by the time I was ten I'd as soon draw a bead on a man as a squirrel. . . . When I was no older than you I was on the road to hell, and I'd be rotting in prison right now—or six feet under—if somebody hadn't come along and put me straight. Yeah, life is tough and maybe you know something about it and maybe you don't. But you make the best of what God gave you, and sometimes, if you're lucky, it makes a difference."

If Angel was surprised by what he had told her, she tried not to show it. But it was hard to remain cool and unmoved beneath the quiet touch of his eyes, and he was standing so close that her skin prickled. Or maybe it wasn't his physical nearness but something else . . . something about his eyes, and the way they seemed to reach out to her, and touch her, and want to draw her in.

She said, as flatly as she could, "So you made good. And now you want to save the world."

"No." He reached out and lightly touched her hair. She couldn't believe it, but he did. And she didn't pull away.

His eyes drifted to the place where his fingertips curled around a strand of her hair and he added softly, "Just one girl."

Angel could feel her heart beating, and the emotion that spiraled up inside her felt like confusion, but it wasn't, exactly. She didn't know what had happened from the time he had jerked her out of the buffet car till now, but it was unsettling. Everything about Adam Wood was unsettling. She should have been furious with him, but she wasn't. She should have knocked his hand away, but she didn't.

His fingertips lightly traced the curve of her ear in a light, breathtakingly gentle caress. No man had ever touched her with gentleness except her papa; she hadn't known that any other man was capable of it. His eyes held her, seeming to ask something from her, seeing things inside her she didn't want him to see . . . but making her feel as though, just once, she might like him to see.

At last she lowered her eyes and turned her face away from his touch. "I'm not worth saving," she said gruffly, and started to move past him.

His hand touched her waist and drew her back in an easy, fluid motion. She should have known what was going to happen next, and perhaps in a way she did; perhaps, for one fleeting moment of weakness and confusion, she wanted it to happen.

It was all very swift and easy, without hesitation or pause, but she could have struggled if she had wanted to. His hand was on the small of her back, his arm encircling her, and in turning her he had drawn her close against him, so that her breasts almost touched his chest. Her hands were braced against his arms but there was an instant in which she was too startled to push away. Then his hand came down and cupped her chin, gently lifting her face. She saw his eyes. His mouth covered hers.

How soft his lips were! They were like velvet, pressing against hers, and so warm, so sweet. His face, which she had thought would be as coarse as sandpaper, was smooth, heated, faintly scented with bay rum. The heat—that was what she had not expected. The heat that rose up inside her, that fanned from him and made her even hotter . . . and the way her heart beat, lurching and slamming against her chest at first, then scattering in broken little pulses so fast that it made her dizzy. The way her throat clenched up and her stomach went hollow with surprise, as though someone had kicked her beneath the ribs, and the strangeness of all the sensations that battered down on her, making her muscles feel like rubber. None of that should have happened just because Adam Wood kissed her.

But it did. She lost her breath and her head spun as his lips drank of her, gently drawing out of her everything that was of importance. His hand was hard on her back, his muscles tight beneath her fingers, and she was like wax melting against him, sinking into him until the heat that burned her face and tingled in her limbs flamed through her breasts and her abdomen, where her body met his. Against the soft parts of her, he was hard. Where she was weak and pliable, he was strong. For one timeless moment he took her mind and wiped it clean, he held her body and made it respond to his command, he filled her with sensation and made her his.

It couldn't have lasted very long. A moment, maybe two. But it was too long. It seemed like forever. He let her go, first with his hands, then with his lips. And she didn't look at him. She drew one shaky breath, and she let the world right itself, and she wanted to look at him but she was afraid of the weakness, the confusion he would see in her eyes. She was afraid of the power she might see in his, and that if she looked at him it might start all over again, and she wasn't sure she wanted that . . . she wasn't sure at all.

So she pushed him aside, and he might have said her name, but she didn't look back. She hurried away, toward the sleeping car where he could not follow. But even in the safety of her curtained cubicle the taste of him lingered on her mouth and the smell of him clung to her skin, and she did not sleep for a very long time.

CHAPTER

Six

ADAM was in the smoking car when Angel came to him. In the middle of the afternoon on a chill, drizzling day in the heart of the Rockies, most of the passengers were dozing in their seats, or reading the newspapers that had been delivered on their last stop, or talking quietly in the parlor car, subdued by the oppressive fog that clung to the windows and muted the scenery. There were a few other men in the car but Adam sat apart from them, leaning back in a big chair by the window, smoking and looking out at nothing.

He had spent a great deal of time by himself since the last evening with Angel, and he thought the smartest thing he could do was to pass the rest of the trip that way. One way or another, any time spent with Angel ended up being more than he had bargained for.

It wasn't that he regretted kissing her. It was just that he didn't understand why he had done it, and trying to figure it out bothered him more than he wanted to admit. Adam knew trouble when he saw it, and Angel Haber was nothing but trouble; he had known it then and he knew it now. He did not, as a rule, go around kissing pretty girls just because they were pretty, and that was not why he had kissed Angel.

The truth was, she had touched something inside him that night and it had surprised and confused him. One moment she was a stranger, the next moment she was not. One moment she was a half-wild, unpredictable, incorrigible child, but when she was in his arms she was . . . something else. And it confused him.

Ethan had often accused him of thinking too much; perhaps that was the problem. Or perhaps the problem was that he knew that given the chance, he would do it all over again.

It was first her shadow, then her scent—like mountain rain—that alerted him to her presence. His muscles tensed, as they always did when she was around, and he glanced up.

She was wearing a brown calico dress and had wound a yellow ribbon around the twisted and pinned knot of hair at the back of her head. There was something about the contrast of that bright yellow ribbon against the jet-black hair that took his breath away, like a shaft of brilliant sunshine piercing the clouds. He sensed the eyes of every man in the room upon her, just as his were, but Angel had that way about her. She was a master of the little things, the subtle, almost unnoticeable nuances that went straight to the core of what made a man forget himself and think only about her . . . a scrap of ribbon, a way of tilting her head, a button left carelessly undone, a flash of petticoat when one least expected it. From another woman these things would have looked contrived, even cheap. But with Angel one was never quite sure whether she was even aware of what she did, and it was that very naturalness that was her charm.

A man would have to be a fool not to find her desirable. Adam was no fool, but he was too smart to walk knowingly into the trap of a woman like Angel. He would, he reminded himself, simply have to be a great deal more careful from now on.

Angel, for her part, seemed little affected by their last encounter. She met his gaze just as boldly, and her tongue was just as sharp. True, she spent most of her days reading to her father and at mealtimes left the conversation to the two men, but there was nothing in her manner to indicate that anything had changed between her and Adam. However, this was the first time they had been alone since that evening.

Adam asked mildly, "Why is it that every time I see you you're somewhere you shouldn't be?"

Angel wrinkled her nose and sat down in the chair opposite him. "It stinks in here."

"That's why they call it a smoking car."

She glanced around, and one by one the other men averted their eyes. Some of them even put out their cigars and left the car. She settled her shoulders and folded her hands, resting them atop the small table that separated her from Adam. She looked at him, and because there was nothing in her eyes to indicate what might be on her mind, Adam felt his muscles tense another fraction.

She said, "I want to ask you something."

He flipped the ashes of his cigarette into a brass spittoon

at his feet, hoping his silence would be discouraging. It was not.

"How do you know you've got the right girl?"

He couldn't hide his surprise. "What?"

"Me," she explained impatiently. "How do you know I'm the girl this woman sent you to find?"

Inch by inch, Adam's muscles unwound. He explained to her how he had traced her down from the mission to which Consuelo had sent her infant, and with each word the puckered line in her forehead grew deeper. She looked almost disappointed when he finished.

"There are lots of orphans in this part of the country," she pointed out dismissively. "More orphans than grown folks. You still could have gotten the wrong one."

Adam was a little puzzled. She sounded almost as though she *hoped* he had made a mistake. "That's true," he agreed. "But not too many of them make it to Catholic missions . . . especially not many with Mexican blood."

Her eyes sharpened. "My mother was a Mexican?"

"Part Mexican," he answered cautiously. "Part Indian."

Her lips twisted in an involuntary sneer of disgust, and her eyes flashed denial. "Then I know you made a mistake. Look at me!" She stretched out her hands for him to see. "I'm white! Any fool could see that!"

"Your father was white," Adam told her, as calmly as he could.

Her lips tightened, and she looked out the window. Adam could not see the struggle in her eyes, but he could read it in the curling of her fingers on the table, in the tightening of her small shoulders and the straightening of her spine. And suddenly he understood why she had never asked these questions before, why she had professed such a disinterest in her mother and her own past history and the life that could have been hers. She didn't want to know. At first Adam didn't understand why, but the courage that it took for her to ask the questions now was obvious as she turned back to him.

Her tone was nonchalant, but a shadow of something very much like fear, or uncertainty, lurked behind her clear blue eyes. "So this place," she said, "this ranch where she lives . . . Casa Verde. Papa says it's a big place. What is she, the housekeeper?"

"No." And suddenly Adam *did* understand. Why had it never occurred to him before, how difficult it would be to explain? How would it sound to her, hearing it for the first time?

He said carefully, "Her—your father always wanted her to live there. After he died, your sister, Tori, asked her to stay."

Her eyes narrowed fractionally, but there was no sign of interest in her tone. "I've got a sister?"

"Half-sister." He felt on easier ground now. "She married my best friend. They have three children . . ." he managed a little smile, "at last count."

She ignored that. "And what about her?" The way she said the word, with a slight tightness to her voice and a curl to her lips, let Adam know she was referring to her mother. "What did she do before she went to live on the big ranch?"

Adam didn't know anything but the truth. "She owned a saloon."

Nothing changed on her face. "And him?" she demanded coldly. "The man that made me a bastard?"

Adam was silent longer than he should have been. Camp

Meredith, one of the slipperiest, most notorious outlaws in the Southwest. His fortune was built on the blood of others. He was a king and his kingdom was what was pillaged and stolen; the soldiers in his army were murderers, thieves, and cutthroats. But he had loved his daughter Tori and protected her with his life. Adam supposed, although it was hard to admit, that he had even loved Consuelo. And in the end even Ethan, who had come to Casa Verde to destroy Camp Meredith, had grown to respect and admire him.

None of that could be summed up in a few short sentences. None of that would answer Angel's question.

He said after a moment and with some difficulty, "Your mother loved him. He was good to her."

"Not good enough to marry her," Angel returned shortly.

Adam couldn't explain that. And Angel was persistent.

"So who was he?" she demanded.

Adam met her eyes. He said, "His name was Camp Meredith. He ran one of the most successful outlaw gangs west of the Mississippi for over ten years. But in the end . . ." And this was hard for him to say, even after all this time. "He was just a rancher."

Angel's hands were now closed into small, tight fists atop the table. She dropped her eyes to look at them, but not a single muscle on her face flinched. Adam felt a hollowness inside.

"So," she said at last, and looked at him. Adam had never seen such emptiness in a woman's eyes, and he hoped never to do so again. Her smile was cold and tight. "The daughter of a half-breed whore and an outlaw. The apple doesn't fall far, does it?"

She stood, her head held high, and left the car.

Adam wanted to call her back, but he didn't know what

to say. He pinched out the cigarette and flung it angrily toward the spittoon.

A voice spoke quietly over his shoulder. "It's hard when you've got nothing to say but the truth, isn't it?"

Adam didn't know how long Jeremiah had been standing there, but obviously it had been long enough. The old man came around the table and eased himself painfully into the seat Angel had vacated. Adam expected to see disappointment on his face, or even accusation, but there was neither. Somehow that made Adam feel even worse.

Adam said, "I shouldn't have told her."

"I don't see that you had much choice." Jeremiah used his hands to adjust his legs beneath the table, and propped up his canes nearby.

Adam dropped his eyes briefly. "I guess I never thought about how it would sound. I never thought about how it would be, not knowing who your folks were or where you came from and then finding out all of a sudden like that. I should've thought about it."

Jeremiah smiled. It was the smile of an old man who has known too much pain to be hurt himself anymore, but who still has room to feel the pain of others. He said, "Our Angel, she's trail-tough. She's had to be. The good Lord knows I haven't been much help to her." He made a small, deprecating gesture toward his legs. "And she's had to do a lot more taking care of herself than she should have. She got tough. But she's got this soft part in her that she doesn't let folks see . . . sometimes I think it's even softer than she knows. I've spent half my life trying to teach her that that softness is the best part of all of us, but it hasn't done any good. Maybe what she needs is for somebody to just break through that toughness and make her look at herself."

"Maybe you're wrong," Adam said slowly. "Maybe the softness isn't the best part."

Jeremiah's eyes gentled. "I think you know better than that. And maybe you're just the one to teach my Angel, too."

For the first time Adam wondered just how well Jeremiah knew the girl he had chosen to call his daughter... and whether the things Angel thought she had kept secret from him were really secret at all, or merely tolerated out of love.

Adam said, "Not many men would've done what you have. She has a lot to thank you for."

He shook his head. "She could have done better. I gave her food and shelter and an education, as best I could. The rest she did for herself. Many's the time I've thought she might've been better off without me... and I do worry about her. About what will become of her when I'm gone. Not because I think she can't take care of herself; she can. But because..." He met Adam's eyes soberly. "When I'm gone, she won't have anybody left to care about. And having somebody to care about, son, that's the most important thing in the world. That's what keeps us alive."

Adam shifted his eyes away from the old man's gaze, suddenly uncomfortable. For three years his life had centered around Angel Haber: searching for her, tracking her, finding her. But he had never *thought* about her. Even after he had found her she had been an obstacle to be overcome, a duty to be executed, an embarrassment to be gotten around. Now that he was being forced to think about her, things weren't so black and white anymore, and it was not a thing with which his mind rested easy.

He was also being forced to think about other things, and see them in a whole new light. About how much alike they were, he and Angel. She reminded him of the worst parts of himself, the parts he had struggled to ignore, and keep hidden, just as Angel tried to hide the vulnerability buried deep within her. She made him angry, she made him frustrated. She made him remember how bad it was to be alone.

And he thought about Consuelo. Looking at her through Angel's eyes was an unsettling experience, and he couldn't make himself do so for very long. Even hearing himself say the words, and knowing how Angel heard him, made him think he was talking about a woman he didn't know. A saloon girl, mistress of a common outlaw. Consuelo was the bravest, strongest, most clean-spirited woman he had ever known, and from the moment he had met her he would have laid down his life for her on command and without question. But now . . . now he couldn't help wondering what kind of woman would give up her baby and not even wonder what had become of it for fifteen years. It was an ugly, insidious thought, like a mud stain on white satin, and he pushed it aside as quickly as he could. But still the doubts, the questions he had never bothered with before, because he thought he had all the answers, cluttered the back of his mind like the residue of something unclean.

It was much easier not to think at all. But he had never learned how to do that.

He glanced at Jeremiah and said, "I reckon she must be feeling pretty low about now. Maybe you should go talk to her."

"I don't think I have anything to say to her." His gaze held steady. "But maybe you do."

Adam didn't think so. He didn't want to. But it was only

another couple of moments before he got up and went in search of Angel.

1868

Everyone in Dry Wells knew it when Camp Meredith and his gang rode back into town. The town, which was dead at all other times, suddenly took on life. There was joyful gunfire in the streets, whoops of victory, drinks poured free, fistfights and broken furniture, and general mayhem. Consuelo Gomez had worked behind the bar all night, pouring those drinks, enduring the filthy jokes, watching the other girls playfully fend off the advances—or, more often, submit to them—of Camp's men. But no one ever laid a hand on Consuelo. She was Camp Meredith's woman, and to offer insult to her was to invite a brutal death.

By the early hours of the morning the excitement had built so high within her that she thought she'd burst. Camp had been away only a few months, but it felt like years. Now he was home, and she would welcome him with her news, her surprise, the miracle that was growing inside her. She was Camp Meredith's woman, and that made her the most important woman in town. She thought she could never have asked for more, but now she had even more. She was carrying Camp Meredith's child.

She knew her lover was married and that he had a child somewhere back east. That meant nothing to her, even as it meant nothing to him. More than a mountain range divided Camp Meredith from what he had left back east, and here, in this time and place, he belonged to her. And she to him.

She went to her room and changed into her prettiest dress. Camp had not been in the saloon all evening, but he would come to her now. Their reunions were always private.

When he burst through the door his face was florid and his eyes were glittering with excitement. He was drunk, but then he often was. He gave a whoop and tossed his hat onto the bed, then picked Consuelo up by the waist and swung her around until she was dizzy.

She laughed and squealed and begged to be put down, and when he let her go she staggered for a moment while the world stopped spinning. It was always like that with Camp. Dizzying.

"By damn, honey, this is the biggest job we ever pulled!" he declared. He strode over to the bureau where she always kept a bottle of bourbon ready for him and poured himself a glass. "Went off as smooth as silk. I'm a rich man, darlin', did you know that? A by-damn for sure *rich* man!"

He bellowed with laughter and downed the bourbon. "Now I can start that ranch we've been talking about. And build that house, a big house up there on the hill. Fine place, big enough for a family—"

Consuelo's heart caught in her chest. She could hardly believe what she was hearing. "A family?" She took a hesitant, joyful step forward. "Do you mean— Oh, Camp . . . does this mean we can get married, and have children—"

His sharp scowl cut her off, and even though he tried to smooth out his features in the next moment it was too late. That look went through her like a knife, and she felt the cut of it all the way to her vitals.

"Now, honey," he said brusquely, "don't start with that kind of nonsense. You know I think the world of you, but it just wouldn't be right. I've got a wife, a fine wife from a good family, got me a fine little girl too. I don't need any half-breed bastards, and neither do you."

The knife twisted, carving out huge chunks of her insides, leaving her bleeding and torn.

Camp must have seen something on her face, because he took a step toward her, and gentled his voice. "Now don't get your back up, darlin'. You know I'm saying the truth. Why, now that I got me a grubstake, I'll be sending for my family pretty soon, settin' them up in that big house, and I reckon things will be changin' a mite between you and me. She don't cotton much to whorin'. Half-breeds, either." And he chuckled. "Can't say's I blame her much at that."

Consuelo felt an awful, burning cold envelop her. Half-breed. Whore. She was Camp Meredith's woman. She was proud, she was protected, she was *important*. No one was allowed to talk to her like that. Not in his presence. Half-Spanish, half-Indian, she knew what she was and she knew what she had done to survive. But no one ever talked to her like that. *No one*.

His chuckles echoed eerily in her ears long after they had faded. And then he came toward her, grinning. "Come on, honey, let's get to bed. We got some celebratin' to do."

Half-breed. Whore. She watched him come toward her with that leer on his face, his arms open to embrace her, his mouth open to cover hers with his smothering, bourbon-scented kisses, and she hated him then, hated him with a blind fury unlike any she had ever known. He couldn't do this to her. He *couldn't*.

There was a paring knife on the table and she grabbed it without knowing she had done so; she lunged at him. She saw the startlement on Camp's face, but even taken off guard, even drunk, his reflexes were superb. He grabbed her wrist, twisting it backward. She screamed in rage more than pain; she fought him, kicking at him, flailing at him with her free hand, and neither of them ever knew how it happened. It was over in an instant.

She felt a sharp, lashing pain across her cheek from temple to jaw and she staggered backward. The knife clattered from Camp's hand to the floor. He stared at her, pale with shock, and she felt blood begin to trickle down her face. She tasted it on her parted lips.

"My God," Camp whispered. "My God, Connie, what have I done?"

He grabbed for a towel from the washstand, upsetting the water pitcher with a crash. She just stared at him. He tried to press the towel against the wound but she jerked her face away.

"Connie . . ."

She would never forget the look in his eyes—shocked, sorry, disbelieving. But neither would she forget the words he had spoken. Nor forgive them.

She turned and walked out of the room, out of the saloon, out of his life.

CHAPTER

Seven

THE observation platform was empty. The mountains were huge amorphous shapes swathed in fog on either side of the train, and the air moved across Angel's face like a clammy hand. Mist dampened her hair and her skin and formed tiny droplets on her eyelashes that blurred her vision. She was cold, and she was angry.

She was angry at herself for having asked, and angry at Adam for having answered. She was angry at the unknown woman who in one wanton act of lust with a worthless, cowardly outlaw had brought all this misery to bear. But most of all she was angry with the child inside her, that stupid, misty-eyed part of her that clung so stubbornly to her coattails no matter how hard she tried to shake it off, which had allowed her to think that the answers to her questions might have turned out differently.

She wasn't surprised. Why should she be? She knew what kind of children were abandoned by their parents: the worthless kind, the weak, the ugly. The used up, the inferior, the kind nobody wanted. A coyote would walk off and leave the sick pup to die. A bobcat would push the deformed kitten from its teat. And the ones that had pushed Angel out of the nest were no better than the animals after which they modeled themselves. She wasn't surprised.

But she wasn't ugly, or a weakling, or deformed. And when she was very small, soon after she learned that the natural order of things was for little girls to have mothers and fathers and beds of their own, she had begun to wonder. And to fantasize. She had imagined that her mother was a princess and her father a sainted knight, off on some holy mission, and that they had left her in the hands of the good sisters only until the kingdom was safe for her again. As she grew older the fantasies matured and she lulled herself to sleep on dreams of holy missionaries who had left her behind temporarily while they went west to make a home for her. The missionaries became bankers, railroad men, famous actors. But always there was a thread of continuity . . . they would return for her.

By the time the mission burned and she realized that no one was going to return for her, the fantasies came less often. The parents of so many of the other children in the orphanage were dead; she could only believe that hers were too. But still she liked to imagine who they might have been, and they were always worthy people, wealthy people, *good* people. After Jeremiah, she didn't fantasize anymore; she knew what her life was. But still in some unsuspecting part of her mind the image clung ... of parents who loved her, who had been taken from her through no fault of her own, who had been, in some way she would never know, special, even great. Then Adam Wood had walked into her life and changed all that.

And that was what angered her most. That even after learning her mother was alive, she hadn't been more prepared for the truth.

She took the daguerrotype from her reticule and looked at it. The woman who looked back had her face and her hair and her mouth, but she was a stranger, and when Angel looked at her she felt bitterness. She felt like a fool. What had she expected, anyway, from a woman who would throw her baby away like a worn-out dishcloth? That she would be a saint?

She closed her fist around the picture and leaned back to throw it overboard. A strong hand closed around her wrist from behind.

"Don't do that, Angel," Adam said quietly. "If you do, you'll regret it the rest of your life."

She whirled on him, jerking her arm away. Suddenly the hatred that was welling up inside her for the woman who had abandoned her was transferred to him: Adam Wood, with his quiet eyes and his low voice, so neat and well dressed and smug. What did he know about any of it? What did he care?

And what did he see when he looked at her now? Her mother?

She flung the picture at him. "Take it," she said shortly. "It means more to you than it ever will to me, anyway."

The small picture struck him in the chest and clattered to

the floor. He made no move to pick it up, so she did, swiping at it first with a vicious gesture, then straightening slowly.

She held the picture in her hand, looking at him. Her heart was beating hard and slowly, and Adam was as solid and unbreachable as the mountains that surrounded them. The mist pulsed around them and danger seemed to echo on the thin, lonely wail of the train whistle. Her hand tightened until the metal frame bit into her flesh. She took a step toward him, very close, and placed her hand on his vest. Lifting it back, she slipped the picture into his shirt pocket. And she didn't take her hands away.

She tilted her head up to him. She said, "You're not the first man that's ever kissed me, you know."

His face remained expressionless. "Is that right?"

She let her hands trail down his shirt front, teasing solid muscle and the lean outline of ribs. "There've been lots."

She could feel his heart beat, and it was power. Her power. She moved her hands down, across his abdomen, and let her body sway closer, touching his. Her hands encircled his waist lightly, teasing, tracing a pattern on his back, and the excitement of challenge tingled in her fingertips. His breathing was faster.

She let her hands drift down, over his belt, brushing his buttocks. His hands caught her wrists, hard. His voice was low, but had an odd, strained sound to it. "What are you doing?"

She tilted her head farther back to look at him, arching her neck, parting her lips just a little. She had seen the whores in the saloon do it that way. She had seen them do a lot of things. She said, "Don't you like it?"

She could see the heat on his face and the darkness in his eyes. He said, very low, "You're messing around with things you don't know, girl."

Her own heart speeded, deep and fierce with triumph. He was bent close to her and his fingers were tight on her wrists, and she could feel his breath on her mouth. She arched closer, and placed her mouth on his. Briefly—very briefly—then she left his mouth and let her lips trail over his jaw.

His fingers loosened a little on her wrists. "Angel, stop it."

She wormed her hands from his grasp and slid them beneath his vest, on his back. She pressed her breasts against his chest, and tasted the firm salty texture of his neck. She could feel his muscles grow stiff and alive beneath her touch, could feel her own heat rising, and when his hands came to her waist she was no longer sure who was master of the game. She wasn't sure she even cared.

She lifted her mouth to his and there was one long searing moment of heat and darkness and pulsing breaths, then abruptly he tore his mouth away. His chest was heaving, his eyes were blazing. "What are you trying to do?" he demanded hoarsely.

Deliberately she pressed her body against his again, sliding her hands up his arms. Hurt and hunger were boiling inside her, all mixed together with what she had been denied—the taste of his lips, the warmth of his arms, the years of being alone. And anger. Anger and hatred, because she was not going to be pushed aside again. "What's the matter, Adam?" she inquired silkily, lifting her face to him. "Don't I do it right? Aren't I as good as my mother?"

She practically spat out the last word, and as soon as it

was spoken Adam's hands grasped her shoulders and shoved her away from him violently. "Stop this!" He shook her once, hard. "Don't you ever talk about her like that again!"

Angel tore herself from his grasp. "Why not?" she flung back at him. "It's the truth! It's just a pity she wasn't around to teach me how to be a better whore, isn't it?"

For a moment the fury blazing in his eyes was so intense that she thought he might hit her. She actually braced herself for the blow, but he turned abruptly on his heel and started away.

"That's right!" she yelled at him. "Walk away! It's the easy thing to do, isn't it? Why should you be any better than the rest of them? You're nothing but a bounty hunter, and you've got your hide. So go!"

He turned around. His fists were clenched and his jaw was locked, but the look in his eyes was not quite so murderous anymore. He said distinctly, "Your mother is not a whore. She fell in love with the wrong man, that's all. And for the rest of it—would you rather I'd lied to you? Is that what you wanted?"

The fury of high emotion drained from Angel in slow, pulsating waves. She leaned back against the rail and looked at Adam for a long time. And in the end she only shook her head. "You fool," she said tiredly. "You think it's because of who they are, don't you?" She looked up at him. "A saloon girl and an outlaw . . . do you really think I expected better for myself? That's not why I hate them. It's because of what they did to me. Because they threw me away, and they didn't have to. Because of all those years I thought they were dead. Because of all the stupid dreams I dreamed. Because of all that time they left me alone, wondering . . ."

She didn't finish. Her head was lowered, her shoulders sagged, and the depth of desolation was as thick as the fog. Adam took a step toward her, then stopped. What could he say to her, what comfort could he offer, what excuses could he make? He had come to her bearing what he thought would be the single greatest gift of her life—her family. He had nothing more to give her. He wasn't even sure he wanted to try.

Suddenly the day disappeared and the train was plunged into blackness. He heard a sound from Angel, a choked cry, a half-scream, and he moved swiftly and instinctively to the place where she had last been. "It's all right," he said. "It's just a tunnel."

"Where are you?" Her voice was thin, frantic, strung out on a note of hysteria he had never heard from her before.

"Here."

He reached out, first one way and then another, and his hand brushed her sleeve. "What happened?" she screamed.

"A tunnel," he repeated, and closed his hand on her arm.

She flung herself against him, her fingernails digging into his arms, small and tight and rigid with terror, and Adam didn't know whether to fight her off or draw her closer. The darkness, the movement , and the thunderous echoing sound of the train in the tunnel disoriented him, and Angel wasn't the same girl she had been a moment ago.

"No." The sound she made was barely a moan, and he could hear her breathing, rapid and jerky. "No, not tunnels . . . Don't make me go in the tunnels."

The sound pressed down on her, the smell of deep dark earth and wet rock, the cold, the dark. Her papa had almost died in the tunnels. She could hear the sound but there was nothing she could do, she could hear him scream but she couldn't find him, she was trapped in the dark of the bowels of the earth and there was no way out. . . . He had promised they would never go into the tunnels again. He had *promised*. . . .

But it was another man with her now, strong and healthy and holding her tightly. He didn't make the dark go away and she couldn't feel his warmth for the cold, but he was a different man and this was a different place and she was ashamed but she couldn't stop the fear; it took all her strength to keep from screaming, from squeezing her eyes closed and just screaming to blot out the sound, the smell . . .

"I hate them," she gasped. She couldn't hear her own voice, the noise was so loud. "I always hated them."

"It's all right." Adam repeated the foolish, meaningless words over and over again. Her body was small and tight in his arms, lifelessly tight, and her breath was choked, hitching. It frightened him. He held her, and when her knees gave way and she sank to the floor, he went with her, holding her and repeating, "It's all right."

"There're rats in the tunnels."

"There're no rats here."

"You can't breathe . . . no air . . . it's so dark . . ."

"Angel, stop it, please."

"Hold me."

"I am." He tightened his arms, pressing his face against her hair.

"I can't feel it!"

And then she began to sob, softly, wetting his shirt with tears that were as cold as rain, too many tears for such a small girl. And the only words he could understand were, "I hate it, I hate it, I hate it . . ." very soft, smothered in his chest.

Sometime later, still in the darkness, she stopped crying. Her fists were bunched against his chest and her head was pressed into his shoulder, and her voice was ragged with emotion as she said, "You don't understand. You can't understand. That's why I hate them. I'll always hate them. Papa almost died in the mines. I had to crawl in the dark to find him . . . in the tunnels . . . so dark . . . so dark . . ."

Adam felt something twist deep and low in his chest. He had no answer. So he knelt there on the floor and held her, and continued to hold her long after the tunnel had passed.

CHAPTER

Eight

ANGEL kept her distance from Adam for the remainder of the journey. Perhaps she was embarrassed by the closeness they had shared in the tunnel, which was deeper than any physical intimacy; perhaps she was still trying to deal with the disillusionment of learning the truth about her parents. Perhaps, like the rest of the passengers, she was just tired. She tended to Jeremiah and spent a great deal of time looking out the window, watching the great West roll by.

Across the plains were reminders of an earlier era in the bleached bones of buffalo and oxen, the broken wagon wheels, the abandoned pieces of furniture and household trails that marked the torturous way west for the early pioneers. Jeremiah found it all fascinating and each glimpse of a new artifact prompted another story. Adam listened with intense interest, amazed at the man's knowledge and with growing admiration for his insights into the past and into human nature, but Angel was distracted and inattentive.

Salt Lake City was a surprise, and their brief stop there lifted everyone's spirits. Many called it the Eden of the West, and it was indeed like a paradise. The land was rich and verdant with flowering plants and thriving orchards in endless, straight rows. Streams from the mountain snows ran along its broad, neatly swept streets to bring water to the lush vegetation, and its elevation was such that the air appeared to sparkle with a crisp, clean freshness. Jeremiah, greatly restored after a few hours away from the soot and closed air of the train, promised Angel that this was only a sample of what they would find in California, and at the mention of their destination Angel regained some of her former vitality and began to listen enthusiastically to Jeremiah's descriptions of the promised land.

But the respite was short-lived. They moved on to Ogden and into Elko, Nevada, and from there began the long trek across the barren desert. They caught their first glimpse of the desert Indians, a band of Paiute on horseback, solemnly watching the train go by, and Adam thought that would generate some excitement from Angel. It did not. Even when a group of dirty, bedraggled-looking Shoshoni boarded the train at a rest stop, causing great consternation among the other passengers, Angel seemed barely to notice.

Only once, in fact, did she speak directly to Adam without being prompted to do so, and that was when they entered the Sierra Nevada mountains.

For Adam it was a relief to be in the mountains after the heat and dust of the desert. The air was clean and bracing, scented with the pine and fir trees that made a stunning contrast of dark green against the rich blue sky. When the train rounded a narrow curve, a spectacular view of Donner Lake spread before them, and Jeremiah told the story of the fabled Donner party, who had been trapped in the Sierras one winter and had been forced to cannibalize the bodies of their dead in order to survive. Angel listened politely, but it was clear that her mind was on other things.

All morning she sat with her hands clenched tensely in her lap, watching the rugged mountainside roll by as the train chugged steadily around the twisting cliffs, and when Jeremiah dozed off, Adam made a point of coming to stand in the aisle beside her, sharing her window view. "Quite a sight, isn't it?" he commented.

She didn't look at him, and her voice was tight. "Will there be any tunnels?" she asked.

"No," Adam replied gently, and didn't know whether he was lying or not. "I don't think so."

Fate must have been with him, because if the train did pass through tunnels it did so at night, while Angel was sleeping. There were no more incidents.

From the summit of the mountains the track dropped seven thousand feet into Sacramento, California, and the engineer ran it without steam, using nothing but the brakes to guide them around the bends as they plunged toward their destination. California greeted the group of tired, dirty, and short-tempered passengers with all its promised sunshine, brilliantly colored flowers, and orchards bursting with blooms. Adam saw Angel's eyes sparkle for the first time since leaving the Rockies.

But San Francisco was still a hundred miles away.

* * *

After the gold rush, San Francisco had been transformed from the sleepy little village of Yerba Buena into a boom town filled with overnight millionaires, rough-and-tumble miners, gamblers, and outlaws. Then came the fire of 1850, and the rebuilt San Francisco blossomed into a city.

By 1886 San Francisco had a theater, an opera company, and a fledgling symphony orchestra. There were streetlights and elevators and a wide variety of newspapers, and the little town that some had thought would never outlast the gold rush was well on its way to earning a reputation as an international city. Here the very rich and influential grew even richer and more powerful, built their mansions and their pleasure palaces, and redefined the terms of obscene excess; at the same time their largess spilled over into the city itself to make it one of the most progressive in the nation.

The cable cars that ran up and down Broadway were clean, cheap, and fast, and the steepest funicular railroad in the world ran from the base of Telegraph Hill to a restaurant at the Summit, while across the city the rich and the elegant commanded Nob Hill. There the Leland Stanfords' huge Italianate frame house loomed behind massive granite retaining walls. Over on California Street the Hopkins mansion of carved and sawn redwood vied for dominance with the Flood brownstone and its $30,000 brass fence.

And lying between the hills, slightly southeast, toward Golden Gate Park, was Chinatown, a rabbit warren of narrow alleys and streets, small shops that sold live animals, herbs, and vegetables and had tiny, dark living quarters overhead. And then there was the Street of Gamblers, teeming with betting parlors, brothels, and opium dens, where anything or anyone could be bought and sold for a price.

But Angel's first glimpse of San Francisco was disappointing, to say the least. After the glory of Sacramento, she expected brilliant blue ocean, lush vegetation, and sparkling skies. What she got was a cold damp fog, the murky waters of the bay lapping against the dock, and the almost overpowering stench of fish. The ferry ride across the bay from Oakland had been tedious and tiring, and Angel was not in the best of moods. Where were the gilded mansions, the elegant shops with plate-glass windows, the perpetual California sunshine? How could her papa have been so wrong? Had she come so far and through such trials for *this*?

She stood on the dock with Jeremiah while Adam went to procure a cab, a valise clutched tightly in each hand for protection against the ruffians who wandered around with sidelong glances and raucous bursts of laughter. Jeremiah tried to smother a cough, but the rattling in his chest had grown worse. The damp, stinking fog seemed to wind its way through her clothing and even her undergarments, making her shiver. How much worse it must be for Jeremiah, already weakened from the trip.

"It's cold!" she exclaimed, scowling with accusation when Adam returned.

"So it is," he agreed mildly, and took one of the valises from her.

Even Jeremiah reprimanded her gently. "Now, Angel, you can't expect Mr. Wood to do anything about the weather." But the statement ended in another choking cough, and Angel quickly took his arm.

"For heaven's sake, let's get out of here," she said irritably. "Does this place even have a decent hotel?"

"Several." Adam led the way to the waiting hansom and tossed their luggage up top. "We might even find one with a working fireplace."

Adam and Jeremiah shared a secret smile, but Angel was not amused. All she knew was that Jeremiah's color was terrible, his eyes were dull with exhaustion, and even his smile seemed weak. Had she been wrong to force him on this trip? Wouldn't they have been better off staying in Denver, no matter what she had to do to get rid of Adam? She had been a fool to believe all those stories about the restorative nature of golden California. And the ocean . . . a cold, smelly harbor that was nothing but a breeding ground for filth and disease. Hadn't she learned by now that nothing—*nothing*—was ever the way it was promised to be?

She had crossed half a country and was tired to the bone. Worry drained her as each day she watched her papa grow weaker and more sallow; she kept herself going by repeating the assurance that the ocean air and bright, warm sunshine would be all the restorative either of them needed. Well, she had adjusted her plans before. One thing San Francisco was bound to have was a bank. She'd pawn the necklace for whatever she could get, and . . .

"Angel," Adam said softly. "Look."

She was fussing with the blanket around Jeremiah's legs and did not respond immediately. It was Jeremiah, who had been resting with his eyes closed, breathing shallowly, who turned his head first toward the window. And he smiled.

Angel looked around. They had left the harbor with its crowds and its smells, and the sun was beginning to break through the fog, and where it struck the broad, recently swept streets it glinted off the cobblestones. The cab was climbing a hill so steep that Angel was pushed back against the seat, but still she strained to catch a glimpse of the fine, three-story houses with their windowboxes and their mani-cured squares of lawn that crowded each side of the street. Then they crested the hill and began the slow downward slope, and came into a business district where the midafter-noon traffic was brisk. Harnesses jingled and freight drivers shouted and tall men turned out in elegant leather and spurs nudged sleek black horses through the crowds. There was a rattling to her left and Angel twisted around with a muffled gasp to see one of the electric cars, painted bright red and gold, lumber by on its track and pole. She stared after it long after it had disappeared over the next hill.

There was a big bank made of white marble, with gold lettering in characters four feet high over its door. There were little shops with tiny plaques discreetly indicating that only the very rich need bother to enter, and there were windows with painted mannequins dressed in the latest fashions. Men in high starched collars and bowler hats swung silver-tipped canes as they strolled down the streets, and the women . . . Angel's eyes ached from taking in all the finery. Bustles two feet wide and drawn up with silk ribbons, smart little hats draped with ostrich feathers, dove-gray gloves fastened with pearl buttons, kid slippers peeking from beneath slim skirts with every mincing step . . . elegance, refinement, and wealth drifted from those women with every move they made.

Nannies in starched gray-and-white uniforms pushed wicker perambulators through the walkways of neatly tended parks as they entered a quieter section of the city. Carriages drew up on the side of the broad boulevard and exquisitely bonneted heads leaned out to chat. Angel gaped at the sight of one very fat, silk-bedecked woman tugging behind her a small, curly-coated dog on a lead. The dog even had bows in its hair.

"Our hotel is right up here," Adam said. "The Washingtonian. It's not the grandest in the city, but they tell me it's right nice. It's across from Washington Square."

The carriage circled the small park that was Washington Square, with its impressive statue of Benjamin Franklin and its ring of low trees enclosing the shady lawns and brilliant flower beds. Fronting the park, and flanked by a row of trees and small fountains, was the tall white facade of the Washingtonian Hotel.

It was a masterpiece of cast iron and stained glass, with a gleaming red mansard roof decorated with dormer windows and an abundance of towers. There were brick walkways and vine-covered arbors, and a green-and-white striped awning over the front. Adam had said that this was not a grand hotel, but Angel had never seen anything quite as grand in all her life.

She would not, however, give him the satisfaction of admitting her ignorance. She merely gave a curt nod as the carriage drew up before the entrance and said, "Well, this is more like it."

A porter came out to take their bags while Adam settled with the cabdriver, and Angel helped Jeremiah out of the vehicle. She could hardly restrain her impatience, or keep her steps slow enough to match his, as they started up the steps. The huge double doors were of yellow and red stained glass with a peacock design, surrounded by dark mahogany and a gilded fresco on the lintel. Inside, the lobby framed a curving dark staircase with an ivory banister and a cage elevator. There were red carpets and plush draperies tied with gold tassels, and groups of overstuffed chairs and little marble tables and gold-framed mirrors, but Angel couldn't take her eyes off the elevator. She watched as a man got inside the peculiar-looking cage, closed himself in, and nodded to the uniformed attendant. And then the contraption began to move upward, off the ground, above the lobby, until at last it disappeared into a hole in the ceiling and, presumably, kept going.

"Something to see, isn't it?" Jeremiah was saying. "Remember I read to you about it from that Denver newspaper one time? Never thought I'd see one working, though."

Angel didn't realize until then how tightly she was clutching his arm, and she quickly released the pressure of her fingers, nodding mutely. She wondered how much it cost to ride in the elevator, and whether Adam could be talked into paying for it. And then her heart seemed to lurch with a surge of happiness, because it was only a matter of hours now before she sold the cross, and then she could ride in as many elevators as she wanted, whenever she wanted.

Adam had gone to the long mahogany bar that served as the registration desk and was returning with their keys. "We're on the fifth floor," he said. "This room overlooks the park, he says." He handed that key to Angel. "Your pa and I will be right across the hall."

He gestured across the lobby. "Are you ready to go up? They've already taken our bags."

Without a word, Angel followed him across the room to the elevator.

Jeremiah made jokes about how much easier the elevator was than walking up five floors, and Angel held her breath and tried not to clutch her stomach. It was marvelous, like flying, like being on top of the world—less so when the view of the lobby disappeared behind a brick wall, but the marvel was restored when the little cage stopped and first the iron door, then a wooden one, opened on a long, carpeted corridor.

There were potted ferns at either end of the corridor and flanking the elevator door, and the ceiling was hung with dropped-globe gas lamps. High stained-glass windows shed a sparkling yellow-and-red light over the patterned carpet, and their rooms were identified with molded brass numbers tacked to the doors. The elevator attendant pointed out a water closet that, he assured them, contained hot and cold running water and full plumbing facilities.

The men saw Angel to her room first, and for a moment she was breathless with pleasure. It wasn't a palace, certainly, but it was a far cry from the dingy boardinghouses—or even the relatively clean Denver hotel—to which she was accustomed. The floor was polished and the white counterpane was spotless. The windows were hung with bright cabbage-rose curtains, and there were lace doilies on the wing chair by the fireplace. The carved armoire was open, and her one extra dress and petticoat were neatly hung inside, her valise stored at the bottom. There was even a little vanity table, covered with a lace cloth, with a mirror above it.

It was with great difficulty that she tore herself away from her wide-eyed appreciation of indulgences to come and turned to her father.

"This must be costing a fortune," he was saying to Adam.

"He can afford it," Angel interrupted rudely. "Now

come on, don't stand around here gawking, you need to get
to your own room and get some rest. Straight to bed for
you, and what do we have to do to get somebody to send up
a hot brick? It's *still* cold!''

Jeremiah began protesting again, however feebly, but she
was firm. The men's room was even bigger than hers, with
a daybed by the window and, she noticed gladly, a larger
fireplace. She got Jeremiah settled on the daybed with a
shawl over his shoulders and a blanket around his knees
while Adam built up the fire. Adam promised to send down
for a hot brick—and a hot toddy, which Angel hadn't
thought of—and when she was certain there was nothing
more she could do in respect to daughterly obligation, she
turned to go.

Adam said, ''I thought I'd take a turn around the city
later. Would you like to go?''

Angel hesitated. That was *exactly* what she wanted to do,
but she had planned to do it alone. Adam probably knew
that, which was why he had made the invitation in front of
her papa.

Jeremiah said quickly, ''Of course she will. Not a word,
miss,'' he insisted when he saw the objection starting to
form. ''I'll stay here all day wrapped in this flannel only if
you promise me you'll be out having a good time with Mr.
Wood. And tell me all about it at supper.''

''Half an hour?'' Adam suggested.

She could see that she had no choice, so she reluctantly
agreed. She turned back toward her room, but Adam didn't
close his door until she had stepped inside hers.

Of course it would be much easier to accomplish her
business without Adam dogging her steps, but that was not
the real reason for her reluctance. She had thought she

would go mad on the train, with him watching her all the time as though he had seen her without her underwear—no, as though he had seen her without her skin, which in a sense he had. She couldn't get that moment in the tunnel with him out of her mind, and at night she lay awake, remembering those blue eyes, that quiet, watchful face. She had shared intimacies with him she had never shared with another man, and they went beyond kisses. She had clung to him, depended on him, for those few moments of blind terror, and she had never done that with anyone, ever before, in her life. He knew everything about her, down to her soul's deepest secret; he knew her weaknesses. She knew nothing about him.

She did not want to spend an afternoon with him. She wanted to get Adam Wood out of her life as quickly as possible.

She closed the door and leaned against it, then on second thought she turned the key in the lock. For a moment she just stood there, letting her shoulders sag with exhaustion and the release of pent-up tension, looking at the lovely little room and allowing herself to believe that at last her dreams and plans were on the verge of coming true.

They had made it to California. The necklace was still safe around her neck. In a matter of days—perhaps even hours—she would be able to trade it in for cold hard cash, and then no one could stop her. Jeremiah would have his house by the sea—even if it was a chill, foggy sea. She would never have to enter another saloon in her life, and as for that woman back in New Mexico and the outlaw who had bedded her and spawned a child he wouldn't have cared about if he had known—Angel would never have to think about them again. If she did think about them, it would only be to laugh in scorn. No one would care who she was or where she came from once she had money.

With a jubilant motion she tossed aside the shawl and grasped the chain of the necklace, pulling the cross out of her bodice and kissing it soundly. She slipped the chain off her neck and held the cross in both hands before the window, admiring it even in its tarnished state. But then the expression on her face grew thoughtful as another problem occurred to her.

It was clear that she would not be able to get any estimates on its value today, with Adam along. For that matter, she probably shouldn't be showing it around at all until she found someone she trusted to do business with. She remembered the ruffians at the dock—and she could never forget the two men on the train or the one who had died in Green River—and realized that while the cross might have been safe around her neck on the train, she couldn't go on taking that kind of risk in a city like San Francisco. What she needed was a good hiding place.

She checked the wardrobe, considered and rejected hiding it under the mattress, looked for loose wall paneling and floorboards, and opened every bureau drawer. Defeated, she stood in the middle of the room and looked around with a scowl. Maybe the cross would be safer around her neck after all, what with people coming in and out of her room anytime they pleased, changing her bed, unpacking her valise, hanging up her gowns. . . .

Her eyes fell on the items some anonymous maid had removed from the bottom of her valise and laid out on the dressing table. Her hairbrush, a few ribbons, the big Bible Jeremiah had given her for her sixteenth birthday. And she got an idea.

She removed her knife from its garter and went over to the Bible, opening the cover. With only a small prayer for forgiveness—to Jeremiah, not God—she stabbed straight down into the tissue pages.

Within five minutes she had carved out a perfect little niche for the cross within the pages. When the book was closed, no one would ever know it contained anything except the Word of God. But when it was open . . . She smiled, admiring her handiwork. It looked right natural, the jeweled cross fitted into the pages of the Bible. And if there was any truth in superstition at all, the Good Book would do its best work right now, protecting the piece of jewelry that represented the rest of Angel's life.

The knock on the door startled her, and then Adam called out her name. She quickly opened a drawer, slid the Bible inside, and returned her knife to its hiding place. When she met Adam at the door nothing showed on her face except the hint of a cool smile, which he was free to interpret any way he pleased.

They took a cab that meandered up and down the steep streets, around the city, and through the park. The midmorning sun had burned away the fog, and Angel had her first glimpse of a San Francisco that was even more than she had imagined—bold, busy, sparkling with life and filled with opportunity. Adam explained to her how the cable cars worked and told stories about how the magnificent mansions on Nob Hill were built on little more than the guts and glory of brash gamblers and miners. Despite herself, Angel was fascinated, and she craned her neck for a better look at the fancy wrought-iron fences and towering palaces. These men had been no better off than she when they started. They came here with a dream and a grubstake, and look what they had become—bastions of society, kings of finance, richer than God. This was a place where fortunes could be made and squandered, a place that smiled on anybody with money or the promise of money; this was the place where Angel belonged.

Her heart was beating fast with excitement and there was color in her cheeks, but she tried to conceal her pleasure from Adam. "How do you know so much about it?" she challenged. "I thought you'd never been here."

Adam shrugged. "You hear things. And I read the papers. It's different seeing it in person, though."

"You're just like my papa," she grumbled. "Always spouting off about things you don't know anything about."

But when they entered the business district and he started telling her about the men who had built the banks and financed the railroads and, in effect, held the financial keys to the better part of the western United States, she listened with every fiber of her attention.

He directed the cab to pull over in front of a row of shops with brightly colored awnings and plate-glass windows. "Do you want to get out and look in some of the stores?"

She wanted to, very badly. But she looked at him suspiciously. "What use have you got for ladies' dress shops and jewelry stores?"

"Not much," he admitted. "But females like them. Being female, I figured you might want to look around."

She wished she could have told him to think again, but there were three jewelry shops within walking distance and she couldn't afford to miss this opportunity. She allowed him to help her out of the cab and waited while he settled with the driver.

"Why are you being so nice to me?" she demanded.

And then he did the most surprising thing. He smiled, took her arm, and replied, "Because I like to see you smile."

The gentling of his eyes, the simple words, did funny things to the area just below her breastbone. She quickly jerked her eyes away from his and determined not to smile again.

But that was easier resolved than done. There were so many glorious things to look at and admire, so many wonderful daydreams inspired by glimpses inside those luxurious shops. Someday she would wear that darling little hat with the spray of cherries, someday she would promenade around town in red kid boots and a tasseled parasol, someday she would know the rustle of silk petticoats against her skin.

But today, of course, she was only an impoverished girl in a worn blue traveling dress and a plain hair net, and every elegantly attired woman she passed on the street reminded her of that fact.

Looking in the windows was not enough. When she had spent a full minute staring hungrily at a frothy little confection of gauze and lace in a milliner's window, Adam opened the door of the shop and gestured her inside. Before she knew it she was sitting at a mirrored table with the hat on her head, staring at the reflection she couldn't believe was her own.

She didn't feel dowdy anymore. Even the faded blue dress with its fraying collar receded into quiet elegance against the background of the hat. Sheer pink gauze framed her face and made her hair glisten. Lace ribbons dangled cockily from the left side. Her eyes looked wider, her skin glowed, her whole face was transformed. She looked beautiful.

"Try this one," Adam suggested, and removed from the clay head of a dummy a blue chip hat decorated with striped ribbons and plumes.

Eagerly, Angel put it on. It sat far back on her head, with a fringe of lace framing its edge, and tied under the chin with a wide, dangling ribbon. It was without a doubt the smartest thing Angel had ever seen. She giggled a little as the white plumes dangled when she tossed her head. "It won't do much to keep the sun out of your eyes, will it?" she observed, and tossed her head again just to make the plumes ripple.

"Of course," the shop girl said coolly, "that is not the point. And it was really meant to be worn with your hair cut in fashionable bangs."

She could see the girl hovering, as though afraid Angel would dirty the bonnet, and the look of disapproving impatience in her eyes suggested that she knew they weren't there to buy. Angel untied the ribbons with a jerk and tossed the hat on the table.

"Let's go," she said. "I don't have any use for this foolishness anyhow."

She left the shop without looking back and had to wait on the street for Adam.

"Don't cut your hair in bangs," he advised when he came out. "Makes a woman look like a curly-horned heifer."

Angel recalled that the shop girl had worn bangs, and she barely restrained another giggle. The girl *had* looked a little like a cow.

"Let's go in here," Adam said. He opened the door of a dress shop.

"What for?" Again she regarded him suspiciously. "You planning on buying yourself a ball gown?"

He grinned. "Depends on whether I can find anything that fits."

This time the woman who greeted them had the warm smile and shrewd gaze of someone who has been in business a long time and knows that in a town like San Francisco, those who had the most money were very often the ones who looked like they had the least. She was stout and matronly, dressed in black satin with white lace at the collar and cuffs, but every move she made exuded elegance and style.

The room was furnished like a parlor, with little settees and chairs and tables displaying bottles of sherry and a silver tea service. Placed discreetly throughout were mannequins dressed up in fashions so stunning that they made Angel's mouth water.

She was immediately taken by a rich green velvet gown with a heart-shaped neckline and a bustle tied with a lighter green bow. It had a panel of green watered silk beneath a draped skirt, and the train was two feet long.

"An excellent choice, my dear," the woman said, and Angel guiltily jerked her hand away from the fold of luxurious fabric she had been caressing. But the woman beamed at her approvingly. "You have just the figure for these long-waisted fashions, don't you? Why, I do believe you could wear that gown right off the dummy with no alterations at all!"

Angel smiled at her a little uncertainly and turned away from the mannequin. *Someday*, she thought.

"That one's right pretty," Adam said, gesturing toward a plain linen skirt and bodice in a rather ugly shade of deep plum, proving that he had no taste at all in women's fashions.

The saleslady pursed her lips reprovingly. "Oh, I don't think so. Not with her coloring and eyes . . . This cream would be much smarter, don't you think?"

It was fun, for a while, letting the woman take them from one display to another, pretending they were real customers . . . pretending that Angel's purse was full of coins, and yes, the dove-gray would be perfect paired with the lace collar, and indeed, the pale pink walking gown did wonders for her skin. . . . She felt like a little girl in a candy store, only this time, when she walked away empty-handed, it wouldn't be for long.

Adam had completely captivated the saleswoman, and Angel left the two of them in deep conversation while she went again to touch and yearn over the green velvet gown. She had never known that there could be so much in life to want, and she had never known that the wanting could actually make her stomach hurt and her throat dry. Not just the gowns and the fancy hats, not even the house on the ocean for Papa, but something deeper, more intangible . . . To be able to walk into a shop like this without pretending. To have saleswomen look at her the way this one was looking at Adam now, as though he were ready money. To walk down the street with her head held high and have people step out of her way. To feel like she *belonged*. That was what she wanted so badly it made her stomach ache. And that was what she was going to have.

When Adam stood beside her, she left the green velvet without a backward glance and stepped out into the sunshine. Her jaw was set and her steps purposeful, and she pushed open the door of a jewelry shop without saying a word to Adam, and strode determinedly inside. For a moment she almost lost her nerve.

She had never seen anything like it in her life. The interior was dark with wood paneling and richly woven carpets. There were paintings on the walls in gilt frames and ornate mirrors everywhere. A huge glass case displayed rings and necklaces and earbobs on black velvet trays. It even *smelled* elegant. Angel, in her tired blue suit and gloveless hands, felt as dowdy as a brown mouse, and just as out of place.

Adam commented, "I didn't know you had a fancy for such folderol."

If he had said anything else, or if he had said nothing at all, she might have turned and walked out of there. But instead she turned on him. "Why?" she demanded. Although her cheeks stung with anger, she kept her voice low and hushed, as she would in church. "Just because I'm the poor offcast of a thief and a whore doesn't mean I don't know how to appreciate pretty things! And it doesn't mean I won't have them someday, either! Let me tell you something, Adam Wood—"

The tinkling of the entrance bell alerted the clerk and he appeared from the back room just then, cutting off Angel's words. She swallowed back her temper, a little alarmed at how close she had come to blurting out her plans for the future. With a jerk of her shoulders she turned away from Adam and looked at the clerk.

He in turn was observing them somewhat skeptically. It was clear that he thought they couldn't afford to be in a shop like this, and that only infuriated Angel further. Still, he inquired almost politely, "Good morning. What may I help you with?"

Angel lifted her head and replied coolly, "We'll let you know when we need something."

Apparently he found her disdain reassuring, because he moved behind the glass case and said to Adam, somewhat more hopefully, "We have a nice selection of rings, sir. Perhaps . . ."

"We're not interested in rings," Angel said, but she came over to the case to examine the merchandise. All of those glittering stones and carved metalwork were enough to take her breath away, but not one piece, she noted with satisfaction, was as magnificent as her cross.

She said casually, "Where do you get all this stuff?"

The little man looked somewhat surprised. "Why, a great deal of it is commissioned from artisans in Europe. Some is custom designed right here in San Francisco. If there is a particular stone you have in mind, we'd be happy to design a setting for it and have it mounted."

Angel pointed to a silver broach, ornately carved and set with a cluster of rubies. "That looks old."

The man smiled and reached beneath the counter for the tray containing the broach. "Madame has a good eye. That piece is, in fact, an antique—seventeenth century. We purchased it from an estate sale in England."

Angel looked at him sharply. "So you do buy old stuff off of people?"

He looked startled, hesitating with his hand on the tray. "Yes, of course. We're quite proud of our collection of—"

"And if somebody was to come in here with, say, Granny's pearl necklace, you'd buy it?"

He returned the tray to the case, growing cautious again.

"It would depend, of course, on the quality of the piece. Does Madame have something she would like to have appraised?"

Angel became aware of Adam's intense interest in the conversation. She pointed again to the broach. "How much does something like that run?"

The man took a card from his pocket, the front of which was imprinted with his name and the address of the shop, and wrote a price on the back. Angel took the card, and it was all she could do to keep from gasping out loud. Seven hundred fifty dollars. Seven hundred fifty dollars for a tiny broach with broken rubies . . . and it would take ten of them even to equal the weight of her cross, much less the pearls and the rubies as big as the tip of the clerk's finger.

Her heart was beating so hard that she was sure he would see it pounding in her throat, and she did not trust herself to speak. So she slipped the card into her reticule without a word and turned toward the door.

Adam tipped his hat to the man and opened the door for her. "What was that all about?" he inquired mildly when they were outside.

"Maybe I'm planning to steal my mama's family jewels and pawn them," she retorted, her heart still pounding. "I'm sure she's got plenty to spare, and I deserve something for all these years I've been scraping by on bacon grease and hard bread, don't I?"

Adam grabbed her arm hard. "Angel, stop it," he said.

Angel started to jerk away. It was not the force of his grip that prevented her, but the look in his eyes—dark and angry, yes, but beyond that something else . . . something that looked very much like hurt.

"Just . . . stop it," he repeated, and slowly released her

arm. She just stood there glaring at him. "Stop blaming your mother, stop blaming yourself. You can't go the rest of your life hating her for something you don't even understand— it's the same as hating yourself, don't you see?"

"You're crazy!"

"No, I'm not." His tone was quiet and fierce, and he wouldn't let her walk away, as she had started to. "What I am is sorry. Sorry about Camp Meredith and about Consuelo and sorry that she had to leave you in an orphanage because she was too young and scared and poor to do anything else. And I'm sorry I had to find you, and tell you, because if I had known it was going to cause you this much pain I never would have done it."

She stared at him. His face was tight and his eyes were clouded with pain, and before she knew it, the words were out. "I think you mean that."

She expected him to look away in embarrassment, but he didn't. He held her gaze with an honesty that was almost frightening, it was so intense. "I mean it," he said softly. "I never want anything or anyone to hurt you again, Angel Haber. And if I have anything to do with it, nothing ever will."

There was something in his eyes—or perhaps it was the words themselves—that made Angel feel as though all the breath had been sucked out of her. It made her feel light-headed and weak, but it was all right to be weak because Adam was there to take care of her. It made her *want* him to take care of her. It made her confused and sorry and it made her ache inside for something more than a new dress or a purseful of coins, and it hurt her because she didn't under-stand the ache. She knew only that she wanted him to look at her like that forever.

But all of that lasted only a moment, and it was she who moved her eyes away.

"We'd better start back," she said gruffly. "I don't like to leave Papa alone this long."

CHAPTER

Nine

ANGEL spent the rest of the afternoon with Jeremiah, and Adam was thoughtful enough—or sensitive enough—to leave them alone. Angel described to Jeremiah every nuance of her tour of the city and entertained him by mimicking the well-dressed ladies and gentlemen she had seen on the streets and the high-falutin' shop girl with her bangs. Her eyes shone when she described all the exquisite shops filled with beautiful things; and when she earnestly assured him that they, too, would one day have all those things and more, he fell into the game and imagined along with her how they would spend the fortune that he, of course, had no idea was really theirs.

By the time Adam returned from wherever he had been, Jeremiah's color was much better and he was coughing less. He enthusiastically agreed with Adam's suggestion that they dine away from the hotel tonight, in one of those fancy supper clubs with a stage where singers and dancers entertained customers while they ate.

Angel went back to her room, pleased with the way the day had turned out despite the fact that she had made no real progress toward selling the cross. Perhaps tomorrow she would be able to steal away from Adam and return to that uppity jeweler who thought he was so smart, just to watch his eyes bug out when he saw what she had for sale. She closed her door and retrieved his card from her reticule, turning to place it safely with the cross, and then she stopped.

Slowly she turned around again and stared at her bed. Upon it was stacked a collection of boxes in varying sizes: round boxes, square boxes, long flat boxes, short narrow ones. Cautiously, almost as though expecting something to leap out from amid the boxes and grab for her throat, she went over to the bed. She lifted the lid of the closest round box, and her heart stopped.

Nestled inside wads of tissue paper was a hat. Not *a* hat—*the* hat. The lovely little froth of pink tulle and lace that made her look like a fairy princess. She lifted it out with hesitant fingers, held it up before the window, wondering over it, then touched the delicate tulle and stiff ruffles of lace. And then, almost as though mesmerized, her eyes went back to the other boxes.

She carefully set the hat aside and opened the lid of a large flat box. Her throat went tight and for a moment she could only stare. It was the green velvet gown, glowing with luxurious invitation against a background of snow-white paper. She touched it. It was real. She lifted it from the box and pressed it ever so carefully against her figure.

She turned toward the oval pier glass and stared at her reflection, all decked out like the Queen of England in green velvet and watered silk. And then with a muffled cry she clutched the gown to her at the waist and whirled around, letting the rich green folds billow about her. She laughed like a child in delight. She draped the gown across the bed and dived for the other boxes.

The cream-colored walking suit. A buttercup-yellow day gown with a matching cape lined in black. The little hat with the striped ribbons and plumes. A pair of black kid boots as soft as butter in the sun, and a pair of pumps tied with white grosgrain ribbons. But that was only the beginning. Petticoats—two cotton and one silk—and stockings so sheer she could see her hand through them. A pair of gray gloves with tiny mother-of-pearl buttons. A darling little reticule embroidered with roses, and a soft white shawl that felt like kitten's fur against her cheek. There was even a parasol, which she unfurled and twirled over her head, laughing in pleasure at the patterns of sun and shadow it made on her face.

It was every Christmas and every birthday she had ever had and never celebrated, it was a stream of girlhood dreams come true, it was like a fairy tale . . . and none of it was hers.

She closed the parasol with a snap and gazed at the array of colorful fabrics and frothy whites scattered over her bed. Slowly her face began to harden. She tossed the parasol onto the bed and turned toward the door. She marched across the hall and knocked peremptorily on the door of the room Adam Wood shared with her father.

Adam opened the door, and Angel did not trust herself to speak—certainly not within hearing distance of Jeremiah.

So she jerked her head at him, indicating that he should follow, and strode back to her room.

She stood just inside the threshold and gestured angrily toward the disorder on the bed. "What the hell do you think you're doing?" she demanded.

Adam followed her gaze, his thumbs hooked into his belt. "Don't they fit? The woman at the shop said—"

"I told you, I got no use for foolishness like this, and if I did I'd buy it for myself! I don't need charity from the likes of you—or from that half-breed whore that's trying to buy my favors, either!"

Adam's face stiffened. "I thought you'd like those things," he said. "I guess I made a mistake." He turned to go.

But Angel would not let it drop that easily. The fury was building in her, an emotion that was generated less by injured pride then by the fact that she had touched all these lovely things, held them in her hands, loved them, and now would have to give them up.

"Is this your way of improving me?" she spat. "Dressing me up in feathers and lace so I'll be good enough to meet my sainted mother? So I won't *embarrass* her?"

Adam turned to her, his face expressionless and his eyes unreadable. "I wouldn't fool myself into thinking you'd accept anything that came from Consuelo, though I know she'd want to give them to you. Those things—all the female fuss and flutter"—he gestured toward the bed—"I thought they'd make you happy, is all. I saw the way you admired them, and seeing as how we're going to be here for a few days, I didn't see any reason why you shouldn't enjoy dressing up in a town that knows how to appreciate a dressed-up woman." He shrugged. "If you don't want them, just pack them up and send them back. Makes no difference to me."

Again he started to leave.

Without meaning to, Angel glanced back at the bed, and felt a physical pang of remorse deep in her chest at the thought of parting with the lovely things. "Wait," she said sharply.

After all, it wasn't as though she couldn't afford them herself. It would be silly to send them all back to the shops only to repurchase them in a few days when she cashed in the cross. And Adam . . . It touched her, in a way she wasn't used to being touched, that he had thought of her and gone to all this trouble. Papa would be disappointed in her if she hurt Adam's feelings by refusing his gesture of kindness. Of course, she wasn't sure what her papa would think about her accepting such a personal gift from Adam Wood, but she could always tell him that the clothes came from her errant mother. He approved of *her*, God knew why.

She lifted her chin and she said, "I won't be obliging to you."

He shrugged. "Suit yourself."

She swallowed. He was not making this easy. "I'll pay you for them, as soon as I can."

She thought she saw the slightest hint of a smile on his lips. "If that's what you want to do. Meanwhile, I think your pa would be right proud to see you in that green dress tonight. I hear folks eat late around here, so be ready about nine."

"I *will* pay you!" she called after him as he closed the door.

She hesitated a moment, wondering if she had done the right thing. Then she went over to the drawer, opened the

Bible, and touched the cross. It felt solid and rich against the palm of her hand. She *would* pay him back. And this was only the beginning. Soon her wardrobe would be filled with velvet gowns and silk petticoats, she would have a different hat for every day of the month and dozens of pairs of kid slippers and gloves with real pearl buttons. . . .

She turned back to the bed, breaking into a smile of pure joy as she surveyed the luxury spread there. Meanwhile, it would be lovely to see her papa's eyes light up when she came down the stairs in that green dress.

She bathed and dressed and spent an inordinate amount of time with her hair, trying to imitate one of the styles she had seen in a portrait in the jewelry shop. But it wasn't until the last button was fastened and the final fold brushed out of the gown that she admitted to herself it wasn't only her papa's eyes she was looking forward to seeing tonight, but Adam Wood's as well.

She was not disappointed. Adam and Jeremiah waited for her in the lobby, and she descended the big staircase alone. They were standing by the door, talking, and Adam was the first to glance her way. Then he glanced again. Then he stared. He touched Jeremiah's arm and he too turned to look at her.

The green gown fit as though it had been molded to her shape. The neckline dipped over her bosom and showed a scandalous few inches of shoulder before forming long, tight sleeves. A panel of pale green silk hugged her abdomen and flared around her ankles and rustled when she walked. The velvet train glided gracefully along the stairs as she descended. She had brushed her hair until it poufed slightly in the front, then had drawn it back into a knot behind one ear with a dangling cluster of curls falling to her shoulder. She regretted that she had no jewelry or hair ornaments, unaware that it was her very lack of adornment that made her appearance so striking.

The green velvet made her skin glow and deepened the color of her hair to a raven's-wing gloss. Her eyes shone with excitement and pride, and her movements incorporated natural grace into the innocent seductive beauty that had always been hers. Not only Adam and Jeremiah but everyone in the lobby—male and female—turned to look at her as she passed by.

But it was Adam whom Angel was looking at. Both men had spruced themselves up with polished boots and carefully brushed hair. Her father's coat was sponged and pressed and he wore a string tie around his neck. Adam had on a fancy city suit of brown wool with a celluloid collar, and he looked as handsome as a picture out of a mail-order catalog. He was looking at her like a man would look at something too good to be true, his eyes deep with wonder and admiration as they moved over her from head to toe and then back again. He took her fingers and bowed over them.

"Miss Angel," he said softly. "You look beautiful."

Pleasure soared inside Angel that was so intense it made her head spin. No man had ever before bowed over her hand. No man had ever before looked at her with such awe in his eyes. She felt like a princess.

And then she turned to her father. His eyes were misted over with pride, and he touched her cheek with an unsteady hand. "I always pictured you like this," he said gruffly.

Angel knew then that it was all worth it, to see that look in her papa's eyes, to hear those words. It would have been worth it if she had stolen the clothes and faced a life sentence for the crime, just to give Jeremiah that one moment of pleasure.

There had never before been a night like that one, nor, Angel was sure, would there ever be another. She had thought she had known grandeur on the train, but that was nothing compared with the opulence and abandon that was nighttime in San Francisco.

They ate at a supper club where a railed balcony overlooked a stage below, and their table was right against the balcony. The table was covered with white linen that was so heavy and stiff it scratched her hand, and the big silver forks had roses carved on them. There were fresh pink flowers on every table, and the huge room glittered with candlelight and chandeliers. Adam ordered a bottle of Mums champagne and Angel delighted in the dry, bubbly taste. The array of dishes that kept coming were enough to dazzle the senses, and not one of them was familiar. Crisp greens topped with vinegar, lobster covered in cream sauce, something called asparagus, which Angel, by watching the other diners, finally figured out was supposed to be eaten with the fingers. Some kind of fish covered with nuts and sliced red meat stuffed with green herbs, and between each dish a little cup of flavored ice. Jeremiah barely stopped her from drinking the little bowl of water and sliced lemon in which other people were cleaning their fingers, but Angel wasn't embarrassed. She was too excited.

And the stage—oh, the wonders that were taking place on stage. Rows of girls in flouncy red-and-white dresses kicked up their heels and showed their ruffled panties, and no one seemed to think it was scandalous...except perhaps Jeremiah, who pretended not to mind. Handsome young men dressed in silver and white danced and sang onstage, and there were jugglers and even a trained bear on a leash. Angel clapped until her hands were sore and her face ached from laughing. The dessert tray was even more dazzling than the ones offered on the train, and afterward the waiter brought a little silver tray with port wine and cigars for the men, and a lace doily containing three Ghirardeli chocolates for Angel. It was magical, magnificent, and Angel wanted it never to end. But when the show was over, Adam glanced at his watch and tactfully suggested they leave, and Angel knew he was concerned about her papa. Although he protested, Jeremiah was looking tired, and Angel was too involved with the dancing colors and sounds inside her head to notice just how tired.

Angel could not bear to go up to her room when they reached the hotel. She couldn't imagine taking off the gown, brushing out her hair, and slipping into her threadbare nightdress just as though this magical evening had never happened. Jeremiah insisted that Adam stay downstairs with her while he saw himself to bed.

She stood on the porch, gazing out over the park, and commented, "You don't have to stay with me. I'm not a little girl." But she didn't really resent his presence. In fact she was glad of it, as much as she tried not to be. It was, after all, a lot harder for a girl to feel like a princess when there was no handsome prince there to admire her.

He stood close beside her at the rail, smelling like wine and cigars and all that was the best of being male. He replied, "Oh yes I do. A man would be a fool to leave a woman who looks as good as you all by herself."

Her face dimpled with pleasure, although she tried not to let him see. "You say silly things."

"I mean them."

She took a breath. The night smelled like flowers . . . and Adam. "You must have a lot of money," she commented.

There was a rueful tone to his voice. "That means a lot to you, doesn't it?"

"It does," she answered matter-of-factly, "when you've never had any."

"Well, I reckon I know how that is." Then he answered her question. "I do all right, I guess. Enough to live it up for one night in a city I'll never see again. It's not like I have anything else to spend on. No family, or anything."

She could feel his eyes on her, and it caused a strange prickling sensation on the back on her neck. She didn't look around at him. The next words were difficult enough for her to say, without having to look at him while she did it. "It was—nice of you, to spend some of it on us. Tonight I mean. Papa—he hasn't had too many good times in his life. I'm glad he had this one."

Adam said softly, "I didn't do it for him, Angel."

The prickling sensation increased, traveling all the way down her spine, and there was a tightness in her stomach, a dizzying expectation, and a wondering. Wondering what she would see in his eyes if she looked at him now, wondering what would happen if she turned to him, wondering what she would do if he laid his hand upon her arm now, or touched her hair, or bent close and brushed his lips against her neck. The night was magical and Adam was part of the magic, and she didn't want to wonder anymore.

But she did not turn, did not look at him. And he didn't touch her. Her hands tightened a little on the railing, and she said, perhaps a bit too brightly, "Papa's looking better, don't you think? I was worried that the trip would tire him too much, but I really think just being here has done him more good than anything else.''

Adam hesitated, and Angel refused to read anything into that uncertain pause. He said, ''I hope he didn't overdo it tonight. I thought tomorrow we'd hire a carriage and take a drive out to the ocean.''

Angel turned to him, her eyes glowing. ''Oh, Adam, can we? That would be wonderful!''

''I promised you,'' he reminded her, and there was something so gentle, so tender and sweet in his eyes, that Angel had to drop her own.

Because if she had looked at him for one more minute, if she had allowed that quiet, soul-caressing smile of his to capture her for even one more second, everything would have changed. And those changes frightened Angel.

She said, ''I guess I'd better get to bed then. Long day ahead.''

''I'll walk you up.''

''No,'' she said quickly. ''Stay out here and—smoke, or whatever it is you do. I'll see you in the morning.''

He did not object as she hurried to the lobby.

She wanted to turn and thank him one more time for the night he had given her. Her footsteps even slowed and she started to turn back, but at the last minute she stopped herself. She went quickly up the stairs, and she could feel his eyes on her until she reached the top.

Angel wore her new yellow dress and the hat with the lace and tulle, and she carried the parasol in her gloved hands. When she walked through the lobby people looked at her as though she were *somebody*, and she responded to those admiring gazes with a cool lift of her head, the way she had seen the quality women on the streets do. But fireflies of pleasure were turning somersaults inside her stomach, and she thought, *This is the way it was meant to be. This is what I was born for.*

And wouldn't she just love for that dark-eyed half-breed who had given birth to her to see her now! As a matter of fact, she thought that she might just pay a visit to New Mexico after all, in her own private railroad car decked out in red and gold and with two liveried servants to wait on her hand and foot, and then she might just invite Miss Consuelo whatever-her-name-was to tea, and she wouldn't even spit in her face because ladies of quality, ladies with money, could afford to be gracious.

The daydream danced inside her head, making her eyes glow and her face flush with anticipation, and she almost laughed out loud with delight at the picture. All of her dreams were coming true; why not this one? The heady glory of her first night in San Francisco still drifted like champagne bubbles through her veins, and the morning was bright and cloudless. Today they would see the ocean. They would actually set foot on golden beaches and hear the crash of waves and see the sparkle of sun on water that her papa had told her about all her life, but which she had never believed, deep inside, she would actually experience for herself. All this and more, and she hadn't even sold the cross yet.

But when she stepped out onto the street where Adam and Jeremiah were waiting with the carriage, prickles of alarm crept through her ebullient spirits, threatening to dissipate her pleasure. Jeremiah looked tired already; his skin was a pasty grayish color and his hand, when he took hers, was cold and shaky. The warm light that always came into his eyes when he saw her seemed filmed and dim.

"Papa," she said anxiously, "we don't have to go out today. You were out too late last night anyway, and—"

"Nonsense!" The force with which he said the word caused him to stifle a cough, and it shook his shoulders. His fingers tightened on hers. "I've waited half a lifetime to show my girl the ocean, and today's the day. Nothing's going to keep me back."

There was a ferocity of determination in his words that frightened Angel. "But—"

Adam touched her arm lightly. "We'd better get going before the sun gets too hot."

She glanced at him, with an automatic retort on her lips, but the words died unspoken. His gaze on hers was steady and seemed to hold an unspoken message—not a plea, but a command. The two men, each in his own way, were aligned against her, and today she would do it their way.

And then Adam smiled at her. "You look mighty pretty this morning. Doesn't she, sir?"

"Yes," Jeremiah agreed, the familiar twinkle coming into his eyes, and it was almost convincing enough to make Angel forget how frail he looked. "As pretty as anything I've seen in a store window. And wouldn't it be a shame not to take her out and show her off?"

Adam agreed that it would, and the two men kept up an easy banter designed to distract Angel as they got into the carriage and left the hotel behind. It did not take long for their strategy to work, and Angel even managed to convince herself that her papa was looking better as the miles unwound behind them.

They went through Golden Gate Park, a fragrant expanse of wooded greenery that was a startling contrast to the bustle and sophistication of the city that surrounded it. There were other carriages, handsomely appointed and laden with smart-looking passengers . . . just as smart, Angel thought smugly, as she was. The clip-clop of horses' hooves were muffled on the road and absorbed by the soft stretches of grass and wild flowers that nestled against the paths. More of the vines laden with purple flower clusters that she had seen all over the city dripped from trees and climbed low walls, and there was a sweet-salty perfume in the air that was unlike anything she had ever smelled before.

And it wasn't just Angel's imagination; Jeremiah's face did grow more animated and his eyes less fatigued as Angel twisted this way and that, pointing out the sights to him and asking a myriad questions. She was glad, selfishly perhaps, that she hadn't been successful in trying to postpone the outing. She was wearing a new dress and she felt beautiful; the sun was shining and the ocean was waiting. This was a day for dreams to come true, and could she really have borne the disappointment of waiting one more day?

She was so absorbed in the journey that she almost didn't notice when they had reached their destination. She heard the distant rumbling and sighing that sounded like a strong wind, she felt the bite of salt in the air, and, leaning her head out the window, she noticed a certain change in the color of the sky, a richer, deeper hue than it had been in the city. Adam drew the carriage to a stop and leaped down to open the door.

"We'll have to walk from here," he said.

Angel sprang to the ground before he had a chance to put the carriage steps in place. "Is it very far?"

"No, but I don't want to take the horses any closer to the cliff."

Angel took a few half-running steps forward and could see where the land came to an abrupt end about two hundred feet forward amid a tangle of broken rocks and scrub brush. The thundering, she understood now, was the sound of the waves crashing below——the sound that had been described to her so often that she could not possibly mistake it for anything else. Overhead the graceful white birds with their shrill voices dipped and soared and the salt breeze tugged at her hat and her skirts.

Excitement propelled her steps as she hurried back to Jeremiah and took his arm. "It's just ahead!" she exclaimed. "Can you hear it?"

His eyes were sparkling as he looked at her, and a warm glow of color had come to his cheeks that banished all signs of ill health. "Music to my ears!" he returned. His hand covered hers on his arm and squeezed tightly.

Adam came around the back of the carriage with a folding chair under his arm. "Be careful," he advised. "The ground is rocky."

But Angel was too excited to be careful and so, she suspected, was her papa. He took up his canes but didn't seem to lean so heavily on them as he had in previous days, and Angel supported him only lightly with one hand on his arm. Adam followed close behind.

The land gave way at the edge of the precipice in a rocky, winding slope lined with jutting overhangs and sharp, irregular protrusions. To their right was a narrow path that led to a small, perfectly protected beach. Below them an avalanche of white foam roiled repeatedly over the boulders, flinging spray into the air. And beyond . . . beyond as far as the eye could see was an expanse of ever-changing shades of blue, of whitecaps rolling toward the shore, of shadows chasing light, of waves swelling and fading, tumbling and splashing in the sun. The sound was like whispered love words lost in the thunder of a heartbeat. The air was like no air she had ever breathed before. And the bigness of it, the color, the movement, and the simple magnificence of it took her breath away.

"Oh, Papa," she said softly.

He squeezed her hand again. "Do you know, Angel, I don't think you ever really believed me when I told you what it was like."

"I didn't." She drank it all in with thirsty eyes. "I couldn't . . . Oh, Papa, it's beautiful!"

"It's like coming home," he said simply, and when she turned to him his face wore an expression of quiet, complete contentment. She had never, in all her years of knowing and trusting and loving him, seen that expression before. His eyes were alive with light and memories, his smile was gentle and relaxed, and the lines that time and pain had etched into his face were eased away. It was the face of a younger man, a man she had never known but wished she had, a man who had no cares, no threats, no responsibilities. A man to whom home was a time and not a place, and who had managed to find his way back there, however briefly, and if only in his mind.

"The smell," he murmured, "the sound of the birds, the wind on my skin . . . I never thought I'd know it again. I'm glad I got to see it all one more time."

Angel lifted her arms and embraced Jeremiah wordlessly, closing her eyes, drinking in the moment with him. *All this and more*, she thought. *So much more, and I'm going to give it all to you. . . . You'll see. This is only the beginning.*

She stepped away from him, her eyes glowing. "Can we go down, Papa? Remember how you told me you used to walk in the waves?"

He chuckled, lightly touching the portion of her hair that was exposed by the hat. "No, child, I'm afraid my days of frolicking in the waves are over."

She tried to hide her disappointment, and then Adam spoke up.

"There's a path down to that little beach there that doesn't look too steep."

Angel was already shaking her head. "No, that's silly. It's too far for Papa, I wasn't thinking—"

Jeremiah insisted, "You go, Angel. I've walked in the surf before, now I want to watch you do it for the first time."

She hesitated. "I don't like to leave you—"

"Go," he repeated firmly. "Don't deprive me of the greatest joy of the day."

She couldn't pretend reluctance after that. She made sure he was comfortable in the chair Adam had brought for him and draped a blanket across his legs. He waved to her as she and Adam started down the path.

On the steeper sections Adam took her arm, and in some place the rocks cut into her new kid slippers, but Angel didn't notice. She moved so quickly that on one occasion Adam had to grab her by the waist to keep her from tumbling headlong down the remainder of the trail, but when he started to scold her she only laughed and moved more quickly.

She was breathless and windblown by the time she

scrambled over a small clump of rocks and stubbly grass to place her feet on the shimmering golden sand of a small inlet. The waves surged and broke and stretched their glassy fingers across the sand only a few feet away. She could feel the spray on her face, and the wind caught her skirts and whirled them around her as she turned and lifted her arm to her papa. She could see him far above, sitting in his chair at the edge of the cliff, and he waved back to her.

She cupped her hands around her mouth and cried, "Watch me!"

When she tilted her head back the wind caught her hat and dislodged it. Laughing, Adam caught it before it spun into the sand, but Angel's hair, freed from the pins, tumbled around her face. She didn't care. She bent over and untied her slippers.

"What are you doing?" Adam demanded.

"I'm going in the water." Her eyes danced with irrepressible elation as she glanced at him, for today she could not be cautious, could not be cool, could not be reserved. Not with Adam, not with anybody. "Are you coming?"

"Are you loco? That water's cold!"

"Coward!" she taunted him over her shoulder, and then, careless of her new stockings and her skirt, she ran toward the water.

He was right. The thin film of water that lapped over the shore was cold as it soaked into her stockings, but the cold was invigorating and she edged forward, closer to the waves that curled and splashed their foam on the sand. She forgot that she was wearing a new dress. She ignored the broken shells and rocks beneath her feet. She was surrounded by the ocean and a childhood of dreams.

She turned again to wave to her papa, and suddenly the

earth shifted beneath her feet. She cried out and flailed her arms for balance as the sand was sucked away by the tide and even the sky seemed to tilt. And suddenly Adam was there, strong hands catching her beneath her arms as she started to fall; she stumbled against him and then both of them were buffeted by a breaking wave that drenched them to their knees.

Angel was laughing and didn't know why. She was wet; Adam was wet. Her new skirt was ruined and her stockings in shreds. But the expression of outrage and astonishment on Adam's face was comical, and his hands were warm and strong as they slid to her waist, and the sun and the water danced around them and she laughed.

After a moment Adam laughed too, and pulled her away from another breaking wave. Impulsively, Angel ducked down and scooped up a shell half-buried in the sand. "Look!" she exclaimed, holding it out to him.

He glanced down at the shell, smiling. "What are you going to do with it?"

"Give it to Papa," she responded immediately, wiping the sand off the shimmering surface. "So he'll have the ocean with him all the time."

The wind whipped a strand of hair across her neck, and Adam pushed it back with his fingers. "You look like a little girl," he said.

A shadow flickered across her face and she said, "I don't think I ever was. A little girl, I mean."

Adam's fingers were damp as they touched the curve of her jaw, and a little cold. The contact tingled through Angel's skin. "I wish I had known you then," he said. "I wish I could have made it different for you."

Angel looked up at him. His eyes were the color of sun

and quicksilver, but soft like shadowed velvet. He was hatless, and the salty wind had tossed his wheat-colored hair into disarray. His face was the kindest and the strongest she had ever seen, and Angel was suddenly swept by wonder that she should be here in this magical place with a man such as he. There was no question of hesitance as his fingers spread along the line of her jaw and slipped behind her neck, no resistance in her muscles as that gentle, almost infinitesimal pressure caused her to lean into him. Her lips parted for the breath that was coming too quickly, and tasted salt only a moment before they tasted his.

She had not forgotten what his kiss was like. A dozen times or more in the time since he had last held her she had relived the sweetness, the weakness, the mind-infusing pleasure. She had not forgotten the yearning pressure that knotted in her stomach or the heat that bubbled in her veins or the way the taste of him seemed to penetrate every pore and blot out everything except the power of him. But now, lost in his arms again, it was as though she had forgotten. It was as though this were the first time, and every memory she had ever had was blotted out by the newness and the wonder of the sensation.

Without hesitation, her arms went around his neck and her body seemed to melt into his. Her head was filled with the roar of the sea and the sighing of the wind, and Adam. He surrounded her, shielded her, filled her with his warmth and his strength. Wonder and dizzying, breath-robbing exhilaration soared through her and she thought that it must be magic, this feeling, this day, this man.

When his lips left hers, reluctantly and with a whisper of breath across her cheek, her fingers tightened on his neck instinctively, wanting more, but then she made herself release the pressure. She opened her eyes and the day seemed to glow with a brightness more intense than before. Light bounced off the rocks and the sand and the edges of his hair, collected in his eyes, and seemed to sear her soul with its brilliance. When she looked into his eyes she saw magic, promises, she saw a moment that could last forever, and she wanted it all.

He said huskily, "Angel . . . I don't think you know what you do to me."

"No," she whispered breathlessly. "I don't."

His fingertips traced the outline of her lips, still moist from his. A shiver of yearning and pleasure went through Angel with the touch. And then he dropped his hand.

"Maybe," he said, "that's for the best."

She could have made him kiss her again; she knew that. But her greed frightened her a little, as though to ask too much from the fairy tale of a life that had become hers in the past few days would be to risk having it all snatched away. So she let her arms slip from around his neck, and, suddenly shy, she looked down at the shell that was still clutched in her hand.

"This is the best day I ever had," she said.

He took her other hand in his, winding their fingers together and examining the joining intently. "If I could, I'd make them all like this."

She looked up at him, her heart skipping and dancing in her chest. "You've done so much for us—for me. Why? I never asked you to. Why are you so good to me?"

There was a moment's quickening in his eyes, and Angel's breath stopped. And then a small smile touched his lips, and she knew that his reply was not what he had originally meant to say.

"I'm not sure I know the answer to that myself." Then he glanced toward the cliff. "We'd better be getting back."

After a moment Angel nodded and went to put on her shoes.

She hurried up the path, spurred by the delight that energized her with Adam's every casual touch on her back or her arm or her shoulders, filled with leftover wonder that made it seem as though her feet barely touched the ground. She called out, "Papa!" when she was halfway up. "Wait till you see what I found!"

He didn't answer, and she moved a little faster.

She tried to ignore the alarm that crawled through her stomach when she called out a second time and still there was no answer. But Adam was moving more quickly too, his arm around her waist, urging her to keep up with his long stride. She needed no urging when the rocky path gave way to scrubby grass and she could see her papa, slumped in the chair where they had left him.

Her lungs were exploding as she broke into a run, her heart a swollen knot of fiery pain squeezing blood through her veins. Her face was hot and slick with perspiration but her hands were cold, her feet numb. The distance between herself and her papa seemed like a gaping hole in the universe, and although she ran as fast as she could it never got any smaller.

She tripped over her skirts and only Adam's strong hand kept her from sprawling. She grabbed her skirts up above her knees and when she tried to call out again it was only a gasp.

And then she saw Jeremiah's face—ash white, stone still, his lips stained with blood. One hand dangled limply over the arm of the chair, and he did not move.

She screamed, *"Papa!"* and fell to the ground beside him. She took his icy hands, she shook his frail shoulders, but still he did not move.

Adam pushed her aside roughly, and she flailed out at him but he ignored her as he bent over Jeremiah.

"Leave him alone!" Angel screamed, pushing at Adam. "Let me see him, don't—"

"Stop it!" He whirled on her, grabbing her shoulders. "Listen to me. He's breathing; he's alive. We've got to get him to a doctor. Go get the carriage and bring the horses as close as you can. Now!"

She watched Adam bend and lift the frail form of her papa into his arms, and then she didn't hesitate. She ran for the carriage.

CHAPTER

Ten

It was a nightmare. Angel had known nightmares before; she was so used to grasping for happiness and having it turn into horror that she had learned to expect it, and she should have grown immune to the effects. But the nightmare had never been like this.

The frantic flight back to the city, with Jeremiah's head in Angel's lap. The blood that spewed from his lips with every coughing, rattling breath, eventually staining her skirt crimson. The pain in his eyes when he tried to speak, the shaking of her own fingers as she stroked his forehead and murmured words, meaningless words that had no comfort in them because she was frozen with terror. The thin, bespectacled doctor they found after an eternal search, who took her papa away behind a curtained divider and left her alone to wait and agonize ... it was all a blur, a foul-tasting, ice-shrouded conglomerate of impressions and half-memories that seemed to belong to someone else.

After a half-hour, the doctor came out with a sad look on his face. He looked at Adam and gave a small shake of his head.

Angel wanted to fling herself on him, to grab his arms and shake him and scream at him to take back that look, to stop shaking his head. But she stood fixed in a cold patch of sunlight in front of the window and her throat was too dry to make a sound; she couldn't move.

"There's not much I can do for him here," the doctor said. "His case is . . . well, it's pretty far advanced. He's going to need constant care."

"I can take care of him." Angel found her voice, although it was hoarse and strained and very unlike her usual tone. "I've always taken care of him. I—"

The doctor took off his glasses and rubbed them with a handkerchief. His eyes were kind and sympathetic. "He needs professional care, Miss, more than you can do for him. We've got a fine hospital in town. St. Mary's. It's clean and quiet and there's a doctor on call almost all the time. Of course . . ." he glanced again at Adam, "it's expensive."

"I can afford it," Angel said quickly, harshly. "If that's where he needs to be, don't worry about money."

Adam asked, "How do we get to this place?"

"It would be better if we didn't move him right now. Let me get an ambulance over here and meet you there in, say, two hours?"

As he spoke he was writing down the address on a slip of paper, and he handed it to Adam. Adam nodded. He touched Angel's arm. "Come on, Angel. I'll take you back to the hotel."

She stared at him as though he had suddenly lost his mind. "I'm staying with Papa!"

"He's unconscious," the doctor said. "He wouldn't know you were here."

Angel jerked away from Adam's touch. "I don't care! He needs me and I'm not leaving him." She started toward the curtain divider.

"Angel," Adam said quietly, "he's going to need you a lot more later. Come on back to the hotel and get cleaned up. Do you want your papa to see you looking like that when he wakes up?"

Angel looked down at her new dress, which was sticky with blood from waist to thigh, splattered with blood across the bodice and sleeves. She felt a wave of sickness and dread, and she shook her head slowly. "No," she whispered. "It would—scare him."

Adam took her arm again. He talked some more with the doctor, but she didn't know what was said. She demanded just as they reached the door, "You'll take care of him? You'll watch out for him till I get there? Because I have money, I can pay you. You tell them that at the hospital, too."

The doctor assured her that he would take care of everything, and she had no choice but to leave her papa in the hands of a stranger.

Angel kept thinking it must be her fault. She never should have brought him here, never should have forced him to make that horrible cross-country trip. The bad air on the train, the fatigue, the cold fog of the bay . . . Staying out till all hours last night, and then this morning . . . She should have known better. She *had* known better, but she was too selfish, too greedy to have it all and have it now, and all this was her fault.

She stepped out of her bloodstained skirt and petticoat and left them in a crumpled heap on the floor, flinging the bodice after them as she reached for her worn blue traveling suit. *I'll make it up to you, Papa,* she vowed desperately. *I will. Everything is going to be all right, you'll see. I'll make everything all right.*

She buttoned up her bodice with stiff, shaky fingers, and wound her hair into a clumsy knot, stabbing her scalp with the hairpins she used to hold it. Then quickly she went over to the drawer and took out the Bible.

The cross was still safe inside. She touched the cold, dully gleaming metal, taking a kind of superstitious strength from what it represented. She started to lift it out, but then there was a knock on the door. She closed the Bible quickly. "I'm ready," she called and hurried to the door.

Adam stood with his hat in his hand, looking grave and sorry, but strong. Always strong. He said, "I thought there might be something your pa would like with him—a book or some such. I didn't know what to pick."

Angel swallowed hard, for what the trauma of the last hour had not been able to do to her, his thoughtfulness did. She felt a quick, hot flooding sensation in her chest and she fought it back determinedly. "Yes," she said huskily. "Books. He'll want his books. And a change of clothes. His are all—ruined. I'll pack some things."

She hurried across the hall to the room Adam had shared

with Jeremiah. Adam started to follow her, but at the last minute he couldn't intrude. She would want to be alone while performing what might well be her last act of service for the man she called Papa.

Adam knew that Jeremiah Haber would not be coming home from the hospital, if he even made it there at all, and he suspected that surely, somewhere deep down, Angel must know the same thing. He had seen many men die in his lifetime, good and bad, fairly and unjustly, and the passing never failed to wrench something within him, leaving him just a little bit more empty than he had been before. But never had any man's death seemed as unfair to him as did this one.

Jeremiah Haber was a good man. Adam had grown fond of him and had learned to admire him, and Adam's admiration was not given easily. Adam had known from the moment he met him that Jeremiah was old and sick and could not be expected to survive long. He suspected Jeremiah himself was neither surprised nor remorseful that the time had come.

But Angel . . . It was for Angel that Adam's throat tightened and his stomach knotted. She deserved so much better than this, she *needed* better than this. She had lost so much already and suffered so much through no fault of her own; was there any justice that the one constant, the only happiness, in her life should be snatched away just when she needed it most?

Adam's eyes fell on the Bible on the bureau, a little surprised to find such a thing in her room, and yet not surprised at all. He picked it up, absently flipping through the pages. He wondered if she had been reading it before he came in, searching for some comfort or hope. Perhaps Jeremiah would like to have it with him at the hospital.

The pages fell open, and he stared.

A dozen questions roared through his head, and with them a dozen possible answers. Her sudden decision to leave Green River. The two men on the train. Her attempt to ambush him in Denver. Her shrill voice insisting "I have money!"

He lifted the cross out of its nesting place, and felt a kind of despair settle deep in the pit of his stomach. The weight of it told him it was real silver, which meant that the stones—dozens of them—had to be real, too. Where would a girl like Angel get her hands on something like this?

There was only one possible answer.

Angel, he thought in a mixture of anger and dismay. *Goddammit, Angel* . . .

If the cross had been legally hers, she would not have kept it such a secret. She would not have suffered such privation and traveled against her will across the country with him if she'd felt she could risk selling it before now.

The man in him—the one who had started to care too much for a woman he knew better than to trust—wanted to confront her with his discovery, to demand an explanation and hope the one she gave was one he could live with. The lawman in him knew better.

The muscles of his jaw tightened and his eyes grew hard as he closed the Bible and placed it where he had found it. He heard Angel close the door across the hall, and without another moment's thought or hesitation, he slipped the cross into his pocket. Then he turned to meet her.

* * *

The hospital was a horrible place, and from the moment she entered it Angel recoiled. The walls were whitewashed but the floors were dull. The interior was dank and smelled of death and dying. Sisters in white habits and headdresses swept along the narrow corridors and with them came a rush of memories for Angel. The mission, small knees aching from kneeling on stone floors, endless prayers, silence, solitude . . .

There was a brief moment when nothing but Adam's firm hand on her elbow kept her moving forward. Somewhere in the bowels of this horrible place her father was all alone, sick and hurting. She had to be with him.

The long room into which they were escorted was lined with beds, and in those beds were men—old men muffling moans, middle-aged men with bloodstains on their sheets, even young men, their bodies twisted with pain and deformity. The room smelled of waste and sickness and was filled with the rattling gasps of the dying.

One of the sisters led them to Jeremiah's bed, and Angel fell to her knees beside him, her legs no longer able to support her. His face was waxy and white, his eyes outlined by two enormous, dark sunken circles. His lips had a bluish tint, but a faint stream of breath still came from them.

A man stood beside the bed, a different doctor from the one they had first seen. He looked at Adam. "You're a relative?"

"This is Miss Haber," Adam said. "His daughter."

The doctor nodded. "We're making him as comfortable as we can, there's not much else we can do. It's a matter of time now."

Angel lifted her face angrily. "Don't say that! How can

you say that? We brought him here for you to make him better! That's your job, isn't it? Make him better!"

The doctor looked uncomfortable, glanced at Adam, then seemed to change his mind about what he was going to say. "We're giving him opium for the pain. He probably won't wake for a while."

Angel turned back to Jeremiah, laying her hand across his forehead. "I'll be here when he does."

The doctor hesitated, then walked away.

After a moment, Adam touched her shoulder. "There's no reason for you to stay, you know. He—"

"I'm staying," she said fiercely, without looking up.

He was silent for a moment. "I have to go out for a while. I'll be back for you this afternoon."

She didn't answer. She was glad when he was gone, because then it was just she and her papa, as it had been in the beginning. As it was supposed to be.

She took his cold hand in hers and waited for him to wake up.

Eliston Lewis, purveyor of fine jewels and master craftsman, removed the loupe from his eye and reluctantly handed the cross back to Adam. "I'm sorry," he said. "I can't offer you what it's worth."

"That's all right." Adam leaned back in the small, uncomfortable chair across the black-swathed table from the man. "I didn't want to sell. What can you tell me about it?"

Eliston Lewis, somewhat relieved to know that the precious artifact was not about to fall into his competition's hands, again took the cross between his long, delicate fingers. "Well, it's Spanish, I would say. Possibly an icon, or even a holy relic. It's old, obviously, ancient. But even if it weren't, I couldn't begin to estimate the value of these stones. To find a flawless ruby of such size, and these sapphires..." Again he shook his head sadly. "It's an honor merely to hold such an object."

Adam frowned. "Icon? What's that?"

"Property of the Holy Catholic Church," explained the jeweler. "Usually associated with a miracle or purported to have special spiritual properties..." He looked at Adam cautiously. "May I ask how you, er, came by such a thing?"

Adam shook his head. "It's not mine. I'm asking for a friend. Any chance of finding out where it came from?"

"I have some books," suggested Lewis, "and I could check with my colleagues... If you could leave it with me overnight, perhaps I could have an answer for you tomorrow. I'll give you a receipt, of course," he added quickly.

Adam nodded and got to his feet. "I'd appreciate it."

He started out of the shop with the receipt in his pocket and the cross locked away in the jeweler's safe, but at the door he turned back. Eliston Lewis looked at him questioningly.

"There's one more thing I'd like you to do for me," Adam said.

Late in the afternoon, Jeremiah opened his eyes. After a couple of hours one of the sisters had been kind enough to bring her a chair, but still Angel's back ached and her shoulders throbbed from bending over him, watching his

chest rise and fall and measuring his every breath; standing
guard over him as though her mere presence could keep
harm from coming his way.

His lips moved dryly but he made no sound. Angel got up
quickly and poured water from a pitcher into a small pottery
cup; he drank a little but spilled most of it.

"Angel," he said. His voice was raspy, little above a
whisper.

"I'm here, Papa." She laid her hand on his brow.

He was too weak for the smile that wanted to touch his
lips, but it was reflected in his eyes, faintly. "You look—
tired. Should go home. Rest."

She shook her head adamantly. "No. I'm not leaving
you." Her mother had abandoned her in a place like this.
She would not do the same to the only parent she had ever
known, the only man who had ever loved her.

His eyes fluttered closed, as though against all efforts to
keep them open. To Angel, it felt as though he were
slipping away, and she tried desperately to think of some
way to keep that from happening.

"Papa, look." She scrambled in her new, embroidered
reticule until she found what she sought. "I brought you
something." She opened his hand and placed the small
object in it. "It's a seashell. I found it this morning. If you
put it close to your face you can smell the ocean on it."

Again the faint flickering of a smile as he opened his eyes.
"I remember," he murmured. "You were so pretty, playing
there on the shore. Just like I always dreamed. Waited—so
long. I'm glad I got to see it, before . . ."

Angel wouldn't let him finish. "You're much better,
Papa," she said quickly. "You haven't coughed all day, and

rest was all you needed. You'll be leaving here soon, and when you do—"

He moved his head feebly back and forth on the pillow. "Angel," he said. It seemed to cost him a great deal to make his voice clear, to hold his eyes open and fixed on hers. "I'll be leaving you soon."

"No!"

He fumbled for her hand. Finding it, he squeezed her fingers. His grip was alarmingly weak. "Yes, I will. But it's all right, Angel. All I ever wanted was to see you happy, and taken care of. Now your mother is waiting for you. You have a home, and a family, and—"

"No," she repeated forcefully. Her voice was low and thick with anger and frightened tears. "I'm not listening to talk like that. You're all the family I need and you're going to get better. I don't need my mother. I don't need anybody but you."

His eyes drifted closed. "So tired. I'm sorry. . . ." His voice grew wearier, fainter. Angel squeezed his fingers harder.

After a moment he murmured, "Your mother . . . She loves you, Angel. And you do need her. More than you know."

And then he was sleeping, with those shallow, rattling breaths of his, and nothing Angel could have said would have made a difference.

After a moment she folded his fingers around the seashell she had placed within them, and slowly dropped her forehead to the pillow beside Jeremiah's face, closing her eyes. "I don't need her," she said thickly. "And I'll never love her. Don't leave me, Papa. . . ."

* * *

1868

Consuelo pushed herself to a sitting position in the hard, narrow bed as the sister entered her room, her hand instinctively covering the newly healed scar on her cheek. In the sister's arms was a small, linen-swathed bundle, and Sister Magdalene smiled as she approached the bed.

"Here she is," she said gently, placing the baby in Consuelo's arms. "Here is your little Angelica."

Consuelo felt the breath leave her body in the wonder of looking into her daughter's sleeping face. So small, so perfect. Already her skin had lost its birth blush and was the color of peaches and cream; the sisters had brushed her thick shock of dark hair into a gleaming wave atop her head. She slept with one small hand curled against her cheek, long delicate fingers curved into a ball, her lips pursed.

"Oh," Consuelo whispered, and for a moment she could say nothing more. Then she looked at Sister Magdalene. "She does look like an Angel, doesn't she?"

The other woman nodded and sat carefully on the bed next to her. "All children are sent from God."

"Yes," Consuelo agreed quietly, and for a moment her face was shadowed with pain. "Even if they do not always arrive according to God's plan."

Sister Magdalene tenderly stroked the infant's cheek with the back of her index finger. "She has a home with us, child, for as long as it takes to find someone—"

"No," Consuelo interrupted. Instinctively her arms tightened around the baby, and the sleeping child stirred. "No, I'll come back for her. I have to find work and—and a home for her, but she's mine. I won't have her given away."

The sister looked disturbed. "Are you sure, child? What you plan is—difficult at best. And she is such a pretty baby. There are many fine couples who—"

"No," Consuelo repeated firmly. "She's my baby. My Angel. I'll do whatever it takes, but I will come back for her." She looked at the sister helplessly. "I love her, don't you see? She's the only person who's ever completely belonged to me and . . . I love her."

Sister Magdalene smiled and patted Consuelo's hand. "I do understand. And for such a love as a mother has for a child, the Blessed Virgin will watch over you, and guide you back to her."

Consuelo looked down at the sleeping infant, touching her tiny hand, stroking her silky hair. "I will come back," she whispered. "I won't live without you. I have to go away for a little while, to find a home for us, but I'll be back for you. I promise."

CHAPTER

Eleven

FOR two days and nights Angel stayed by Jeremiah's side. She did not eat, and if she slept it was only for a few seconds at a time, dozing off in her chair. Even though Jeremiah was rarely conscious, she talked to him constantly; she talked until her voice was hoarse and then she whispered. She talked about the times they had shared together, about what they were going to do when he got well...about a house on the ocean with sunshine in every room, walks on the beach, and long drives in an open-topped carriage.

Adam watched her with a mixture of frustration, despair, and a heartbreaking empathy that he tried to ignore but could not. It didn't matter what kind of woman Angel was or what she had done, there was something inside her he understood too well. Beneath the bravado was the defenselessness of a girl who needed too much and had too little, and now she was facing the loss of the only thing she did have. Adam wanted to make it easier for her, but he couldn't.

She was short with the nuns and questioned their every attention, making the job of caring for their patient much more difficult. She complained about the noise and the smell and was constantly suspicious of the cleanliness of the place. She was merciless to the doctors. And perhaps worst of all, she flatly refused to hear what any of them tried to tell her. She would not allow for the possibility that Jeremiah would never leave this place, and she became furious when anyone suggested it.

Adam could see that she was near collapse. She might have a will of iron but her body was just as subject to limits as was that of anyone else. He knew it was unfair to take advantage of the confusion and weakness brought on by fatigue, but when it became apparent that she didn't have the energy to fight him—or anyone else—he took her firmly by the arm.

"Angel," he said, "go back to the hotel. Get something to eat and some rest. You're not doing anybody any good like this."

She tried to pull her arm away but couldn't even manage that. Her eyes were puffy and undercircled with dark pockets; the fragile skin around her cheekbones looked tight, translucent, pale. "No," she said dully. "He needs me."

"He's sleeping. He's going to need you more when he wakes up."

Angel stroked Jeremiah's forehead. "He will wake up, won't he?"

"Yes." Another lie. How many had he told her in the last few days? "And he doesn't need to be worrying about you on top of everything else. He will if he sees you looking like this."

Angel pushed her hand across her face as though physically to wipe away the fatigue. Her voice was flat and stripped of emotion. "This is an awful place. I've got to get him out of here. There must be a better place."

Adam said, "I'll sit with him while you're gone." She was already shaking her head and he added, "I've gotten you from Colorado to California and haven't let you down yet. Don't you trust me to sit with him for a few hours?"

That seemed to confuse her, and she thought about it for a long time. "He does like you," she admitted. "Maybe . . . it would be all right."

"Of course it will."

She got to her feet a little shakily. "I've got—there's some things I have to do. This place—we need better doctors. I won't be gone long."

"Take your time. I'll stay." He took the chair she had abandoned. "Get some sleep, Angel. Everything's going to be all right."

She didn't believe him; he could see that in her eyes. But she didn't have a choice. She leaned forward to kiss her papa on the forehead and then she left.

It was dark when Angel stepped outside. The street was shrouded with a misty, foggy rain and she was not sure whether it was twilight or dawn; she was disoriented. She couldn't recall the name of the hotel and she was too tired to try. So she simply started walking.

The air smelled of horse manure and wet stones, cooking odors and coal smoke and—so very faintly—the ocean. Was it a lifetime ago that she had felt the sand beneath her feet and the ocean spray on her face and held, for such a brief moment, magic in her hands? Had it ever happened at all?

Adam had kissed her then. His lips had been soft and his arms had been strong and within them the entire world had spun and faded away. Oh, how she needed to be held tonight. How she needed someone to make it all right. She had to sell the cross and get a lot of money, and get Papa out of that awful place. She would take him to Baltimore or Boston, or London if need be, for the finest doctors and nurses and miracle-working medicines that only the very rich could buy.

Her papa was very sick, she knew that, but he wasn't going to die. If he died she would be all alone in the dark and she wouldn't allow that.

The drizzle clung to her face and dampened her skirts, making her hair curl and escape from its pins. The sound of hooves and the rattling of wheels were eerily magnified on the streets, and every streetlamp was surrounded by a yellow halo that illuminated nothing. Her legs ached and her breath was short from climbing hills. She didn't know where she was, and she didn't care. She was so tired.

After some time the wide boulevards and quiet homes gave way to narrow, winding streets where the buildings were close together and the storefronts were shabby and leaned. The air smelled of fish and oil and exotic spices, and there were shapes in the darkness, bold eyes staring at her, sly forms slithering away. Her heart started to beat a little faster, for danger was a palpable thing that challenged all her senses—not with fear but with excitement. Life began to trickle back through her veins, the necessity of alertness pushing back her fatigue.

Some of the buildings were brightly lit, and she could hear voices and bursts of laughter inside. Foreign tongues reeled off syllables she couldn't begin to understand, and in the reflected lights of windows she could see faces in the streets . . . yellow-cast skin, dark slanted eyes, men with long pigtails. A group of them were gathered in front of a bonfire in the middle of the street, passing around a bottle and shouting out in that mangled, exotic language of theirs. The firelight danced garishly across their strange forms and lit up their dark eyes, and it was like a scene from hell. And hell, at that moment, was exactly where Angel felt like being.

A shadow fell over her, accompanied in an instant by a thick muscled arm that stretched out between Angel and the wall of the building by which she was standing, blocking her way. A big man leered down at her.

"Well, little lady," he drawled. "Where're you bound for?"

He was a seaman, from the looks of him, with a shaggy blond beard and a broken eyetooth and breath that was thick with the smell of whiskey. He didn't look like much, but she knew about sailors in from exotic ports with their pockets bulging with money. Tonight she had a taste for a little of that money herself. She had a taste for a lot of things.

She looked him over measuringly. "That depends," she replied. "You in the mood to buy a lady a drink?"

He grinned and took her arm.

* * *

Adam didn't know how long he sat there, listening to the sounds of men dying and suffering all around him, watching Jeremiah drag in one slow, rattling breath after another and certain that each one would be his last. How had Angel stood it for so long? How had she sat there hour after hour, and not gone mad?

He didn't know why he was sitting there at all. There was nothing he could do for Jeremiah Haber, nothing anybody could do. He shouldn't have let Angel leave on her own. He should go back to the hotel and check on her. He should check on a lot of things. But he stayed . . . because he had promised Angel.

While he sat, he wrote. Trying to put into words for Consuelo what he had found in Angel, trying to prepare her in some way for what *she* would find . . . but it was impossible. Writing came hard to him; words had never been his most efficient tools. Perhaps he could have told her in person . . . or perhaps not.

She looks a lot like you. . . . That was true enough. *Feisty . . .* That was an understatement, and anyway, he didn't know how to spell it. He tried to think of other words. Brave. Beautiful. Smart. The way she looked with the ocean sunlight sparkling in her eyes and her face all aglow, that dark, silky hair whipping around her shoulders . . . The way she felt, like windsong in his arms. The way *he* felt, as though he could never hold her long enough or kiss her thoroughly enough or keep her close enough.

He scowled at the paper. Angel Haber was a liar and a thief and God knew what else. A man would be a fool to trust her out of his sight, and yet he couldn't get her out of his mind. How was he supposed to explain to Consuelo what he himself couldn't understand?

It's your fault, he thought suddenly, staring at the paper. *Yours, Consuelo, for loving that thieving outlaw Camp Meredith and turning your back on your own child. She can't help what she grew up to be, it's a miracle she grew up at all. It's your fault . . .*

He cut the thought off sharply, shocked and horrified at the betrayal of his own mind. Was this what Angel was doing to him, then? Turning him against the woman he had devoted his life to from the moment he had met her, a good woman . . .

Good, that treacherous little voice whispered inside his skull, *but not perfect . . .*

Abruptly he crumpled up the sheet of paper, and then there was a stirring on the bed. Adam stood up, looking around for one of the nuns, but it was late and the long room was deserted.

Jeremiah opened his eyes. Adam went to the head of the bed, bending over the prone figure so he could hear if Jeremiah wanted anything.

Jeremiah stared at him for a long time with hazy, drug-fogged eyes, then said, "Adam."

Adam felt a stirring of relief that Jeremiah had recognized him. "Yes, sir. It's me."

He tried to speak, but the effort stirred a weak, wheezing cough. Adam started to move away, in search of a nun or a doctor, but Jeremiah plucked feebly at his sleeve. Adam stayed.

"Angel . . ." Jeremiah managed at last.

"I sent her back to the hotel to rest. I can send for her if you want."

"No . . ." He tried to move his head on the pillow. "Better. Want to talk—to you."

Adam leaned down closer. He could hardly make out the words.

"Angel . . ." the old man whispered. The effort it seemed to cost him to form the word, or even the thought, was enormous. "I worry—about her. So headstrong. Needs somebody—to look after her."

Adam wanted to assure the old man that Angel could look after herself just fine, but it would have been the wrong thing to say. And it wasn't true.

"I can't—look after her any more. So much—" The words were cut off by a sharp crease of pain that divided his forehead from brow to brow; his hand tightened on Adam's arm as he struggled to subdue it. "So much I wanted—to teach her," he finished in a gasp.

Adam covered Jeremiah's hand with his own and didn't know what to say or do.

Then the older man's eyes focused on him. They seemed clear and bright and strong with purpose for the first time since his collapse. "You—understand her," he whispered. "You know . . ."

And then Adam found his voice. It was hoarse. "Yes. I know."

"I give her to you," Jeremiah said steadily. "You'll take care of her."

"With my last breath," Adam whispered thickly, and he didn't realize how deep the truth was until he spoke the words, or how long he had been trying to ignore it. His hand tightened on the other man's. "I'll take care of her. I promise."

Jeremiah smiled and closed his eyes.

* * *

The little tavern was close and smoky, tended by a Chinese man with mean eyes and occupied mostly by sailors who looked even meaner and were a great deal drunker—some of them on opium, some on the same brand of cheap whiskey Angel had been drinking. The mood was volatile, swinging from violence one moment to outbursts of ribald songs and laughter the next. From a curtained-off room Angel heard a woman scream and it was a horrible, soul-chilling sound, but not as chilling as the silence that followed.

This was a bad place, the worst place Angel had ever been in. Danger was as thick as smoke in the air, and the men who looked at her, even the one who sat across the scarred table from her and kept filling her glass with whiskey, grinned and licked their lips, like a pack of coyotes circling a crippled rabbit. Something bad was going to happen to her before she left this place, Angel knew that. And she didn't care. She waited for it, welcomed it. Because nothing was as bad as what waited for her back in that hospital ward, and here at least she had a fighting chance.

The whiskey flooded her mind and numbed it to the pain, making her reckless and wild. Desperation thrummed through her veins and the noise, the smoke, and the danger were like intoxicants, sealing her in a narrow, barricaded world of her own where death and loneliness could not invade. Here she was in charge. Here she could control her own fate. Here she could take what she needed and no one and nothing could stop her.

When the big ragged-bearded sailor flung his arms around

her and hoisted her to her feet she went laughingly, with her head thrown back and her heels kicked up to flash her petticoat, which brought hoots and howls from the other patrons. He whirled her around the room in a clumsy, impromptu dance, muttering something through that drunken grin that was probably obscene but she couldn't hear and didn't want to. She just laughed and wrapped her arms around his waist and pretended she was having the time of her life while she slipped her hand into his pocket and closed it around the bundle of bills there.

There was a lot, more than she had hoped, and her heart speeded with the excitement of triumph as she slid the money out of its nesting place and folded it into a secure packet that fit into her fist. It didn't matter how much there was, really; what mattered was that she had done it, she had won. . . .

Then suddenly the sailor grabbed her hair and jerked back on it with a force that snapped her neck backward and startled a cry from her. He was still grinning down at her, still smothering her with the whiskey fumes of his breath, but his eyes were malevolent with cunning and grim intent.

"Think you're so smart, do you, bitch? Picking my goddamn pocket when you think you got me so worked up I won't notice? Well, I'll pay the price, by God, but not before I get the goods!"

He lunged at her and she saw her chance, her only chance. She kicked out forcefully and her foot slammed into his groin. He doubled over with a howl of pain, but her own instincts were dulled with alcohol, fatigue, and simple shock; she whirled for the door but a moment too late. Someone grabbed her arm and snapped it up behind her; she screamed as she felt the tendons stretch and bones lengthen and the pain sent a paralyzing numbness down her spine. Her fist tightened around the money. She could smell the sweat and hear the laughter of the man who held her, and her one futile attempt to break away almost caused her arm to snap in two.

The sailor, still half bent over, swung toward her, his eyes dark pools of rage as his arm arced up and out. The blow caught her across the mouth and she tasted blood; pain exploded in her head and left her momentarily blind and deaf. She lashed out instinctively, kicking and flailing with her free arm, and in one wild, desperate moment she thought one of her blows must have struck home because the pressure on her arm was suddenly released.

She staggered forward as needles of pain surged into the arm that hung uselessly at her side. Still she would not release the money. She swung her shaking legs in what she thought was the general direction of the door and suddenly she was slammed back against a wall, an iron hand closing around her throat.

She had a blurred impression of the sailor's bared teeth and glittering, lustful eyes as he loomed over her. Her fist tightened on the money even as his hand tightened on her throat, choking off her breath, crushing her windpipe. He was speaking but she couldn't make out the words for the roar of blood in her ears. Her lips felt numb and swollen; her head throbbed. She gasped but drew no breath. She clawed at him with her free hand. He only grinned and tightened his grip.

There was a gunshot. She heard it clearly, like an explosion amid the seemingly distant voices that surrounded her. The pressure was released and air flooded her lungs, her head swam. Another gunshot and the big sailor swung around. And, incredulously, Angel heard her name called.

Adam was standing near the door, his back protected by the wall, the gun in his hand moving slowly from the sailor to his companions to anyone who looked as though he might move. His eyes were like ice.

"Angel!" he commanded sharply again. "Get over here!"

She stumbled toward him.

The room was quiet now, sullen, wary eyes fixed on Adam, and she moved quickly. When she reached him she wouldn't have stopped, she wanted only to get out of there, she had eyes for nothing but the door. But his hand suddenly shot out and grabbed her wrist, twisting it around and jerking it downward with such violence that she cried out and her fist opened; the bundle of bills scattered on the floor.

With a hoarse roar of outrage, she actually lunged toward the scattered money, but Adam jerked her up and pushed her hard, out the door, down the street, into an alleyway, his ruthless grip on her upper arm propelling her forward and then dragging her when he broke into a run. Perhaps he heard what she was too infused with rage and terror to hear—running footsteps, shouts, the sound of gunfire. She didn't care. She knew only that he was here and he shouldn't have been, she was running and she shouldn't have been, she had *lost*. . . .

When he pushed her around the side of a building and flattened her against a wall she struck out at him, lashing her nails across his face and drawing blood. "You bastard!" she screamed. "You had no right! That was my money—"

"Shut up!" It was a furious hiss through ragged breaths, and he clamped his hand hard across her mouth, pushing her head against the cold brick wall. She struggled and he leaned his weight against her, pinning her tight with his hips and his chest.

She couldn't breathe. Her throat ached with the residual effects of near-strangulation and her head pulsed waves of pain. Adam's fingers dug cruelly into the bruise on her face that the other man's blow had left. His breath steamed in the cold damp air and his body pressed a hard, heated imprint into hers, his chest crushing her breasts, the sharp points of his hipbones digging into hers. Terror was a thick black brew inside her that bubbled and gurgled and spread its noxious broth into every corner of her mind. Not for what had happened in the tavern, not for the danger that was still pursuing them, but because Adam was here and he shouldn't have been; Adam had come looking for her and he shouldn't have, he wouldn't have ...

Adam's face was half-turned from her, his head cocked in an intent listening pose, his gun still drawn. At one point she saw the puffy clouds of his breath stop but she couldn't hear what he heard; her heart was beating too loudly, her blood roaring in her ears. But then whatever he was listening for must have passed; slowly the tension in his body relaxed and he eased away from her. He reholstered his gun, then removed his hand from her mouth.

Without his weight to support her Angel sagged against the wall, gasping for breath and choking on a sudden, spasmodic contraction of her throat. "How did you find me?" she demanded. Her voice was hoarse and broken, choked with fury. "You shouldn't be here, you—"

"I know you too well, Angel," he said, his voice low, his breathing uneven. "It wasn't hard."

"You were supposed to stay, you promised you would—"

"Angel—"

She saw it in his eyes and wouldn't let him say it. "Liar! I trusted you and—"

"Angel, listen to me—"

"No!" Hysteria fought its way to the surface with mad, knife-sharp claws. "No, I won't listen to you, everything you say is a lie! I'm going back to Papa, he needs me!"

She started to push past him but he caught her shoulders. "Angel, he's gone."

Spoken quietly, finally, and with the hollow solemnity of rain dripping from the eaves into the darkness. So quiet were the words in fact that she didn't hear them, refused to hear them.

"I never should have left him in the first place. You shouldn't have left him. What if he wakes up and I'm not there? I can't leave him alone!"

"Angel—"

"Let go of me!" Her voice was shrill and she tried to jerk away from him. "You can't tell me what to do! You can't keep me away from him! You left him there! You left him there to die—"

"Angel, stop it, for God's sake!"

"I won't, I won't! You're a filthy liar and I won't listen to you! I—"

He closed her mouth with his own. His arms were hard around her and her body was rigid as it struggled against his; the night was electric with wild emotion and raw desperation. He saw the terror in her eyes and all he knew to do was to draw her closer, to still her struggles, to hold her tight and keep her safe, and then his mouth was on hers.

She pushed against him at first, but then she clung to him. Her mouth opened beneath his and she made a sound, a sob or a smothered cry; he was drawn into her, and desperately, hopelessly, he drank from her. It was not passion that fueled their embrace but another, deeper, more primitive need. Their hands clutched and their bodies strained against each other, propelled by madness, by hunger, by an urgency raw and wild... the need for life, for hope, for certainty, for an anchor in the darkness. Her fingers dug into his neck and his fingers pressed into her hips, pushing her against him. Madness, need, a roaring blackness in his head. He tasted the blood on her lips and knew this was wrong. He tried to stop, he had to stop...

But when he dragged his mouth away from hers she caught his face and sought his mouth again. His mouth, on hers, could not speak the words. His body against hers was hot and strong and filled with life. When he held her, she wasn't alone. When he kissed her, she wasn't afraid.

But it was no use. He took her face in both his hands and moved his lips away from hers. "Don't leave me," she whispered desperately.

"I won't. I'm here."

She started to shake. She couldn't help it. Her legs wouldn't support her and she brought her forehead slowly to Adam's shoulder. "I left him," she whispered. "I left him alone to die."

He drew her into his arms, tenderly, securely. His lips touched her hair. He said nothing, just held her there in the dark for a long, long time.

It was dawn by the time Adam got her back to the hotel. No one was in the lobby, so he carried her from the carriage to the elevator, and she didn't protest. She seemed not even to notice when he took her to his room instead of her own. He bolted the door and laid her on the bed, and she curled up on her side, not saying a word. Adam sat beside her and stroked her hair until her eyes closed. She didn't say another word.

He covered her with a quilt and went to sit in the chair by the door, watching over her while she slept.

CHAPTER

Twelve

CASEY was about to decide for certain what he had suspected for a long time: he was the only one with any brains in the outfit. Jenks had been beaten up pretty bad in the fall off the train; he had snapped something in his foot and it had swollen up to twice the size of his boot. He still didn't walk right and complained about it constantly. A gash on his head had kept him delirious for two days, and Casey figured that same injury was responsible for scrambling his brains even more. He was like a mean dog whose only worth had been his meanness; now with all the spirit whipped out of him, he wasn't worth much at all.

Casey would have left his partner behind to fend for himself but for one thing. He had broken his own arm in the fall and needed Jenks to be his hands. Casey could hold a gun in his left hand, but he couldn't fire it with any accuracy, and if he got into a fistfight he'd be a goner. He could have handled the girl—maybe—but now that she had two male protectors he would have been easily outmanned.

He couldn't wait for his arm to heal, although he was sorely tempted to do so. His quarry was in San Francisco; that much he had been able to determine from the train schedules. How long they would be there—if they still were—or how long before they sold the cross—if they hadn't already—was anybody's guess. Every day he wasted narrowed his chances of getting back what was rightfully his.

"It's a curse, I tell you," Jenks whined, absently rubbing the knot on his forehead. There was no bruise, and the scab had fallen off a couple of days ago, but the knot was as big as a hen's egg and wouldn't go away. It looked like a horn trying to sprout right over his left eye. "Stealing from a church, it ain't right, it ain't smart. You know what happens to folks that steal from a church, Case. Look what happened to us."

"Shut up about your goddamn curses. Ain't no such thing, and if you had half the brains God gave a turnip you'd know that." The curse had been a recurrent theme with Jenks since the train, and it was starting to get on Casey's nerves . . . perhaps because he was starting to wonder if there might not be just a little bit of truth there.

"You know what that priest said," insisted Jenks. "He said it was a holy piece of work—"

"Goddamn priests think everything they touch is holy," muttered Casey, pacing the narrow length of the room to peer out the grime-encrusted window. San Francisco was a cold, filthy, godawful-ugly little town and he couldn't wait to see the last of it. Chinamen everywhere he looked. Rain every goddamn day. And it smelled like rotten fish. The room they had taken was over some kind of food shop; it was crawling with bugs and he had slept in stables that smelled better.

"Said the cross had miracles in it," Jenks went on nervously. He sat on the edge of the creaky little cot that served as a bed, paring his fingernails with a buck knife. He had been doing the same thing for two hours; it was a wonder he had any fingernails left. "Said whoever took it would draw down the power, and bad trouble would come. Said the cross would protect itself."

"The only bad trouble I see is you, blathering like a goddamn moron." But that wasn't strictly true, and maybe that was what bothered Casey the most.

They'd staggered out of the Nevada desert into the shelter of the mountains and had been found by Indians who took them to their village. Casey and Jenks had repaid their kindness by stealing their treasure. It should've been the easiest job they'd ever pulled. Who would ever have thought an adobe hut of a church in the heart of a forgotten mountain range would be the resting place of something as rich as that cross? Who would've figured they would just leave it out, protected by nothing but a glass case, for anybody to just walk in and take? It had been too good to be true. If anything, it was a job sent from heaven.

But they'd barely even gotten out of the mountains before their own partner turned on them. They'd ended up having to kill him, and for what? They still didn't have the cross back. They'd chased that girl halfway across Colorado and what did they get? Casey had a busted arm and Jenks had gone soft in the head and they were still just as poor as they'd started. They could've robbed half a dozen stages in the time they'd wasted, pulled two good bank jobs, and been living it up south of the border on tequila and high-priced whores, instead of sitting around this filthy hell-hole waiting for word that might never come. It had seemed like easy money, but now Casey was beginning to wish he'd never heard of that pissant little church in the Sierras and had never laid eyes on the cross. It was turning out to be more trouble than it was worth, particularly for a man who was used to taking what he could get the easiest way he could get it.

And what if they had missed the girl? What if she had already disposed of the cross and had lit out for parts unknown on the money that should have been theirs? How much longer was he going to chase that piece of silver and rock?

"If I'd wanted to work for a living, I'd've been a goddamn bank teller," he muttered out loud.

That struck Jenks as extremely funny and he started laughing in that nervous, high-pitched giggle of his. Casey wanted to backhand him.

There was a scratching on the door. Casey spun toward it, his gun sliding out of his holster. Jenks's craziness seemed to begin and end with the subject of the cross, for he hadn't forgotten how to take care of himself. The laughter ceased abruptly and he went to stand behind the door, knife at the ready. Casey went forward and opened the door cautiously.

He pulled the boy inside roughly and closed the door just as Jenks stepped out with the knife aimed for the boy's throat. Terror bulged the little Chinaman's narrow eyes and Casey slapped Jenks's arm away. "What you got?" he demanded of the boy.

The boy looked warily from Jenks to Casey and swallowed hard. "The woman you seek, with the crippled elder and the yellow-haired man, she is here."

Jenks glanced uncertainly at Casey. "Maybe it's the wrong woman, Case. Lots of black-headed females around, you know."

Casey gave him an impatient look. He sounded as though he *wanted* it to be the wrong woman.

"You sure, boy?" he demanded. "You sure it's the one we want?"

The boy drew himself up proudly. "My people, we work in the kitchens and hotels and rooming houses of every street in this city. There is nothing we do not know. Here is the address." He took a piece of paper from inside a shirt that was too baggy on his thin body, and Casey snatched it from him.

"The money, if you please," the boy said politely.

Casey scowled at him. "Give him the money, Jenks."

"Why don't I just slit his throat?"

"Give him the goddamn money. If he's got the wrong woman, I want him to know we're gunning for him."

Sullenly Jenks withdrew a silver dollar from his pocket and tossed it at the boy. He caught it deftly in midair and bowed deeply from the waist.

"You will be pleased you did not kill me," said the boy, unperturbed. "For I have more information for you. The woman, she was here only two nights ago. She danced in the tavern of my uncle's cousin. The yellow-haired man came for her and there was shooting."

"Did he get kilt?" Casey demanded eagerly.

The boy shook his head soberly. "There was no killing. But the elder who was her father, he has died."

Casey frowned distractedly. That was one less problem he had to deal with, not that the old man had ever been much of a threat anyway. "All right, boy, you did good. Now get out of here." He jerked his head toward the door. "We'll let you know if we need you again."

"So pleased to serve." Again the boy bowed deeply as he backed out the door.

Casey was glad to see him go. All that bowing and scraping, not to mention the mangled English, made him nervous.

"Shoulda asked him where the place was," he mumbled, squinting over the handwriting on the paper. "Jesus, I hate a town where I don't know my way around."

Then he looked at Jenks, his face setting in determined lines as he saw the end of the chase nearing. "What're you waiting for?" he barked. "Get your boots on. We got her now."

The dream that had begun with bright skies and ocean breezes ended on a gray and weeping day that was as cold as an empty heart. That was appropriate. California was a lie. The good life was a lie. Jeremiah Haber had never dreamed anything in his life that turned out to be true.

There were three people at the open grave in a corner of the city cemetery: Angel, Adam, and a Methodist preacher. The preacher asked if she wanted to scatter the first handful of soil over the coffin. Angel stepped to the edge of the grave and paused there for a moment, looking down at the cheap pine box. Then she opened her hand and let the seashell fall. It made a dull thud on the wood, and she turned away before the gravediggers could emerge from the shelter of a nearby mausoleum to finish their job.

Angel walked away from the grave, weaving her way aimlessly through the stained and leaning tombstones as she headed toward the street. Adam stayed beside her; she didn't know why. Looking back, she realized he had been beside her every minute of the past two days, although her recollection of that time was indistinct. The time since Adam had dragged her from the tavern was a blur, a nightmare that seemed to have nothing to do with her. But the nightmare was over now. She was wide awake, the world was cold and harsh, and she had to make her plans.

This was an ugly city. Why had she never noticed that before? It was cold and foul-smelling and it rained all the time. The first thing she was going to do was get out of this place. It reminded her too much of Jeremiah and his stupid dreams that never came true.

Adam touched her arm and gestured her to the waiting carriage. She would have walked, but the rain was coming down harder now and she didn't want her dress to get splotched. It was the cream-colored one, inappropriate for a funeral but the only clean dress she had left. She climbed inside the carriage and leaned back against the leather upholstery, listening to the erratic plopping noises the rain made on the roof. It was a desolate sound, and she was glad when Adam signaled the driver and the horses lurched into motion, blotting out the noise.

"I want a drink," she said abruptly.

"No," Adam answered. The word was not unkind. "We're going back to the hotel and pack. Then we're going to New Mexico."

"Like hell. This is where you and me part company, mister. The deal's off. I don't need you anymore."

Her voice was harsh, but her face was tired, devoid of emotion . . . devoid of everything except that thin hard core of brute determination that had enabled her to survive all these years on her own. Adam's heart twisted to see her like this and he cursed Jeremiah for dying and Consuelo for deserting her, and himself for being helpless to do anything about it. He had seen this coming. He'd known what this would do to her. But he hadn't been able to stop it.

He didn't know what to do for her, so he hardened his voice and spoke to her in the only language she would understand. "You're into me for a lot of money, lady. The deal stands."

Her jaw tightened and her chin jerked upward, but she said nothing.

"Look at me, Angel."

When she refused to comply, he took her chin in his hand and firmly turned her face to his. Her eyes were shadowed with hollow mauve circles, and the sparkle that usually gave them such life had dulled to a hard glint. The small cut on her lip from the sailor's blow had almost healed, but the side of her face was still slightly swollen and discolored by a faint blue bruise. When he touched that bruise with his forefinger, she jerked away.

"Why do you do it, Angel?" he asked, frowning. "Why do you keep doing this to yourself?"

"You'll get your money," she spat, tightening her gloved fists in her lap. "Leave me alone."

"You're not a stupid girl. You knew what would happen in a place like that. You went looking for a fight."

"What else do you expect from the daughter of a whore

and an outlaw?" she returned spitefully. "I was bred in the sewer, wasn't I, and I don't like to be too far from home!"

He said coolly, "Maybe you're right. Maybe the sewer is where you belong."

She turned angry, glittering eyes on him. "I can take care of myself. I don't need anybody to—"

"Is that it?" His voice was growing harsh now. "You have to keep proving you don't need anybody—even if it means risking your life to make a point? I was wrong. You *are* stupid."

"Maybe I just get tired of people trying to change me!" Her cheeks were blotched with color, her eyes icy-bright. "That worthless old man—you—even that saloon girl you say is my mother I never even met, and she's the last person in the world that's got a right to sit judgment on me! Maybe I just don't want to be a part of somebody else's dream, did you ever think of that?"

Her voice was shrill enough to crack glass, and so were the emotions that lashed out at him. Adam reached out a hand to her, as instinctively as he would to a wild-eyed horse, but she jerked away.

"I'm sick of it, do you hear? I'm sick of pretending and I'm sick of taking care of the do-gooder weaklings in this world that don't have the sense to take care of themselves. I'm *me* and I don't want to be good and kind and careful— that old man spent his whole life turning the other cheek and look what it got him!" She made a choked, disgusted sound and gestured violently toward the back window. "It was all lies, anyway, all of it! The only way to get along in this world is to fight dirty and fight hard and look out for yourself first because nobody else is going to do it for you. Do you hear me? Nobody!"

Her voice broke then and her hand flew to her mouth, but she couldn't stop the sob that choked its way to the surface; she couldn't stop the tears that flooded from her eyes and wet her hot face. Adam took both her hands in his and she tried to pull away, but not very hard. He held her hands firmly, and her effort to keep from sobbing out loud shook her shoulders.

"Angel," he said earnestly, "it doesn't have to be that way, you know it doesn't. You've got a family, and they want you—"

"I don't want them! I don't want—anybody!"

"And you've got me."

There was a catch in her breath and she wanted to spit back something spiteful and shove him away from her, but she couldn't. The tears flooded through her in slow, insistent waves and she was too tired to fight them. She was too tired to fight anything anymore, and when he drew her into his arms she rested her face against his shoulder and let the tears soak his coat and it felt like coming home. Because the truth was, she did want him. He was the only thing left in this world worth wanting.

From the moment he had stormed into her life he had been there, fighting at her side, pulling her from danger, charging to her rescue when she least expected it. She hated him for that but she was helpless to do anything about it. She supposed she would spend the rest of her life, in dark moments and bright, looking over her shoulder, expecting him to be there, *wanting* him to be there . . . She didn't want to depend on him, didn't want to need him. He was soft, like her papa, too good to last; she had no business with a man like him, and he had no right to worm his way into her life, making her need things she could never have.

But when she lay in his arms he was the only thing that stood between her and the gaping pit of dark emptiness that threatened to consume her; he held her tightly and kept her safe and in his arms she was not alone. For a little while, at least, she was not alone.

Angel felt Adam's lips on her hair, the deep expansion of his chest with a breath. And he whispered hoarsely, "Oh, honey. What can I do? What can I do to make it easier for you?"

Just hold me, she thought. *Hold me and keep me safe, close the bad things out, don't ever let me go . . .*

The carriage swayed and rocked with the rhythmic sound of the horses' hooves as the team slowly negotiated its way through the heavy afternoon traffic. The rain on the roof was like the distant whisper of the ocean, sealing them inside a soft and secret world of their own. The tears faded, but Angel did not move from the circle of his arms.

She felt Adam's hand lightly caressing the coil of her hair, his fingers stroking the back of her neck. The tingles of warmth drifted through her, blotting out the pain, blotting out fear. When he touched her, he could make everything go away. She wanted his touch; she needed his touch, and not with the passionate impulse of a girl on the verge of discovery, but with the quiet surety of a woman who has already discovered the only truth that matters.

Her voice was husky with the residue of tears, but steady and a little wondering. She did not lift her face from his shoulder. "You took me to your room. To your bed."

His hand stopped moving on her hair.

"But you didn't touch me." Slowly she lifted her face to look at him. "Why?"

His hand dropped to her shoulder, fingers brushing against her neck. His voice felt thick, every nerve and cell fiber in his body responding to her upturned face, her tear-ravaged eyes. Eyes that were now clear and unafraid and so completely stripped of artifice that his stomach ached with desire simply from looking at her.

He said steadily, "It wouldn't have been right."

"I wouldn't have stopped you."

The words were difficult to form. "I know."

She lifted her hand and touched his throat, where heated flesh met stiff white collar. "I would have been glad," she added simply.

The collar was choking him; fire trickled from her fingers into his skin. He should have stopped her then; he should have said something harsh and dismissing or kind and noble; he should have pushed her away and saved himself, saved her, from this moment that would change everything between them for better or worse. But it had gone beyond that. Every time they came together the fire that was kindled only flamed brighter and now it was very nearly out of control. It was his fault. He knew better. But he wanted Angel with a fierce intensity that blocked out common sense; he wanted her wild and beautiful and tender and vulnerable, he wanted to protect her and tame her, he wanted her because she was *his*. And as hard as he tried, he couldn't stop the wanting.

His fingers drifted down, across the lace fichu that cupped her throat, along the breadth of delicate bones and fragile flesh that defined her chest. The swell of her breast was only inches from his fingers. Inches. His loins ached and burned; his heartbeat counted off heavy, suspended moments of decision. Her small hand, all the more arousing for its guilelessness, slid down across the shape of his shoulder to rest upon the heavy thunder of his heart. The breath he drew was deep and unsteady, and her perfume—innocent, unadorned female—filled the humid air like a drug.

I would be good for you, Angel, he thought. *Let me be good for you . . . .*

Her lips parted, and he was helpless. His hands moved to her head, tilting it back, drinking of her first with his eyes, flooded by her, aching for her. He bent his head toward hers, and then the carriage swung to a stop.

Their lips never touched.

He could not release her. He heard the creak of the springs as the driver prepared to dismount the carriage box. Her eyes searched his, waiting, wanting. She whispered, "Take me to your room again, Adam. I could . . . Let me be your woman."

Heartbeats. Coiling, throbbing need. And Adam heard himself say softly, "Is that what you want, Angel? To be my woman, like your mother was Camp Meredith's woman?"

She did not recoil; her position remained unchanged. But everything within her froze, and he saw it in her eyes.

Adam knew what he had said, he saw his words sink into her like small poison arrows. But he couldn't stop. The time for coyness and games had passed; it had gone too far. His fingers tightened on her skull and he said hoarsely, "I can teach you love, Angel. I can show you the best of what it's like between a man and a woman, the best it can ever be. I can make you my woman, and you won't be sorry. But I've got to know. Is that what you want?"

Angel pulled away from him slowly and sat in rigid, aching silence until the driver came to open the door.

Inside Angel spun turmoil, shock, and confusion, but not

for the reasons he thought. Had he meant to hurt her? Did he think she had come to him now as she had that other time on the train, to mock herself and mock him, to punish herself for being the daughter of a whore and him for making her aware of it? It almost didn't matter what he thought. Because his words had not hurt her, and the confusion was not from his rejection, if that's what it had been. What was storming inside her and casting her emotions into chaos was a sudden and unwelcome understanding.

Had her mother felt like this when she went to the outlaw's bed? Had she known, as surely as she knew night from day, that this man would destroy her, but had her heart melted at his touch and her senses exploded with need when she looked at him? Had she felt empty when he wasn't there and had she believed that one night in his arms was worth all the world well lost?

Because Angel did. Because the emotions Adam Wood aroused in her were tumultuous and undisciplined and lacked any basis in common sense. She refused to trust him, but he was the most trustworthy man alive. She despised his calm strength and his even temper, but she relied on it for every breath she took. She hated him for what he did to her, yet he was inside her skin, inside her soul, and she wanted him; for now or all time, she simply wanted to be a part of him.

And if, at length, a child were to swell and quicken inside her, what would she do, where would she go? Would she count it all well worth it then?

She knew the answer to that. It pained her and it frightened her, but she knew.

Adam walked her to her room, and she did not look at him again. His skin was tight, his throat dry, and every part of him still strained with need for her, yet the hollowness of loss almost engulfed him. He wanted to say he was sorry, but he wasn't sorry. He wanted to try to make her understand but he didn't understand himself.

She opened her door, and he touched her shoulder.

She turned to look at him.

Then suddenly she spun away from him. No, she was jerked away from him, stumbling backward across the room, her face a startled mask of shock and horror. Adam lunged for her and the door slammed behind him. He had half a moment when his hand slapped for the gun that was not on his hip and then a brilliant white light exploded inside his head.

CHAPTER

Thirteen

THEY caught her off guard. It never would have happened if her reflexes hadn't been so dulled by fatigue and grief, if her mind hadn't been so distracted with confusing, disturbing thoughts, if her senses hadn't been reeling from memories of Adam's touch. But before she could cry out or strike back or duck for the knife that was, even with her fancy clothes, strapped to the inside of her leg, a wad of cloth was crammed into her mouth, rough hands pushed her face down on the floor, her arms were jerked backward, and she felt the sharp bite of rope on her wrists as her hands were tied behind her.

The room had been torn apart. The mattress was dragged half-off the bed, tables and chairs were overturned, bureau drawers upended, the slim contents of her wardrobe scattered everywhere. Her eyes went in panic to the Bible, which, although it had been cast aside on the floor, had not fallen open. The cross! Even before she recognized the two men from the train, she knew that was what they had come for. She hadn't looked at the cross in days; there had been times—long, dark, empty times—when she had forgotten about it altogether. But now they had come for it.

But they weren't going to get it. Adam . . . Adam was lying face down on the floor near the door, motionless, and the sight of the dark red stain soaking through the golden hair on the back of his head made her heart pound with fear; made the whole world dim and blur in stark, unrelenting terror. No. He wasn't dead. He would get up, any moment he would get up and come to her rescue, just as he always had. But he didn't move.

Adam! she screamed inside. *Adam, don't die, please don't die! Get up, please, I need you!* But the cloth they had stuffed inside her mouth pressed against the back of her throat, choking off all but the thinnest breaths, and she couldn't make a sound.

The man finished tying her hands and jerked her cruelly to her feet by the hair. Her eyes stung with pain and he shoved her into a chair. She sat down hard, her arms twisted painfully behind her, but she didn't move. Her eyes were fixed on Adam, begging, pleading . . . .

The other man, the one with his arm in a sling, pressed the barrel of a pistol roughly into her temple. "All right, little lady," he said, "I'm gonna take that gag out of your mouth so's you and me can have us a little talk. But I'm telling you now if you scream or even breathe hard, I'm gonna make a mess of your pretty face all over these here walls." He jabbed the pistol into her temple for emphasis. "You got that?"

His partner, younger and leaner, walked with a limp.

He went over to Adam and nudged him contemptuously with his boot. "He don't look quite dead to me, Case. You want I should finish him off?"

"Tie him up." Casey did not look at Adam. "We might need him later."

Angel couldn't take her eyes off Adam as Jenks began to wind the rope tightly around his hands and feet. He didn't move. *He didn't move . . . .*

Casey grabbed her chin roughly and forced her to look at him. "You listenin' to me, woman? You make a sound, and he's dead for sure!"

With terror clawing at the back of her throat like a sharp-taloned bird, Angel nodded her understanding.

Casey thrust his fingers inside her mouth and jerked out the cloth. Her throat constricted into a series of involuntary gagging sounds as she gasped for breath.

"Where is it?" demanded Casey. "What'd you do with it?"

Jenks propped Adam into a sitting position to get him out of the way of the door in case they had to make a quick escape, and Adam's head lolled. He moaned.

Angel's head jerked around and the wash of relief that went through her made her dizzy as she saw Adam's eyes struggle to open. He moaned again. He was alive!

She swiveled her eyes back to Casey. She made her heart stop thundering and forced cool contempt into her face. She said, "I don't know what you're talking about."

She thought he was going to hit her and she braced herself for it. Instead he moved his eyes to Adam and made a sharp gesture with his gun to his partner. The other man drew back and kicked Adam gleefully in the stomach.

The smothered cry of pain that tore through Angel's chest was only a thin echo of Adam's groan. He sagged against the wall, his lips white.

Casey grinned. "Got a throb for 'im, do you? Well, that oughta make things easier all the way around." The grin faded and he jammed the barrel of the gun into her throat. "Now where's the goddamn cross?"

The metal pressing into her windpipe hurt and made it hard to talk, but Angel refused to show it. Her mind was racing feverishly. They hadn't found it. They had torn the room apart, they had cast aside the Bible, and they hadn't found it. She had kept her future safe across half a country and two brutal attempts to take it from her and no one was going to rob her of it now. Not if she was smart.

She lifted her chin, arching away from the pressure on her throat, and said, "I don't have it anymore. I sold it."

"Lyin' bitch," Casey said softly. "If you'd'a sold it you wouldn't still be hanging around here. Where is it?"

"I told you, I—"

Casey said abruptly to his partner, "Kill him."

It all happened in an instant, but with the infinite slowness with which a person's entire life can unfold before her eyes. Jenks drew his gun in a single smooth motion. Adam's eyes were open, fogged with pain, and he was looking at her. She remembered the way the cross had felt in her hand, heavy and warm, the glint of jewels, the mind-staggering promise of wealth. Jenks cocked the hammer. Fancy gowns and gloves with pearl buttons, ornate railroad cars and faraway places. It was hers, she had won it fair and square, she had kept it and protected it, she deserved it, she had built a future on it . . . it was *hers*. She had scraped and scrimped all her life waiting for something like this and never believing it would come, but it had; it was hers and no one could take it from her . . . .

Jenks swung the gun into a dead aim on center between Adam's eyes, and a small smile curved his lips as his finger tightened on the trigger. A house on the ocean, sunshine in every room . . .

"No!" she cried. "I—I didn't sell it. I still have it."

"Angel," Adam said hoarsely. "Don't—"

She was breathing hard as she watched Jenks slowly, reluctantly it seemed, ease back the hammer on his gun. Casey leaned back, waiting.

She watched all her dreams, all her bright promises of the future, dissolve into dust around her in those few interminable seconds before she could get her voice to work again. But it didn't matter. They were just dreams.

"The Bible," she said. She was amazed at how steady her voice sounded. "I carved out a hole in it. The cross is inside."

Casey's slack, ugly face broke into a slow grin. "Well now, ain't that clever? Never would've figured it."

He jerked his head at his partner. "Keep your gun on her." He walked over to the Bible.

He opened it up, and found the carved-out hole. Angel couldn't see what he saw, but she could see his face harden. He lifted the Bible by the corner and shook it. Nothing fell out. He whirled and flung the Bible at her. It hit her on the shoulder, a glancing blow that shocked more than it hurt, but that was not what caused Angel to gasp out loud. The Bible fell open at her feet, the cross-shaped, carved-out niche plainly visible.

It was empty.

Casey's face was furious, but it was his voice that

frightened Angel the most. It was cold and deliberate, yet hiding a sort of demented pleasure as he said, "Hey, Jenks. You wanna have a little fun?"

Jenks looked at him uncertainly, then licked his lips as understanding began to dawn. He holstered his gun and drew from his belt a heavy, businesslike buck knife. He advanced on Angel, his eyes glinting.

Adam struggled to hold on to consciousness. The pain in his head was not just a pain, it was a series of explosions, each one worse than the last, following the beat of his heart and every infinitesimal movement of his neck. His eyes kept fading in and out of focus, and every time he forced them into focus, nausea, sick and unmanning, swept over him and he had to grit his teeth to hold it back.

He struggled against his bonds but the outlaw had done a thorough job; even if he had been in good shape he couldn't have budged them. Rushing them was out of the question; his feet were tied, and even if he could have gotten his rubbery legs under him he couldn't have made it across the room before the big one shot him or the other one plunged his knife into Angel's throat.

He watched in helpless fury as the man with the knife moved toward Angel, his legs apart, grinning madly. Angel muffled a cry as he sat astride her legs, twisting her face away from him.

"Lie to me, will you, bitch?" Casey said softly. "We'll see how much you feel like lying when my buddy gets through with you."

"I'm not lying!" There was real panic in Angel's voice. "I thought it was there! I put it there! I don't—"

Jenks grabbed her face and brought the tip of the knife to

the outside corner of her eye. "Gonna pluck 'em out, one by one." His voice rippled with low pleasure. "Gonna—"

"Stop it!" Adam shouted hoarsely. "Leave her alone! She doesn't have it—I do."

Casey looked at him.

Adam struggled with dizziness, with the throbbing, paralyzing pain. "In my coat pocket," he said. Breathlessness made his voice weak. "Inside."

Casey glared at him. "I ain't falling for no tricks, mister. I come too far and worked too hard."

"No—tricks," Adam said tiredly. "Search me. It's there."

Casey gestured to Jenks. "Hold him down."

It was a long time before Jenks obeyed, and then with an obvious, sullen reluctance. He sheathed the knife and squatted beside Adam, pushing him back roughly against the wall with one hand on his throat. Casey tore open his coat with his one good arm, and found the cross in the hidden right-hand pocket almost at once.

His eyes glittered as he drew it out, the chain swinging from his fist. "Well what the hell do you know about that?" He glanced at his partner. "You and your goddamn curse. I told you we'd get it back. I told you."

When Jenks looked at the cross, he swallowed hard. His hand eased its pressure on Adam's throat. He said, "We gonna kill 'em now?"

Casey got abruptly to his feet, dropping the cross into his pants pocket. "Don't be a ijit. You fire a shot in a place like this and every lawman inside a mile'll be on you. 'Sides," he grinned again as he looked at Adam, "we got what we come for. Ain't nothing they can do to stop us now. They tell anybody about this, *they'll* end up in jail for stealing

the goddamn thing in the first place, while we're living high
on the hog down in Rio De Janeiro.''

Jenks frowned. "Where?"

"Just shut up and get out of here," Casey said sharply.
He opened the door and peered out cautiously. Then he
looked back at Angel. "You can scream all you want to
now, little lady. Won't do you a damn bit of good."

And they were gone.

But Angel didn't scream. She just sat there, stunned,
disbelieving, shocked. It was gone—her fortune, her future,
her one chance in this world to *be* somebody, to have
something. . . . Adam had stolen it. *Adam*.

The grand and glorious dream had swept down on her like
a gift from heaven, and piece by piece it had been destroyed.
She shouldn't have been surprised. She had known, hadn't
she, that it was too good to be true? First Papa, now the
cross. But Adam . . .

"Mr. High and Mighty Lawman," she said softly. "Nothing
but a common thief and a liar, just like me."

Adam didn't look at her. He couldn't. "Come over
here." His voice was roughened with pain and effort and he
twisted his hands inside the ropes. "We've got to try to get
each other loose."

She didn't move. "All that fine preaching of yours,
nothing but words. You come in here while I'm not looking
and you steal the only thing I have that's worth anything at
all. You just plain out steal it."

"Goddammit, Angel!" The sound of his own voice sent
fireworks of pain through his head. "I'm not perfect, I
never said I was! It was wrong, all right? I did it and it was
wrong and if you want to hate me for it you can do it later

because right now I'm all you've got left and we've got to help each other!''

"Yes," Angel agreed slowly. "You are."

After a moment she got up and went over to him. "Are you going to go after them?"

"Just sit down." Painfully, he shifted around, his breath coming in gasps. "Here, with your back to me. Try to undo the knots on my ropes."

She just stood there, looking down at him thoughtfully. "My knife," she said without expression, after a moment. "You'll have to reach it."

He tilted his head up to look at her and her face swam dizzily. For a moment he didn't know what she was talking about. Then he remembered the knife she kept strapped to her leg.

He swallowed back a hotness in his throat, and his head gave a magnificent throb. "Sit down," he responded hoarsely. "As close as you can."

She lowered herself unsteadily to the floor, at right angles to his hands, which were tight behind his back. She shifted forward until he could feel her skirts against his fingers. Adam shifted his hips and stretched his torso, feeling for the hem of her skirt. The movement made him dizzy, and his heart was pounding anvil strokes through his body, making his limbs shake. Effort, exhaustion, and the pain in his head formed thin lines of sweat on his hairline and his upper lip.

She said, "I don't hate you." Her voice, strangely devoid of emotion, was distant and almost contemplative. "I reckon . . . in your own way, you thought you were keeping me out of trouble. You wouldn't think about it any other way, not right off anyhow. And you don't need the money. You're rich."

"I'm not—rich." He felt the top of her boot where it hugged her ankle; he shifted downward a few inches and worked his fingers beneath her skirt. He would have to shift his body again to move his hands upward, but he had to rest for a moment first.

"I knew it wouldn't really happen," she went on in that same detached, faraway voice. "Things like that don't happen to girls like me. But for a while . . ."

Christ, Angel, he thought in despair, but to speak required too much breath. He steeled himself to move his hands upward.

Her ankle was a small, fragile work of tendons and bones; his rough hands snagged on the delicate fabric of her stockings. Her skin was soft, steamy warm beneath the secret shelter of her skirts. Against his will, his mind formed pictures; his throat grew dry. He twisted his body again to move farther upward.

"It was all for Papa anyway," she said quietly. "Now it doesn't matter."

Adam stopped moving, paralyzed by the wave of remorse and fierce determination that went through him. *Never again, Angel,* he thought. *Nothing is ever going to hurt you again . . . .*

He set his teeth and moved his hands upward, tangling in the material of her petticoat, dragging up her skirts. His fingers traced the shape of her calf, firm, smooth, and silky, until they met the resistance of hard metal sheathed in leather.

"I'll try to be careful," he said, breathing hard. "I don't want to cut you."

He felt her muscles tense as his fingers closed around the hilt of the knife, slowly easing it out of the supple scabbard.

The point caught on her petticoat and he almost lost his grip on it. He tightened his fingers and moved away from her, then sat there with his shoulders slumped and his head spinning, trying to breathe deeply.

Angel slid around, her shoulders against his, and he was glad to release the knife to her. He didn't feel steady enough to try it himself.

As Angel turned the blade in her hands, applying it to his ropes, Adam strained his wrists apart to apply more tension. It seemed to take forever, but at last the ropes began to fray and, with a snap, fell apart. Angel let the knife clatter to the floor and Adam moved to untie her hands.

"You're not going after them, are you?" she asked with a faint note of anxiety in her voice.

Adam turned stiffly to untie the ropes that bound his feet. His head roared when he bent over. "Do you want me to?"

"No." The answer came quickly, more quickly than Adam could have expected, and was accompanied by a quick hand on his shoulder. "You're in no shape. You'd just get yourself killed."

"Thanks for the confidence," Adam said, but when he tried to stand up the blood drained from his face and he didn't feel very confident himself.

Angel knelt beside him, putting her arms around him and helping him struggle to his feet. Adam caught his breath and sheltered his middle with his arm; the kick had caught his stomach, so no ribs were broken, but it hurt like hell. He cursed the weakening waves of nausea and the dancing spots before his eyes that made him lean on her so heavily, but without her he never would have made it to the bed.

"Wait."

She left him for a moment to tug the mattress back onto

the bed, and he sat down on it heavily. She swung his feet onto the bed and placed a pillow behind his head. Until that point he was too sick to protest, but when she started fumbling with the buttons of his shirt he caught her hand.

"Stop it. You don't have to fuss over me."

"I'm used to it," she said briskly. "I need to see your belly, where he kicked you. Does it hurt much?"

"Not much," he lied; and he didn't try to stop her as she pulled his shirt open, because he could see her hands shaking and hear, behind the bravado, the fear in her voice. She was used to taking care of things, to fighting off death and starvation and the dark of night with her bare hands, and she needed to be doing that now. She needed to feel she was doing *something*, and he knew how that was. So he wouldn't try to stop her, even if he had been strong enough to do so.

Angel did need to keep busy. As long as her hands were moving her mind wasn't reviewing the horror of the last few minutes; she wasn't trying to make sense of all the things she had learned about Adam, and about herself, that clearly did not make sense. As long as she could feel for herself the warmth of his skin and see with her own eyes the rise and fall of his breath she could forget, for a moment, how close he had come—they both had come—to death, and that awful sense of helplessness as she watched with her hands tied and her throat paralyzed while Jenks pulled back the hammer.

She unsnapped Adam's collar and tossed it aside; the back of it was soaked with blood. She eased his coat off his shoulders and tugged his shirt out of his trousers. His shirttails were warm and wrinkled with the heat of his body, and when she unfastened the lower buttons there was a strange catching sensation in her chest, like nervousness. She quickly removed the shirt and discarded it with his coat. He had a fine, strong chest, with a light pattern of blond hair spreading from the center to nestle around flat brown nipples. Just below his rib cage, near his belt, was a wide, pale blue bruise, the flesh surrounding it was already beginning to swell. When she touched the area lightly she felt his muscles tense.

She looked at him quickly. "Does that hurt?"

"Some." This time she could not tell whether he was lying, and the intense, alert light in his eyes caused her to move her hand away quickly.

She moved to the washstand and poured a basin of water over two towels; one she wrung out, and brought to him, the other she set on the hearth to warm.

Adam said, "I'm sorry I wasn't more help with those outlaws. Maybe you should've let them shoot me."

She shook her head tersely and sat beside him. "You've done nothing but save my life since I met you. I reckon I owed you one. Can you ease up a little? I need to get this on your head."

Adam pushed himself away from the pillow, trying not to wince as she began to clean the blood from the wound on his head. It didn't hurt quite as fiercely as before, but that might have more to do with the gentleness of her touch than the severity of the injury.

He said, with some difficulty, "Angel, I need to explain to you about the cross. . . ."

"It's stopped bleeding, but you've got a lump the size of a hen's egg." She wadded up the bloody towel and stood, returning in a moment with the warmed towel, which she spread across the bruise on his middle. "That should feel better in a minute."

It was already beginning to feel better. "Angel, listen—"

She shook her head firmly. "No. Not now. We've both done enough talking for one day, and I'm not interested in any explanations." She walked over to her wardrobe, rummaged around the back for a moment, and brought out a half-filled bottle. "You can tell me later if you still want to. Right now you need to rest."

She poured some of the liquid into a water glass and brought it over to him. "Drink this."

Adam eyed her skeptically. "Where'd you get this?"

She shrugged. "Off a snake-oil salesman. Sometimes it helped Papa's coughs."

Adam tasted it cautiously. Beneath the slippery licorice flavoring was the unmistakable bite of alcohol. He drank the rest down in one gulp and it spread tentacles of fire through his veins, stinging his eyes. One hundred proof.

She replaced the warm towel on his abdomen with a cold one, and he sucked in his breath, swearing softly. Angel smiled and took the glass from him. "You'll feel better after you sleep awhile."

"Dammit, Angel, what was in that stuff?" His voice sounded thick, and already a pleasant numbness was flowing through his limbs, like the residue of three good whiskeys swallowed fast.

"It'll help you sleep," she replied complacently.

A needle of panic—or the closest he could feel to one— went through him, and he grabbed her wrist hard, struggling to sit up. "You're not leaving this room," he gasped. "Dammit Angel, it's not worth it. If you'll just listen to me—"

She looked surprised. "I'm not going anywhere." She released his hold on her wrist with amazingly little effort. "I wouldn't leave you like this."

He abandoned his efforts to sit up. When his head fell back against the pillow it was like sinking into clouds. Everything seemed distant and disconnected, even his thoughts. He groped for her arm again but found only her fingers, and they entwined tenderly with his. "Don't do it, Angel," he said huskily, and the moment the words were spoken he couldn't remember what it was she should not do. "Blast it to hell . . . I'm supposed to be taking care of you. I promised . . ."

But his words trailed off, and his eyes drifted closed, and he didn't say anything else.

When she was sure he was asleep, Angel pulled off his boots and covered him with a quilt, then crossed the room. She picked up her knife and spent a moment staring at it contemplatively. She couldn't explain why she made the decision, nor was she aware of consciously making a decision at all. But after a time she put the knife on the table, and returned to change the compress on Adam's stomach.

Then she pulled up a chair close to the bed, and she stayed there while day turned to night, watching over him while he slept.

CHAPTER

Fourteen

THE smell of coffee woke Adam. Tantalized by the scent, he drifted for a moment back to better days, easier places. The headache was little more than a foggy memory, and when he cautiously stretched his arms and legs he found that only a slight stiffness remained of the afternoon's peril.

Peril. His eyes snapped open and he swung his feet to the floor in a single motion, his heart slamming with alarm. The curtains were drawn and the room was bathed in the soft glow of a single lamp and a low-burning fire. Angel was bending over a small table in front of the window, pouring coffee.

He took a breath, drawing a hand across his bleary eyes and forcing his heartbeat to slow down. He said hoarsely, "You didn't go after them."

Angel turned with a cup of coffee in her hand. "Did you know that if you ask that man at the desk downstairs he'll send a boy out for any kind of food you want and bring it right to your room?"

She spoke as though that were the most incredible notion she had ever heard, as though there were nothing of more importance than that discovery. She pressed the coffee cup into his hands and he took it, blinking to clear his head as he looked around the room.

She had straightened everything up, and no signs remained that anything untoward had happened in the room. On the table with the coffeepot were covered dishes of food, and one used plate that signified she had already had her supper. Adam sipped the hot, strong coffee, shaking his head a little. "You never stop surprising me," he muttered.

She went back to the table. "Are you better?"

"Why didn't you go after them?" he asked quietly.

"I got you some soup."

"I'd rather have a big beefsteak."

"Maybe. But this is better for you."

She sat beside him on the bed, the bowl of soup in her hands. "Here. Have some of this."

He took the bowl from her and set it on the floor. "You don't have to take care of me, Angel," he said firmly. He would have said more, but he held her eyes and thought she knew his meaning. He was not her father; he had no intention of taking his place in her life. He didn't need that from her and wouldn't tolerate it; and although he probably could have been gentler about letting her know, there was no point in playing games. Not with stakes as high as this.

Her eyes shifted away briefly and her voice was a little defensive as she replied, "I know that."

He took another sip of his coffee. She had done up her hair, and it glowed softly in the lamplight. The top two buttons of her bodice were broken, likely from the struggle with the outlaws, but she seemed innocently unaware of the few inches of skin that were revealed by the parted lace and linen. She sat close to him, whether by accident or design, and he was acutely aware of his nakedness from the waist up. He imagined he could feel the warmth of her small arm radiating toward his shoulder.

He said, "I asked you a question."

She looked uncomfortable. "What difference does it make?"

"A lot."

She could have told him a facile lie; she could have told him to mind his own business; she could have refused to answer at all. But somehow none of those solutions seemed quite as easy as they might once have. And, by the same token, telling him the truth didn't seem as much of an admission of weakness as she had thought it might.

"Maybe I didn't feel like getting myself killed either," she admitted. She folded her hands in her lap, looked down at them briefly, and met his eyes again. "What you said before—about me looking for fights so I could prove how I could take care of myself—well, it didn't seem so important to prove it this time. It seemed like the important thing to do was to stay right here and make sure you were going to be all right."

She lifted her shoulders again and forced nonchalance into her tone. "I reckon they're long gone by now, and the cross with them. Maybe it's for the best. That piece of tarnish and rust has brought me nothing but trouble since I laid eyes on it. I never would've brought Papa all the way out here if I hadn't thought I could sell it, and now he's . . ." Her throat closed up briefly.

"Now he's dead. I almost got myself killed twice. And you . . ." She looked at him, hoping he could read in her eyes the depth of what she was feeling. She wasn't used to letting anybody see that much of her, and it was hard to allow herself to be so vulnerable. "I'm sorry for what they did to you, Adam. It was my fault, and—I'm sorry."

Adam brought his hand up to cup her face. There was so much he needed to tell her, to explain to her, even to ask her. So much inside him that was straining to be said. But he never should have touched her. Because the moment he felt the silkiness of her skin beneath his fingers, the moment he looked into her luminous eyes, all the words went out of his head. All he could do was look at her and feel her and marvel over her.

She didn't protest or try to move away. His eyes drifted to the small, faint bruise on the side of her mouth, and he couldn't help it: he leaned forward and kissed the spot gently. He could feel the small catch of her breath, and her lips were parted a mere fraction of a inch from his. He could taste her, and he wanted to taste more of her. He wanted to gather the taste of her on the tip of his tongue, to trace the shape of her lips, to explore the rich moist recesses of her mouth, and in a moment the wanting would be more than he could bear.

He dropped his hand and moved away from her, trying to clear his head. He said thickly, "I'd best be going."

But go where? His own room wasn't far enough, another hotel wouldn't be far enough; New Mexico wouldn't be far enough to get Angel out of his head.

He put the coffee cup aside and started to get up, and then she said simply, "Why?"

He looked at her and found that he couldn't think of a single reason. There were dozens of reasons, of course, and she knew them as well as he did, but none of them seemed important right now. Maybe that was the trouble.

He couldn't stop looking at her. He couldn't make himself get up and walk away from her. He said, "It's been a rough day, Angel."

She nodded.

He made himself go on, with difficulty, "You've lost a lot, the past couple of days. I reckon you're feeling kind of empty and—lost inside right now. But in a few days maybe you'll look at things different. Maybe you'll look at me different."

"I look at you different every time I see you," she answered.

It was so hard not to touch her when she was so close. So hard not to draw her into his arms when every bit of his skin tingled with the need to feel her against him. So hard not to kiss her when he saw in her eyes how much she wanted him to.

He stood up and turned to search for his shirt. His voice was gruff as he said, "It'll be a lot different if I stay much longer. And maybe you'll hate me for it."

"You thought I was going to say no." Her voice was soft, surprised.

Adam turned, his shirt clutched in his hand, to stare at her. She sat on the bed, her hands clasped in her lap, looking at him with a kind of hesitant amazement, and the faintest tinge of embarrassment colored her cheeks. "Before—

when you asked if I wanted to be your woman, you thought I was going to say no.''

Angel's voice choked up inside her, because now that he was looking at her, waiting for what she was going to say, she wasn't sure she could say it at all—not in the way a man like Adam would want to hear it, if he wanted to hear it at all. But she was equally sure that these feelings were not going to go away, and if she didn't speak them now, when would she? Everything had changed, and maybe they had changed too fast or maybe they had been too long in changing . . . maybe it had begun that day he had held her in the tunnel and she had known safety, for the first time, in his arms. The changes had frightened her, and they still did; but it frightened her more to think that one day he might just disappear from her life, and she would never know what she might have had if he had stayed.

Her fingers laced together tightly in her lap and her cheeks were hot, but she didn't know any other way except to blurt it out. She went on in a rush, "You think it's because of my mother, a way to get even or prove I can be as bad as she was . . . and I guess maybe I am bad, but I don't feel like it, when I'm with you. Or maybe you think that now that Papa's gone I'm feeling lonesome and scared, and I guess I am, but don't you see I've always been scared and alone . . . until I met you. You make me feel different about everything, and I—I want to stay with you. But maybe . . ." She searched his face anxiously. "Maybe you don't want me."

Adam's blood pumped through his veins in heavy, sluggish waves, and with each pulse was a new crest of desire, of wonder, of helplessness. She looked so small, sitting there, so vulnerable, offering herself to him. She didn't know what she was doing. He didn't know what he was doing. But not for all the kingdoms of a thousand kings could he have walked away from her then.

He let his shirt drop to the floor and he went back to her. He sat beside her and touched her face, threading his fingers through her hair. And all he could say was, huskily, "I want you."

Her eyes changed from dark to light on a small intake of breath, and he needed no kisses to arouse him. Just looking at her, just brushing his fingers along the texture of her skin, doubled the knot of need within him. He felt the pins that bound up her hair and released them with fingers that felt twice their normal size. Her hair, as dark and glossy as the finest satin, tumbled around her shoulders in waves and curls. He gathered up handfuls of it, inhaling the fragrance, reveling in the texture of it against his face. He felt her soft sigh and her hands rested on his bare arms, slipping upward in a shy caress. Her touch sent pinpricks of heat along his skin.

For Adam, coupling with a woman had always been the easiest, most natural thing in the world. There was pleasure in it beyond the satisfaction of urgent need, and none of the women he had lain with had ever been the worse for having known him. He had always thought that was enough. But with Angel it was different, and he was surprised to recognize a slight edge of nervousness beneath the desire.

It was easy to find his own pleasure, and until now that was all that had mattered. For Angel there should be more. He did not want her to regret this night with him. He did not want her to hate him when it was over. He did not want to lose her, now or ever.

He pushed aside the material where the two top buttons of

her bodice were broken and with his fingertip traced the narrow path of flesh that was exposed there. He felt her stiffen when he unfastened the next button, and he stopped, raising his eyes to her face.

"You don't have to do this, Angel," he said. His voice was somewhere between a whisper and a murmur, and it sounded rough and uneven. "Don't do it because I'm making you, or because you think I want you to."

Her cheeks were bright with warm color, her breath coming quickly between parted lips. Her eyes searched his with a mixture of curiosity and uncertainty. "It feels—strange."

"Yeah." He stroked the curve of her jaw with the back of his knuckles. "I reckon it does."

After a moment, she lowered her eyes and unfastened the next button, and the next, until her bodice was open from neck to waist over the creamy transparent material of her chemise. Adam held his breath as he took the material and drew it gently, carefully, over her arms and away.

He could see the shadow of her breasts, the reflection of pale pink skin, and the rise and fall of her chest with each breath. The drawstring tie of her chemise was impossibly tiny; it slipped through his unsteady fingers twice before he managed to unfasten the bow that loosened the material. His heart was pounding and perspiration dampened the back of his neck as he hooked his fingers beneath the shoulder strap and pushed the garment slowly down to her waist. And then with a slow, deep intake of breath, he gathered her into his arms and lowered her to the bed.

Angel felt a rush of heat with his embrace, with the contact of his bare skin against hers, the softly abrasive texture of his chest hair against her breasts, the solid length of his abdomen against hers. There was a breathless, spinning sensation as she sank back against the pillows, wrapped in his heat and strength, as though her mind was being flooded with too many impulses to absorb at once. She had been shy at first, but now, locked in this secret intimacy of touch and texture, she was swept outside herself, overwhelmed and infused by him.

His hands cupped her breasts and she lost her breath, suspended with the strangeness of his touch there and the response it generated within her. A dizzying, tingling flood of heat, a tightening low in her abdomen, an uncertain yearning . . . and then she felt his lips there, feather kisses rich and moist, and the pleasure was more intense than anything she had ever known before. Pleasure, yes, but a blossoming ache for something undefinable made her smother a moan deep in her throat.

Shyness was forgotten as her hands moved over his back, exploring the slippery smoothness, the flexing muscles, the knots of his spine. How strange and wonderful it was to know a man in this way, to hold him so close that their very skins seemed to blend, to feel his touch ignite fires in her blood, and to let his kisses drink away her thoughts, her cares, her very essence.

She did not object when his fingers fumbled with the buttons of her skirt, or when he lifted himself to draw the garment, and her undergarments, down over her hips, leaving her naked against him. Her heart was beating hard, pounding waves of dizziness and dark, hot anxiety through her head, making her tremble. He murmured her name and stroked the shape of her leg, and she went weak with his touch. He held her close, the soft texture of his flannel trousers feeling infinitely strange against her bare legs, her naked stomach. And then he moved to unfasten his trousers, and she had to look away.

She thought she knew the pinnacle of wondrous pleasure already, that she had touched with him the deepest of intimacies in a simple embrace, but nothing could have prepared her for the sensation of his body, fully naked, drawing her against him. The alien nature of the male, now revealed for a woman to know, to touch, to see: muscled thighs and hard calves, flat planes and sharp angles, the parts of him that were smooth and the parts that were dusted with hair; his breath, his heartbeat, all were a part of her. She was enfolded in him, intoxicated by him, helpless to the wonder of discovering him.

How gentle he was when he held her, when his fingers caressed those parts of her that were so sensitive they were hardly familiar even to herself, yet every part of him was coiled strength, controlled power. The ache inside her was a feverish thing that spread from deep in her belly to secret nether regions and burned there. She strained for his kisses and shivered with his touch; the heat left her senseless to everything except the growing urgency inside her. When Adam's thighs began to nudge hers apart she tensed, resisting him, but instinct ruled the wiser and she gradually began to yield to his insistent pressure. His breath was quick and hot on her face; she could see the brilliance of his eyes and the flush of desire that colored his skin. He whispered something but she couldn't hear him through the roaring in her head.

His entry into her body was a shock and it made her cry out softly, but it wasn't a brutal shock. It was powerful and singular and deeply pleasurable in a way her untutored senses could not define. It caused her to tighten her arms about him, hold him closer, and she gasped as he slid even deeper inside her and, slowly, began to move.

So many things she learned that night, so many things she had not even thought to imagine until Adam taught her they were possible. How it was to be part of another person, not just in body but in mind and in heart. What it could mean to share so deeply, to give so freely, to want to give as desperately as she wanted to take . . . to depend on another, to cling to another, to take a man deep inside her soul and know that there was a place there that would never belong to anyone but him, that would always be empty when he was not there. How it was that the awful, agonizing ache could build and build until she wanted to cry out with the need of him—and how it could suddenly disperse into shimmering waves of pleasure so sweet, so intense that everything inside her, everything she had ever known or thought to know, was forever changed.

But perhaps the most wondrous thing of all was lying in his arms, feeling the thunder of his heartbeat and her own, washed in warmth and dazed with sensation, wanting to shout her joy to the world, wanting to say a hundred things to him, a thousand, and knowing she did not have to say anything at all. He held her. He kissed her fingers and he stroked her hair. And she fell asleep, secure and untroubled, in his arms.

When Angel awoke the next morning she lay with her eyes closed for a long time, wondering if she was supposed to feel bad. She wondered if she was supposed to feel ashamed or sorry or if she was now in the same class with

those saloon girls she used to regard with such contempt—
and her mother. She wondered if Adam now thought of her
in that way. She decided she probably was and he probably
did, but it didn't matter as much as she'd thought it would.
Because his arms were still around her and as long as he was
holding her she didn't care what she had become, or what
anyone else thought.

"You're pretty when you sleep," he said. "I've been up
since sunrise, watching you."

It felt so odd to be naked beneath the sheets and hear a
man's voice. A little thrill went through her, and she opened
her eyes drowsily. She couldn't stop the little smile that
curved her lips. "How did you know I was awake?"

He bent down and kissed her tousled hair softly. "I heated
up some of that coffee from last night. Do you want some?"

She noticed then that he had put on his trousers and was
lying atop the covers, holding her against his bare chest.
She could see the darkening bruise on his midsection and
that brought back memories of a time so long ago it seemed
almost not to have happened at all. But it had happened, and
a smoky tendril of unpleasantness slithered into the perfect
wonder of the morning.

She sat up, bringing the sheet with her to cover her
breasts, and combed back her hair with her fingers. She
never slept with her hair unbound. It felt wanton.

She looked at him uncertainly and decided that this must
be the hardest part—not knowing what to do or say in the
morning, not knowing what he expected of her. She wished
he would take off his clothes and come beneath the covers
with her; then she would know. But he simply returned her
gaze with quiet, morning-soft gray eyes, and said, "We've
got a lot to do today, Angel."

She was disappointed. That was not what she had expected him to say. "Like what?"

"Like find a preacher, and get married."

Her eyes, which had been restlessly following the motions her fingers made as they straightened out the pleats and folds of the sheet, flew to his in blank astonishment. "What?"

He smiled, coiling a strand of her hair around his index finger. "You said you wanted to be my woman," he reminded her gently. "Do you think I would've done what I did last night if I hadn't planned on making it permanent?"

Angel's head reeled. Married. Married to Adam. Her, a married woman, keeping house and having babies . . . Adam's babies. Respectability, security, permanence, things she had never imagined before because it simply hadn't occurred to her that they might one day be hers. But Adam wanted to marry her. He didn't want to use and discard her, like that outlaw had used her mother; he didn't want to keep her around to sleep with until he grew tired of her. He wanted to *marry* her. *Her.*

He must have taken her stunned silence for uncertainty, because he went on quickly, "Look, I'm not saying I've got much to offer. I've been a roaming man most of my life, a law-man and not much else. But I've got a fine strong cabin back in New Mexico—not much to look at, but I reckon a woman's hand could fix that—and a good piece of land that's starting to turn out some of the best-looking quarter horses this side of the Mississippi. You won't be rich, but you'll never want for anything I can provide, either. I'll do my best to—"

"Oh, Adam." The words were barely a whisper, and broken between one syllable and the next. She closed her eyes against the happiness that brimmed there and threatened to overflow and she threw her arms around him. "I never thought— I didn't mean for you to— Yes, I want to marry you!''

She felt his deep intake of breath and his arm tightened around her, holding her in a fierce, loving embrace that filled Angel with such incredulous joy she could hardly breathe. "We'll have lots of babies," she whispered, "and they'll never be hungry or cold or alone. We'll have a house with real dishes and a cloth on the table and glass windows. Can we have glass windows?"

His strong hand tangled in her hair. "Glass windows," he repeated thickly. "And as many babies as you want."

And then she hesitated as a tiny pinprick of doubt threaded through the wonder that infused her, a touch of reality. "Maybe . . ." She forced herself to move away from him a little, and to look up at him. "Maybe you ought not to be so quick," she said. "Maybe I won't make such a good wife. I don't have any manners and I'm used to having things my own way and I've never stayed under one roof for more than half a year at a time. Maybe I'll embarrass you in front of your fine friends."

A slow grin stole across Adam's face and it filled Angel with a glorious, weakening joy. "You're going to fit in just fine with my friends. One of my best friends is your own sister, and she's more like you than you'd believe if I told you."

Her sister. Her mother. A whole built-in family was waiting if she married Adam. And even if she didn't, they'd still be waiting. The prospect of meeting them, of even trying to like them, wasn't as hateful as it once had been. She still wasn't sure exactly how she felt about it all, but as long as she was with Adam maybe it wouldn't be so bad. Nothing could be bad as long as she was with him.

And, for all he had given her, she owed him one more thing. She didn't want to bring it up, she wanted to wipe away the past as one would sweep dust under the rug—but like the dust, it was sure to be scattered again by the first strong breeze if she didn't deal with it now. So she took a breath, she held his eyes, and she said, "I want to tell you something. That cross—I didn't steal it. I know you think I did, but I didn't. I won it fair and square in a poker game. I didn't even know what I had until—well, until all the trouble started in Green River."

Some of the light faded from Adam's eyes as he too was brought back to face the unpleasant reality of the past. He said quietly, "I know you didn't steal it, Angel. And now I've got to tell you I didn't plan on stealing it from you. I guess you know that, don't you? I didn't plan on even finding it, but when I did I knew it was trouble. So I took it to a jeweler to see what it was worth."

A needle of greed that Angel could not control pricked at her. "What did he say?" she asked eagerly.

Adam shifted his weight, settling back against the headboard with Angel in his arms, her cheek resting against his shoulder. "He said," he went on matter-of-factly, "there was no telling what it was worth. More money than he had ever seen, anyway."

Angel drew a sharp, pained breath.

"He said it came from a church. Stolen, most likely, from some little place in the Sierra Nevadas called Milagros. It's a poor little village way out in the middle of nowhere; most folks wouldn't even know it was there. But the church, it's been there since the Spanish came through three hundred years ago, and the way they tell it, this Spanish soldier brought the cross all the way from the old country, to protect him in battle or something. Seems that while him and his company were up there in the mountains they got caught in a flash flood and he called on the power of the cross to protect them. The flood just about tore the side off the mountain, but it parted around him and his men, leaving them high and dry. He called that spot the Place of the Miracle, and he built a church there, and left the cross and a priest to look after it. That's the legend, anyway. As long as the cross is there, the village'll be protected. But if it ever leaves the church bad things are supposed to happen. A kind of curse, I reckon.''

Angel studied on this soberly, speechless for a moment. What impressed her most was not that incredible nonsense about miracles and Spanish priests, but the fact that an object of such incredible worth would have been left all these years to rot away in a little church nobody had ever heard of.

After a moment she said, "Well, I guess those thieving outlaws got what they deserved, anyhow. If it's cursed, I mean." She didn't sound as sure as she wanted to. It still gave her a pang to think of her cross—*hers*—in the hands of those filthy bandits.

Adam was silent for a moment. Then he shifted her away from him and swung his feet to the side of the bed. "Not exactly."

He got up, crossed the room, and opened a drawer. The curtains were drawn and the room was dim; Angel couldn't see what he had until he sat beside her again and opened his hand to her.

It was the cross.

Her breath left her lungs in an involuntary gasp and she

reached out her hand for it—and then stopped, and withdrew. It couldn't be. How had he . . . ?

She raised her eyes to him in uncertain question, and he explained, "I had a copy made. I figured . . ." He looked uncomfortable for a moment, and dropped his eyes briefly. "I figured it might not be so easy to talk you into giving it up, so I was going to put the fake back in the Bible till I figured out what to do with the real one. I just got it yesterday. The outlaws got the fake. This one—the real one—was down in the hotel safe all the time."

Most of what he said went out of her head in the rush of incredulous joy that went through her. She reached for the cross, closed her hand around it; she stared at it, counting the rubies, marveling over the dull luster of pearls, recalling every tarnished line and swirl. For good measure, she impulsively bit down on it hard, and then she laughed out loud. It was! It was her cross; it was back, it was real, it was *hers!*

"Oh, Adam!" she cried. She bounced on the bed with excitement, pressing the cross to her chest, to her cheek. "You are the smartest man that ever lived! You did it, you fooled them both, and it's ours now! We *are* rich!" She flung her arms around him, laughing, hugging him, almost weeping with joy.

But strangely, there was a slight stiffness to Adam's muscles as he took her arms and moved her gently away from him. His eyes were sober, and perhaps a little confused, as he looked down at her.

"No," he said simply, "we're not. We're taking it back where it belongs."

CHAPTER

Fifteen

FOR a long time she stared at him, one hand still clutching the cross, the other dropping limply from his arm to rest against her thigh. She thought she must not have heard him right. Then she thought he must not have said it right. Take it back? That made no sense. It *was* back. It was back with her, where it belonged. It was hers, he had tricked the outlaws out of it and returned it to her, and *that* was the right thing to do. What on earth could he be talking about?

Adam was looking at her oddly, and his voice sounded a little strained as he explained, "It was stolen, Angel. Maybe by those two outlaws—maybe by somebody else and they stole it him—but we can't keep it. It's not ours. It belongs in that church up there in the mountains, and that's where it's got to go."

"You're crazy," Angel said flatly. For a moment the two words, and the stunned, disbelieving expression that backed them, were all she could manage. And then her breath came back in a rush and she exclaimed, "That's got to be it—that knot on your head scrambled up your brains, that's all! You can't mean what you're saying! You don't even *know* what you're saying!"

"I know." A guarded expression descended on his eyes, and his voice was quiet. Too quiet. "Maybe you're the one that needs to think about what you're saying. That cross doesn't belong to you, Angel. You don't have any right to sell it, and if you did you'd be living on stolen money— money stolen from a *church*. Do you want that on your conscience for the rest of your life?"

"I didn't steal it!" she cried indignantly. "And what do I care about the church? The church never did anything for me and if they cared anything about this cross they wouldn't have let it get stolen in the first place!" Her fist tightened protectively around the cross, and without realizing it, she had leaned away from him, so that they were no longer touching at all.

His face softened with what looked like a touch of pain, and he lifted his arm, cupping her bare shoulder with his hand. "Angel," he said softly. "Honey, I know how it is for you. I know how hard it's been and how scared you are of being poor and alone, but you're not alone now, don't you see? I can take care of you. We don't need this." He gestured to the cross. "We have everything we need back in New Mexico, a good life that's going to get even better. *We don't need this*."

Angel tried to think about what he was saying. She tried to think about a snug little cabin and a big sprawling ranch and nights spent in the warm security of Adam's arms. Children, and supper on the stove, and curtains in the windows. But what did she know about any of those things? No one had ever taken care of her before, no one had ever even tried. People had used her and depended on her and pushed her aside and left her behind, and maybe that was what Adam was doing now. She tried to think about the promises Adam had made, tried to believe in then, but all she could really think about was how vulnerable she felt with only a thin cotton sheet shielding her nakedness, and how firm and heavy the cross felt in her hand.

She shook her head, her voice sounding thick with urgency. "No, you don't understand. We don't have to go to New Mexico, you don't have to raise horses for the rest of your life—with this we can go anywhere, do anything! We can be rich, Adam, the way fancy bankers and railroad men are rich—we can *buy* a railroad if we want to and build a big fancy house right here in San Francisco or anywhere you want and we never, ever have to worry about being poor again! Don't you see? That man—that jeweler you talked to—he said even *he* didn't know how much it was worth, maybe more than the biggest bank in San Francisco even has, and you can't just throw that away, Adam! How can you think about throwing that away?"

Adam's hand dropped slowly from her shoulder. The imprint of his warmth lingered for a moment and then began to fade—just as the last remnants of warmth faded from his eyes and was gradually replaced with something she could not quite name . . . something very close to disappointment. Why should he be disappointed in her? She was the one who had been betrayed. She was only holding on to what was rightfully hers, while he was trying to take it away from her, so why was he looking at her like that? She only knew that it made her feel cold inside, and angry, and the chill of aloneness that had been banished so thoroughly last night began to creep over her again like a damp draft from an open window. He had no right no make her feel that way. He had no right to look at her that way.

Adam stood up and walked away from her, his strong, bare back etched in perfect silhouette against the morning light from the window. Angel felt a sudden pang of remembrance—the texture of his skin beneath her fingers, muscles straining at her touch, the wonderful intimacy that had been theirs. And with the remembrance came loss, because those broad shoulders were set against her now, the column of his neck stern and unyielding.

He said, "I thought it would be enough for you. That *I* would be enough." He stuffed his hands into the pockets of his trousers and the muscles of his shoulders bunched with the motion. "I guess I was wrong."

She wanted to cry out that he wasn't wrong, that he was enough, was more than enough and all she could ever ask for. She wanted to stumble from the bed and fling her arms around him and show him it was so; above all things in the world she did not want Adam to despise her. She did not want to lose him.

But the cross . . . It was all she had ever had that was hers alone. It was more than just metal and stones, it was her life. It meant freedom and luxury and never having to worry again about the next meal or the next cold winter; it was her future. And it was more, even, than luxury: it meant being safe, never being looked down on again, never being afraid of what tomorrow would bring. How could he ask her to give it up? How *could* he?

She said, trying to keep her voice gentle and persuasive, "It's for both of us, Adam, don't you see? The money—it's yours, too, I don't mean to keep it all for myself. I want us to have a good life, and we can if only—"

"That's the difference between you and me," he interrupted shortly. He turned, and in his eyes was exactly what she had expected to see, and dreaded: contempt, and beneath it the shadowy caldron of anger. "I don't want the money. I couldn't live with myself if I took it."

"And that makes you so much better than me, doesn't it?" she cried, abandoning any attempt to control her anger and hurt. "You've always got to be throwing that in my face!"

"Yeah," he replied coolly. His eyes, as they measured her, were so distant that they seemed almost not to see her at all. "I guess it does make me better than you. I didn't used to think that was so, but it looks like that's just another thing I was wrong about."

She could feel him retreating from her, slipping through her fingers like fog in the wind, and the agony that went through her was like something being torn apart, deep down inside her. But she held on to the cross with both hands and returned hoarsely, "You're a fool. You think your high-sounding rules about right and wrong are going to fix everything, but they won't put meat on your table or wood on your fire or—or me in your bed! I should have known better. I thought you were different but you're just like Papa—giving your last dime to some thieving beggar on the street while your family goes hungry, just because it's *right*!"

His eyes sparked with embers of anger. "My family will never go hungry."

She ignored him, her hurt and anger—and fear—boiling inside her until it blotted out everything else, even her dread of being alone again. "Well, I'm not like that and I'm proud of it," she cried. "And I'll tell you something else—you don't have to worry about taking care of me because I don't need you!" She shook the cross at him defiantly. "I've got this and that makes *me* right, do you understand? I don't need you!"

The ice in his eyes was white-hot, searing cold. It formed a brittle shield between them, like that which the first breath of winter spreads across the land on a moonless night. It felt, when Angel looked at him, as though all the light and all the warmth in the world had been sucked away when she wasn't noticing, and the emptiness that was left inside her throbbed painfully.

He said quietly, "That's it, isn't it, Angel? Last night meant nothing to you. I asked you to be my wife, and it meant nothing to you. Because you don't need anybody. You don't *want* to need anybody."

She wanted to cry, *No, that's not true! I do need you, and I'll do anything, anything in the world to make you stop looking at me like that* . . . . But she couldn't say that, because the one thing he wanted from her was the only thing she couldn't do.

She looked at the cross in her hand. This was real, this was solid. This meant forever.

This she could trust. And Adam . . . he wanted her to give up everything for him. *So close*, she thought. *I was so close to having it all* . . .

Her mother had abandoned her, leaving her to fend for herself. Her papa had died, leaving her to make her way the best she could just as she had done all her life. And now

Adam expected her to believe that, just because he said so, he would take care of her? That, because he said so, she was supposed to give up the one thing that could ensure her future—*both* their futures—and take her chances with whatever life had to offer?

Adam was the best thing that had ever happened in her life. The one good, real, wonderful thing that had ever carved its way through the murky fog of struggle and disappointment that had shrouded her since birth. He was a miracle she had never thought she would deserve, he was glorious, he was certain, he was hers . . . and so was the cross. How could he ask her to choose between them? How *could* he?

But that's what he was doing.

She lifted her chin and tightened her fist around the cross. "What I need," she said, "I've got right here."

He looked at her for a long time, so long that it took all her courage not to cringe from his gaze. Then he said, "It's not that simple, Angel."

In two swift strides he was upon her, seizing her wrists, wrenching the cross from her hand. She cried out and lunged for him, but he swung away. The sheet slipped down, baring her breasts, but she didn't care. With a shrill cry of fury she sprang across the bed, but the covers tangled around her legs and she almost fell. She grasped the bedpost, jerking at the tangled covers, breathing hard. "Give it back to me!" she demanded hoarsely. "It's mine. You can't take it! Give it back!"

His own breath was coming none too steadily and his face was strained. "That would make it easy for you, wouldn't it, Angel? You made your choice, and now you expect me to just leave you with what you chose and walk away. Well,

I have a say in this too, and I'm not going to make it easy; if I have to drag you to hell and back, I'm not going to make it easy!''

He was standing less than half the room's length away from her, the cross gripped so tightly in his hand that his knuckles were white. She could have flung herself at him, could have kicked and clawed and hit and tried to wrestle it from him, but she knew she would not get it unless he wanted her to. And the expression on his face was so cold and angry that she knew she would have to kill him before he relinquished it. Not because he wanted the cross, but because he didn't want her to have it.

''You can't do this!'' she screamed.

''The hell I can't. There's a train leaving at noon and we're going to be on it.''

''I'm not going anywhere with you! You won't get away with this! You can't do this to me!''

He drew a sharp breath. ''Yes,'' he said, ''I can do this to you. And to myself. I'm taking this cross back where it belongs, and you're coming with me.''

''I won't! You can't make me give it back, you can't!'' She clung to the bedpost, wanting to hit him, wanting to beat her fists against him and sob out her rage and frustration but knowing it would be like throwing herself against a stone wall. She had not expected this from Adam. She had not expected this *at all*. Last night he had opened a world for her she had never imagined and today he had torn that world apart. ''Why?'' she demanded hoarsely, and her voice sounded weak with the torrent of confusion and betrayal that battered her. ''You don't even want the cross, it has nothing to do with you! Why are you doing this?''

He looked at her steadily, and then all the anger, all the

hurt and disappointment and raging emotion, seemed to drain out of him, leaving him only tired. "Maybe," he said, "I still think you're worth saving."

And then he turned toward the door. "Get dressed," he added. His voice was dull and emotionless. "I've got promises to keep."

The door closed with a muffled click behind him, and Angel was alone.

It was not easy for Casey and Jenks simply to walk into a shop like the one owned by Mr. Eliston Lewis as it had been for Adam. In the first place, they probably would not have been allowed to dirty the carpet in one of those fancy High Street shops, and second, they didn't know it was even possible for men like them to do business with people like Eliston Lewis. They were dealing in stolen goods—that much would have been obvious to even the most unsophisticated of buyers—and they were accustomed to doing business with men who had too much to hide themselves to ask questions.

Had they gone to Mr. Lewis, or any of his colleagues, the entire transaction could have been completed within an hour. But in a strange city where, it seemed to them, only one out of ten people spoke American English, they had to feel their way around. It was late into the second day before they made contact with the man who was known only as Red Eye.

With a name like that they had half-expected an Indian, or an old outlaw with a bad alias. It was therefore with some dismay that Casey parted the curtain that separated the outer shop from the back room and discovered a Chinaman.

He was sitting on the floor on a pile of cushions, behind a low black table upon which were scattered bits and pieces of unidentifiable junk. His arms protruded from the oversized sleeves of a red silk robe like a frail bird's wings, and his head was completely bald. He was bent over the table when Casey and Jenks came in, squinting through a magnifying glass at some of the pieces of junk there, and he did not look up.

The sign over the doorway purported this to be a clock shop, and the outer room was crowded with dusty clocks: big ones, small ones, cuckoo clocks and chiming clocks. The asynchronous ticking sounded like the clicking jaws of insects, and it penetrated the thin curtain into the back room as though there were no barrier at all. The sound was starting to get on Casey's nerves, and Jenks had been jumpy from the minute they'd opened the door.

When the little man continued to squint through the magnifying glass without looking up or acknowledging their presence in any way, Casey cleared his throat and said what he had been instructed to say: "Your nephew sent me."

The man pushed aside the small mechanism he had been examining and picked up another. It occurred to Casey that they might have the wrong place, that the stupid Chinaboy who had sent them here had made a mistake or played a joke, and this skinny little man in the woman's night dress might be nothing more than he claimed—a clockmaker.

His temper began to rise, and the ticking of the clocks set his teeth on edge. The only thing that stopped him from pulling his gun and putting a hole through the ceiling—or anything else that was handy—was the thought of having to start all over again in his search for a man who knew his way around this heathen-infested city enough to sell what didn't belong to him to somebody who had no business buying.

He could feel Jenks's eyes darting around nervously, as though looking for an escape, and he could smell the other man's sweat. If the silence had gone on another two seconds, he would have shot something no matter how much trouble it caused, but just then the Chinaman put down his magnifying glass. "You have something for me," he said.

It wasn't a question but a statement, and Casey's relief in discovering that the man at least spoke passable English was mitigated by the flat, disinterested way in which he spoke it and by the utter lack of expression in his narrow black eyes.

He said cautiously, "Depends. What we got to sell ain't no clock, and it don't go cheap. I hear tell you know folks that'll pay premium for quality goods."

"Give it to 'im, Case," Jenks muttered, licking the sweat off his upper lip. "Get it done with and let's get out of here."

Casey ignored him, and continued to stare at the little Chinese man. He had never realized before how hard it was to stare down somebody who wouldn't blink. "Before I show you what I got, we better have a couple of things straight. Anybody ever finds out where this here object come from, and you're a dead man. Try to cheat me and you're dead a lot quicker. We understand each other, do we?"

The Chinaman simply held out his hand, palm up.

Jenks nudged him in the ribs, and Casey glowered at him. But the truth was, he was kind of anxious himself to have the whole business done with. He hadn't slept a wink since they'd gotten it, and he told himself it was because he was too busy planning how he was going to spend all that money. The truth was, he'd spent more than a little time jumping at shadows and listening to every creak on the stairs and thinking, as hard as he tried not to, about that goddamn curse Jenks kept harping on. It would feel good to have the thing out of his pocket and replaced with cold hard cash.

He jerked his head to Jenks, who took up watch at the curtained doorway, his gun drawn. He looked jumpy enough to shoot a stray cat if it happened to slither in through the curtain, and that was good. Casey removed the cross from his pocket and laid it on the table.

The little man took his magnifying glass in one hand and the cross in the other. He spent a long time studying it, turning it over, holding it to the light, drawing the magnifying glass down its length and up again, examining every curve and crook. He took so long, in fact, that Casey felt a prickle of nervous sweat break out on his lip. The clocks were starting to sound like thunder.

At last Red Eye put down the magnifying glass and said, "Good piece of work, very good. Sayers, I should say. One of the best in the business."

Casey cast a triumphant glance at Jenks. "The best, huh?"

The little man nodded sagely. "Each piece a work of art, and always in demand. This one, of course, is somewhat unusual, but I can probably move it for you."

"How much?" demanded Casey, trying not to sound too eager.

The other man met his eyes, still without expression. "You realize there is a fee, of course."

Casey nodded impatiently.

"It is my policy to tell my customers exactly what I expect to make from the transaction. It avoids misunderstanding later."

"How much?" repeated Casey.

"I can probably sell this . . ." he made a strikingly graceful gesture with one long-fingered hand to the cross on the table, "for twenty-five American dollars. I will give you ten for it."

There was a space of time, marked by the ever-increasing raucous ticking of the clocks, in which Casey thought he had not heard him right. And it was even a longer collection of *tick-tock, tick-tocks* before he could get the words out of his mouth, hoarsely, "*What* did you say?"

Red Eye's face remained expressionless. "A fair price, I assure. You can ask—"

"Twenty-five dollars?" roared Casey. "For goddamn genuine silver and rubies—"

"Tin," corrected Red Eye, and Casey thought he was talking about the price. Ten.

"Ten *thousand*, maybe! What kind of fool do you think I am? I ought to shoot you dead here and now!"

Red Eye shrugged. "As you please. I don't usually deal in items of such low value, anyway, but as it is a Sayers . . ." He shrugged again and pushed the cross across the table toward him. "You should have no trouble selling it yourself. Good luck, gentlemen."

His hand was already on the butt of his gun, but when the man pushed the cross aside Casey froze in the movement, staring. He couldn't believe it. The Chinaman didn't even want it. He had offered him ten dollars for it and that could have been a con, but now he didn't even *want* it. Something was wrong here. Very wrong.

"What the hell is going on?" Casey growled. "You said it was good. Best in the business."

"So it is," Red Eye assured him. "Mr. Sayers is a fine artisan, much sought after—particularly by rich American women who worry about having their fine jewels stolen. He makes copies so fine only an expert can tell the difference. He's very proud of his work. You might find he would be willing to buy it back from you," he offered helpfully.

The word stuck in his head: *copies*. But still Casey didn't make the connection. Still it made no sense.

Jenks had abandoned his vigilance at the door and was watching the interchange intently. Now he said softly, "Cursed. I told you it was cursed."

If he had been closer, Casey probably would have backhanded him, but he didn't have time for that now. He tried fiercely to concentrate, to make sense of what the Chinaman was saying. It was like trying to piece together a broken pane of glass.

"What the hell are you talking about?" he demanded furiously. "This here didn't come from no shop in town, it—well, you just never mind where it came from! And even if it did, I know what silver is worth and it ain't no twenty-five dollars, not for something that big!"

"Ah," Red Eye said softly, and for the first time Casey saw him smile. It was not a very pleasant expression.

The Chinaman picked up a small hammer with a rubber tip and drew the cross close to him. Before Casey could stop him or even guess what he was going to do, he brought the hammer down against the cross.

Dumbfounded with horror, Casey watched as one of the

rubies popped out and rolled across the table. When it hit the floor it shattered like . . . glass. Casey forced his eyes back to the cross and couldn't believe what he saw. Even after the ruby, he couldn't believe it. The rubber-tipped hammer had left a dent in the silver the same way a stone would leave a dent when tossed up against a tin can. The very same way.

"Jesus God Almighty," murmured Jenks. "It's a fake. It was a fake all the time."

Tin. Tin and glass. After all this, after everything they'd been through, it was *worthless*. Halfway across the country, one man dead, his own arm broken, and Jenks soft in the head—all for a piece of tin and glass.

Casey wanted to kill something. It didn't matter what or how, but red spots danced before his eyes and he had never wanted to kill so badly in his life. The Chinaman was the closest and the handiest, and, with an inarticulate roar of rage, Casey took one lunging step toward him. Like magic, a long, sharp-pointed stiletto appeared in the other man's hand.

"I think," he said mildly, "our business here is finished." He was no longer smiling.

Casey's head pounded out those red dots of animal rage, and he whirled to Jenks, expecting backup. Jenks was standing there with his gun slack in his hand, grinning from ear to ear.

"It was a fake!" he declared, as though that were the most glorious news he had heard in years. "Tweren't no curse after all, never was, 'cause all the time it was a fake!"

"Shut up, you slack-jawed ijit!" Casey shouted at him. "It was that cowboy that stole it from us, stole it and slipped us this fake! I'm gonna kill him, if I have to chase him around the goddamn world, I'm going to kill him! Nobody makes a fool of me and gets away with it, do you hear? He's a dead man!'' He shoved Jenks hard on the shoulder. "Let's get out of here. We got some hard riding to do.''

The expression of sheer, stupid pleasure slowly faded from Jenks's face. "You goin' after it, Case? You goin' after that cross again?''

"You're goddamn right I am, and I'm gonna get it, too! But not before I see that cowboy drown in his own blood.''

He pushed through the curtain and had taken three furious strides before he realized that Jenks wasn't following. He spun back. "What's the matter with you? We're mounting up!''

Jenks swallowed hard, and it caused a clicking sound in his throat. His face looked wet and pale, and his eyes were hollow. He said, "I ain't going, Case. I ain't having no more truck with that cross.''

Casey figured he should have shot him them, the way a man would shoot a horse with a broken leg or a dog that barked too much. But just then every clock in the place started wheezing and grinding and striking and chiming, all at once but not all at once, and it was enough to make a man in much better shape than Casey temporarily lose hold of his senses. He whipped out his gun and fired it till it was empty, but his aim with his left hand was no better than he knew it would be and he only hit two of the clocks; missed Jenks entirely.

He flung his gun back into its holster and pushed out the door with the sound of those clocks still ringing in his ears and Jenks staring after him, looking apelike in his shock. It didn't matter; Jenks was worthless anyway and Casey, when he could think straight again, decided he was better off without him.

It took a long time for the clocks to wind down, and even longer before Jenks turned back into the little room where Red Eye still sat at the table. A little hesitantly, he walked over and picked up the cross, turning it over in his hand.

He looked at Red Eye. "Five dollars?" he said.

Red Eye smiled and reached for his cash box. Jenks left the shop feeling like he'd just made the best deal of his life.

CHAPTER

Sixteen

I N the days of the forty-niners Orion had been a boom town as hundreds of thousands of men and women poured into the Sierra Nevadas in search of gold. Overnight, hotels, livery stables, brothels, and bars had sprung up in ugly profusion along the western slope of the great mountains.

But now the gold rush was long past, and Orion was barely hanging on. Nothing was left of its former prosperity but a few shabby buildings huddled along the railroad tracks; its streets were littered with tumbleweed, and its residents—what few remained—had the look of dull-eyed defeat about them, as though the only thing that kept them tied to a dying town was a lack of will to go any farther. There was still the occasional miner who panned for gold deep in the mountains, refusing to believe that the once great mines were played out. Now and then timber cutters passed through, outfitting themselves before heading to the big-tree country of pine and fir and sequoia. And there were always the drifters, some running from the law. Some just running.

Charlie O'Neal had owned both the livery stable and the dry goods store in Orion for forty years, and he had seen them all. He watched them come and go with the singular lack of curiosity that was born of the knowledge that whether they came or not, he would still be here, tied to this place, which was slowly fading away around him, until the day he died.

But the young couple who had gotten off the train that morning were not miners, drifters, or loggers. They had headed straight for his store, as most folks did, to outfit themselves for a trek into the mountains, and despite himself his curiosity was aroused.

The woman—although he thought of her as more of a girl—bought a boy's shirt and trousers and a heavy jacket; even though it was coming on summer there was still snow in the high mountains, and her companion, the man, was smart enough to know that without being told. She looked sullen and resentful and didn't say much; it was the man who was making all the decisions and asking the questions.

Well, Charlie had the answers, just as he had had for other travelers over the past forty years. He leaned back in a frayed cane-back chair, watching the man pile his purchases on the counter, and spat a neat stream of tobacco juice into the brass spittoon at his feet before he spoke. "Yep," he answered the man's question carefully. "I know where that Ciudad des Miracles"—he didn't bother putting the Spanish pronunciation on it—"is. 'Bout four days' ride on the other side of El Diablo. That's the big peak you'll see just left over the train station. Still got snow on the top.''

The man looked a little disturbed by this and cast an uneasy glance toward the girl. He probably hadn't figured on it being so far. He glanced back at Charlie. "Which road do we take?"

Charlie chuckled. "Road? Hell, there ain't been a road to Diablo in thirty-five years. Not since some damned fool mine company tried to find gold up there—drug their drills and picks and a whole squadron of diggers up there and left the goddamn mountain shot full of holes, but didn't come out with nary a speck of gold." He shrugged. "Might be a trail left over you could pick your way through, but don't get your hopes up on what you're gonna find. Like I said, nary a speck of gold."

Of course, he knew the two weren't looking for gold; they hadn't bought so much as a pickax. But he had to admit that he was getting mighty curious about just what it was they *did* expect to find up there.

The woman shot her companion a bitter look and spoke her first words since entering the store. "Did you hear the man? There's no road, there's no town. This whole thing is a wild goose chase!"

Charlie looked at her with renewed interest, then drawled, "Oh, there's a town all right. More of a village I'd say. Just a church and a bunch of Indians."

The girl repeated in a shocked tone, "Indians!"

Charlie nodded sagely. "Yep. A couple of hundred years ago, some Spanish priests built a church up there, claimed it was on the site of some miracle or t'other—reckon that's how it got its name. They was going to Christianize all these mountains, build a whole string of missions. But the land

was too hard for 'em and things changed. So the town—
Ciudad des Miracles—just stayed there, kinda keeping to
itself. Still got a priest and a school, but not much else.''

"Indians," the girl said again, and looked as though she
might choke on the word.

"Right peaceful kind," Charlie assured her, "you don't
have to worry about that. Call theirselves the Miwok, not
many of 'em's left. What the white man didn't kill off,
disease finished. Guess they thought they was safe up there
in the mountains and there they stayed. They don't bother
nobody and nobody bothers them.''

He cocked an eyebrow at her and couldn't keep his
curiosity to himself any longer. "What business you got up
there, anyhow?''

The woman turned away—angrily, it seemed to Charlie—
and it was the man who answered. He looked stiff and
unhappy. "We have to deliver a message to the priest.''

That might have been true, Charlie observed, but it was
only part of the truth. "Must be an important message.''

The woman strode out, letting the door bang behind her.
The man looked after her for a moment, then turned back to
Charlie. "Very important," he said grimly. He indicated the
supplies on the counter. "How much?''

At least a dozen times since he had dragged Angel from
the hotel room in San Francisco, Adam had asked himself
Why? The more times he failed to come up with a satisfactory answer, the more disgusted with himself he felt.

Why had it been so important to him to bring the cross all
the way back out here himself? That had never been his

original plan. He could have turned it over to the law, or even to any church in San Francisco—they would have seen that it got back where it belonged. Angel was right; this had nothing to do with him. It wasn't his job.

But that morning in her hotel room he had watched her hands tighten around the cross and watched the hard gleam of avarice take over her eyes and everything had come unraveled. He had loved her, but she was no longer the woman he loved. He wanted her, but she didn't want him. Rage and betrayal and hurt had gotten all tangled up inside him and he hadn't known what he was doing anymore.

He could have just left her there. His first inclination, his strongest impulse, had been just to walk away and leave her with that stolen artifact and its promises of wealth that she wanted so badly. The outlaws would be back as soon as they discovered they had been duped; he knew that and so, most likely, did she. They would kill her without a qualm, and he told himself he couldn't just leave her there to a certain death.

But he hadn't had to take her with him. He could have sent her someplace safe, turned the cross over to the police, and been done with it all. Bringing her along was the first true act of stupidity he had performed in a long, long time. Now here they were out in the middle of nowhere facing a four-day trek into some of the most unforgiving mountains in the world and he still didn't know why. The more he thought about it, the angrier he got.

From the moment they got on the train he had expected her to do something—to try to steal the cross from him, make a break from the train; he was beyond trying to predict what she would do. And in a way he almost hoped she *would* do something, anything to break that awful, sharp-as-glass tension between them. Something that would make it clear to him why he was doing this, and why the love and hate he felt for her were all mixed up and boiling inside him like acid slowly eating a hole through his gut; something that would give him an excuse to shout at her, to grab her and shake her till her teeth rattled, as he had wanted to do since that first morning in the hotel . . . or something that would just make the anger and pain go away, fading into emptiness and apathy, allowing him to turn his back on her and walk away like he should have done in the first place, and put her out of his mind. But she did nothing.

On the train, he had dozed once—lightly, always alert, as he had done in his Ranger days. He had felt her move in her seat beside him, and he had thought with a kind of heady relief that this was it: she was trying to slip the cross out of his pocket. He was awake in an instant, his hand clamped around her wrist with the swiftness of a striking snake, his eyes fastened on hers.

She looked at him with cool disdain and slowly, deliberately twisted her arm from his grasp. Then she bent over and reached for the timetable that had fallen on the floor between his feet, which had apparently been her intention all along, and leaned back to study it. That was the worst of it; she had done nothing.

No, the worst of it was her silence. She hadn't said a word to him until that brief, bitter outburst in the Orion dry goods store, and had kept her face so closed and masked that it was impossible to know what she was thinking. But he could guess. She too was wondering why, and was probably marking him down for just as big a fool as he had already decided himself to be.

He came out with their bundles of provisions in his hands:

two sets of saddlebags filled with foodstuffs, two bedrolls, Angel's clothes. The horses, which he had picked out before they went in the store, had already been saddled and brought up, their reins wrapped loosely around the hitching post in front of the store.

A man was sitting in the shade of the narrow porch, his hat pulled down, a bottle between his feet. Adam glanced at him briefly, but he seemed harmless. Angel sat on the steps, staring at the mountains. And Adam knew the time for wondering why and feeling anger was past.

He dropped the saddlebags and the bedrolls onto the porch with a thump. The man with the bottle didn't even look up. Neither did Angel. Adam sat down beside her.

He said, "You could've stolen that cross from me anytime before now."

She replied diffidently, "Maybe. But I wouldn't have gotten far with it on the train."

"Am I going to have to sleep with a gun in my hand for the next four nights?"

She looked at him. Her eyes were clear and as blue as a Colorado summer, but otherwise expressionless. "You wouldn't shoot me."

Adam said softly, "What about you, Angel? Would you shoot me? Or take that knife of yours to my throat while I was sleeping?"

She looked at him for just a moment longer, then away. "You're a fool," she said roughly, "and I'll take that cross from you if I can. You know that. Anybody who'd ride four days into those mountains to take something worth thousands—*millions*—of dollars back to the Indians deserves what he gets."

She turned her eyes on him again, and this time they were

kindled with little sparks of blue fire. "Indians!" she repeated scornfully. "What do they need with it anyway? They don't even know what it is! They left it lying out to be stolen and it'll get stolen again—you know that, don't you? And what will all your fine ideas about right and wrong mean then?"

In the distance the train was chugging steam, having completed its water stop and delivered the few goods it had brought from bigger cities. Adam reached into his pocket and took out a wad of bills and a few silver pieces.

"Here," he said, grabbing her hand and thrusting the money into it. "The train is getting ready to pull out, and if you miss it you'll have to wait two days for another one. You'd better get going."

She looked at the money in her hand but did not close her fingers about it.

Then she said, her voice hoarse with incredulity, "That's it? You brought me all the way out here just to send me back again? Where am I supposed to go?"

"I don't care where you go," he returned shortly. "You've got money, that's all you care about. So just go!"

But in his heart he *did* care, and he suddenly had the answer to the question that had been plaguing him. He knew why he had brought her here. It wasn't because he had promised Consuelo, or Jeremiah Haber. He could have left her in San Francisco; but if he had done that, with matters standing the way they were between them and hatred boiling in his soul . . . she would never have come back to him. It would have been over, finally and forever, and *he wasn't ready to let her go*. It was as simple as that.

Maybe she would try to run away from him on the trail. But if she took the money and got on that train now, it would be over just the same. She would be gone forever. And though he could feel his skin tightening and his heart pounding hard in his chest, he had to know now. He had to give her that chance.

He said gruffly, "There's enough there to get you back to San Francisco. If you need more, wire Tori Cantrell or Consuelo Gomez in Casa Verde, New Mexico. You've always got a home there. I'm not turning you out. You know what to do. Like you said, you don't need me."

She kept staring at the money in her hand. And then, slowly, she closed her fingers over it. Adam felt whatever hope had been left in him drain out in a cold, dull wave.

She tossed the money back at him. Some of the bills scattered on his lap, the coins bounced on the porch. "I don't want to go back to San Francisco. And that"—she gestured disdainfully at the scattered bills—"isn't near enough to pay for that cross. As long as you've got it, mister, I'm your shadow, and you're dumber than I thought if you think different."

"And that's it?" he asked quietly. "That's the only reason?"

He saw her throat move as she swallowed, but she would not look at him.

"I won't kill you in your sleep," she said, "if that's what you're worried about." Her voice sounded husky, and she kept her eyes determinedly fixed on the distant mountains. "But aside from that, I'm not making any promises."

Adam began to gather up the spilled money, returning it to his pocket. "I could force you to get on that train."

"You could have left me in San Francisco."

And then she looked at him, and there was a moment when their eyes met that hovered on the edge of truth, pushing aside the veil of anger and hurt just long enough to remember another time, another place, and the people they had been then ... eyes laughing on the beach, an embrace that was sweet and strong, words whispered in the dark. It was all still there, hovering just beneath the surface of the angry words and violent suspicions that kept them apart, and a touch, or a word, could have brought it back to life again.

But Adam didn't have the words, and after a moment, Angel turned away.

Adam swallowed hard to clear his throat and said, "You'd better find a place to get changed." He thrust the bundle of clothes at her. "We've got a full day's ride ahead of us."

Then there was nothing left to do but get moving.

The first part of their journey took them through scrubby chaparral and across streams lined with live oak, blue oak, and willow. It was big, empty country and it resounded with loneliness; the two horses, whether walking side by side in the blazing sunshine or dipping into the black shadows of trees, were dwarfed by the vastness of the land that surrounded them. Up ahead, the mountain the storekeeper had called El Diablo rose like a giant, jagged tooth splitting the sky. Angel had traveled hard country before, from town to town and camp to camp on broken-down mules and pinned-together wagons, but nothing like this. She was glad she was not alone ... yet she had never felt quite so alone in her life.

She had never really believed it would get this far. She had thought that surely Adam, if left alone long enough, would come to his senses and realize what a stupid, point-less thing he was doing. Maybe there was a part of her that still believed he had never been serious. She had made him mad in San Francisco, and although she still wasn't sure exactly how the disagreement about the cross had ever gotten so out of control, she had said some pretty rough things there at the end, and so had he. So now he was mad, and he wanted to make a point or teach her a lesson, the way men, when they got their backs up, were prone to do. She'd thought that was really all there was to it . . . until this morning.

He had wanted to send her back. He hadn't been fooling or making a point when he put that money in her hand; there had been no humor in his eyes then. He was dead serious. And in that moment a chill had swept through her soul like none she had ever known. Even now, with sweat trickling down the back of her neck and sunshine bouncing off the baked ground to burn her eyes, there was a cold clamminess inside her that wouldn't go away. Adam didn't want her anymore.

Perhaps what shocked her most, what made her feel so scared and angry and desperately confused, was that it mattered so much. She had known from the beginning, hadn't she, that a man like Adam could never be a perma-nent part of her life? She had taken what she could get from him—one night of loving, one night of feeling she belonged, one night of sheer ecstasy that hovered on the open edge of a whole world of possibilities. She had offered to be his woman for as long as he would have her . . . but then he had asked her to marry him. He had known what she was from the beginning and *he had asked her to marry him*. That's what hurt her the most. That's what made her so angry—with him for pretending, with herself for believing.

And then there had been that moment when he placed the money in her hand and looked at her with hard, distant eyes and she had known it was over. Another dream dissolving into the mist, and she should have expected it. She should have known all along that nothing so wonderful could ever be real, that things like that didn't happen to girls like her.

But nothing had ever hurt her as much as the moment when that particular dream had been torn from her grasp. Nothing had ever left her feeling so empty and shattered inside.

Maybe she should have gotten on the train. There was nothing for her here. Even the cross . . . the only way she could take it from him was by force, and she wouldn't do that. Adam must surely know that she wouldn't, she couldn't do that. Maybe there was still some small part of her that held out hope that he would change his mind. Maybe she had half-convinced herself that somehow, over the course of these next few days, she would be able to steal it back from him. But she doubted it. And somehow the cross didn't mean as much to her as it once had.

So why hadn't she gotten on the train?

She looked at Adam's strong, broad back, now in the lead as he guided his horse carefully up the small incline that took them out of the foothills, and she knew the answer. It made no sense, and it hurt her to admit it, but she knew why she was still with him.

They camped beside a scraggly oak tree near a stream, and the sun went down with fearful abruptness. Adam opened a can of beans with his knife and balanced a skillet of bacon over the fire.

"It's going to burn that way," Angel said. She wrapped the hem of her oversized jacket around the skillet handle and moved it off the center of the fire, slapping at the tiny flames that had already begun to catch on the bacon fat.

Adam glanced at her. "I was going to make coffee. I can't hold the skillet over the fire and fetch water at the same time."

"Here, I'll do it. I never did know a man who could make a decent cup of coffee. Hold this."

After a moment he squatted beside her and reached to take the skillet from her hand.

"Careful, it's hot."

There was some difficulty unwinding her jacket from the skillet handle and for a moment her fingers got tangled up with his. It was only a moment, but it seemed like more that his rough, manly fingers lay against hers, and she wasn't prepared for the darts of remembrance and longing that accidental touch sent through her . . . remembrance of things that were no longer hers, longing for things she could never have. She jerked her hand away and the skillet almost fell into the flames. Adam rescued it quickly, hissing as the handle burned his hand.

Angel got to her feet and her throat felt thick with words she dared not say, and the warmth that stung her cheeks was more than the lingering effects of the fire. She grabbed the coffeepot and went quickly to the stream.

Adam concentrated fiercely on the flickering flames, determined not to watch her leave. But his ears strained for her and the back of his neck prickled when she returned and her shadow fell over him again.

The shapeless men's pants and the too-big coat hid most of her figure from him, but her scent was warm and musky and female on the crisp night air, and it went through him with a shiver of awareness, teasing his senses. When she bent down beside him to place the coffeepot over the flames he could see the way the material of her pants tautened against one thigh, outlining its slender, feminine shape perfectly, and he had to jerk his eyes away.

"I'll take that now."

Her voice sounded muffled as she reached for the skillet, but it might have been no more than the pressure of Adam's blood in his ears. He turned over the skillet to her, careful not to touch her this time, and left the fire. He was beginning to understand that he had made more than one error in judgment in bringing her along.

They ate on opposite sides of the fire, in a strained silence that was magnified by the wildly jumping shadows the flames cast off and by the echoed stirrings of animals foraging in the brush. A chill had come over the land with the setting of the sun, and Angel shivered inside the big coat, inching closer to the fire. She wasn't sure whether the cold was coming from the night air or from Adam's wintry silence.

He said at length, "Good coffee." The words startled her so that she jumped. "Want some more?"

He lifted the pot, and she held out her cup. He refilled her cup first, then his own.

A sudden screeching howl from somewhere up the mountain caused the coffee cup to jerk in Angel's hand, sloshing hot coffee on her wrist. She cried out and dropped the cup on the ground. Adam was immediately beside her.

"Are you burned?"

She looked around anxiously, holding her injured wrist. "What was that?"

"Just a bobcat, or a cougar maybe. It won't come near the fire. Let me see your hand."

He pushed up the sleeve of her coat and examined the reddened skin of her wrist in the firelight. It wasn't a bad burn, but it stung like a thousand crawling ants and Angel had to press her lips tightly together to fight the childish instinct to bring her scalded wrist to her mouth.

"Better get some cold water on it," Adam said, "or it could turn nasty."

He was still holding her arm, bent over her so that not only his shadow but all his body warmth enfolded her, and when she looked up at him his face was close enough to touch her own. His face was planed by the firelight, his eyes a soft blur of lights and dark, of mystery and uncertainty; for the first time since San Francisco she was looking at an Adam she knew and her instinct was to sink gratefully into his arms, to let his warmth and strength wash away all the hurt that had sprung between them.

The moment went on for an eternity of heartbeats, their eyes locked and their breaths merging, and she thought, *Kiss me. Just . . . kiss me.* She thought he would. She knew he wanted to.

The he said, a little gruffly, "Take care of that arm. I'm going to get some shut-eye." He stood up and went to gather some more sticks for the fire.

Disappointment and loss tasted bitter in Adam's throat as he spread out his bedroll near the horses, leaving the place closest to the fire for Angel. The disappointment was not with her but with himself, for coming so close . . . for not coming closer. She still had that much power over his senses. She was poison, but he was lying on the cold hard ground thinking how easy it would be not to sleep alone tonight.

He could see her shadow moving back and forth in front of the fire as she prepared her bed. He could hear her movements—the creak of her boots, the rustle of her clothing—before she lay down and pulled the blanket over her. He was straining for those sounds, searching the dark for the shadow of her movement. Sleep had never been so far from coming.

When he moved his head he could see her, in a faint pool of flickering light from the fire, lying on her side with her knees drawn up.

She was as cold as he was. He could make her warm. He could make them both warm. His skin grew tight, his heart beat heavily. She was so close. He had made her his, nothing could ever change that. There was no reason for him not to reinstate that claim, to continue what they had begun in San Francisco. She would expect no different. She had asked to be his woman.

Maybe she no longer wanted him. But Adam could make her want him; he had always known how to make women want him, it was as natural as breathing. And the way she looked at him . . . She wouldn't be sorry.

He fancied he could hear her soft breathing above the sounds of the night, and she looked so small and alone huddled there in the pool of dying light. He was helpless against the hardening of his loins, against the slow, steady pulses of wanting that heated his blood. And he was disgusted with himself. Because it would be wrong, and there had been too much pain and betrayal already. For what he was thinking and feeling now he had no right to sit in judgment on her. He had never had.

He was using his saddlebags as a pillow, and tucked deep within them was the cross. She knew that, and now he half-wished he had left the bags with his saddle so that if she was going to steal the cross, she would do it tonight and he would know. Then it would really be over. But would it?

She could still leave him. She could slip off in the night and be gone long before morning, and it really wouldn't surprise him. And if she did?

I'd go after her, Adam realized suddenly. *God help me, I'd go after her and start it all over again . . . .*

The yowl of the cat came again, making the horses snort alarm and toss their heads. Angel's voice came swift and frightened across the darkness, and she sat up. "Adam? It sounded closer!"

He sat up too, and touched the stock of the rifle at his side. It did sound closer. He knew the cat would be much more likely to go for the horses than for the two people sleeping by the fire, and he started to tell her so. But something stopped him.

She was afraid. She needed him. He should take his bedroll closer to hers, lie down beside her, touch her hand for reassurance. Talk to her. Put his arm around her, draw her close. Hold her. It would be so easy. He would stroke her hair, kiss her face, and then . . .

He said, "I'd better sleep nearer the horses." He got up with an abrupt movement, and it took more strength of will than he knew he possessed to walk, not toward her, but away from her.

He did not sleep much that night.

Neither did Angel.

CHAPTER
Seventeen

CASEY thought the hardest part would be tracking them out of San Francisco. That they had left the city he had no doubt; they had probably hightailed it out by the nearest conveyance the minute they had gotten themselves untied, and it made his head pound with fury to think that they had gotten such a head start. It didn't matter, though; he would find them. If it took the rest of his life, he'd track them down and he'd kill them, slowly, one by one: first the man, because he thought he was so goddamn smart, then the woman, because it was all her fault.

They had shown a preference for traveling by train, so he started at the station first. Dozens of people left and entered the city every day and he didn't hold out much hope, but he had a good story ready just in case. The difference between him and that lunatic Jenks, after all, had always been brains.

He put on a good face and told the man at the station that he was looking for his daughter, who had been stolen away from him against her will by a tall blond-haired man. For good effect, he added that the bastard had broken Casey's arm when he tried to stop him. He described them both as best he could and said that they had left the city on the twenty-third.

It was a stroke of genius, and Casey spent the better part of two days congratulating himself on it. The window clerk didn't ask why he hadn't brought in the law, didn't even ask why it had taken him this long to get after them. But he did remember a couple fitting that description, and he remembered clearly because the girl was so striking to look at and because it was obvious she didn't want to go where the man was taking her. He had thought at the time that something underhanded was afoot, but he was just a man who sold tickets and he couldn't go interfering in the private business of everybody who passed through the station.

The clerk went on to say that they had bought tickets south, not east as Casey had supposed. The clerk remembered that because their final destination had been a little nowhere town called Orion, in the foothills of the Sierra Nevadas, and he had wondered at the time what they planned on doing up there. Orion was nothing more than a water stop for a spur line, and the only thing that ever got off the train in that town these days was mail—and precious little of that. Casey was confused too, and he thought maybe the clerk had put him on the trail of the wrong couple. But then the man told him something that made him decide to take the chance. The man and woman hadn't left on the twenty-third, as Casey had supposed, but on the twenty-fourth. That put them only a couple of days ahead of him. And if Casey took the stage, which didn't make as many stops as the train, he could cut that head start by another day.

He took the stage as far as North Fork, its last stop, then stole a horse in the dead of night and took off riding. By the time the liveryman noticed that the horse was missing in the morning, Casey was far, far away.

It was a fast horse and he pushed it to the limit, riding hard all night and most of the next day until the horse began to heave so that he knew if he didn't give it a rest he'd be walking the remainder of the way. He arrived in Orion in the middle of the afternoon, and a kind of sick dismay filled him as he walked his horse down the empty, littered main street. It was nothing but a ghost town. Somebody had been pulling his leg. He'd ridden hell for leather all this way for nothing; they had never been here, wouldn't have come anywhere near here. They would have done just like he'd thought at first—head east to some big city like Boston or Philadelphia and sell the cross, then disappear the hell out of the country. That's what *he* would do, and that's what they had done. Unless . . .

Unless they had sold the cross in San Francisco. Unless they were trying to throw him off the trail by hiding in the mountains. Unless they were lying in wait for him, even now, expecting him to track them down, getting ready to blow his head off when he came around the next corner. Unless they were stupid enough to think he *wouldn't* track them down . . .

He was in a fine lather when he strode into the dry goods store, the only business that appeared to be open on the godforsaken little street. It was opposite the train station, and if anybody fitting the description of the two people he was hunting had gotten off, somebody in that store was sure to have noticed it.

He was in no mood to be subtle, and he went in with his gun drawn. There was nobody in the store except the storekeeper, just as there had been nobody on the streets. If there had been, Casey probably would have killed them on the spot.

Charlie was pouring out coffee from a fifty-pound bag into one-pound ones, and when the man came slamming through the door with his gun drawn, his hands shot into the air immediately. The fifty-pound bag tipped over and coffee spilled all over the counter.

Instinct made him put his hands up; a man came breaking into your store at gunpoint and that was what you did—if you had any sense. But then he looked at the coffee spilled all over the counter—ten pounds worth, if he was any judge, and that was a small fortune these days—and he got mad. There was no law in this town—hadn't been for years—and little hope that anybody would come to his rescue even if he yelled for help, which he wouldn't do. What few folks were left around here took care of themselves and stayed out of other folks' business. Charlie O'Neal did the same. But the sight of all that spilled coffee made him mad.

Not quite mad enough, however, to take his hands down.

Casey advanced on the old man slowly. "That's right, mister. You just stay where you are like a good fella. I got some questions for you and you're gonna answer them, then I'll be helping myself to a few things and be on my way. All right with you?"

Charlie said nothing. He thought about the shotgun he

kept loaded under the counter, just a few feet away. But he didn't dare drop his eyes to it.

"I'm looking for some folks," Casey said. "Man and a woman. She's black-haired and real pretty, you'd know her right off. He's a yellow-haired man, tall and rangy. They got off the train here yesterday or the day before. I wanna know where they went from here."

Charlie looked at the gunman and looked at the coffee. He'd lived here forty years, and some of those years had been rough and wild. But not once in all that time had any man been able to come into his store and take what was his without paying for it. He'd lived his life by taking care of himself and his own, and he'd be damned if he was going to die a sniveling coward at the feet of a thief with a gun.

So Charlie met Casey's eyes and said coolly, "Ain't nobody like that been in here, mister." It did no good to lie; he had no reason to lie for a couple of strangers he didn't even know. But he was mad, and the gunman wasn't getting a thing from him. Not even the truth.

Casey took two furious strides toward him, pressing his belly up against the counter with the six-shooter less than three feet from the old man's face. Even with his weak left hand, Casey wouldn't miss at that range. He said, his voice low, "Don't you waste your breath lying to me, mister. Ain't but one goddamn train through here and it stops right outside your goddamn window. They got off it, all right. Now you tell me where they went or I'll blow you to kingdom come."

Charlie said, "I'm seventy-five years old. I been working hard and making nothing in this dead-hole town for the last forty of 'em. You kill me now, I reckon you'd be in the way of doing me a favor."

Casey pulled the trigger.

The old man's face disintegrated into an explosion of blood, but Casey had swung around and headed for the door before the sight even made an impression on him. He burst out the door with his gun drawn and breaths of ragged fury parting his lips, half-expecting—although logic rejected the notion, in a town as empty as this—a posse to be bearing down on him. Instead he saw only one man, rising slowly out of a cane chair on the porch, and Casey would've shot him, too; he was cocking the hammer to do so, but the man spoke.

"You do that, and you ain't never gonna find them two."

Casey hesitated, not because of the words, because he knew he wouldn't have quite the advantage with a moving target as he had before, and this man was wearing a gun. He was lean-faced and bearded, but his eyes were sharp and the way he flexed his fingers against his hip told Casey that he wouldn't have any trouble getting his revolver out of the holster.

He went on, "I was sitting here yestiddy. They didn't notice me. Most folks don't. Heard it all. Some kind of cross, ain't it. The girl said it was worth millions." He shrugged. "Maybe, maybe not. The man what was with her, he sure seemed anxious enough to keep it away from her. Tried to put her on the train. She wouldn't go."

"Where'd they go?" Casey demanded hoarsely.

The man continued to gaze at him with a lazy lack of concern, his fingers flexing. "Name's Briggs," he said. "Turned it over in my head as to how I'd like to go after them myself, just to see what it was they was carrying that could be worth as much as all that. But a man'd be a fool to go up in them mountains all by his lonesome, not knowing for sure if there was anything to what they said.

"*Where did they go?*"

Briggs nodded his head north. "Up yonder trail. Mining country. Little village up there full of Injuns and missionaries." And then he glanced at Casey's arm, still bound by its dirty bandanna sling. "Looks to me like you could use yourself an extra gun."

Casey stared at him for a long time. Village—Indians...He couldn't believe it could be that simple. Then he looked up and saw it, white-capped and towering—El Diablo. He'd seen it from the east, from the Nevada side where they'd stolen the cross. Now he was seeing it from California, but there was no mistake about it. It was the same place. They were taking the cross back to the Indians.

"You got a horse?" he demanded.

"There's a stable right there chock-full of 'em."

"Then get one. Let's ride."

By the second day Adam and Angel had left the scrubby grass of the low country behind. The mountains were thick and wooded, redolent with the smell of pine. Cottonwood and maple lined the streams and for long stretches at a time the traveling was almost pleasant, sun-dappled and rich-smelling, cooled by the higher elevation and the thick foliage. But the streams were deep and steeply banked, and the horses were skittish about crossing them. There were often unexpected chasms of rock that split the terrain and caused them to backtrack and go around. In places the ground was so thick with spiky thorns that the horses couldn't pass, and more backtracking was required. By the end of the day they were both exhausted. They ate little and slept heavily.

As they climbed higher, the trees grew denser. Big red firs formed a ceiling where their crowns touched, admitting a glimpse of the sky only in scraps and patches. Blue jays and squirrels chattered overhead; occasionally they could hear the crash of a running deer in the underbrush, but aside from that there was no sound, no sign of life at all, except the steady crunch of their horses' hooves. It was eerie.

The ground was covered with litter; broken limbs and uprooted trees blocked their way more than once, and the going was hard. Despite the coolness of the increased altitude and the deep shade, perspiration gathered repeatedly on Angel's face and the back of her neck, and by midmorning she was exhausted. She kept thinking, *Why am I doing this? Why am I here in this awful place, for what? Why would anyone want to do this?*

Most of her life had been spent on the move; campfires by night, rickety wagons by day. Aching muscles, thirst, and fatigue had been her constant companions by day, and worry and watchfulness had invaded her nights. She was tired. She had been tired of it all for a long time and now all she wanted was to go home.

And when she thought of home, she thought of a cabin in New Mexico. She thought of sunny windows and the smell of baking, of floors to polish and hems to mend and a fire crackling in the grate. She thought of someone coming through the door at night, glad to see her . . .

And the thinking did nothing except form a hot knot of pain in her stomach that gradually flooded her chest and closed off her throat. Because that place didn't exist for her.

Her life consisted of rutted roads and leaky shacks and feeble fires to ward off the chill. She should never have counted on anything more.

The higher they went into the mountains the more heavily defeat weighed on her. She had been a fool to come this far, ever to think that anything good would come from this. Even if she had the cross, she couldn't get out of these mountains by herself. Once before she had run away from a man who had offered her nothing but kindness. The three nights she had spent lost in the mountains before Jeremiah found her again were enough to convince her that she never wanted to repeat that experience.

Adam had won; she had lost. The only question that remained was: What now?

Angel could hear the rush of water that signaled the presence of a stream up ahead and her horse quickened its pace a little, kicking up debris as they moved through a stand of quaking aspens. Adam drew up his horse in front of her and dismounted.

"It's too steep." He took off his hat and ran his fingers through the tangle of his hair before replacing it. He looked down at the rocky embankment that guarded the stream. "We're going to have to walk the horses across."

Angel wearily pushed a hand over her damp face. She was so tired, and it was hard to breathe. When she swung down from the saddle she actually saw spots before her eyes for a moment. The last thing she wanted to do was to drag her horse down an embankment and then plunge waist deep into an icy stream.

But she wound the reins around her hand and followed Adam's lead as he cautiously led his mount down the bank. The horse half-climbed, half-slid down the bank and

Angel struggled to stay out of its way. The water wasn't just icy; it was paralyzing. The shock struck her legs, soaked through her trousers, numbed her thighs. Even her horse rebelled, tossing its head and snorting in protest at the rush of cold water and slippery stones beneath its hooves. Adam's face was grim as he pulled his mount across, splashing and struggling for balance.

"Don't rush him," he called. "Take it easy; you don't want to spook him."

Angel set her teeth against the cold and pulled on the reins. Her nostrils were flared with harsh breaths and her heart thundered with strain as she fought the current and the cold and the stubborn horse, which would take one cautious step forward and then two backward. "Come on, you ugly beast," she muttered, and, bracing her feet, she jerked hard on the reins.

The horse reared, jerking the reins out of Angel's hands. She stumbled forward, trying to catch them, and the horse reared again. She was gasping. Following the horse with her eyes, she saw the pale, shivering underbellies of the aspen leaves, saw a dark tangle of spiky firs against the sky, saw dancing sparks of blue and red. She lunged forward, and then she saw nothing but gray.

When she opened her eyes it was to a sickening, swirling headache and a nauseous collage of running colors—blue and green, red and black. The red, she gradually began to see, was Adam's shirt; the black was the hat he was fanning back and forth in front of her face. She was lying on the ground; the dried carpet of leaves was rich and musty-smelling. Her skirts were still cold and wet, but her head was cradled by something warm . . . Adam's lap, she realized. He was holding her.

Weakly, she reached up to stop the fanning motions of his hat. The effort cause a renewed onslaught of nausea, and she swallowed hard against it, closing her eyes.

"I thought the horse had hit you," Adam answered her unspoken question when she opened her eyes again. "You were lucky he didn't. You fainted. It's the air up here, too thin. It takes some people longer to get used to it than others."

She felt sick and weak and his words didn't have much meaning to her. But his voice . . . she could lie here forever, cradled in his warmth, listening to his voice. His face, tight with concern; his eyes dark and anxious—just looking at him made her stronger, and she wanted to do nothing but gaze into those eyes, memorize that face.

But after a moment she braced her rubbery arms beneath her and struggled to a sitting position.

"Careful," Adam said. He held her shoulders lightly. "Not too fast."

"I'm all right," she muttered. She took a deep breath and waited for the world to right itself again, but when he took his hands from her shoulders the world did not feel right at all.

She took another breath, trying to sound strong, trying to sound competent. She did not want his pity, and she did not want to be a burden. That was the last thing she wanted. "I'm sorry," she said. "That was stupid. I've been in the high country before. I should have thought about the air."

"No." His tone was tight as he got to his feet, slapping his hat against his thigh in a gesture of restrained anger.

"I'm the one who was stupid. And I'm the one who's sorry."

He walked a few steps from her, his motions taut and controlled, his stance radiating tension. "I'm sorry for getting you into this—for getting us both into this. It was crazy, making this trip. If I had any sense I'd—"

He stopped, and Angel's breath caught in her throat. She watched him, hardly daring to hope. "You'd turn back?" she prompted softly.

For a moment longer, hope was suspended, and then she saw his shoulders sag, slowly and by degrees. He turned to look at her, and his face was set, but there was a hardness in his eyes.

"No," he said quietly. "I can't do that. You know I can't."

And Angel did know. Because if he relented now, if he admitted he had been wrong and turned back, he would be giving up more than the value of the cross. He would be admitting defeat, and no man would allow himself to do that.

And yet, Angel realized slowly, it was more than pride that kept him going when he knew it was stupid, admitted it was crazy. It was Adam himself, the type of man he was . . . the man who did the right thing no matter what the cost, the man she had mocked and derided and tried so hard to hate, but had ended up falling in love with. If he turned back now, he would be giving up himself, and although Angel wanted more than anything in the world to be out of this place and rid of this hateful mission, she did not want him to do that. She could not *let* him do that.

And so she was trapped; they both were trapped in this place they did not want to be, doing something neither wanted to do. Why, she did not completely understand yet. She knew only that he had no choice, and neither did she, and weariness ran through her like a chilling fog.

She drew up her knees and rested her head on them. "So," she said after a long time, tiredly. "What happens next?" It was the one question she had been afraid to ask even to herself, the question she didn't want to hear answered. But the words came out, and perhaps it was time, after all, to know the answer. "After you get to the Indians and give them their cross, what then?"

His response was slow in coming, and his voice sounded heavy with quiet finality. "I don't know. I'll go home, I guess."

There was nothing complex about those words, nothing momentous or surprising. But they seemed to hold within them all the misery and defeat of her short life. He was going home. He had given up on her. She thought she had known emptiness before, but this was more than emptiness. This was the absence of everything: will, purpose, hope. The future was a gray, gaping hole somewhere in the distance because he was going home and she had no home to go to.

Her throat was so tight and full that it hurt to speak, but she tried not to show it. She did not meet his eyes. "What will you tell my mother?"

She heard his footsteps crunching on the leafy ground as he came over to her. He sat down beside her—not too close—and rested his arm on one raised knee, looking out over the dense woodlands ahead. A warmth crept over her with his nearness, but it was not the kind of warmth that brought her pleasure. It was an aching, tingling awareness of loss, poignant and painful, and she tried to steel herself against it but could not.

"I'll tell her the truth," Adam said quietly, at last. "As much as I know of it, anyway. I thought I could make you go back to her, I thought I could make you *want* to . . . I thought it would be as easy as bringing in a stray calf, or breaking a mustang . . . I don't know what I thought. I reckon a man who's lived as long as I have ought to've figured out there's a difference between people and live-stock, but it took me a little longer than most."

He looked at her, and Angel could no longer avoid his eyes, as much as she wanted to. What she saw there broke her heart just when she thought there was nothing left inside her to shatter. It was sadness, and longing, the look of a man who has reached for some great prize only to find it snatched away just as he closed his fingers on it and knows he will never have another chance.

He said, "I can't change you, Angel. I can't make you think about things the way I do, or want the things I do, or care about the things I think folks ought to care about. I guess . . . I don't know, family's always meant a lot to me, and I figured everybody was the same way. A while ago you told me I hadn't lived your life, I didn't know anything about you, and I reckon you were right at that. I wish it was different but wishing don't make it so. And I can't make you want to go home, any more than I can . . ."

He stopped, and moved his eyes away, and Angel thought he wouldn't finish. He then glanced down at the hat in his hand and added, very quietly, "Any more than I can make you want me."

She wanted to cry, *You're wrong! I do want you, I want everything about you, you're the only thing I've ever wanted*

*that was worth anything. I want to go home, I want what
you promised, I just want to be with you for the rest of my
life.*

Maybe if he had looked at her then she would have told
him that and so much more. But he would not look at her,
and the words lodged in her throat.

It was a long time before she could speak, and then it was
only to say gruffly, "We'd better get moving."

"No." His voice now was easy, and he got to his feet as
though nothing of any significance had passed between
them. "We'll rest here for a while. The air's not good for
the horses either. No point in wearing them out."

He walked away from her and began to unsaddle the
horses.

They lost half a day, but Adam was no longer on a
schedule. In fact, the closer he got to his goal the longer he
seemed to want to postpone it, and the less important it
became. City of the Miracles. It was beginning to seem, in
his mind, more like a place of damnation. When he reached
it, there would be nothing left for him. Angel would be
gone, and the quest that had consumed his life for three
years would be over, wasted. He would go back to Casa
Verde with nothing more than he had started, and Angel . . .
Angel would be gone.

They camped that night on a slope ringed with aspens;
they made a shivery, haunting sound with every breeze that
stirred. Tomorrow's traveling would take them into the high
Sierras, and after that he figured one, maybe two more
days. Angel was quiet, moving around the campfire like a

ghost, tired and drawn into herself. It worried Adam. Tomorrow they would travel more slowly.

He walked away from the camp to smoke, thinking about promises made and promises broken, wondering what he would tell Consuelo, wondering what would happen to Angel, wondering how he would be able to let her go. Wondering if there was anything he could have done to make it turn out differently, and deciding there were probably a hundred things. But there was nothing he could do now except to move slowly, and make this time before the end last as long as possible.

And then he noticed something that made him realize that they could not afford to move slowly anymore.

There was a faint tinge of woodsmoke on the air, and it did not come from their own fire but below them and to the east. He stood stock-still for a long time, not wanting to believe, cursing himself for not suspecting it before. But there was no mistake.

They were being followed.

CHAPTER

Eighteen

ADAM and Angel moved out of the wooded mountains and into the high-plains country. The ground was covered with low-growing grasses and dwarf flowering plants where there was ground cover at all; most of the time they spent negotiating boulders and sharp cliffs without seeing much more than an occasional stunted tree. The air was so thin and clear that it almost seemed that one could see to the end of the world, and Angel noticed that Adam spent a great deal of time looking back over the trail they left behind.

Angel began to notice signs of mining: abandoned shafts with the boards rotting away, deserted tools, rock piles, and gaping holes drilled into the mountain's face—the refuse of another time. She knew they were getting closer.

Over and over she thought about it, tried to make some

sense of the whole mess. But the only conclusion she came to was that, despite the foolishness of this mission, despite its utter stupidity, Adam was determined to see it through. She had to admire him for that. She couldn't have loved him for anything else. But loving him had brought her nothing but pain, and he didn't want her love. He didn't want her at all.

When they reached the village, Adam would turn over the cross to the ignorant Indians and she would be alone again. Then what would become of her? She had struggled all her life to stay out of those rooms above the saloons where men doled out a dollar at a time for a few minutes under the sheets. But now what was left for her?

She thought about her mother and the place Adam called home. But that avenue was closed to her now, even if she wanted it. Because Adam lived there too—or if not there, then close enough that the difference didn't matter—and because those were his people, that was his home, and she didn't belong there. And because of something else, something she had known for a long time, perhaps from the very beginning. And it was that one thing, perhaps more than anything else, that had kept her from agreeing ever to meet this woman who called herself Angel's mother.

As the afternoon heightened the sky darkened, and before long they were riding through a cold, misty rain. The horses' hooves slipped on steep, rocky inclines, and at one point they picked up a trail that was little more than a footpath along a narrow ledge that circled and climbed the mountain. The going was treacherous, and it required all of Angel's concentration to keep her horse hugging the rock wall, away from the sheer drop below.

The ledge was littered with loose stones and dried debris,

and once, when her horse slipped on some loose gravel, she jerked back so hard on the reins that the animal screamed and threatened to buck. With her heart slamming in her chest, she managed to calm him, then looked anxiously ahead, expecting Adam to turn back with a reprimand. But Adam had come to a complete stop about ten feet in front of her, and he did not look back.

Cautiously Angel guided her horse forward. It was raining harder now, the droplets spattering her wool coat and dripping off her hat to creep inside her collar. She could hear thunder in the distance, and the day was like twilight, gloomy and hard to see. She shivered.

Adam dismounted, and as Angel drew up behind him she could see that the path was blocked by a rockslide. It was only about four feet high, but it was far too treacherous to trust the horses to climb, and there wasn't an inch of room in which to go around.

"We'll have to go back," Angel said. But an unexpected roll of thunder swallowed her words and she repeated, raising her voice a little, "We can backtrack down the trail—it's only a couple of miles. We might as well make camp."

But Adam was shaking his head. "We can't turn the horses around here—it's too dangerous. I'll have to try to move it."

"In this rain? Why don't you just wait until—"

"No time! We've got to keep moving."

His words stung, making it plainer than she wanted to see what a hurry he was in to get where he was going and be rid of her. When he offered his reins to her she jerked them away and retorted, "Well, don't expect me to help!"

She forced the horses to back up a few steps, closer to the

rock wall, then stood there shivering in the cold rain while he bent his back to the work. Thunder boomed again, making her start, and the horses shifted and whinnied nervously. Angel tightened her grip on the slick reins, sliding farther down the trail a few feet to avoid the danger of being pinned against the wall by the frightened horses.

And then her eyes fell on Adam's horse. His saddlebags. The cross was in there; he had never made any secret of where he kept it. He knew she wouldn't run away in the middle of the night, not in these mountains. But as far as she knew, he hadn't checked it since they had begun this journey. There was no reason to think he would check it until they reached their destination.

Angel pressed her lips together against another shiver, and tasted rain. She looked at Adam. He had cleared most of the rubble away by kicking it and tossing it by handfuls over the ledge. Now there remained only the biggest boulder. It would take him a long time to move that.

If she slipped the cross out of his saddlebags and into her own, he wouldn't know. He wouldn't know anything until she disappeared, and if she waited until the village was in sight, until they reached something resembling civilization, she could hire a guide to get her out of the mountains. She might not even need a guide. The storekeeper had said there was no road leading from Orion, but that didn't mean there wasn't a trail down the other side of the mountain; towns and villages even closer than that little dust hole they had come through. It was not only possible, it was likely.

Angel glanced at Adam again. He had braced his back against the rock wall and his feet against the boulder, trying to push it over the edge. As she watched, the boulder slid a few inches along the muddy ground. He would have cleared the path before long, and if she was going to do this thing, she would have to do it now.

Her mouth went dry with anticipation and nervousness. It would be so easy. She deserved this. It was hers and she had nothing left and she *deserved* it.

Adam's attention was focused on his work. Through the rain she could see his face straining and his muscles bulging as he applied force to the boulder. He had it almost to the edge now, and bent down, bracing his legs to push it the rest of the way. If the ground hadn't been so slippery the job would have taken a lot longer, but as it was he would be finished in only a few more minutes. He wasn't looking at her. He couldn't see her behind the horses even if he did happen to glance her way.

Swallowing hard, watching Adam out of the corner of her eye, Angel slid her hand over the horse's neck, reassuring it with a stroke, and then down to the saddlebag. Her fingers were numb with cold and slippery with rain as she fumbled with the buckle. The wet leather stuck. She tugged it open. She slipped her hand inside.

It was only a flash of movement, a half-choked cry or grunt of surprise, followed by a scrambling, crashing sound. She jerked her hand out of the bag guiltily and whirled around just in time to see the boulder tumble over the edge and Adam, his boots losing their purchase in the mud, slip forward, plunging after it.

She supposed she screamed. There was no other explanation for that high ringing sound in her ears. But for the longest time she couldn't move; her feet were rooted to the ground while rain pounded on her hat and blurred her eyes and she stared at the place where Adam had been, expecting him to reappear again, expecting the next flash of lightning to show her that it had never happened at all.

But thunder cracked and lightning flashed, jolting her out of her paralysis, and Adam was not there. She dropped the reins and stumbled forward, slipping once in the mud and going to her knees. "Adam!"

There was no answer.

It couldn't be. It couldn't end like this, not after all they had been through. He couldn't be dead, he *couldn't* be.

"*Adam!*" She reached the edge of the ledge and felt her own boots begin to slip in the slick track left by Adam's fall; she flung herself back just in time to stop herself from tumbling over the edge. Her heart was pounding, shattering in her chest as she dropped to her belly and inched forward to the edge.

Beyond her was a tangle of rocks and ragged growth, dropping down so far and so dramatically that she couldn't see the bottom through the pounding rain. It was as though God had cut a hunk out of the world with a meat cleaver, scooped out the remains, and left nothing but ragged edges to mark his passing. Just looking made Angel dizzy, and she dug her fingers into the ground in desperation and fear.

And then there was a movement below and to the left of her.

"Adam!"

She never knew whether she cried the word or only breathed it as relief washed through her and took her strength. He had caught the root of a scrubby pine tree and was holding on grimly. His face was streaked with mud and blood and the tracks of rain, and there was a gash in the arm of his coat. But he was alive. Against all odds, by a miracle she couldn't name, *he was alive*.

She moved toward him quickly, stretching out on her belly again, reaching out one arm. He was not more than three feet below her. "Grab on!" she cried. "You can reach me!"

He shook his head, and his reply was punctuated with gasps of exertion and desperation. "You're not—strong enough! I'll pull you—over too!"

"I'm strong enough! I can do it!" She stretched out her arm farther, holding on to the cliff edge as tightly as she could with the other hand. "Take my hand!"

Holding on to the root, Adam got his feet under him against the cliff wall, and tried to push himself upward. If only he could straighten his knees, his shoulders would be almost within reach. She could steady him while he grabbed on to the ledge and pulled himself over.

Angel gritted her teeth, straining to help him as he began to straighten his legs, pushing himself upward. But the extra pressure applied to the root was too much, and Angel saw it begin to loosen.

"Take my hand!" she screamed at him.

A clatter of loose rocks pulled away from the root and Adam lost the purchase of his feet on the cliff wall. He flung his hand upward and Angel grabbed it, winding her fingers into his coat sleeve as he closed his hand around her wrist. The momentum of his sudden weight jerked her forward and lashed through every muscle of her body, but she braced herself and held on desperately to the ledge with her other hand. But she couldn't pull him up. She would have to let go to do that, and if she did they both would fall.

Adam braced his feet against the wall again, trying to relieve her of some of his weight, but even then she could feel herself slipping, inch by inch, closer to the edge. Her arm was numb and a hot ribbon of pain seized her spine and her legs; a few more pebbles gave way at the base of the root Adam was holding.

Tears mingled with the rain on her face and she cried, "Hold on, Adam. Use me to climb. You can do it!"

He shook his head. His face was pale, his lips tightly set. "Let me go."

"No!"

The root gave way again and he lurched down a few inches, sending a wrenching avalanche of pain through Angel's body. She cried out. Her breasts were over the edge now, and the root to which Adam held was attached to the mountain face by only a few stubborn feeders.

"Goddammit, it's going to give!" he shouted. "Let me go!"

"*No!*"

Suddenly he wrenched his hand away, kicking out with his feet, and the root pulled free of the mountain. Angel screamed, and the scream seemed to go on and on as she watched him fall—tumbling over, slipping out into the void, his body growing smaller and smaller against the jagged edges of the cliff face, the looming chasm below . . .

Except that he didn't fall. He *jumped*. He tucked his legs beneath him and lowered his head, and his feet struck the edge of a narrow, shrub-covered cliff about six feet below. His shoulder bounced against the wall, flinging him forward; he lunged back and struck his head. He collapsed onto the ledge.

Angel's scream turned into a sob—of hope, or despair, or desperation. "Adam!"

There was no response except a booming, rolling shudder of thunder and the lashing torrent of rain in her face.

She dragged her hands across her face to clear her eyes and leaned over the ledge, too far for safety but not caring anymore.

"Adam!"

He moved, pushing himself to a half-crouch, weakly lifting his hand to her.

Sobbing, gasping, Angel pulled herself back from the ledge and scrambled to her feet. She stumbled toward the horses, half-expecting them to have bolted through the storm by now. But they were still there, huddled against the rock wall, their heads down, looking miserable. Her hands were shaking so badly that she could hardly control the movements, and she couldn't see through the driving pellets of rain and her own hot tears. But, somehow she got the rope uncoiled from Adam's saddle and grabbed the bridle of his horse, urging him forward.

She secured the knot around the pommel as well as she could; she would hold it with her own hands if she had to. Adam was not going to die down there all alone in this wilderness with no one to help him. Not after all this. Not *now*.

She tossed the rope over the ledge. "Adam! Can you hold it? Try! Please try!"

Adam got to his feet with what appeared to be a great effort, his back against the wall, and reached out for the rope. It was swinging too far away. Angel pulled it back, sobbing with frustration, and tossed it down again. This time he caught it.

She watched as he circled the rope beneath his arms and knotted it. It seemed to take forever. At last he lifted his hand to her. His voice sounded weak, muffled by the rain. "All right! I've got it!"

Angel ran back to the horse and grabbed his bridle. The horse took a few backward steps and then balked, frightened by what it couldn't see. "Move, blast you!" Angel screamed at the animal. "Back up!" The horse snorted and tossed its head, and Angel slapped it forcefully on the neck. The horse took a few more hesitant backward steps.

It was like that for what seemed like hours. A step backward, stop, another halting step. And the worst was that Angel couldn't see. She struggled with the stubborn horse, she cursed and kicked and pulled at it, and she couldn't see what was happening to Adam. She couldn't hear him if he called to her. She wouldn't know if the rope began to fray or the knot to loosen until there was a sudden slack in the rope . . .

And then the rope went slack. She saw it fall and curl in a muddy puddle at her feet and her heart stopped. She turned.

Adam was coming toward her, limping a little, bruised and muddied and bowed with exhaustion, but alive.

With a cry, Angel ran to him. Heedless of his injuries she flung herself against him. His arms went around her and they held each other with ferocious, bone-crushing strength, clinging to each other while the rain pounded down on them and the thunder cracked around them, until the storm, at last, passed away.

A few hundred yards farther the ledge widened to a comfortable degree, and they found shelter beneath a rock overhang. Angel built a fire at the mouth of the indention and they sat close to it, drying their clothes and watching the curtain of rain that sealed them in grow fainter and foggier. Occasionally a raindrop would splatter onto the hot sticks with a sizzling sound, and the steady sigh and patter of the rain seemed to seal them in, protecting them.

Adam reached for the coffee ration in his saddlebag and then paused, his hand on the open flap of the bag. Angel returned from the opening of the shelter, where she had collected rainwater in the coffeepot.

"You should take off those wet boots," she advised. "They'll dry faster by the fire."

Adam withdrew the cross from his saddlebag. "You had your chance," he said. "Why didn't you take it?"

Angel dipped a cloth into the coffeepot and wrung it out. "Seems like I'm forever cleaning you up," she said, beginning to wipe away the dried mud and blood from the cut on his forehead.

Adam stopped her hand. His eyes were deep blue, almost black, as he looked at her, and his voice was very quiet. "You could have left me there."

Angel met his eyes and answered steadily, without evasion, "No, I couldn't."

Angel dropped the hand that was holding the cloth to her lap and glanced down at it. "I don't know. Maybe— maybe there is something special about that cross." She looked at him again. "I was going to take it. I had it all planned out. And then you fell and—you should be dead, but you're not. I should have stolen it, but I couldn't." She shrugged. "I don't know."

Adam lifted his hand and touched her hair, cupping the rain-damp curls lightly.

There was nothing awkward about the gesture, nothing startling. The changes that had taken place between them in the past hour were subtle but sure, and there was no denying them. Too many choices had been made to turn back now; too many certainties had been uncovered to allow either of them to retreat again.

Adam looked at her, his face streaked with mud, his hair still dark with rain, and Angel saw in that face all she had ever wanted or needed or could treasure in her life. But in his eyes she saw hope battling with need, trust struggling with suspicion, and she understood, because the same war was taking place within her. She wanted so much and expected so little; the discoveries they were making about themselves were still too new to be embraced without caution.

Then Adam dropped his hand and turned his face a little away. "Ah, Angel," he said softly, "I don't know what to do with you."

And that, then, was the final truth, and Angel could no longer avoid it. She said quietly, "It's because of her, isn't it? My mother. You're in love with her."

The look of surprise in his eyes was unfeigned, but beneath it there was something else—a touch of guilt, and it was the last thing Angel wanted to see. Pain clutched at her throat, and she turned away.

"Hand me that coffee," she said dully. "I'll put some on to brew while we wait out the storm."

Adam said, "Angel, let me explain—"

"No." Her voice was a little shrill, a mere reflection of the fiery pins and needles that were scraping along the paths of her nerves, and she deliberately tried to calm it. Still, her words came too quickly, a little breathlessly, and she was afraid that if she stopped talking she would burst into tears, and she refused to do that.

"No, it's all right, I understand. I've known it from the

first. The way you talk about her, the way you look when you talk about her——I know, I've always known. It doesn't matter. It's better this way. She wouldn't want me around, and neither would you, I understand that. Give me the coffee.''

Adam seemed not to have an answer. Angel couldn't look at his face, couldn't bear to see that final, insurmountable admission of truth there, the one thing she could never fight, the one thing they could never overcome. Adam turned slowly to take the coffee from his saddlebags and Angel was glad, because if he had spoken to her, had continued to look at her for another moment, she knew her control would snap, all the pain and humiliation and betrayal would come flooding out of her, and it would be a vile, horrible, helpless thing that would shame her and win him nothing but her pity. She couldn't stand it if he pitied her.

And then his shoulders squared, and he said softly, ''No.''

He turned back to her, and Angel tried to avoid his eyes but he grasped her chin, making her look at him. She pressed her lips tightly together, trying to hold back the tears, and jerked away.

He caught her face between his hands, holding it steady, pinning her in his gaze, and his eyes were dark with emotions she didn't understand. ''Listen to me,'' he said intently. ''Once, a long time ago, I fancied I was in love with Consuelo. She never felt that way about me. Never. And over the years I started to realize what I felt for her wasn't love but friendship——''

''Don't,'' Angel said hoarsely, almost begging him. ''Don't lie to me.''

''And then I met you,'' he went on fiercely, as though she

hadn't interrupted, "and I saw that—" He drew a breath and released it, almost as though he was surprised by the course of his thoughts. "That all the things I thought I loved about Consuelo were just a shadow of what's real about you. Your spirit, your courage, the way you move and hold your head, the way your eyes flash when somebody goes against you—the way you talk, even the way you *breathe*, dammit, that's what I love!"

She drank in those words like a parched desert creature thirsting for rain. She needed them so badly that the ache was in her skin, her muscles, the very marrow of her bones, and she was desperate to believe them. Yet she was afraid.

She tried once again to turn her head away but he held it firm. His voice was lower now, edged with a faint trace of huskiness, as his eyes searched hers—probing yet tender, hesitant but strong, as though he were trying to burn his words into her brain. "I'll tell you what else I love," he said. "The way you fight. Your stubbornness. The way you get an idea in your head and you don't give up, even if it's an idea I don't like—even if it means lying and cheating and stealing I don't care, because that's *you*, and it's a part of what I love. Can you understand that?"

She shook her head slowly, but there was a heat in her cheeks, and a burning in her eyes—tears, but they were tears of joy, of wonder, of awe. He meant it, she could see it in his eyes, feel it in his touch. He didn't hate her at all. He loved her.

"I never understand you," she whispered.

And then he kissed her, and the rain faded away, the hurt and doubt and pain of all these past days faded away; and the heat of the fire paled in comparison to the heat that exploded inside her. Joy, pure and unadulterated, need that sharpened to an agonized pinpoint and then blossomed like overblown petals against a clear blue sky, bigger than life, more vibrant than wanting . . . Adam's touch, Adam's taste, Adam blending into her and making her whole.

They sank back onto the ground in a blur of weakness and spiraling colors. His hands traced paths of heat beneath her damp clothing; she greedily, instinctively sought the contours of his muscles and the slickness of his skin as she pushed away the hindering fabric that separated her from him. Their merging was swift and poignant yet wholly natural; a coming home, a rejoining of two souls that had only been temporarily separated, a finding of what was lost, a fulfilling of need so consuming that, in its completion, it was without measure. Its power was like the wind that sweeps across the desert, wiping out everything in its path and changing the face of the land; like an island rising from the ocean in an explosion of volcanic fire and ash; like the floodwaters that carve away whole mountainsides and leave the world born anew. They became one and the strength of their oneness was fire and wind; it wiped away the past and left them reborn.

Afterward they lay in the tangle of their clothing, holding each other tightly; stroking occasionally or touching fingers to lips, but mostly just holding each other and listening to the sound of their mingled breathing and blending heartbeats. *I am not alone*, Angel thought. *Whatever happens now, I'll never be alone again.* And the strange thing was, she had known that from the beginning. Adam was the other half of her—good where she was bad, steady where she was impetuous, strong where she was weak—and they needed each other, just like sunshine needs the rain or nighttime needs the day. It was so simple. And so beautifully clear.

After a long time, she murmured, "I still think you're crazy, you know."

She thought she felt him smile against her hair. "I know."

She lifted her face a little, looking at him anxiously. "But I think you're right, too. And I guess . . . that's why I can't help loving you."

He stroked her hair. "Angel," he said quietly, "I guess you know I'd do just about anything for you right now. All you have to do is ask, and I'd get it done, I'm that scared of losing you again. But I need you to tell me—what do you want?"

It did not take her very long at all to reply. "I want to get rid of that cross. You were right the first time, we don't need it, and I would have agreed with you a lot sooner if you hadn't made me so mad. And then I want to go to that ranch of yours, and I want you to marry me like a decent man would a decent woman; that's all I ever wanted. Right from the very first that's all I wanted."

She felt his deep inhalation, and his fingers were strong on her cheek as they turned her face to his. He kissed her. "Me too," he said softly. "That's all I ever wanted too."

And then he held her gaze, his eyes asking the question before he spoke. "And your mother? Will you see her first? Do you want to?"

This time Angel's answer was a little slower in coming. This was the first time she had ever faced that question honestly, and it was difficult to break down the barrier that had guarded the most vulnerable parts of her for so long. "I—want to see her," she admitted. Her voice was a little muffled. "I guess I've wanted that since the first day you told me about her. I just . . .'' She looked up at him hesitantly and forced herself to go on. "Maybe she won't like me. She doesn't know me, like you do, and—maybe she's like me, building up all these pictures in her head over the years about what I'd be like, just like I built up pictures of her. Maybe she'll be disappointed.''

Adam simply smiled, tenderly and adoringly, and cupped his fingers beneath her chin. "I know there's no way I can make you believe this, you're going to have to see for yourself. She already knows you, Angel—better than I do, better than even you do yourself. Because she *was* you, twenty years ago. She'll like you, honey.'' He leaned forward and kissed her lightly on the forehead. "That I can guarantee you.''

Angel lowered her eyes. "I've made a lot of mistakes. Done some bad things.''

"So has she,'' Adam responded quietly. "I guess maybe nobody in the world knows more about making mistakes than Consuelo Gomez. And I think maybe that's why you two need each other.''

After a moment Angel forced a weak smile and glanced at him again. "I hope you're right.''

1871

Dry Wells had not changed much in three years, but Consuelo had not expected it to. Towns like that didn't change, just as women like her didn't change.

The last three years had been hard for her. She had tried, desperately, but there was only one kind of work for a girl such as she, and she had never been able to put enough money together to buy more than a meal, not in all this time.

Her baby was gone.

Her little Angel of the perfect skin and raven's hair and deep, vibrant blue eyes—Camp Meredith's eyes—was dead, or sent away, no one would tell her. She had gone back for her, just as she'd promised, and it hadn't mattered that she had no money, hadn't mattered about her pride or her independence. She would take her to Camp and make him acknowledge her, she would plead if she had to and threaten if she must, but she would have her baby with her. She would take care of her.

There had been a fire at the mission more than a year before she arrived. No one was left. The few children who survived had been shipped to orphanages around the country, the nuns reassigned. In her heart Consuelo knew that her child had survived; she would have felt the stab of truth like a knife in her gut if she had not. But it didn't matter, for to Consuelo she was lost. And she could only hope that her Angel, wherever she was, was happy, and well taken care of, and loved. . . .

She had been drawn to Dry Wells like a magnet, perhaps because she had no place left to go, perhaps for deeper reasons. She had no idea whether Camp Meredith was still there, or whether his wife had come out to live with him, or whether he would remember her at all. But she had to come back.

She found him in a saloon. It was just as she remembered it: sawdust floors, greasy tables, scarred bar. And one man leaning against the bar, a glass in his hand. There were one or two gray hairs in that vibrant mane of red, and his beard was thicker, his skin darker. But he was just as tall as ever, just as broad-shouldered and powerful, and when she looked at him her heart stopped and then swelled to bursting with longing.

She didn't say a word. He turned slowly, and looked at her, and the emotion that surged between them was like a physical thing, audible to the ear and hot to the touch. It seemed to suck all the air out of the room and all the motion out of the world; they were frozen there, eight feet apart but locked body and soul to each other.

And then he began to cross the room toward her. He swept her into his arms and his embrace was fierce and strong, tight enough to bruise. But Consuelo didn't care, she held him just as fiercely, and inside she managed only one desperate prayer: *Don't let me do this. Don't let me lose myself to this man, not again* . . . .

But it was a futile prayer. She was lost already.

He pushed her away, holding her face, staring intently into her eyes. And then his gaze fell upon the scar that marked her cheek and she saw the pain lash through him and felt a small satisfaction from it.

He traced the scar lightly with his fingertip, punishing himself with the touch, and then he let his hand drop. "Connie," he said hoarsely. "Connie, you're back." His eyes were eager and searching, as though hardly daring to believe what he saw. "I've missed you, girl. I thought—I thought you wouldn't forgive me."

"I can't forgive you, Camp," she said softly. "But I can't—stay away from you either."

His hands tightened on her arms. "You're back now, that's all that matters."

She wanted then to tell him about their child, wanted it

more than anything in the world. Camp, so strong, so powerful, could make everything all right. He would want his daughter, he would find her....

But then Camp rushed on, "So much has happened. My wife—my wife's dead, Connie. But my litle girl, she's here now. Living at the ranch. Ah, she's a fine girl, Connie." His shoulders swelled with pride, and his eyes took on a light she had never seen before. "You're gonna like her. A real Meredith, she is."

And then Consuelo knew. Camp Meredith had a daughter. A fine, redheaded daughter by his fine, cultured Virginian wife; he would have no use for the offspring of a half-breed whore. She would never tell him about her Angel. He would never know what he had lost, and that would be her punishment to him. That she was punishing herself as well did not matter. Angel would be hers, and hers alone, until her grave.

"But she needs a woman's touch, Connie," Camp said. "All girls do. And now that you're back, you come on up to the ranch, you—"

"Are you asking me to marry you?"

A change came over his face. "Is that what you want?"

She had her answer, and her smile was bitter. "No. Not anymore. But I won't live in your ranch house and raise your daughter for you like a squaw. I'm not the girl I was three years ago, Camp Meredith. I'm not yours anymore."

She started to turn away, but he caught her arm. His grip was hard, and there was something in his face that she had never seen before. It closely resembled desperation.

"You're not walking out! You're not leaving me again!" He lowered his voice until it took on a husky edge, and his fingers pressed so hard she could feel the imprint on the bones of her arm. "I need you, Connie. I've always needed you, you know that. You can't leave me again."

Her heart was twisting in her chest. She wanted to throw herself upon him, to pour out her need for him, to promise him anything. But she lifted her chin and said quietly, "I'm not going back to being a saloon girl, Camp. I'm not going back to being your whore. I deserve more than that. I *need* more than that."

"Hell, I'll buy the saloon for you! You can be anything you want, have anything you want, just—" His voice lowered another fraction, almost breaking. "Don't leave me. Connie, don't do that."

She looked at him, and she knew why she had come back. She had never really left him at all, and she couldn't do it now. She was bound to him, now and forever, and there was nothing she could do to change that. She loved him. She wasn't proud of it, or happy about it, but she could not stop it. She was his, and he was hers, for all time.

She loved him, but she could not forgive him. And the one thing that could have brought them completely together was now the secret that would keep them forever apart.

Angel. Her Angel. Because someday Consuelo would find her and bring her home. She would love her and protect her and no one would ever call her daughter a half-breed whore.

But until then, there was Camp, without whom she could not survive.

She looked at him quietly for a long time. And then she said, "I'll stay."

CHAPTER

Nineteen

CASEY could not believe his luck. It had been hell, trying to make time through the mountains, riding long after it was too dark to be safe, stumbling along where there wasn't even a trail. By all odds, he should never even have spotted them; in fact, he should have lost them back in San Francisco. But over and over again luck had intervened, and now he knew not only where they were headed; he had them in his sights.

He had worried that if they managed to get the cross back to the village, it wouldn't be so easy to steal again. He didn't want a shoot-out in the middle of a street thronged by Indians, not even with an extra gun riding by his side. But he had resigned himself to the fact that that was how it was going to be—and then he spotted them.

He had spotted fresh horse droppings early that morning,

and even then he couldn't believe his quarry was that close. By his figuring, they should have been a day or more ahead, but he and Briggs had ridden through the storm yesterday, while they must have waited it out. He took a chance that that was exactly what they had done, and he chose a parallel, upward course around the mountain that—if his luck held—would bring him out above and in front of the two riders.

His luck held. They were in high country now, distinguished by flat mountain meadows and jagged rock overhangs. Casey sat atop a wooded, rocky outcropping and looked back. About four hundred yards below and two hundred yards behind he could see them, riding side by side on the open plain, resting easy in the saddle and walking their horses just as though they were on their way to a Sunday picnic. Casey barely repressed a hoot of triumph.

"We got 'em now, Briggs," he said softly. "We damn sure got 'em."

Briggs folded his hands on the pommel and leaned forward, his narrowed eyes scanning the two people below. Briggs was a man of few words, and in that Casey had again been lucky.

"We gonna kill both of 'em?"

Casey's face tightened grimly. "Damn right. Shoot 'em right out of the saddle."

Briggs nodded. "Just one thing we ain't discussed." He kept his eyes on the two below. "How're we fixin' to divide up this cross?"

Casey had an answer for that, the same one he had given Jenks—and long ago a man named Riley, who lay dead in a barn. "We got to sell it first. Then it's right down the middle, fifty-fifty, fair and square."

Again Briggs nodded. "Best get to it, then." He nudged his horse down the deer path that curved toward the meadow.

Casey let him take the lead. All in all, he figured he could have done worse when it came to picking a partner at the last minute like that. Luck had been with him, and Briggs was a pretty good man. It was a shame he was going to have to kill him.

Adam was uneasy. He did not believe that he had lost the pursuit of whoever was following him, nor did he believe that he had been mistaken about being followed. Yesterday, before the storm, he was certain that the stalker had still been on the trail. Today there had been no sign.

He supposed that whoever was following him might have run into an accident, or even a landslide like the one that had almost killed him yesterday. But it seemed to him that anybody who had been able to track them this far wouldn't have that kind of luck. He was still out there, somewhere. The fact that Adam didn't know where was what worried him.

He and Angel weren't far from the village. Ten miles, maybe. Another night on the trail, and they would reach it before noon tomorrow. It couldn't be soon enough for Adam. Yesterday, before the storm, he had wanted to drag out the trip as long as possible. But now he just wanted to get Angel safely out of here as quickly as possible.

"Adam, look."

Angel had nudged her horse over to one of the abandoned mine shafts. They were in the heart of mining country now, and Adam had been amazed by the network of holes and tunnels that defaced the mountainside. Some were elaborate, with tracks for ore carts and heavy shoring, while others were mere bore holes in the rock. This one was large enough to have been a railroad tunnel, crisscrossed with iron tracks, and the abandoned ore cart outside was almost half the size of a rail car.

"If they were getting enough ore out to fill that car, I wonder why they closed the mine," Angel said.

"Maybe it played out." He didn't want to linger here, but he didn't want to alarm Angel with the knowledge that they were being followed, either.

"Or maybe the tunnel goes all the way through the mountain," Angel suggested. "That man back at the store said the reason they cut the road to the village was because they were mining there. Maybe the real ore is on the other side—or they thought it was, anyhow. That's why all these shafts are up here in the middle of nothing—they cut clear through."

"Maybe." Adam tried not to let his impatience show. "Listen, Angel—"

The first shot skimmed off the rock wall above the mine shaft and left a white scar there. Angel stared at it uncomprehendingly; for an infinite moment they both were shocked beyond reaction, holding on to their startled, rearing horses, perfect targets for an unknown assailant. The second shot tore a hunk out of Angel's jacket, knocking her sideways in the saddle. And then Adam was on his feet, abandoning his horse, dragging her from the saddle, pulling her into the mine shaft. Two more bullets dodged their feet as they stumbled inside. Adam pushed Angel to the wall and fired two blind shots from his six-shooter into the daylight outside.

There was no return fire. Adam flattened himself against the wall, and for a long time there was nothing but the sound of his own harsh breathing and Angel's, and water dripping somewhere far in the distance. It was pitch black inside, cold and earthy-smelling.

Angel whispered frantically, "Adam!"

"Here," he answered swiftly. He reached out his hand, found her, and drew her into the circle of his arm. "Are you all right? Are you hurt?"

She shook her head against his shoulder. "Did they go away?" Her voice sounded high and tight. "Did you hit one of them, or scare them away?"

"No." He hated the way his voice echoed hollowly in the blackness. He hated what he had to say to her now, but he wasn't going to lie to her. If he had told her the truth about being followed before this, they might not have had such a close call. They might not be trapped now. "I think they're coming closer. That's what I'd be doing. They've got us where they want us."

She was silent, seeming to accept this. Her voice was a little stronger as she said, "We need light. Do you have any matches?"

He shook his head. "No. We strike a match in here and we only give them something to shoot at. Don't look at the opening. Let your eyes adjust to the dark."

"Adam, we can't let them come in here! It's dark, we can't see, we—"

He tightened his arm around her, and he could feel the tremors in her shoulders. "They won't come in here. They wouldn't be able to see either. But they might start firing just on principle. Stay close to the wall."

"I'm not going anywhere," she whispered, winding her fingers into his jacket.

Adam stared straight ahead, forcing his eyes to adjust to shades of black and gray, trying to think. They'd move closer, all right. Then they'd start firing at the mine entrance, pinning them in. On the other hand, if they got close enough, Adam would have the advantage—he would be able to see them, but they couldn't see him. He might be able to pick them off . . . if they got close enough.

The least he could do was hold them off. Angel was right. They couldn't let them gain access to the mine; it would be slaughter. As long as he kept firing they wouldn't come in . . . But the only ammunition he had was on his belt, and his rifle was still strapped to the saddle of his horse.

"Angel," he said. "I've got to go out there."

"No!" Staring up at him in the darkness, she could feel him stiffen. "You're crazy! You don't know where they are, or how many, or—"

"I've got to get my rifle," he explained, still breathing hard. "And my saddlebags. We're under siege here; they know that without food or water they can keep us pinned down as long as they like."

"But the horses might not even be there! They probably ran away when—"

"Let's find out." He started inching toward the entrance of the mine.

Angel was close beside him, her fingers digging into his arm, even when they were close enough to the entrance for the light to guide their way. He stayed flat against the wall, and kept her back, too. The silence from outside was profound.

And then he heard what he had been waiting for. The

jingle of a bridle, the snuffle of horses. Their mounts were still there.

"They're waiting," Angel whispered. "They're just waiting for you to do something like this."

"Or they haven't gotten into position yet. This might be the only chance we get."

"Adam, don't—"

He pressed the revolver into her hand. "Don't shoot unless you have to. Don't draw any attention to me. And stay against the wall."

He pulled his arm away from her and for a moment he was silhouetted in sharp relief in the patch of daylight at the entrance. Then he slipped away.

Angel licked at the sweat that filmed her upper lip and shivered in the cold. The revolver felt heavy and unwieldy in her hand, but she knew how to use it. And she wasn't going to stay here in the dark while Adam risked his life out there. She cocked the hammer on the revolver and moved forward.

Adam's horse was about ten feet away, munching grass in the meadow. It had been too much to hope for that the animal would have stayed nearby and Adam could have used the mountain face for cover. He would have to make a run for it across open ground.

He couldn't see anybody, but there were a thousand places for a man to hide up here. Behind that clump of bushes, on the other side of that rise, behind a hundred boulders, or even on the ledge above his head. Without his rifle and saddlebags, he and Angel didn't have a chance. He ducked low and broke into a run.

He expected to feel the slam of a bullet in the next second, or the next. But he was almost to the horse before the first shot skittered into the ground to the left of him. Angel returned fire. He thought with a fierce surge of pride, *Good girl!* and flung himself at the horse.

He could tell where the shots were coming from now and he used the animal for cover as he jerked off the rifle and the saddlebags. He cocked the rifle and fired in the general direction of the gunfire. The horse bolted, and he had to trust Angel to keep the gunmen busy as he broke for the shelter of the mine.

There were two of them, he could tell that much. They were using rifles, not six-shooters, so they weren't close enough for Angel's fire to do any good. But if Adam could just see where, exactly they were...

Just before the mine entrance, Adam paused and half-turned, sweeping the countryside with his eyes. It was an instant, nothing more, and then something slammed into his back, knocking him off his feet. He heard Angel scream, and he was up again before he drew another breath, diving into the mine, grabbing Angel and shoving her back.

"Move!" he gasped. "Dammit, I told you to stay back! Run!"

"You're hurt—"

"Run!" He pushed her hard, and they both stumbled back into the depths of the mine.

About twenty feet back into the darkness, Adam stopped and sagged against the wall. He let the saddlebags drop to the ground as he struggled to regain his breath. "Angel, listen," he managed after a moment. "They've got us pinned in here pretty good. We can hold them off, but that's all we can do, and sooner or later we're going to run out of ammunition. Then they'll come in."

Angel's voice sounded surprisingly strong; stronger than

his, and reasonable. "Then we have to find a way out of here. Some way they can't see."

Adam nodded, still struggling for breath. "These mines—they always have more than one entrance, don't they?"

"Usually." She sounded a little doubtful. "But it might be boarded up, or caved in—"

"Then an air shaft, something. We need an ace in the hole." He drew a deep breath and was surprised by a dull ache in his chest. "You're going to have to stay here. If you hear anything from the entrance, shoot. I'm going to have a look around."

He expected an argument from her. He could barely distinguish her face, a blur of white against the shadows, upturned to him and without expression. Then she said simply, "Did you bring your rope?"

"What?"

She knelt down, feeling around on the ground for where he had dropped his saddlebags. "You can't go back there without a rope. You might not be able to get back." She found the rope, which he had jerked off the pommel with everything else he could unloosen, and handed one end of it to him.

"Good thinking," he admitted. He should have thought of it himself, but his thinking seemed to be getting fuzzy. Then he touched her cheek and smiled. "Glad I've got you along."

"Yeah." Her voice was husky. "Me too."

He wanted to draw her into his arms and hold her forever in the dark. Their chances weren't good. They had come so far and still she might be snatched away from him, and he wanted to hold her. But he made himself drop his hand, and he said strongly, "Do you know how to use a rifle?"

"Some."

He doubted that she would admit it if she had never held one in her life. He shifted the weapon to her hands. "It doesn't matter. You fire this thing and you'll blow whatever's in your way to kingdom come. *Stay here*. You're close enough to hear if they start coming in, and then you just start firing. Don't let them get close enough to have to use the pistol."

"I won't."

He smiled again in the dark and, catching her face in his hand, kissed her hard on the lips. "I won't be long."

"Adam—" She wanted to catch his arm, to pull him back, to argue with him. She didn't want him to leave her, didn't want to feel as though this might be the last time she would see him.

But when he hesitated, she said only, "I'll be here."

It was foolish to worry. He would be back. After all, he only had a couple of hundred feet of rope.

So she shifted the rifle under her arm, took the other end of rope in her hand, and watched him walk off into the darkness.

When Adam was within five feet of the end of the rope, he let his end drop to the ground. That way Angel wouldn't feel the tautening as he reached the end, and would never know how far he had gone. He had moved cautiously, staying against the wall, but so far the tunnel seemed to be a straight shot. Its walls narrowed in places; at others he had to stoop to get through, but he had felt no offshoots or forks.

He was far enough from the mine entrance to risk lighting

a match, and he did so, holding it aloft and glancing away from the glare. He caught his breath sharply when he glanced down.

Less than half a step to the right of him was a sheer drop into blackness. Another step and he might have gone over. He edged away from the gap and held the match higher. It looked as though somebody had tried to drill another tunnel and a whole section of the mountain had given way. Perhaps that was why the mine had been abandoned.

Curious, he dropped the match over the edge. It went out immediately, of course, and when he tossed a pebble over he never did hear it hit the bottom.

He struck another match and moved on.

By the time he had gone another hundred yards the pain in his shoulder was intense, and he could feel blood running down his side. He knew he'd been shot, he'd known it the minute it happened, but there was nothing that could be done about it now. The first thing, the only thing, was to find some way out, or some place to defend, or else Angel . . .

He didn't like leaving her alone. His ears strained over the hiss of his own stertorous breathing for the sound of gunfire—and if he heard it, would he be able to reach her in time? But he had to do this thing. He couldn't send her back here, through the tunnel.

He tried to save his matches, knowing he'd need them for the walk back. He found himself needing to rest more often, and by the time he'd lit his tenth match his head was spinning so badly he had to shake it out and lean back against the wall until the vertigo passed. He went another five or six yards in the dark, and struck the last match he'd allotted himself.

Air was coming from somewhere. He could smell it, and see it in the slight flickering of the flame whenever he lit a match. There was an opening somewhere up ahead, but it could be miles away, it might be only six inches wide. He couldn't go much farther, but he couldn't return to Angel with no hope. Then he glanced down, and he could hardly believe what he saw.

Footprints were tracked into the dust in front of where he stood. And they were leading away from him.

Adam had been gone for hours. A small bit of logic within Angel told her that that couldn't possibly be so—it wouldn't take him more than a few minutes to go to the end of the rope—but a bigger part, the part that was a child sitting in the dark, buried underground, listening to the water drip far away and fighting back panic with all her strength, knew he was gone forever.

She held on tightly to her end of the rope. It should have tautened by now. It *should* have. And then it should have slacked again as he turned back. She kept her face turned toward the entranceway. She couldn't really see the light outside, just a lighter patch of gray, but she knew it was there. She wasn't really buried underground.

It was a big tunnel. At least there was that. The walls weren't squeezing against her on every side, and she wouldn't bump her head if she looked up. And there was lots of air. She was close to the entrance. If she had to, she could run . . .

He had been gone too long. What if he'd had an accident? What if the rope had broken? What if he was lost?

"Adam?" she called out softly. And then, more sharply, "Adam!"

There was no answer but her own echo.

Tentatively, she tugged at the rope. It gave easily. She pulled again, and there was no resistance. There was no one on the other end of the rope.

Her heart felt like a water-filled pouch expanding and releasing and expanding again, filling up her chest, crowding into her throat. Droplets of sweat formed on her forehead and trickled from her armpits, while her fingers were numb with cold. She stared into the darkness where Adam had gone.

"Adam," she whispered hoarsely.

She had to go after him. There were rats in the tunnels, and falling rocks, and dirt slides that could suck out all the air in an instant. It was dark and cold and wet, and who knew what else was in the tunnel? But Adam was there, all alone. . . .

Desperately she looked back toward the patch of gray that marked the entrance. Out there were men who would shoot her down the minute she stepped into the light. But she wasn't afraid of them. She was afraid of what she might find in the tunnel.

She wanted to run toward the light, to get out of this awful place, and she didn't care what happened then. She couldn't *think* here. She couldn't breathe.

She took a stumbling half-step toward the entrance, then heard a sound behind her. She whirled, clumsily angling the rifle into position, and in her panic she might have shot him had he not called out her name just then.

Angel let the rifle clatter to the ground and ran toward the shadow in the darkness, flinging herself against Adam. "I was so worried—thank God—"

But his returned embrace was weak, his breathing labored. She felt something wet on her hands, soaking through his clothes, and the relief she felt was stabbed through with alarm.

"Adam, what's wrong?"

"Nothing. Listen—"

"It's blood!" she cried. "You're hurt—"

"Listen to me!" He forced strength into his voice and his hands closed hard around her arms. "Listen," he repeated more calmly. He was still breathing raggedly, but his words were distinct. "You were right. The tunnel goes straight through—probably comes out right by the village. There were footprints in the ground. I don't know how old they were, but we've got to take the chance. Angel . . ."

He sagged and Angel quickly pressed her body against him, supporting him, easing him to the ground. His coat was wet with blood.

She propped him against the wall and began to peel away the layers of his clothing, examining by touch rather than sight. She felt his sharp inhalation of pain as her fingers skated over the ragged edges of the wound just beneath his shoulder blade, and her stomach twisted into a breathless knot.

"Oh, Adam," she whispered. "You shouldn't have gone on. You've lost so much blood . . ."

Even as she spoke she was pulling off her coat, ripping at the wool lining with shaking fingers.

"I didn't—know it was this bad."

A shot skidded across the entrance of the cave, making

both of them jerk. It was followed by another, and another. The men were moving closer.

Adam fumbled for the rifle Angel had dropped.

"No—leave it! You can't—"

"We've got to return fire! Otherwise they'll come in."

Angel took the pistol he had given her and fired blindly toward the light, twice in succession. The noise ricocheted and amplified and exploded in her ears. Trickles of dust scattered from the tunnel's ceiling.

There was more gunfire at the entrance. Angel fired again, then tossed the weapon aside. She returned to trying to bandage Adam's wound, although her efforts were greatly hampered by his attempts to reload the pistol.

"Angel, listen to me," he said. "We can't hold out here forever. I don't know how long this tunnel goes on—or even if it's clear on the other side—but I know I can't make it."

Angel's hands fell still. Her eyes had adjusted to the darkness well enough to see Adam's face; she even imagined she could see his eyes.

"You have to go through without me," he said.

She whispered, "No."

"You have to." She could hear the effort it took for him to keep his voice steady and strong, but it was all but lost in the roaring in her ears. "You have to get out—get help if you can. But *get out*."

"No!" Panic, dry and sharp-clawed, tore its way through her. "No, you can't make me. I won't leave you here, you can't ask me—you can't make me go through the tunnel! Adam, don't make me do that!"

His hand closed around hers. His grip was strong though his fingers were cold. "I have to," he said quietly. "You have to. If you don't, we're both going to die here."

The words sank like stones through the swirling waters of cold fear that surrounded her. She tried to push them away but couldn't. She tried to deny them but couldn't. She tried desperately, through the pounding of her heart and the dry clutching in her throat, to think of some other way, some other hope . . . but she couldn't.

Adam was badly hurt and weak from blood loss. Perhaps they could wait until nightfall, but by then he might be unconscious. By then the horses would surely be gone. If she tried to make a break for it now, in broad daylight, she would almost certainly be shot. Had she been alone, she would have taken that chance, but if she couldn't get help Adam would be left alone there to die.

She had to go through the tunnel. There was no other way.

She finished packing his wound as best she could, then brought his rifle and saddlebags close to him. "I'll be as quick as I can," she said. Her voice was not quite steady.

"I'll hold them off until I run out of ammunition. That'll give you a good head start. Stay up against the left wall; there's a bad drop-off on the right. And, Angel . . ." He had opened his saddlebags and now reached painfully inside. "Take this with you."

He brought out the cross.

She shrank back as though it were a deadly object, as though the curse attached to it were real instead of a legend, as though he were offering her poison. "No." Her voice was hoarse, and she shook her head violently. "No, I don't want it."

"This is what they're after," he explained patiently. "If they get in here, I don't want to have it on me."

"If they get in here, *give* it to them!" she cried. "I'd throw it outside myself right now if I thought I could get close enough! No, I won't take it. It's caused enough pain and—and dying and it might be the only thing that can buy your life if . . ." She drew a choking breath, and her next words were muffled. "Keep it. Give it back to the Indians yourself."

She started to rise, then turned back. "Adam," she said brokenly. "I do love you."

He caught her fingers and held them briefly against his cheek. "I know."

She drew away from him slowly and started off into the darkness.

CHAPTER

Twenty

CASEY grinned and wiped the sweat from his hatband. "I think we got him, ol' hoss." The return fire from the mine had been sporadic over the last hour, and Casey knew the signs of a man running low on ammunition. Their last five volleys had not been returned. "I surely think we do."

"Could be he's just laying in ambush," suggested Briggs, "waiting to lure us in."

Casey shook his head. His luck was running one hundred percent gold today. "That slug you put in him hurt him bad. He was wasting shots, not thinking right. He's either dead by now or too close to matter."

"There's still the girl."

"Yeah." A greedy look came into Casey's eyes as he

wiped a hand over his mouth. "If she's smart, she saved her last bullet for herself."

"We goin' in, then?"

"Yeah," Casey said grimly. "We're going in. I'm tired of wasting time on these two."

They had been able to get within a few yards of the mouth of the tunnel; flat up against the mountainside, all they had to do was angle their weapons out every once in a while and fire off a round without fear of being hit themselves. Going into that dark place would be different, and they both knew that. But the two people inside were at their mercy; if Casey hadn't been sure of that he never would have gone in.

Casey let Briggs go first.

"You been a mighty big help to me, Briggs," he said sincerely. "I want you to know that. One of the best partners I ever took up with."

And he put a .45 slug into the back of Briggs's head.

"It's just that I ain't never been partial to sharing," he added. He stepped over the body and into the mine.

Angel felt she had been in this dark, evil place for years. Her tears had congealed on her cheeks, and mud encrusted her eyes. Her fingertips were raw from gripping the wall, staying to the left as Adam had warned her. The coldness racked her, from within and without, and sometimes the shudders were so bad that they robbed her of breath; at such times she had to stop and *command* herself to breathe, to hold a picture of Adam in her head, and to remember his warmth and pretend that somehow, some way she would get out of there. And then she had to make herself move on.

It wasn't so bad. The walls weren't crushing her. There was plenty of air. She kept telling herself that. And she kept moving. Because somewhere, back there, Adam was dying.

At first she could hear the gunfire. Every explosion rocketed through her body as though the bullet had penetrated her flesh, and she thought, *Was that it? Was that the one that got Adam? Is he dead? Is all this for nothing?* Or had he killed the outlaws? Had he lured them in and killed them and could she go back now? She had to fight each step to keep from turning back.

Now she couldn't hear the gunshots anymore. But she heard other things. Scuttling things, slithering things. Things that she could step on in the dark, things that could get tangled up in her skirt, things that could crawl across her hand or brush against her face, and she wanted to scream. She wanted to scream and scream and never stop, and in just another moment, one more step, she *would* scream. But she never did.

It was so dark, and in the dark was timelessness. Eternity was a great black tunnel filled with fear and Angel was trapped in the middle of it. She walked with one hand pressed against the wall, her feet shuffling, the other hand stretched out in front of her and swinging back and forth. If that hand should touch something, she didn't know what she would do. She thought her brain would simply explode from terror.

And then her hand did touch something. It was solid, flat, hard-packed earth, as far as she could feel. A dead end.

Angel didn't scream. She leaned her head against the rubble and sobbed.

* * *

Adam didn't know how long he had been trapped in this dark place. He was sweating badly, and his hands were shaking. He kept fading in and out, losing great chunks of time, it seemed to him, and when consciousness returned he kept expecting everything to be different, but it never was. The same colorless void all around him, the same dank smell, the same pistol gripped in his hand.

He had emptied his rifle some time back. He didn't know how. He shouldn't have done that, he wouldn't have done that if he had been in his right mind. But a fever was burning in his brain and his shoulder was a mass of icy-hot agony and the sweat that was pouring from him felt like blood. He had one bullet left in his pistol. He heard Casey enter the mine.

He kept thinking about Angel. He had sent her into the tunnel. He had probably sent her to her death. She was afraid and alone, and he couldn't help her. He had *done* it to her. He had made her go through the tunnel.

He heard the footsteps stealthily approaching. He tried not to breathe. And then he wasn't sure whether it was footsteps he heard at all, or rats . . . the rats in the tunnels, the rats of which Angel was so afraid. He blinked the sweat from his eyes. He held the pistol steady, braced against his upraised leg. He didn't move.

Come on, he thought grimly. *Come on* . . .

A shape took form among the shadows. A man's shape, moving closer. The man didn't see Adam pressed against the wall; he was only another part of the blackness. Adam waited. The hammer was cocked. The man moved closer, moving carefully, quietly. But Adam could see him. Close enough now. A clear shot. Adam squeezed the trigger.

And missed.

Angel could feel air on her face. Frantically she felt along the solid embankment toward the source, and then her hand went through the dirt. An opening. There was an opening, it wasn't entirely blocked . . . but it was so small. It was barely wide enough to get her shoulders through, and who knew what was on the other side. She couldn't go in there. She *couldn't*.

Darkness all around her. Darkness in front of her. And Adam . . .

She began to dig away the loose dirt with her fingers, trying to widen the opening. She couldn't go into that tiny place, couldn't make herself go. And then she hoisted herself through the opening on her belly; but when she tried to straighten up on the other side, she couldn't.

The cave-in had left a tunnel less than three feet wide, one foot tall. The ceiling was against her head, the floor pressing into her belly, her shoulders crushed on either side. There was dirt in her mouth. She couldn't breathe, couldn't move, she was *trapped* . . . .

But she could move. Inching along like a snake, she wriggled forward, digging in her toes, pulling with her fingers. She couldn't turn around, there was no room, she couldn't go back, and she had to keep moving.

Adam, why did you do this to me? Why did you make me go into the tunnel?

Hours passed. Days. Blackness around her, blackness behind her, and she wasn't moving at all, she only imagined that she was. She was trapped there forever, she was going to die with the earth crushing down on her, and when she went to hell it would be like this, a long dark tunnel that never ended.

Mama, why did you send me into the tunnels?

After a time she couldn't even hear the sounds of her own sobbing, or the slide of her body or the pebbles she scattered with her progress. She just kept moving without moving and she never got any closer, for she had forgotten what she was moving toward.

And then she remembered. A ranch house in New Mexico. A cabin with glass windows. It was in a green valley, bathed with sunshine. Light danced on every surface, glinting from the windows, shining from the ponds, playing in the grass. And Adam was there, waving his hat to her as he rode in. And a woman. A woman with dark hair and eyes and a face that looked very much like Angel's. She was smiling, and holding out her arms to her. New Mexico was just at the end of this tunnel. And she could reach it, if she just kept moving.

New Mexico. Home. It was a beautiful place. And she knew it was home because of all the light, the sunshine that never ended . . . a light so bright that it warmed her cheeks and hurt her eyes. Home. She had always pictured it like that. Bathed in light.

But it wasn't as far away as she had thought. The light *did* hurt her eyes. She could feel it on her cheeks. And she could hear things—voices, movement. The tunnel took a sudden downward slope and she slid, landing on her hands and knees. She began to crawl.

And then the light was everywhere. A blinding white light filled with moving shapes and murmuring voices, and she knew she was home. She had made it. She was safe. She was home.

She tried to stand up but her muscles betrayed her. She thought she felt a hand on her shoulder. And she made out one of the shapes before her—a pair of dark-booted legs. She fell upon those legs, half-sobbing, half-laughing.

"Help me," she gasped. "Please—help me."

Adam stumbled along the rock wall, half-running, half-staggering, making enough noise to wake the dead. But it didn't matter. He was as good as dead himself. He was leaving a trail a blind man could follow in the dark, and the outlaw was right behind him. The only thing he didn't understand was why he hadn't been killed already.

When he paused, bracing himself against the wall and making himself still his breathing, he could hear footsteps all right . . . but they were far behind, moving cautiously. At first Adam was confused, and then he realized that the outlaw must have stopped to search his saddlebags. And why should he hurry? He knew every step Adam made from the sound of it. He knew he'd catch up with him eventually.

Adam didn't want to die. Not now. Not with Angel still lost in the tunnel. Not with Angel waiting for him. He couldn't die now.

He plunged on, no longer caring how much noise he made. When at last he came to rest, his legs buckled beneath him and he pressed back against the wall, waiting, listening.

Casey stealthily approached the sound of the last footsteps, his gun drawn. He had seen Adam's discarded rifle
and pistol, but he was taking no chances. The damn fool
had surprised him once today, but Casey's luck had held. He
wasn't about to push it too far.

He heard a pebble tumble and he whirled toward the
sound. A grin split his face as he made out the man's shape
huddled against the wall.

"Well now. Got you, didn't I?" His voice echoed in the
stillness, and he rather liked the sound. "I reckon you
expect I'll finish you off now, and so I will. Gonna get right
to that. But first . . ." his voice harshened, "you got something I want."

Adam could barely make out the words through the roar
of blood in his ears, the rasp of his breath. "Yeah," he
responded, and was surprised at the strength of his voice.
"I've got it."

Casey looked around suddenly. "Where's that little gal of
yours? No tricks, now."

Adam said, "No tricks." He reached inside his coat with
a great effort and took out the cross. It weighed his hand
down and was hard to lift. "I'm done in. You can have it."

Adam could see the glint of greed in Casey's eyes as he
took a step forward. He guessed that until that moment the
other man wasn't really sure that he'd ever see the cross
again. "Hand it over then," he commanded. "Let's have
it."

"Here it is."

Adam drew back his arm and threw the cross.

Casey whirled and grabbed for it as it went over the
chasm; he pivoted on his feet and his gun went flying as he
flailed for balance. For a moment it seemed he would be

able to right himself, but then his luck failed him. A piece of the precipice crumbled beneath him, and he plunged into the darkness after the cross.

Adam never heard the end of the scream. Another darkness had come to claim him.

When he opened his eyes there was light everywhere. Small flickering lights, large glowing lights, lights that floated and wavered, suspended in space. He thought he must be dead.

And then something touched his face. It was a hand, soft and warm. He tried to focus, but all he could see was a blur above him, almost a face but not quite, the amorphous shape of an unearthly being. An angel.

And then she spoke. "I'm here, Adam. These people— they came to help you. You're going to be all right. It was all there, just like you said—the village, the priest. They came to help you."

Adam tried to make sense of it but the mere effort of holding on to a thought was exhausting. Angel was there. Whether he was dead or alive didn't matter. Because she was there.

He mumbled, "The cross. I lost it. It—went over the cliff. Gone."

He heard a murmuring that gradually turned into a buzzing in his ears. Then a man's voice spoke with quiet assurance. "Perhaps it is best. After all these centuries—perhaps it has served its purpose."

Adam felt himself begin to drift away, and his last coherent thought was that perhaps the man was right. The cross had served its purpose. It had brought him Angel, and it had kept them both alive. That was enough of a miracle for his lifetime.

Strong hands reached and lifted him to safety.

Casa Verde was the most magnificent house Angel had ever seen. It was posed like a castle on top of a hill, dominating everything for miles around. Angel had been watching it grow closer and closer for the past half-hour, and she couldn't quell the fluttering sensation in her stomach.

Adam glanced at her. "Nervous?"

"You never told me it was so big."

"I guess it never seemed big to me."

"I wish we could have gone to your house first."

He chuckled. "It's nothing like this."

"I don't care." She looked at him. "It's where I want to live."

He smiled at her, and the fluttering inside her calmed down.

She reached in her pocket for the daguerrotype, as she had done at least a hundred times since they had begun this last half of the journey, reassuring herself with the face there, trying to project herself into the thoughts, the hopes, the expectations of that woman.

Adam said, "Don't worry."

"I just don't want her to be disappointed in me."

Adam smiled and didn't say anything. He had said it all before.

They passed beneath the wooden arches and the house was before them. Angel's heart began to beat hard, then gradually slowed down. It wasn't a castle after all, just a house—stone-hewn, broad, solid. There was a wooden rocking horse in the yard, and a plank had been fastened to a sawhorse to form a child's teeter-totter. Several puppies ran around, yipping excitedly and weaving in and out of the horses' legs.

The door opened and two women came out. The first was tall and red-haired, with three children clinging to her skirts and watching the approach of the riders with shy excitement. *My sister*, Angel thought, filled with awe. *My sister, and my nieces and nephew . . . My family. And they've been here all the time.*

The red-haired woman smiled as she watched her approach, and then Angel's eyes were drawn to the second woman. She was dark-haired and beautiful, not much changed from the daguerrotype Angel carried in her pocket. She moved with a quick, fluid grace as she lifted her skirts and ran down the steps and partway down the drive, and then she stopped, her hand touching her throat, watching Angel ride forward.

Angel's heart began to pound again as she slid off her horse. But then she saw the glow on the woman's face, the tears in her eyes. And she wasn't afraid anymore.

Consuelo opened her arms to her. "Angel," she said. "Welcome home."

Adam watched as Angel went into her mother's arms. "Hello, Mama," she whispered.